NOTHING EVER HAPPENS HERE

ANN FOWERAKER

Living in London suddenly becomes too uncomfortable for the attractive Jo Smart and her sixteen year-old son, Alex, after he is beaten up, so when they are offered the chance to take an immediate holiday in a peaceful Cornish town they jump at it. But not all is as peaceful as it seems as they become involved in a murder inquiry, drug raid and abduction.

DI Rick Whittington has also escaped from London and the reminders of the death of his wife and child, and through his investigations finds himself meeting Jo and being drawn into the events surrounding her.

Crime, romance, smuggling and Cornwall all come together in this light thriller set in the early 1990s

NOTHING EVER HAPPENS HERE

First published 2011 in eformat by AnnMadeBooks

Set in 12pt Garamond

Printed by: Lightning Source

Paperback Edition 2014 Pendown Publishing
Cornwall, United Kingdom

www.pendownpublishing.co.uk

Cover : NJM Designs

NOTHING EVER HAPPENS HERE

ANN FOWERAKER

To my husband who has always supported my writing

CHAPTER ONE

He heard their feet first, their heavy-booted feet, scuffing and ringing on the pavement. It was only as they neared, and he could make out the murmured chant, that he knew they were after him.

He knew it wouldn't be a good idea to turn round and face them, they'd love that. They'd love it too if he tried to run away. His bag, stuffed full, was already pulling at his muscles and bruising his shins as he slightly increased his speed.

'Smart Alec. Smart Alec. Smart – ' the chant became more rhythmic, louder, as they moved in for the kill.

Two Asian women rounded the corner ahead of him. He breathed lighter, they weren't quite stupid enough to do him in front of witnesses. The pair walked with eyes cast down, with only a furtive glance to the future, they did not look at him, or those behind him. They walked close together their peacock saris bright in the sunshine, exotic against the grey of the wall, the grey of the pavement.

'All right mate?' a breezy voice edged with razor blades blasted in his ear as an avuncular arm slapped across his shoulder.

'Yeah, all right Smart?' hissed another voice from the other side, and he could still hear the sound of boots behind him.

He could sense them grinning at the Asian women as they passed, a great joke between friends.

'Weren't nice of you was it?'

'Grassing – that's a – punishable crime – innit?' Alex kept on walking, steadily, as if alone, not answering, praying for someone else to appear in the street. How could anywhere be so empty in London?

'Oi! I asked you a question, Smart,' Skells said digging his elbow sharply into Alex's side. Alex turned, his eyes bright with anger, and it all went out of control.

*

'Bye, Miss,' the cheeky face of Kylie Burns smiled at Jo. Kylie, eleven going on twenty-one, was leaving her primary school for the last time. A little madam and too knowing for her age she had none the less done well in the lessons that Jo Smart, deputy head of Sir John Liddle Primary, took with the top juniors.

'Bye Kylie, I'm going to miss you.'

'Miss Smart?'

'Yes?' Jo looked interested, wondering what important thing Kylie wanted to ask to her.

'Who's that in your photo?'

'Who?' began Jo, then realised Kylie was pointing at the small frame that she kept on the bookshelf behind her.It had been one of very few 'new-baby' gifts and was just the right size to take the standard school photo. In it, each year, she put a new one of her son. Sixteen now, he looked older than his age and remarkably like his father had when Jo had first met him, dark and sultry. She'd met Alessandros at school, in her first teaching post, both new probationary teachers they'd been thrown together, and that's how they'd stayed. He had an English mother and a Greek father, the combination had gifted him the looks of a Greek god, beautiful, dark and strong to her blonde and fine, intelligent yet wildly impulsive – she'd fallen in love almost at once.

'Oh, that's my son,' Jo smiled, 'he's sixteen.'

'I didn't know you had any children miss, he don't look like you.'

'No. Not a bit. He looks just like his father though,' she said softly. Just like his father in looks and intelligence, but she'd never describe Alex as impulsive, but then perhaps that was her input.

'Okay. Bye then miss,' Kylie said, spinning on her heel and heading for the door.

'Bye, and you work hard, you've got the brains to do well if you work hard.'

Kylie pulled a funny face, shrugged and vanished from sight.

*

Like some ghastly vicious ballet, the gang worked as a remarkably co-ordinated unit. Raikes stuck out his leg and one of the others shoved Alex from behind and, as he fell, Skells snatched at his bag, twisting Alex's body so that it crashed undefended to the coarse concrete. Even as he landed they were reaching for him.

'Oh dear, the poor boy's fallen over,' Raikes snide voice sang out, 'Help 'im up,' he added as he scanned the still deserted street. They frog-marched Alex a metre or two up a back lane and dragged him into a yard behind a take-away, where the rank smell of oil and rotting waste from the row of bins permeated the air and the ground was slippery with decaying debris.

Barden and Skells linked their arms in Alex's and twisted him round to face Raikes. Raikes stood squarely in the gap in the wall, legs astride, fists clenched and with a mockery of a smile on his face. Suddenly Alex knew exactly what was going to happen. It was just like a scene from a hundred old films – the henchmen hold the victim while the boss thumps hell out of him. Almost as the thought came into his head Raikes strode forward, and Alex instinctively tried to curl up, to protect himself from the fist that hurtled towards his stomach. It hurt, God it hurt, but they were pulling at him to force him upright again, and the fist thumped again. Raikes' face was glowing, his eyes glittering with power. And again. Alex's stomach muscles, strong for a boy of his age, screamed with the tension that he was holding them in, and the pain flared across his body.

Another scene from the old films flashed across Alex's brain. It was worth a try, he thought, as Raikes' disgustingly delighted face came into close-up with the next thrust. Judging his moment, Alex threw his weight back onto his captors, and kicked out his leg, straight at Raikes' crotch. He had time to see Raikes' eyes turn black with uncomprehending pain before Barden and Skells toppled back into a heap, dragging Alex with them.

Was it worth it?

'Get the bastard!' Raikes screamed, doubled up in the doorway. And Alex disappeared under a rain of fists and boots allowed their fun at last. He took a blow on his cheek, another in his stomach; he curled tighter wrapping his arms around his head, and forced himself into the corner, to protect his back, to make a smaller target. Everywhere hurt, everywhere was battered. By the time Raikes had recovered, and had them all stand round to deliver the coup-de-grace, Alex was unconscious.

*

Detective Sergeant Kelvin March perched on the corner of the desk as his Detective Inspector, Rick Whittington, carefully emptied drawer after drawer.

'I can't believe you're really doing this? You'll be buried there – whoever made good down in the sticks?' he said as he watched Rick select some things to go into a box, some in an office tray and dump the rest in the bin. 'And don't tell me promotion isn't everything – it was you who used to push so. Go for it, eh? You, damned near dragged me up to D.S.'

'You deserved it,' Rick spoke quietly, his voice, almost always soft, had its own subtle nuances, some as hard as granite, some as silky as the finest sand. Kelvin had heard them all, knew how Rick could inspire confidence with one, and fear with another, yet seldom had he heard that voice raised in anything but song.

'That's not the bloody point, the point is you could go far. Star rated you are. The Met's the place to stay, you know that, you'll make bloody top brass.'

Rick shoved the last empty drawer back in place. He looked at his old friend. Somehow they'd managed to travel the same way since leaving police college and joining the Metropolitan

Police. True, Rick had made it one step higher in the time, but there was no resentment, and they knew each other well. Leaving Kelvin was about the only thing that Rick regretted as he'd put in for a transfer. He just couldn't stand another year in London. He knew he certainly couldn't stand another New Year's Eve.

'I've told you why. It's no use staying – nothing'll ever come right if I do.'

Kelvin looked contrite. 'I know,' he sighed, 'but you could have said like, earlier – eh?'

'Never knew when it'd come off.'

'I'd have understood.'

'Look, I'll meet you for a pint later, seven at the 'Dog' ?' he said using the nickname for the local pub

Kelvin raised a smile, 'Yeah. See you later,' he said and pushed himself off from the desk and with a glance at his watch left the D.I.'s office.

*

Mr. Ahren opened the back door to let some air through the stuffy back store and into the kitchen. As soon as the smell that came from the over-heated yard reached him he wasn't sure it was such a good idea. He was just about to step back inside, thinking stale air better than smelly, when he noticed a book lying in the yard, its pages flapping lazily in the light breeze. He stepped out of the door, eyes on the book as if it might suddenly flap its wings and take off. He was just stooping to pick it up when he heard a sound. He froze, the sound, a small groan, was coming from behind him, barely discernible from the background hum of traffic but different enough to be noticed. With a prickle of fear tightening his spine he looked round.

The corner beyond the bins was a confusion of fluttering paper and a knot of clothing that emitted, as he stood transfixed, another moan and shifted to reveal a face.

'Oh! My God!' gasped Mr. Ahren, stumbling forward towards the boy.

The boy's face and the sleeve and front of the white shirt were bright with blood. File paper had been tipped out all over him, sticking to his frame, the wall, the ground. Broken empty files rested at crazy angles where they'd landed, pencils, split and bright, lay like broken firewood, and a gutted bag hung from a bin.

As Mr. Ahren stepped forward the sweet, acrid smell of urine enveloped him and he noticed the pages of writing were smeary. He crouched down.

'Are you all right? I'll phone for an ambulance.'

The boy's eyelids opened and closed twice as if it was all he could manage. Mr. Ahren stood quickly, making his head swim. He looked at the boy for a second and decided he'd better phone first and make him comfortable afterwards.

*

Jo pulled another pile of forms towards her and yawned. It was the last day of term before the Summer holiday, just one more day for administration then the bliss of no school work for at least five weeks and, towards the end, a fortnight in Greece. It might be the last holiday that Alex took with her, or the second to last, whichever, it wouldn't be long before holidays would mean going off somewhere with his friends, not with his mum. She'd decided to leave visiting Greece until he was older, for a time when he might appreciate it more, she'd told herself, for a time when she could really explain things.

She yawned again, the heat of the summer making the room as dry as chalk dust, the air heavy. She wondered if Alex would remember to pick up some salad stuff to go with their evening meal, he usually did, he was a good boy.

The phone rang, she finished filling in the line while it rang twice more.

'Deputy Head's office,' she said as she scanned the next line to be completed.

'Jo? Sally. I've got a call for you – it's the police.'

Sally's voice sounded unusually tight. Clicks sounded on the line and a new voice began.

'Mrs. Josephine Smart?'

This wasn't right. Usually if the police wanted to impart or gain information about a pupil they referred to her as the Deputy Head. That it might be a personal problem concentrated her mind.

'Yes.'

'I'm D.S. March, Mrs. Smart, you have a son, Alexander?'

'Yes, yes. What's happened?'

'I'm at St Stephens' Casualty.'

'Casualty?'

Sally appeared at the door, her round face set in a frown.

'I'm sorry to inform you that your son has been assaulted – he's expected to be okay though,' D.S. March added quickly.

'I'll be there – now!'

'Give you a lift?' Sally offered, knowing that Jo never drove to work.

'Oh God, Sally – he's been – assaulted.' The term sounded vicious and perverted.

Jo grabbed up her bag and together they ran from the room, skittering down the echoing stone steps and out into the glare of the asphalted playground.

The drive was interminable, Jo trying to hurry the rush-hour traffic forward with willpower. She hadn't even stopped to ask when or where it had happened. Could she have prevented it if she'd gone straight home after school instead of staying on to fill in forms? What had happened? Why were all the traffic lights red?

Sally swung her Metro round to the Hospital entrance and paused, where bright painted notices screamed NO WAITING, just long enough for Jo to leap from the car.

Running, Jo headed for the large 'Casualty' sign and burst into the waiting room at a trot. Inside everyone was still. Sitting waiting, standing at the desk, waiting, or moving slowly and carefully around. The coolness of the room after the heat of the street immediately calmed her. Yet to wait while the receptionist filled in a form for the person in front of her was agony

'You've got my son. Alex – Alexander Smart?'

The receptionist looked down at her screen and up, past her, and gave a small nod, before returning her gaze to Jo.

'Yes, Mrs. Smart. This officer would like a word.'

'When can I see him?'

'Now,' said a stout, smartly-dressed man at her elbow. 'D.S. March. We spoke on the phone?'

'Yes – what happened? When?' all the questions she had failed to ask poured out.

'It appears he was set on by a gang – he's not said much yet. The doctor says he's taken quite a beating, it's mostly superficial, but it was a nasty attack – one we'll need to investigate. Go in and see him now, I'd like a word after.' Kelvin tried to sound gentle; he could see the pain in Jo's large grey eyes. He'd been taken aback by her appearance. He'd seen the dark-haired son and he knew that the mother was a deputy head at a large primary school, so he had expected someone different, someone a bit more domineering, not this young blonde bit that stood before him.

A nurse let Jo into the cubicle where Alex lay. He looked small as she entered the room, her little boy. She caught her breath as she came close. Half of his face was shiny, white and red, swollen. One eye almost closed with the swelling, the kiss of butterfly plasters on his cheekbone.

'Mum,' he mumbled as his eyes filled with tears, and she was by his side. Tears were trickling down her face while anger filled her.

'Oh Alex. Who did it? Oh.'

'Raikes' lot.'

'Are you – anything broken?'

Alex raised half of his mouth towards a smile, the other half stiff with swelling.

'They say not – mum?'

'Yes?'

'The police want to talk to me – don't they?'

Jo nodded.

'Won't do any good. Their word 'gainst mine. No one saw. Besides...'

'Besides?'

'Ohh,' why couldn't she see, it hurt enough to talk as it was, 'they'll still be about, won't they?'

'Not if they get done for – for assault – whatever. They'd be away.'

Alex shook his head a fraction, the pain whirling with the motion, 'Doubt it – nothing much happened to Jenkins last year, and he beat up a teacher.'

Jo nodded. He was right. That little brute had received a reprimand and little more, the teaching union press had made it sound like the courts had declared an 'open season' on teachers.

'But you'll listen to him, the policeman?'

Alex nodded a fraction, it hurt. It all hurt, and he could still smell the stink from the yard on himself, despite having been cleaned-up by the nursing staff.

'Mum?'

'Yes, darling,' she said, her throat tight as she touched his coal-black curls gently, where they lay matted on his forehead.

'When can I come home?'

*

'Sorry I'm late!' Kelvin said as he landed heavily on the old plush seating of the 'Dog', 'Had a GBH on a young lad to see to.'

'What'll you have? Lager?'

'God! Yeah – that'll be fine.'

He watched Rick standing at the bar. Somehow he already seemed more relaxed. He was dressed casually, jeans and Tee shirt, but it was more than that, his long, lean frame looked less angular, more at ease than it had seemed for ages. Rick's Mediterranean good looks were holding out well too, scarcely a grey hair in sight, Kelvin thought, considering his own spreading waist and the grey that seemed to have multiplied in his hair since his fortieth birthday last year.

'When you off then?' Kelvin asked as Rick returned with his drink.

'Report on Monday. I'll pack up tomorrow and leave on Friday. It'll give me the weekend to get settled in, some digs sorted out.'

'Digs?'

'I intend to buy something down there eventually – plenty of small places around Plymouth.'

'Right – I'll come for m' hols then shall I? Book me in last week in August.'

Rick grinned. 'I'm only going to miss one thing about London – and that's you!'

'Don't be daft – you'll be back, won't you? You'll never stand the boredom down there. Mrs. Minnie's cat going missing, great blag at the sweetie shop?'

'Huh – if only! No, I won't be back,' he shook his head slightly.

'You could always transfer too!'

'What would my missus say? Dragged away from her beloved shop!'

'She might say "Thank you!"'

'No way – she couldn't live away from it now – it's in her blood.'

'They do have shops down there – she could open a branch of 'Tats' in Plymouth.'

14

Kelvin seemed to consider this for a moment. 'Nah – Josie says you can only make money out of being exclusive in the capital.'

All 'Tats' hats were exclusive. Catching on to the new concerns about sun-induced skin cancer she'd developed a stunning range of hats for all sunny occasions, each hand finished by herself. That each hat was unique and each carried her own designer label meant that they had become one of *the* fashion accessories of the last couple of summers. Sheer time had kept her business small but exclusive, now it was paying off as her prices became exclusive to match. Their house always smelled of raffia and straw and in every room were sheaves of colour, piles of glistening fruits, bundles of plasticized wire and hats – hundreds of hats, in all stages of creation. They filled the house like the children they did not have.

'Holidays then.'

'Rick? I hope it works mate – but I don't know, seems like – ' Kelvin tried to find the words to express his feeling that Rick was trying to hide from the facts.

'Like I'm running away?'

Kelvin nodded, shamefaced.

'More like running home. It's just, down there I have other memories, things to fill up the spaces. Here? Here nearly every other street reminds me of them.' Rick felt his throat tighten against his will, and swallowed to release it.

He should have put in for a transfer long ago, he'd not felt settled for the past year and a half. New Year's Eve had confirmed his feelings. The first anniversary of their death – his loss; wife and child together, gone in an instant. His request for transfer landed on the Chief Super's desk as soon as he was back on duty but it had taken six months to work through. He'd kept it quiet, not even telling Kelvin, knowing that every discussion of the transfer would bring him back to his reasons for leaving, and that would bring back the pain and the futile anger. It was better this way, one session of justification and it would all be over.

*

'You ought to take him away from here.' Sally said quietly over the cup of coffee she'd just put down on the desk.

Jo looked up startled. She'd been miles away. It was her very last day in school, supposedly a whole day of administration. In reality she was just 'being there' in between visiting Alex in the hospital. They had decided to keep him in for a day's observation, though they'd assured her that he was very lucky to have nothing more than some cracked ribs and severe lesions.

'I was just thinking of that, sort of. We're off to Greece at the end of the summer, but that's too late, I need to get him away now, really.'

'Any ideas?'

Jo shrugged and gave a rueful smile. 'Greece will just about clear me out for this year – and that's going cheap, a non-resort place I know. I don't know where we could go, it's pricey this time of year.'

'Relatives?'

Jo shook her head. Relatives might as well be non-existent, a long story she kept to herself.

'Hmm..' Sally mused, 'There's – it's only an idea mind – my sister, down in Looe? She might know somewhere – not too expensive, might be a bit rough and ready though.'

'Looe?'

'In Cornwall, fishing village – on the south coast. Don't you know it?'

'No, I've been to Devon, but that's it.'

'Oh, you'd like it. I wish John could find work down there. It's where I come from, well   St. Austell really. But Sylvie lives in Looe. Shall I give her a ring?'

'Okay. Thanks Sally,' the idea of an immediate break growing on her. 'Only if she happens to know of somewhere really cheap, we don't need anything fancy – just peace and quiet.' Sally smiled, thinking of the unusual holiday place on the cliffs, and trotted off back to her own office to put through a call that wasn't strictly school business.

*

'Smug bastards.' Kelvin muttered to himself. He'd just finished interviewing the last of the gang named by Alex Smart. It hadn't surprised him that they all swore to being elsewhere, nor that some of them were the alibis for the others, but they'd obviously worked on a few of their 'friends' too, just to make sure that their story stood up. What irritated him most was their cockiness, the way they almost swung on their chairs, lounging back and sneering. Trash, rubbish he'd be sweeping in time and time again, and a nice lad like that Alex gets the shitty end of the stick. 'Good record,' his school had said, 'expected to get top grades on all ten of the GCSE's he'd taken – had even been in until the end of term helping out in the Science and Technology departments.' As for the others he asked about; the school just seemed glad to be rid of them.

It was strange to walk over to Rick's office and see a different face. The new D.I. seemed a pleasant enough bloke, but the reputation that had preceded him was that of a paper shuffler, unlike Rick, who'd rather have been out following up leads than sitting behind a desk.

'Not much joy on this one, sir, as it stands,' Kelvin March said as he offered his report to D.I. Williams.

'No?' Williams replied, raising his eyebrows. 'Why's that?' he added, not making any attempt to take the sheaf of papers.

Kelvin stood up straight and withdrew the file, glancing at it then tucking it under his arm.

'The gang who beat Alexander Smart up were his contemporaries, from the same school. They've got themselves pretty well covered and there's no concrete evidence and no witnesses to actually link them to the assault – on the surface. If forensic were let loose on their clothes, boots, whatever, it's my guess they'd find evidence.'

'Forensic? What were the injuries?'

'Minor – but,'

'Minor. I'm sure we have more serious detective work to spend money on than sorting out teenage fights. File it.'

'But if – '

'File it.'

'Sir.'

Kelvin stood for a moment looking down on the balding spot on the top of D.I. Williams' head, and congratulated himself on not going bald, even if he was going grey!

*

'Do I really have to?' Alex asked the nurse who had brought a wheelchair to his bedside.

'Yes, we have to take you down to the car in the wheelchair. It's policy.'

It seemed ridiculous. Getting dressed caused much more pain than walking, it was moving his arms that hurt the most not his legs. His mum had gone back down to move the car to a collection space, he picked up the sports bag with his pyjamas in and sat in the wheelchair. He felt such a fraud as a grey-haired old porter arrived and began to push the chair out of the ward and down the corridor. It was only as they came out into the light that he suddenly felt nervous. A feeling of being exposed, of being suddenly visible to unfriendly eyes, ran through him. He shuddered despite the heat of the day.

He climbed into the car, wincing as he did so, and pulled the seat belt across. Jo, noticing his pain, took the end from him and slotted it into the catch. He sat with the belt held slightly away from his chest to ease the pressure. They waved goodbye to the porter and were off.

'Okay?' Jo asked as she pulled out onto the main road.

'Yeah,' he said softly, feeling nervous about everybody they passed.

'I've got a surprise for you. You know we're going to Greece at the end of the summer? Well, at the beginning we're off to Cornwall! In just under a week!'

He didn't say anything; his throat seemed to have a lump in it.

'Alex?'

He drew in a loud breath.

'Alex?' she said, stealing a quick look at him. His dark eyes were full, shining with un-shed tears.

'Oh, great. I mean – I really mean it. I didn't want to be around here – for a bit.'

'Oh Alex. It's a friend of Sally's sister – down near Looe in Cornwall. She says it's a bit primitive – but I'm sure it'll be okay. It should be really quiet – Sally says nothing ever happens down there.'

'Good.' Alex's voice sounded small and tight. It hurt Jo just to hear him.

They turned off the main Fulham road and were on home territory, turned right just past the church and then it was just straight down the street. Parking, as usual, was difficult, but Jo found a space almost opposite their door. She leapt out of the car to go ahead and open the door calling for Alex to take his time, to be careful.

The sun had been shining on the front of the house all afternoon and the light bounced off her brilliant-blue front door. It had been the finishing touch, after years of re-decorating she had at last finished with the bright flourish of a beautifully glossed door. She sniffed. The heat of the sun usually rekindled the scent of new paint, but as she lifted the key to the lock she registered a quite different smell. She glanced round at the steps and pavement, and tipped up each foot in turn to check that she hadn't stepped in something unpleasant, something she certainly wouldn't want to walk onto the recently laid carpet. All clean. She smiled back at Alex, as he clambered out of the car, pushed the key in the lock, turned it and opened the blue door.

Then it hit her.

CHAPTER TWO

The first time she saw that small terraced house Jo knew it was right for her. It was tucked in behind the Fulham road where the roar of Chelsea's victory could be heard from the Stamford Bridge ground. Almost on a junction with the incongruously named Farm Lane it had one eye-relieving view across the railway track to the patch of green offered by the Cemetery.

What a gamble! Four years ago, as the housing market had taken a steep nose-dive and bottomed out at prices that seemed derisory to the purchasers of only a couple of years before, Jo had bought. It had been a terrifying experience, but one that she was glad she had taken. Prices had steadied since then and, here and there, even begun to tentatively rise again.

Number 38, or 'Homeleigh' as some previous owner had dubbed it, was anything but, when she first viewed it. It was a sad house, dark and musty, trapped in time. The new owners, inheritors, were desperate to sell before a 'poll tax' was levied on it. The old gentleman had scarcely changed a thing since his wife had died thirty years before, she was told, and she could readily believe it, but the house itself was sound. With a little downward negotiation, a horrifying mortgage and all of her savings, she bought 'Homeleigh' determined to make it live up to its name and Jo was nothing if not determined. It was the last piece of proof that she needed: successful teacher with a top job; handsome intelligent child; home owner. That would show them, everyone of her family who had turned their backs and stuck up their noses, who had told her she was stupid and worse and who hadn't wanted to acknowledge her baby.

With very little left over after paying the mortgage, Jo had worked on the house herself. Alex had helped as much as he could, and in the last two years he'd really made a difference to how quickly they'd finished. Started with a general clean;

scrubbing all the paint-work, tearing up layers of crisp linoleum, washing down the walls, until the house smelled fresh, then, month by month as there was enough money for each job, they began to repaint. Jo had decided against wallpaper as it seemed so expensive and, after having read some books and bought a basic kit, she decided to paint the walls and stencil designs onto them for decorative effect. It had the extra benefit of costing nothing to spend three weeks painstakingly removing the wall-paper and not too much to roller all over with a 'white-with-a-hint-of-colour' emulsion. Each room she finished with a stencilled border in one colour to enhance the colour hinted at in the base paint and a new, but usually cheap, carpet.

She'd started in their bedrooms, to get practise before moving on to more public rooms, and she'd needed it, even now she winced at the heavy stencilling that was her first effort in Alex's room. After that she'd moved down to the kitchen, no longer able to stand the cracked and crazed surfaces of the yellow and black melamine-faced worktops and doors. It had been the slowest room to come right, and the most expensive, but she was so proud of her efforts. The kitchen now had a country look about it that would belong in a house just off 'Farm Lane'. She'd retained the cupboards, as they were sound in themselves, but had stripped off the doors and worktops. She'd bought a length of new 'marble' faced work top ready cut to fit and some cheap solid pine doors to fasten to the fronts, with the aid of Alex's technology teacher. All at once, the room looked both more wholesome and more homely. With more advice, an adventurous bit of tiling and more paint and stencil it had only taken the introduction of a few plants to make the kitchen one of her favourite rooms.

The tiling she undertook in the bathroom had been limited but effective, in a bold, deep red and black it made so much difference to the plain white suite which, as it was still good, she kept. In the past year she'd finished off the dining-room and sitting room. Each was now a pleasant, light room in soft shades and with simple furnishings. The hall she had left until last. Feeling quite accomplished in the art of stencilling she designed and created something special. Her whole hall was an experience in light and shade. She'd taken her ideas from the water-side, from the light cast by sunshine on ripples and dappled shade through fresh green leaves. Everyone who'd visited her since she'd finished had been amazed, had suggested she could do interior design as a side-line, had laughed with her, knowing how little time she had left in a day as it was. Since she'd completed the hall, opening her front door was an experience she always enjoyed; refreshing and pleasing.

She turned the key and pushed open the door. The stench hit her. A stench that she'd merely suspected as being somewhere outside surged out from her hall assailing her senses as a physical force. She staggered back, gagging, her eyes trying not to register the desecration, her hand waving Alex back behind her.

'What is it?' Alex began, before the stink of faeces reached him. He stepped back as if someone had hit him, found hot tears rushing into his eyes and an intense anger lodged somewhere in his chest.

'Go back – Alex – in the car,' Jo snapped, stepping backwards as if she couldn't bear to take her eyes from the open front door. In her mind the dull brown smears were crawling out and streaking everything, muddying the brilliant blue of the door as it stood in the shadow. She shuddered. They stood at the car and stared at their home.

She put her hand to her mouth and tried to breathe. The air seemed full of the foul smell even here on the other side of the road.

'I – I must phone,' she muttered. 'Stay there *please* Alex.' She didn't want him to see any more than he had already. She steeled herself and having taken a breath, as if about to dive under water, strode across the road and straight up to the door.

The peace of the hall was destroyed by streaks and circles covering the walls, drawn in excrement. The telephone was on the kitchen wall, she hurried forward towards it. She came to a halt at the door of her favourite room with tears running down her face, and even so she tried not to breathe too hard, tried to block out the smell. The scene was bizarre: a mountain in the middle of the kitchen floor. Everything, almost everything that belonged in all the cupboards, had been hauled out and smashed on the floor, heaped up in a sticky, crunching, powdery heap. Moving carefully, trying not to slip, feeling the crunch of cereals beneath her feet but not permitting herself to stop, she reached for the phone. It was slippery as she picked it up and she almost vomited as she realised that even the hand-set had been smeared with shit. She wiped it with a kitchen towel and scrubbed at her hand for a moment before punching the number for the police. 'At least it still works' she thought as she heard a distant ringing tone and tried to work out what she was going to say.

Replacing the hand-set she turned to go back outside to wait. Alex stood in the doorway, his face a shadow against the back-light from the open door.

'Alex – I said not to …'

'It's me.'

'What?'

'See what it says? Grass!'

Jo stepped back into the hall and looked up at the wall where Alex was pointing. The streaks and circles at that point resolved themselves into the word. She allowed her eyes to move round the hall, stepping back to see other smeared words, foul four-lettered obscenities.

Just as the stench had overcome her senses so that its strength seemed diminished in her mind, now she found herself becoming detached from the personal effect of the attack. She found herself wondering whether they'd gone round collecting dog-mess or had 'manufactured' it themselves. She wondered if they'd come prepared with rubber gloves to protect themselves or had merely scooped it up in wodges of paper, and she wondered about the handprint on the wall halfway up the stairs.

'They didn't break-in,' Alex said as they stood outside in the sunshine, their backs to the door.

'They must have got in somewhere. I don't know. I haven't, couldn't go round everywhere.'

'Won't be a break-in – they had a key.'

'Alex?'

'Bloody Raikes ...' Alex voice broke as tears coursed down his face and he tried to hide them from his mother.

'You don't know Alex – it could just be a coincidence.'

But he was shaking his head. He knew they'd gutted his bag and remembered seeing the baseboard, where he kept his key hidden, tipped out amongst the other debris. It had seemed a safe hiding place, buried under all his files and stuff, and had been until then. Now it made him feel responsible.

'Is there someone you could go to, Mrs. Smart?' The young constable asked kindly, looking definitely a little green after his first sortie into the house.

Jo thought for a moment. He was right of course, though she'd not thought past calling the police, they could not stay there tonight – and there were so many other things to consider: Alex; cleaning the place up; insurance; getting away, getting away.

'I'll ring – ' she began, then the thought of actually speaking into the shit-smeared phone again made her feel sick. She looked round, tears forming in her eyes, wondering where she could phone from. She caught sight of a neighbour standing at her door, arms folded, leaning against the doorjamb, watching the police activity. Jo had no idea who she was, she knew only one of her neighbours, the rest seemed to be either out most of the time or securely locked indoors, there wasn't a great community in this street; undeterred Jo headed for the woman. As soon as the woman became aware that Jo was coming towards her she straightened up and stepped back into the shadow. Her hand was on the door, ready to close it, as Jo reached it, instinctively putting out a foot to keep the door open.

'May I? I live just over there, Jo Smart – may I use your phone? Please?'

'What's going on?' the woman asked, thin and pale with eyes too large for her face, like a creature that lives in caves.

'We've been broken into by – vandals. I just need to phone someone urgently – my phone's – out of order.'

The woman's face wrinkled a little. Jo wondered if the stench clung to her, hung about her like a cloud.

'It's there,' she said pointing at a phone fixed to the wall near the stairs, and stepped back to allow Jo to reach it. She moved no further as if barring the way to the other rooms of the house, almost as if Jo carried the danger with her.

'Thanks, I won't be a minute – thanks,' Jo said steadying herself against the wall as she pressed in Sally's home number.

*

He'd been living in an empty house for almost a week. As soon as he knew that the transfer was through, Rick Whittington had packed up his home and sent it into storage down in Plymouth, to wait for him. A fortnight ago he'd used the couple of days he had off to take a drive down and look around some of the estate agents, to collect sheaves of details on 'desirable' properties, to check some of these out and to get the flavour of some of the areas. It had been years since he'd been to Plymouth and he'd never really known it well, so it had been a useful exercise. His last few belongings were crammed into his trusty Carlton estate, luckily it always held more than he thought it could.

Rick looked round the empty rooms, one by one. Stripped bare, they seemed impersonal, yet they still echoed with memories of the eleven years they'd had together there. Elise sitting in the living room sewing new curtains, bright curtains that changed the rooms where they were hung. Louise running to meet him at the door and tripping over one of her own toys, knocking out a tooth. Bathing Louise on the evenings when he was home early enough, too few, when they'd splash water all over the place and both be in trouble with Elise. Eating late with Elise, dinners fragrant with herbs or sizzling with spices, or early, en-famille, joyously and easily. The bedroom. He closed the door. It hurt too much to even think now. He closed the front door of their police apartment and walked away.

As the miles rolled by under his wheels he began to feel better, as if layers were being left behind, strewn on the hard shoulder. A fresh start. Though they would always be there, always be part of him, he could try to begin again and wipe the bitter taste from his mouth that arrived every time he came home, every time he 'saw' them in a familiar place and every time he had to pass the junction where Kensington High becomes Hammersmith Road. He allowed the miles to unwind the years, to take him back to the time when he had first seen Elise. He'd had enough girlfriends in his time, but none had proved to be stronger in their attraction than his work and none had been able to share him with it. For Elise he thought he might have given it up completely, had she not been quite happy to be the wife of an irregular time-keeper.

He'd seen her as soon as he arrived at the club. He could hardly miss her, standing as she was in the centre of the small stage. She had a fine willowy figure with high carved cheekbones that accentuated her dark eyes under her glossy black hair. Her voice had seemed to belong to someone else, someone a lot bigger and stronger, as she galloped with the horsemen in the folk ballad that she was completing. All at once, under the spell of the song, she was transformed as her voice fell to that of the lady-love that the knight sought, calling to him from beyond the grave. 'Alas! My Lord, where I am gone, you may not follow. Alas! My Lord, where I am gone, for me you must not come.'

The applause had been effusive, and Rick joined in as, on unaccustomed impulse, he pushed his way to the front and round to the side of the stage to congratulate her on her voice as she stepped down. She'd smiled up at him, her dark eyes shining, and asked him to join her party. Captivated, he'd followed her to a group of young people sitting against the wall. Everyone had shuffled about a bit to squeeze in Elise and her new friend. Introductions were made, a quick round of first names or nick-names, and they settled back to listen to the next singer to take to the stage. Whether Rick's ears had become deafened by love already or whether the next singer was truly dull he was never to discover as the general decision was taken to move on. Politely they'd waited until the dirge was complete before standing en-masse and leaving the folk club.

Rick had found himself walking through the cool evening air beside a woman who made him feel lit up. She told him that she worked as a translator, working on texts, often on deadly boring technical texts like those for instruction leaflets. He'd laughed and pointed out that she must be the one responsible for many an abandoned self-assembly kit. She'd laughed and told him he must be responsible for all the burgled apartments in London! It was the beginning of a year-long courtship, as they worked all round the fact that they had both fallen for each other in an instant on that first evening because they just couldn't believe it. They created a beautiful duet, a pair of complementary voices and eventually they married, Rick was twenty-eight and Elise two years younger. Louise arrived after a year and they settled in their new Police apartment as a family. Now they were gone, so suddenly, gone. 'Alas My lord where I have gone you may not follow. Alas my Lord where I have gone, for me you must not come.'

It had been New Year's Eve, but the New Year was still a few hours off. Louise had been invited to a party in Kensington, her first teenage party. He was on duty late that day so Louise had given him a fashion show the evening before. It made him smile as she paraded her fineries. Except for the ugly heavy boot-like shoes, the black and white dress could have been something one of his girlfriends would have worn back in the late sixties. Louise had suddenly grown, the prototype of the young woman she would be in a few years. The puppy-fat had left her cheeks giving naturally fashionable high cheekbones, just like her mother, and even taking the prejudice of a father, she was all set to be a stunner.

The party finished at nine, a sensible and respectable time for an eleven year-olds' disco-party. He wasn't due off duty until ten that evening so Elise had gone to collect Louise. They were on their way home when it happened. Head-on smash. Two survivors. The back-seat passengers of the Lotus. Not the right ones. The police were on the scene in an instant. They would be, they'd been chasing the stolen Lotus for the last mile or two.

The police had called in the numbers of the cars. One was registered in his name; and his name was recognised. They radioed him on his way home. They told him to pull over a moment, and checked that he was ready before asking him if his wife and daughter had been out in the car that evening. With a lump settling in his throat he'd answered them, knowing that this was just a pre-amble, a check, before his world broke apart and because he knew, he sounded in control when they said there'd been an accident, a fatal accident at the junction of Kensington High and Hammersmith Road, and that all the casualties had been taken straight to hospital. The heavy pause told him that the next words to be spoken would be the death sentence. The driver and passenger in the white Metro were not among the survivors. He signed off in a voice that belonged to someone else, then screamed and shouted until his throat felt raw with the harshness; then the tears came instead. He felt trapped in a vacuum, in a bubble of time, he'd sat there for half the night screaming, but barely ten minutes had passed since he'd pulled over. Through misted eyes he pulled back into the traffic, and headed back through the dark of the last hours of the Old Year towards the hospital.

He really should have put in for a transfer straight after the funeral; instead, he'd struggled to pull his life back together. The effort had been too much; so often pieces would fly away just as he'd almost got them tied down, too many memories crowded in on his quiet moments. This New Year's Eve had been the breaking point, full circle back to the realisation that he had to start again, somewhere where the memories could be brought under control, somewhere where he could concentrate on his work – it was all he had left. Plymouth forty-six miles the sign said – nearly there.

*

'What did I say? Henry's not the only one, I have my contacts too,' Detective Constable Fuller expanded, gangster-like in stance, dress and looks. 'Well do you want to know about the Lord Mayor of London – or don't you?'
'Okay – give,' sighed D.C. Lewis. She was curious, they were all curious about the new D.I. they were getting from London. After all, they all had to work with him and it made a big difference to their lives if they could get on with the man. Fuller's manner irritated her, but she had come to accept it as an intrinsic part of his personality and like it or not, when pushed he was a good man to work with. All they'd been told was a name. Richard John Whittington. In an instant Fuller

had picked on the name, Dick Whittington – Lord Mayor of London, and had run with it to find out what he could.

'Our Dick is a good-apple. No sideways demotion job at least. Mind you it makes you wonder whether he's been sent or has jumped – doesn't it?'

'That all?'

Fuller shrugged. 'I could have got tied-in with a pal – he didn't seem too forthcoming – leaving for personal reasons, his wife and kid were in a car smash last year, that's it, except to say he was – quote – "one of the best".'

'Poor guy.' Glenda mused as she glanced out of the window, past the burned-out church, out to sea. 'Why Plymouth – did they say?'

'Nah. No doubt we'll find out soon enough once he's here,' James remarked acidly.

Glenda turned and glanced at him sharply, it wasn't a tone she was used to from James.

*

Jo put the phone down and put her hands flat to her face, hiding every feature. She sighed deeply and slid the palms down until she could just see over her fingers.

'Problems?' Sally asked, her face furrowed by worry was curiously creased in a manner it wasn't designed for.

'You bet,' Jo said, removing her hands from her face and interlocking her fingers in case they tried to escape. 'It seems that I will probably not be covered by my household insurance because there was no forced entry. They make it sound as if I had left the doors wide open or something!' She heard her voice rise with the indignation that she felt and breathed deeply to bring it back under control.

'But you told them, about Alex – the attack. What did they say?'

'They said that I should have notified them and had all the locks changed – under the insurance! They say they would have paid for that.'

'But you had so much to worry about.'

'Doesn't cut any ice with them. Besides I didn't even know the key was missing – don't think Alex even realised until after we went home and saw that - that – I will never, ever, understand it! You know at college we used to do child psychology – and how the baby goes through all these little stages - anal obsessive, that was one – just about describes this bunch. Sorry Sally – I'm talking ugly.' I haven't said that for years, she thought, thinking about Greece must have brought it back. "Don't talk ugly – ugly is as ugly says." Alessandros had said that day when she bitched about her parent's attitudes, comparing them to the open-arms welcome she'd just received from his family.

'No – it's okay. What are you going to do?'

'Get some cleaners in – I don't really want to – it's not like me – but I couldn't look at it again. It's sort of scarring. I'm rather hoping that when I see it again I'll be able to pretend it was just a dream – correction – nightmare!' Jo laughed, feeling the tension slightly ebb away. 'I'm just so grateful to you for putting us up like this.'

'Nonsense, it's a pleasure. And while you ring round some cleaners I'll go and put the kettle on.' Sally beamed, her face regaining its usual shape and optimism.

'That's Greece gone!' Jo said as she heard Sally come back into the room. 'With the new locks and a bill from one of that lot we'll only be able to do Cornwall if that! Perhaps I ought to just knuckle to and do it myself.'

It wasn't Sally.

'No mum! You mustn't do that – that'll really please them. Forget Greece…'

'Alex! – I thought you were Sally – I didn't mean. It's not as if they'd be there, watching.'

'So.'

'Don't say 'so' like that!' Jo snapped, then instantly relented and added softly, 'I know what you mean – it's okay – I couldn't face it anyway. Anywhere else – perhaps I could do a swap – I'll clean up someone else's mess and they can do mine,' her voice tapered off as she noticed how tired Alex looked. 'We'll get away, just the minute the house is clean enough to lock up and leave, we're off. Okay?'

Alex smiled – it was enough.

*

'Mum?'

'Yes?'

The traffic moved slowly, fumes belched from the cold exhausts all round them, insinuating their stifling odour into the fully closed-up car. Jo looked sharply and briefly at Alex.

'Nothing,' he said, shaking his head.

'It's silly but I'm really nervous about going back home,' Jo said softly, feeling she understood Alex's wary look.

'Mm,' he acknowledged.

'Be okay though – 'all clean and fresh' they said, with an emphasis on the fresh!' Jo grinned ruefully. 'Better damn well be – at that price! Oh I must be mad – I could have – '

'No!' Alex shook his head violently. 'No – I can't forgive myself as it is – not that.'

'Oh Alex – I've told you – it's not your fault that there are such disgusting creatures in the world.'

'Just mine for knowing them.'

'But you don't. Forced acquaintances.'

'Yeah, but if I'd just kept quiet ...'

'No Alex – you were right about that. It's important that you – that people stand up for what is right – or else – else – we might as well give up and go back to the jungle right now.'

They pulled up in the nearest space to their home they could find. Jo switched the ignition off and they sat as each waited for the other to move first. Jo sighed. Alex moved and opened his door. With a quick grin at him, Jo did the same.

The sun beamed down the street and shone its sideways glance on the bright blue door.

Jo sniffed – she consciously tried not to – but as the gleaming new key reached the shiny circle of the new lock – she sniffed.

There was a smell. A smell usually described as being the essence of the pine forest – pungent and acidly green. It increased in strength as she opened the door, her eyes unwillingly seeing the brown smears her memory painted, before she could wipe it clean with reality.

She sighed, Alex was at her elbow and she turned and looked up at him. It was, as they had said, clean and fresh, but she felt it would never be quite the same. They moved through to the kitchen and found a similar transformation. Jo flicked open a cupboard. Empty. As was every one in the kitchen, not a plate, not a cup, not a can of beans remained.

'Well we better get packed and on the road before we fancy a cup of tea,' she said with more light-heartedness than she felt and led the way briskly up the stairs to drag the suitcases down from the tops of the wardrobes. She was thankful that the handprint halfway up the stairs had not been a way marker of their trail of desecration, but apparently a full stop. Why, she could never be sure, but she had been convinced that they would have trashed Alex's room, yet it remained, as did all the other upstairs rooms, untouched. Had they been disturbed? Was it not Raikes and Co but someone else who had the key and address? Impossible to say now, but she was thankful as she laid clothes from the wardrobe and chest of drawers into her case.

Alex finished before her, came in and watched as she packed a few more pieces, squeezing them into a sports bag.

'Finished already?'

He nodded.

'Nearly done – take the key – put yours in the car – I'll just be a minute.'

Alex left and Jo quickly checked all round the house, paid a last visit to the loo, and locked up her bright blue door. As she turned she felt a deep sense of relief and strode towards the car with a feeling of optimism.

*

'Where exactly are we staying?' Alex asked as if he had just woken up. They had been travelling for three hours, listening to the radio, playing the odd cassette, but not talking much.

'At Sally's sisters – just for,' Jo reached forward and pressed the off button on the radio. 'Just for the three days until this chalet place is empty.'

'Where's that?'

'The chalet?'

'Sally's sister's.'

'Oh, in Looe itself. Um, West Looe – next to a pub – I've got the instructions in the back, we'll look at them when we stop for some lunch. Soon!' she smiled, knowing that he was probably feeling ravenous by now. She felt, rather than saw him nod his approval of the idea of lunch.

'Ah! Services five miles – Plymouth sixty-eight,' Alex read out with a certain degree of satisfaction, 'nearly there.'

CHAPTER THREE

It was his eyes that really attracted her, green and sparkling, like sunlight on the sea. They'd arrived in Looe mid-afternoon, glad to reach the small town after the winding country roads, greeted by the sight of gulls wheeling, and houses perched up the hillside, beaming down on the harbour. Following the instructions they'd crossed the bridge and swept up to West Looe and round to the point where the sight of the Smugglers Inn told them they'd arrived. They stretched their limbs as they climbed out of the car and headed for the door of the house. Before they reached it the door was suddenly thrown open and Sylvia Gold beamed a welcoming smile at them.

Jo was momentarily taken back, and at the same time glad that she wouldn't have to ask if this woman was Sally's sister. Sally of the ample figure, round face and mousey-blonde hair had a sister who looked nothing like her – except for the smile. Sylvia was slim, to the point of thinness, and her hair was a dry ginger.

'Come in- come in,' she said, 'and this must be Alex,' she paused a second to take in his still bruised face. 'Poor love.'

Alex cringed inside 'love!' – and he'd hoped he could forget last week – that there'd be no one round to remind him – did everyone know?

Sylvia moved quickly, bird-like, so different to the gliding movements which Sally engaged, that Jo could not help wondering at the amazing combination of genes that could make two so different sisters.

'It's really good of you,' Jo began as they were sat on the soft floral lounge suite, cup of tea in hand.

'No! Not at all, Sally explained everything. You couldn't stay *there* a moment longer. I don't know how Sal sticks it myself – but there it is. Still, after all you've been through it was the least we could do.'

'Sally said you'd only got the one spare room, I'm happy to..'
Jo started to explain how she wanted Alex to have the room
with the bed that wouldn't aggravate his cracked rib and
bruised body, and that she'd make do.
'It's all fixed – can't have guests on a put-you-up. Tamsin'll
move out for the couple of nights. No!' she added quickly,
noting Jo's immediate start of a refusal, 'It'll do her no harm.'
Sylvia finished thinking of her sulky fifteen year old daughter.
It had been the usual toss of the head and the pouting lip when
she'd been asked to vacate her room. She was up there now,
ostensibly clearing it up a bit for a guest.

Tamsin had been sitting on her bed reading an old Cosmo
magazine that Michelle had lent her when they'd arrived. She
was playing a game of brinkmanship – wondering whether her
Mum would come up and give the room a quick tidy if she
didn't bother – or whether she'd blow her top first. She heard
a car draw up and glanced out. Not that she really expected it
to be the visitors, not so early, all the way down from London.
But it was.

She watched the small blonde woman climb out, stretch her
back then dive back in for something – then she saw him.
Even at twenty metres she knew she was in love. If that was
the visitor then he could have her room anytime. By the time
they'd reached the door and she heard her mother's voice, her
face was pressed against the cold window in an effort to get a
better look at him. Her face flushed with a deep heat as she
glanced round the untidy room. She set to tidying it furiously,
aiming to clear weeks of mess in ten minutes.

She could barely think where to store all her clutter for trying
to remember what her mother had said about the visitors.
Friends of Aunt Sally's – from London. HE was from London!
That was glamorous enough without being tall, dark and
handsome with it. She wondered how old he was – he looked
about eighteen. What else had Mum said while she wasn't

listening? She swept her make-up and hairbrush off the dressing-table and into an old wash-kit bag. She dumped an armful of clothes in the bottom of her wardrobe, and old trainers and magazines on top. The major clutter removed she glanced around the walls. It was awful! Absolutely kitsch, from the roundel picture of kittens her mum had hung on the wall when she was small, through the fading posters of 'Take That' to her latest 'Guns 'n' Roses', that she was suddenly sure must be 'old-hat' by now. She peeled the yellowing tape holding up the 'Take That' poster as carefully as she could, trying not to pull paint off the wall as she did so. That was why they'd stayed up so long – Dad had gone bananas when she'd left great holes in the paint before, now 'the kittens' and the 'Guns 'n' Roses' were covering them so couldn't take them down! A last glance at her tape deck revealed too much – she grabbed some of the sick-making juvenile stuff and tossed it on top of the pile in the wardrobe.

'Blow!' a red-faced Tamsin said to the mirror as she realised her favourite black Tee-shirt was in the pile she'd deposited in the wardrobe. She dragged it out, hearing a clatter of cassettes rattle down the back of the wardrobe. She tugged it on and checked her profile, pulled a face and reached for her brush, recovering it from the wash-kit she brushed her long hair. She bent over forwards and let it fall around her head, brushed it vigorously, then, in one arching movement, swung her hair high back over her head to fall cascading over her shoulders and down her back. Long heavy auburn waves that shone as she gave them a final surface brush set off the few pretty freckles on her pale skin. She couldn't wait any longer – she daren't, she didn't know whether at any moment her Mum might bring them up and really didn't want to be in her room when he saw it, she needed to create a good impression first.

The chatter sounded light and easy as she crept down the stairs. She waited a moment at the bottom before turning into the living-room. Her heart was thumping. She swallowed and made sure her face felt cool. She was dying to see him close-up.

It was true – she tried not to stare – her eyes had not deceived her – he was really gorgeous a drop-dead looker. He was leaning forward, elbows on knees – eyes on his coffee cup, but she could see most of his face without him noticing. Wow.

'Ah, Tamsin.'

She jumped. Sylvia had suddenly noticed her daughter standing quietly just inside the door. Tamsin, to her horror, felt a warmth spreading up her neck as they all turned to look at her. She'd meant to give a bright beaming smile – people had said she had a lovely smile – but it came as a tight lipped grimace. She knew it, saw the slight narrowing of her mother's displeased eyes, and heaved a sigh. It was so stupid, she felt on the brink of crying now.

'Tamsin – this is your Aunt Sally's friend, Mrs. Smart and her son, Alex.'

Tamsin nodded and squeezed out 'Hello,' aiming it at Jo rather than Alex.

'I was just telling them that this is the place to be for peace and quiet – as you keep telling me,' she smiled an encouragement at Tamsin to finish the line.

Tamsin looked blank.

'In common with most of the youngsters down here, Tamsin's always saying,' Sylvia put on a voice, ' "there's nothing to do, it's bor- ring, nothing ever happens here".'

How could she! Tamsin felt the blush hit her cheeks. 'So?' she said, vehemently.

Jo laughed. The universal teenage 'so'.

'Suits me,' Alex said so softly that Tamsin only just heard him. She glanced at him, thinking he was making fun of her too, and met his deep brown eyes, and knew he wasn't.

*

Rick knew his way around in Devonport and finding the Mount Wise area was easy. Which of the roads lined by long yellow-striped blocks of flats was Cloncy Street he wasn't sure and slowed a little to read the barely-legible defaced signs.

'Next one, sir,' D.C. Glenda Lewis said suddenly. This was her first time out with the new D.I. and she'd surprised herself by checking her appearance before they left the station. He flashed a grin of thanks and turned slowly into the street. The flats crowded in on both sides, each identical in paint scheme, each as depressing as the other. They pulled into the side between a battered Ford Capri and a chassis up on blocks. The smell of the area should have been of salt and sea, considering the Hamoaze was less than five-hundred yards away, yet the air hung heavily with the rancid scent of decay as if it were trapped between the blocks of flats.

The police constable on the balcony walkway indicated the flat they had come to view. He straightened fractionally as he watched them approach. The flats seemed deserted, no curious faces at windows, no one lounging in the doorways.

'Quiet isn't it?'

'Keeping out of the way,' Glenda shrugged.

'Bedroom at the back, sir,' the constable said as he opened the door for them to go in, 'Dead, I'd say.'

The hall was narrow, claustrophobic, it felt as if it brushed both of his shoulders as he walked down the middle. The carpet was a greasy red, the walls beige marked with scuffs at various levels, he expected the bedroom decor to be much the same. The door was, had been, a cheap flat hardboard faced door in pale pink. It hung loosely from one hinge, a number of gaping dark holes had been smashed through its smooth facade.

He stopped a moment to sense the air. Stale tobacco, sweet wine and the iron-filing smell of blood. Then he stepped inside; into a different world. The room was lit by a single window hung with flounced lace curtains, framed by heavy burgundy velvet drapes. The bed, centre stage, was a delicate four-poster turned in a deep rich mahogany, draped with brilliant white broderie anglaise . The coverlet had once been of the same pure-white ornamental material. The dark stain that streaked across and over the side of the bed appeared like a crevasse in a snowy plain. Stepping carefully, Rick moved around the bed to the end of the bloody trail and the body slumped on the floor. A mass of dark hair surrounded a delicately shaped face, pale and slack in death. A young woman, fully dressed in fashionable clothes, drenched in darkening blood. He heard the wail of the ambulance siren as he confirmed for himself the police constable's immediate diagnosis of death.

Pulling on a pair of gloves he quickly turned on the light, a miniature chandelier, and together they began to search the room. All was immaculate, tidy, clean. Not a thing out of place.

The doctor arrived and was almost dismissive of the murder. 'Straight stabbing, single blow, long – um – ' He tipped the woman's body forward a little, supporting it so that it didn't fall. 'very long weapon. I'll be able to tell more later. Professional job, or very lucky.'
Rick thought 'lucky' a strange term, but acknowledged the instant diagnosis. It was important not to ruffle the feathers of the doctor too much, it could make all the difference between a quick start and a delay.

Forensics came and took photos, fingerprints and fibres, the medics came and took the body, Rick and Glenda concentrated on the other rooms.

'It's weird,' Glenda said as they returned to the hall after checking the sitting-room. 'That room's been ransacked – just about anything that comes apart, has been taken apart, yeah? Yet the bedroom was untouched. And the furnishings! They must've cost a packet – look past the wreckage and here's some poky flat that's been done up like a place in the Ideal Home magazine.'

Rick nodded his agreement. 'Okay, kitchen and bathroom left, your choice,' Rick smiled. Glenda pulled a face, wrinkling her diminutive nose. 'Kitchen – get it over with.' It would take ages if the kitchen had been ransacked in the same way.

The find came in the bathroom, the once immaculate bathroom. It was a fluke that they found it at all. The medicine cabinet, the only container in the room, had been tipped out. Lotions and pills filled the hand-basin, empty bottles littered the floor, and as in the other rooms, there seemed nothing left to search, someone had been doing their job for them.

The bathroom had been done out in style, if a little over the top, like the bedroom. More Viennese-draped lace curtains, blue and white tiles, a mock marble-topped washstand in dark wood with a hand-basin sunk into it and a Victorian style cast iron bath with an old-fashioned shower head, like a huge watering-can rose, hanging over it.

'I can't understand this – you just don't change the bathroom suite in a council flat – there's probably rules about it,' Glenda said wearily as she stood in the doorway.

'It's certainly different – and with the hall left just about as grotty as you can get,' Rick said, idly turning on the shower tap, curious as to the effectiveness of such a large shower-head. Nothing, no water, not even a dribble. He tried the bath taps below, they worked fine, gurgling and spluttering water forcefully. He looked again at the shower-head. It appeared to screw on, no other fixings, he gave it a gentle twist and it moved easily. As he turned it a little more he felt a tingle run round his frame. How many parts of a plumbing system move so easily?

'Glenda?'

'Sir?' she stepped over beside him.

He turned the shower head, once, twice, three times. It came loose and was heavy in his hand. He lifted it down, a globe filled with a plastic bag stuffed with white.

*

Sylvia was burbling on about some of the places to see, some to avoid. Tamsin scarcely heard until her own name was mentioned again.

'What?'

'Pardon! – I said you were working for your Uncle over at Millendreath this summer.'

'Yes,' her voice sounded unenthusiastic – when only the day before she'd been delighted and more – triumphant – when she told Michelle that she had a holiday job. Jobs of any type were hard to come by – especially for someone not yet sixteen. Now she thought her time might be better spent showing Jo and Alex, or rather Alex and Jo, around Cornwall. 'Only a bit – though – part-time,' she smiled at Alex for the first time. Alex caught her smile, and returned a shy one of his own.

The waves were almost lost in the dimness and the thin mist that was creeping round the bay as the last rays of the sun lost their strength. Sylvia, her husband Tom, Jo, Alex and Tamsin sat in the warmth of the evening outside The Smugglers and sipped their drinks. Alex and Tamsin leant back against the wall of the pub, cokes in their hands, listening to the adults' conversation, but not taking part and not daring to chat to each other.

'I've a confession,' Jo smiled, shaking her head. 'I would never have picked you out as being Sally's sister – put you in a crowd and I'd never have guessed.'

Sylvia laughed, 'I s'pose Sally never said. No, it's a bit of a joke in the family. There's three of us, right, Sally's the blonde, I'm the red-head and Richard's dark – real Spanish-Cornish. We always says that the milkman kept changing,' she laughed quickly, 'before anyone else suggests it!'

'And your parents' colouring? Stop me if I'm being nosy.'

'Nosy nothing. No, Mum was blonde as a girl – real blonde, not like Sally's. And Dad was dark like Richard – they say it can throw up these mixes.'

'Mmm,' Jo nodded, 'All sorts of permutations – fascinating isn't it?'

'What's fascinating round here then – apart from you?' a rich warm voice cut in.

'Evening Rod,' Tom said with a small salute of his beer glass. Rod pulled up a chair and joined them amid smiles of welcome.

'Well then – aren't you going to introduce me?' He smiled across at Jo, she found herself smiling back at a ruggedly handsome face, sun-tanned and framed by chestnut brown wavy hair.

'Jo, this rogue is a friend of ours, Rod,' obliged Tom.

'Hello, Jo,' Rod said and held out his hand to her. 'Here on holiday are you?'

'Pleased to meet you,' Jo said as she took the proffered hand and shook it, a hand that was warm, dry, hard and extremely masculine.

'Here to escape London!' Sylvia said with feeling, 'You've no idea what she's gone through in the last couple of weeks.'

'Really?' Rod turned his eyes on Jo once more. They sparkled as they caught the light from the pub window. They sparkled green like the sun on the sea, and Jo felt herself begin to float. 'Tell me about it,' he invited.

CHAPTER FOUR

Pete Austin steered the little boat out into the darkening water. The lights of Looe were hazily discernible in the distance. The bulk of Looe island, a darker splodge in front of the mainland, helped to give him his position. The sky became a deeper dark blue and the stars became visible directly above, being swallowed by the sea-mist on the horizon.

He cut the engine and turned off all the lights. Almost immediately, before the clatter of the big out-board had completely left his ears, the boat began to ride the swell, rising and falling with the waves. He hunched forward in the small cabin, allowing his body to get accustomed to the movements, and fiddled with the radio. He moved the dial: listening; listening.

He could have been wrong, though he thought he'd decoded the message he'd heard a week before. Listening; listening.

With a grunt he heaved his bulky frame out of the cabin and braced himself against the cabin as he lifted the heavy night-sight binoculars to his eyes. He scanned the waves finding himself alone with the slap and roll of his small vessel against the whole sea.

*

'So who is he?' Jo asked, 'The local Casanova?' hoping despite herself that Sylvia would not say that he was.
'Who? Rod? No – not really, just on his own like after he split with Mary a while back. 'Tis a laugh, as they always said as East shouldn't marry West.'
Jo looked puzzled.
'East Looe – West Looe. Fearful rivalry there was in past. Now they all goes to the same school, tin't quite the same – but the saying sticks. Mary's East Looe – lives over there now and our Rod, West.'

Jo was surprised to find herself relieved. She'd enjoyed his gentle flattery and warm sense of humour. There was something comforting about his easy Westcountry manner. He'd offered to take them both out on a fishing trip the next day. They'd be in company he'd said, as he ran fishing trips for tourists in the summer months, but they'd be his guests. Jo had, of course, demurred and insisted on paying if they came. Rod had said that they couldn't come at all if she was going to be like that.

There had been friendly banter, a warm battle of wills between them and Jo had found that she liked that too. Perhaps she would allow herself the luxury of a small dalliance, she was, after all, on holiday. Jo settled into sleep smelling salt and seaweed drifting through the open window, feeling comfortably safe as she snuggled down into Tamsin's bed.

*

'Cocaine, and a high quality batch. We've matched it to some taken last month in Dorset at that festival, but that's the only thing I can tell you,' Jim Hines said as he dropped his chemical analysis report on Rick's desk.

'Thanks Jim,' he looked thoughtfully at the paper lying there, 'Do you suppose it's coming in through our end?'

'Only guessing mind, but we've too much shore-line for our own good down here.'

Rick grinned. 'Don't I know it? You know I'm from St. Austell way – originally.'

'Oh! Really? Local boy then. Still must be a bit different. How do you find it after the Met?'

'Cleaner – but the crime's no different. I'd sooner be here I think.'

'P.M. boss,' scowled D.C. James Fuller as he came into the cramped office. He laid the post-mortem report on top of the chemical analysis without a look or sign of acknowledgement for Jim Hines.

Rick looked up at the two men, there could have been a brick wall between them for all the notice they took of each other. It was fortunate that they didn't have to work together as it was obvious that there was bad feeling between them. Rick made a mental note to find out what it was all about later.

'I'll be off then – you'll let me know if we can tie it in with any other finds, won't you?'

'Sure – thanks Jim,' Rick said making eye contact, but his mind was already absorbed by the words that had leapt from the page of the new report. He looked up at James.

'Interesting, Eh?' James said with his characteristic shoulder hitch.

'Interesting. Weapon used between 200 and 250 millimetres in length,' he spread his hand. 'Mm – eight to ten inches say – forty-five millimetres circumference, smooth, round and tapering to a point,' he read. 'What's that sound like to you – not a knife.'

'No sir, Not really sure what – I just get the feeling it might be something like an ice-pick?'

'Ice-pick? Who goes round Plymouth with an ice-pick?'

'Sir.'

'Sorry, James, I didn't mean it like that, kick the ideas about – you never know what it'll trigger off,'

'Yes, sir,' he grinned.

*

'You suggested what? That it might be an ice-pick? You're crazy – you read too many American thrillers!'

'No, Glen you've… '

She darted him a look, he knew she didn't like her name shortened.

'Glenda! You've got it wrong. He like, listens – he said it was good – throwing up ideas – even if they seem crazy.'

'All right. I know what you mean – he makes you feel as if what you've got to say is really important – must make a big change for you!'

'Fun-ny. No, I think I'm going to get on all right with our Lord Mayor.'

'Not if he hears you calling him that – nor 'Dick' mind, Rick to his friends – okay?'

'Familiar aren't we?'

'Get lost,' Glenda waved him away with a laugh but to her annoyance she could feel her cheeks begin to warm.

'Cheers Glen – da, da!'

She shook her head at his retreating form, smiling to herself and wondering when he'd ever grow up.

*

'Eleven o'clock from the harbour,' he'd said. Lucky that she had thought to ask Sylvia where exactly to find Rod, for there were far more fishing boats than she'd thought there would be.

The smell of fish and seaweed was strong around the cluster of boats, the water dark and sheened with oil. The valley side rose steeply from the town, houses perched on the steep sides like a colony of gulls. Then the sun came out. A warmth spread through the town, lighting the dark corners, bringing a sparkle, and with it Jo saw Rod, tanned and grinning at her from the stern of a medium sized vessel, painted in blue, white and black. Rod's boat, especially smartened up for the summer trade, even had a name painted on her prow, 'The Merlin'.

Before they reached the mooring Rod had come round and jumped off to meet them. He shook hands with Alex swiftly, giving Alex a good feeling, a welcome between men. Rod was just as charming as he'd seemed the evening before, taking her hand for a second in welcome, letting his wonderfully green eyes look into hers for a moment, before sweeping both Jo and

Alex on board. Jo felt a tingle of excitement and told herself it was the prospect of going out fishing.

'There's a mackerel line for you each,' Rod said quickly, 'You'll excuse me just a moment – I've to get the rest on board and kitted out, okay?' he smiled at Jo and Jo felt the touch of his care in his voice.

The boat filled with the fee-paying passengers and Rod got 'The Merlin' underway with the smell of diesel permeating the air before they could move out of its pall. Steadily, the boat moved out of the harbour, East and West Looe on either side, until it broke free of the bordering land and was surrounded by the sea. The breeze increased to a blow that cleared the fumes away, but Jo could still taste them in her mouth, and the throb of the engine was echoing in her stomach.

'Eddystone light,' Rod said, leaning close to her ear so that he didn't have to shout, and nodding in a south easterly direction, 'Were going for a shoal off to this side – usually offers good fishing with mackerel on top,' he added flicking the switch on a black box in front of him.

The small screen glowed and a profile began to move across it, and a series of dots passed, then another, which suddenly stopped and whizzed back across the screen.

'Echo-sounder, sonar. It's a fish-finder,' he grinned.

The engine slowed, but remained just ticking over.

'Ladies and gentlemen, as you can see we are just west of the Eddystone light. This dangerous bank of rocks have seen the demise of many ships in the past, and beneath these waves the rocks stretch out to provide an excellent shelf or shoal for us to fish along, not to mention the odd wreck to attract conger and the like. I'll come round and help anyone who needs it, if you'll bear with me, anyone starting with a mackerel line can begin to unwind it and let it over the side.'

The waves lifted the boat, and let it drop, gently, repeatedly. Rise and fall, lift and swoop. Jo clenched her jaw and swallowed. She looked at the lighthouse, tried to keep it steady in her view. Rise and fall, lift and swoop. Her hands began to feel ice-cold.

'Mum – look!' Alex wound the rectangular frame around in his hands and held up a line alive with black and silver mackerel, flashing the colours of the rainbow into Jo's jaundiced eyes. Jo opened her mouth to speak but instead threw herself against the side of the boat, just in time to empty her stomach onto the waves. And she felt so stupid, unaccountably stupid. She was shivering. Then she felt his strong warm hands on her shoulders, and felt the warmth of his breath as he leaned close.

'Don't worry – it's okay – it'll pass. Sit here,' he whispered as he pulled the stool over to her. The shaking eased, though she still felt cold. He reached into the cabin and pulled out a coat and wrapped it round her shoulders. 'Back in a minute,' he said softly.

*

For the umpteenth time that morning Pete Austin had found himself standing looking out to sea and wondering what he'd missed. He had been so elated, so certain that he'd cracked the code, but last night had yielded only emptiness and a coldness that had permeated his bones so much that he felt the chill even as he stood on the sun-drenched cliff.

It really was so beautiful, the sun glinting on the waves, the island, like an emerald set in billowing, diamond-starred silk, if only Julie were still here to share it with him. He turned his back on the siren sea, snatched up the buckets and strode away. The geese greeted him with sinuous necks and a low hissing that had no venom in it as he was their friend. They dipped their heads and chortled among themselves as they gargled the fresh water he'd provided. He entered their house, ducking down low through the door and careful not to slip on the green goose-squat that layered the floor. Once inside, he straightened up the little he was able to under the low roof and reached over the door frame. His thick fingers found the edge of the packet and eased it from its hiding place. Slipping it into the pocket of his fisherman's smock he ducked out of the door again, breathing the fresh air in deeply as he emerged into the sunlight. As he passed the geese, sitting in a circle and gossiping round the bucket, he promised them a clean floor by the evening and hurried on down to the house.

*

Jo shivered. The sun struck through the window of the small cabin and filled the air with dust motes dancing in the light, but she shivered again as another spasm clutched at her stomach and squeezed her skull. She'd never known such sickness, such an unrelenting urge, as if her stomach was in revolt against the rest of her body and her head was out in sympathy. Rod had been so good, had wrapped her up warm and provided a clean damp cloth for her to clean up with. He'd encouraged her to sip a drink, to replace the liquid she'd lost, but after the third try at keeping some down she'd given up. The muscles in her stomach screamed with each squeeze. All she wanted was to be back on land – but good as he was Rod had promised a boat-load of people a day's fishing, and that was what was expected of him. She didn't even ask that he turn back.

Alex had caught enough mackerel by the second wind of his line and had moved on to a proper sea-rod. Rod had instructed him quickly on how to use the sea-rod and had moved on to his other customers. Alex caught on quickly and landed a good sized ling shortly after being left. Another ling and a pollack later he felt confident enough to help the youngster next to him who was having some difficulties. His easy manner and helpful disposition was quietly noted by Rod as he moved about the small boat. Every now and then he'd rev the engine and move them round a little, bringing them back over the best part for the fish, every now and then he'd pop into the cabin and check on Jo.

'You're not the first you know?'

Startled, Jo looked up at his smiling face.

'Most trips we have someone who's sick – I've got used to it. I'm just so sorry it's been you – you'll not fancy coming out again now I suppose?'

Jo raised a wan smile for him, but shook her head.

'That's okay, but I'd gladly take your boy out again though – he's a real help.'

'He's welcome to it,' Jo managed to grin.

'That's better – we'll be heading back in ten minutes or so, okay?'

Jo nodded and smiled at him again, the smile warming her up a little as she watched him through the cabin door as he moved around the boat helping reel lines in and stow the gear away.

*

Rick pushed the pile of files away. While he'd been out the sun had heated his small office beyond endurance. He'd opened the door to a wave of hot stuffy air and though he'd opened the window and turned the vertical blinds enough to throw a shadow, the room still created a torpor in his head. He'd be sure to leave the room in shadow whenever he went out in future. The words had begun to shift and swim and he knew he needed to give it a rest.

They were already getting nowhere fast. The community around the flat where they'd found the murdered woman were almost all blind, deaf and dumb, excepting those few favoured words 'Don't know.' Discreet enquiries about the cocaine side of the business had led to an equally dead end. No one knew of a supplier or user who knew the dead woman. Nor had anyone anything to say about the incongruous decor, the grotty entrance, entirely in keeping with what was expected and the over-the-top interior design pinched from half a dozen copies of Interiors magazine.

Lastly, and more interestingly, almost nothing was known about the woman. One, surprisingly well-spoken young woman, with two toddlers hanging on her skirts, did have a little light to shed, when pressed. Living in the opposite block she wasn't so close to the scene in one way, but had a view that included the balcony entrance to the woman's flat.

'People, men, came and went frequently, but I didn't notice anyone in particular, there's nothing strange about that around here,' she'd said in answer to his questioning about the comings and goings across the way. 'And I was away, visiting relatives, when it happened, so I can't really help you there either.' So he'd asked her if she'd known the murdered woman. Her face registered distaste. 'I don't mix,' she said. Pressed on how long she'd lived in Mount Wise the woman's eyes clouded and she looked briefly down at her twin daughters. 'A year, next week, but not for much longer, thank God.' And the murdered woman? 'Oh she arrived about six months ago, shortly after the last one left, another one of them,' she'd finished with an eloquently raised eyebrow.

According to the council, however, the previous tenant had never left, the name on their books had been the same for years. The rent was always paid, there had been no need to look into it. The name on their books matched the name on anything that might identify the woman in the flat, Jane Smith, a name as innocuous as it seemed phoney when its veracity was challenged.

Jane Smith had a bank account, Visa card, building society account, and membership of the National Trust, all with a starting date of the twentieth of January, this year. Old statements suggested that Jane Smith had a regular income, the same amount of money paid in each week, in cash, and that she was careful to pay all bills by standing orders or direct debits. Nothing left to chance. Her Halifax book showed savings of nearly four thousand pounds, not too incredible, a steady amount, about five hundred pounds deposited each month, after opening the account with one thousand. And that was it, a regular source of income and no sign of a regular job. Being on the game certainly wouldn't have kept her in the manner she had obviously enjoyed, for added to the money recorded had to be the furnishings in the flat, unless they'd been put in place by the previous 'Jane Smith', wardrobes full of expensive looking clothes and her general living expenses.

It was enough for one day. Rick stretched as he left his chair. He thought of the house he'd been to view a couple of days before. The more he thought about it, the more he felt it would suit him. He decided to drive out round that way, have another look and make a decision on his way back to his digs.

*

Pete blinked, the day had disappeared and the room had become dark around the glowing computer screen. With a start he left the table and moved to the window. Another promise broken. He returned to the desk and exited from the program. Within minutes he was striding through the dusk towards the goose-house, calling them in out of temptation's way, calling a promise to the other animals that he'd be with them soon.

*

Jo sipped the hot tea as if it were nectar. The warmth transferred itself to her frame, warming the cold aching core that had been her stomach. It was with relief, almost amazement, that she found the liquid did not cause her any discomfort. Now she could scarcely wait for it to cool enough to drink properly.

Yesterday evening was a blur. Rod had helped her from the boat to his Landrover, she had never felt so weak in her life but she was past caring about her image. Alex squeezed in beside her to support her as Rod swept the car up to the Gold's. 'It'll be all right, Mum.' he repeated like some mantra, and the sound of his voice made her head ache even more. Sylvia's voice had scratched on the high notes, but she knew what to do, warmth and liquids. Jo was obviously dehydrated and despite Jo's protestations they managed to get her to drink, and keep down, a couple of glasses of flat lemonade. Sleep had been her escape. She'd closed her eyes and stopped fighting the terrible sense of continued motion to allow herself to sleep, the sofa riding up and down on the waves. Rod and Tom helped carry her up to Tamsin's room and then left Sylvia to minister to her guest.

The morning had come bright and startling, her head ached as if hung-over, the light made her wince. She'd showered and realised that beneath the ache of over-exercised muscles her stomach was telling her she was hungry. Downstairs she'd noticed the speculative look that Sylvia gave her before asking how she felt. She proclaimed herself quite recovered and automatically apologised for any trouble she might have caused, as if she'd really been intoxicated by drink and didn't know what she'd been up to.

Jo sipped the tea and looked up as Alex came in. He flashed a smile at her, and she knew she must be looking a lot better than she did last night. They ate a full breakfast and sat looking out of the window at the sea. There was a tap and the back door opened.

'All right Sylv? Thought I'd come and see – ' Rod said, 'Ah! Morning Jo, how are you?' he added softly as he stepped in and saw her sitting at the table.

She grinned. 'Fine – I can even look out at the waves with no ill-effects!'

'That's what I like to hear. Look I've got a trip out later, but this evening, would you mind, would you like to come out for a drink with me?'

He looked apologetic and shy at the same time, yet his eyes still held a twinkle.

'I'd like that, yes, thank you,' she said smiling at herself coming over all shy.

'Mr. Pentewan?' Alex began.

'Rod.'

'Rod – er, could I come today? To help I mean – '

'Sure – you could crew – help out a bit with the fishing if you like. I'd said to your mum here, that you'd be welcome.'

'Thanks, what time? Is it okay?' he added looking at Jo.

She nodded, 'Just as long as you don't expect me to come too!'

'Eleven then, see you at 'The Merlin',' and to Jo he added softly, 'See you later,' and slipped out of the door.

Jo hugged her cup of tea unaware of the smile that lit her face, Sylvia raised an eyebrow and turned back to her washing up thoughtfully.

*

'Stanton and Crowber.'

'Good morning. I have the particulars of one of the properties on your list and I'd like to put in an offer for it.' Rick said.

'Thank you sir, I'll put you through to Mr. Washrook.'

'Mr. Washrook.'

'Richard Whittington, I viewed 34 Crownhill Lane last Tuesday, I'd like to make an offer, if it's still available.'

There were sounds of a keyboard being tapped.

'Yes sir, er, asking price is £56,500.'

'If you'd put an offer for £55,000 in for me, please – it's as far as I can go.'

'Yes, sir. I'll see what they say.'

Why do the estate agents always send out houses that are above the price limit that you have set them? Rick mused as he drove into the city centre, fifty-five thousand was the most he could manage, yet only two of the properties that they had given him were at that price, all the rest have been two or three thousand over. If they wouldn't take it he'd just have to look elsewhere, after all he only had himself to please.

'Dick – a word,' Superintendent Williams said, catching up with him in the corridor.
'Sir,' he felt himself tighten at the use of the nick-name.
'How's this murder going? I hear that you found cocaine there, sufficient for supply?'
'Yes, I'd say so – there may have been more, it may have been taken by who-ever wrecked the rest of the place,'
'And the weapon?'
'No sign – as yet. It's difficult to say exactly what it is we are looking for, not a knife – more a spike,'
'Mmm? The cocaine dealing, part of an organisation, do you think?'
Rick felt pushed, not ready to jump to conclusions as there was no evidence to suggest others as yet.
'Not as – ' he began
'Must be. Quantity; quality. Keep me in touch,' he ordered, 'By the way – settling in all right? Good,' he added as he disappeared down the corridor.
'Slimy basket,' a voice muttered behind Rick. He looked round in quiet surprise at James.
'Special reasons?'
'Watch him when you bring them in, always centre of the photo, Mr. Crime-buster himself,'
'Like that is he?'
'Can fish swim?'
Rick grinned, he was beginning to like D.C. Fuller after all.

*

The green gloop glistened in a heap outside the goose-house as Pete brushed the bucketful of water he'd thrown down, across the floor and out of the doorway. Next he shovelled the muck into a wheel-barrow and ran it dripping across to the compost heaps. He was sweating, small trickles ran down his face and he swept them away with the back of his hand. He was getting out of condition, too much stodge to eat, he never seemed to have enough time to cook proper meals lately. He'd already cleaned out the goats, ducks and chickens, but the mucking out wasn't over yet. The last bunch in the chalet had moved out at lunch time and the next were due in tomorrow, which meant that place needed cleaning thoroughly too. If only it was as simple as the goose-house.

The groups of people that used his chalet had fossilised, as had the charges. Each year it was the same, each year they'd book the same-week-next-year before they left. This year, however, the Farquahars had phoned to cancel, saying that they were heading off for France and leaving an unexpected gaping hole in the summer. So when Sylvia had asked, she was in luck. Just a woman and her son, friends of Sylvia's sister – it'd be a change, almost strange to show someone new around the 'farm' after so long.

'There you are – promise kept,' he said to the geese as he passed. The geese muttered amongst themselves, the goats pricked their ears and watched as he put the bucket and brush away and headed off in the direction of the chalet.

CHAPTER FIVE

Julia had always liked to call it the 'chalet' and the name had stuck. In reality it was a form of barn conversion, but not from a rugged stone built place but from a wooden faced intensive rearing unit for chickens. Unlike the comfortably Cornish-stone barns which clustered around the old farm house, the chalet stood away from the main farmyard, closer to the cliffs. Here, the visitors could involve themselves as much or as little as they wished in the running of the 'farm'.

Bodrigga Farm was in reality only a small-holding now, the vast majority of the land having been sold off to wealthier farmers in the vicinity years ago. When Pete and Julia Austin had bought the place it had been run down and all but deserted. Their vision, Julia's vision, had been of a rural retreat, a place where people like themselves could come to live in tune with the earth for a while, to get to grips with the land. Here they would grow organic vegetables, run free-range poultry, milk their own goats and share this life with their holiday makers each summer – and Pete could continue his new work from home.

He was one of the first technological home-workers. A natural with computers he sorted out software. He could somehow sink his mind into the computer to fathom what went wrong when there was a bug in a program, which small digit or symbol threw it all out of balance and caused it all to lock up when certain combinations of events were asked for. De-bugging was not so much a science as an art: and he was good at it, really good. Top secret disks came to him, games disks that the creators had spent months producing, worth millions world-wide – when the tiny glitch in their operating system had been sorted. He wasn't cheap, but he was recognised as one of the fastest and the best, and that was all he needed. In the main Farmhouse one whole room was taken up with computers. Two RISCOS machines, one the new

RISC-PC; an Apple-Mac; two standard IBM compatibles and one research model, ranged round two sides of the room. The third, covered by an enormous shelving system, was full of disk boxes, books and magazines. It was his domain.

The Stewarts had left the chalet tidy, as usual, but the basic cleaning still had to be done. He pulled out the bucket and cloths ready to start on the bathroom, wondering, not for the first time, why he had carried on letting the chalet, now that Julia was gone.

*

'Jim Hines?' Rick started, 'Not a lot of love lost between him and James, is there?'

'That's one way of putting it,' Glenda said with a small laugh.

'Well, at least they don't have to work together – is it a history I should know about?'

Glenda pondered this as she changed down to take a tight corner.

'Yeah, perhaps,' she began, thinking that, at the root of it, there was a problem that may come up again and again. 'James is single, okay, and er, he has an eye for the ladies. Problem being they also seem to have an eye for him – regardless of whether they ought to, if you follow. This doesn't excuse him, mind, just – he's a liability to himself, can't resist a come-on.'

'And Jim Hines?' Rick asked, even though he thought he could guess.

'You've not met Jim's wife. She's a bit of an ice-maiden type,' Glenda permitted herself a small flash of bitchiness, 'but she melted as soon as she set eyes on our James. Then came the odd bit, after what one gathers was a single, non-consummated tryst, the ice-maiden is about to throw out Jim and replace him with James. James, not really being ready for commitment calls a halt and beats a rapid retreat.' She was really getting into the swing of the story, as difficult as it was to believe, 'Now you'd have thought Jim would be delighted, but somehow he feels slighted by James turning down his wife! There was a 'weird row' – that's how James describes it anyway – where Jim kept yelling 'So what's wrong with Helen? eh? Why don't you want her?' James got the hell out of it and they've never spoken since – least, not if they can help it.'

There was a silence. Rick shook his head, it sounded so odd that it had to be true.

'Does he give you any trouble?'

'Who James? Nah – I'm one of the lads, doesn't even notice me,' she said with more bravado than she felt. James was like an itch with her, irritating, annoying, but she'd got used to him being around, he made her want to scratch. Rick raised an eyebrow, 'one of the lads' Glenda might be, but she was also an attractive woman and he was surprised James hadn't noticed.

*

'Sylvia tells me you're moving up to Bodrigga farm tomorrow,' Rod said softly. They sat side by side looking out over the sea, glasses in hand.

'Yes, seems we were lucky, someone cancelled.'

'Pity, in a way. Can't just drop in there like I can here.'

'Oh, but we couldn't stay here, poor Tamsin's on a put-u-up until we go,' she smiled to herself, poor Tamsin had seemed wretched earlier when she'd learnt that Alex had gone out on the boat again, and it being her day off from the Cafe at Millendreath, 'Surely you could come up to the chalet – it's not in a fortress is it?'

Rod gave a slow smile and shook his head. 'Not that – I don't get on with Pete Austin too well these days. Can't blame the man, but he don't like to see me round, reminds him you see.'

'Reminds him?'

'Ah, 'bout Julia. Before she disappeared, Julia, that's his wife, was doing a bit of fishing an' that. Used to come out with me sometimes too, fishing mind, nothing else. She weren't like that. Don't know what happened, freak wave may have swept her off rocks, she may have slipped and got drowned,' he drew one hand down his face, wiping the memory from his features, 'Who knows?' he added with a grimace.

'When?'

'Winter before last, they never found her though, bit of a problem that.'

Jo shuddered, 'And they say nothing ever happens here.'

'Don't though, do it – woman goes missing, no proof of anything. But you see, Pete doesn't like to be reminded.'

'No I see, but,' she found herself feeling as if she were about to lose something.

'Well, we can still meet, can't we?' he said in just the way she would have liked to.

'Sure, I'd like that, assignations!'

'Oh! I don't know about that – sounds a little up-market for me, does that,' he grinned happily, his eyes sparkling at her.

*

She was shown the location of Bodrigga on the map by Tamsin, who was keen to show Alex the coastal path that made it a short trip down to Millendreath. From the map Bodrigga sat almost on the cliff edge, all alone, with Millendreath off to one side and a Monkey Sanctuary on the other.

'A Monkey Sanctuary?'

'Oh yeah, its been there for years, Woolly Monkeys, I think they breed them to release back in the wild,' Tamsin said, realising that she knew very little about the place. Last time she'd been there was from primary school and her abiding memory was of bare footed long-haired men with monkeys climbing all over them. 'Would you like to go and see? It's not too far a walk from Bodrigga and it's been years since I bin there,' she added hopefully to Alex.

He smiled and gave a slight nod finding himself tongue-tied again in her presence.

'That would be lovely,' Jo said.

Tamsin smiled, a threesome wasn't what she'd had in mind, it was one of the few places they could go without transport.

Jo looked at the map again. The roads wound all over the place and it looked as if she'd have to go a long way round to find the lane that led to the farm. When it came to the actual journey it seemed miles. Miles of narrow lanes that brushed both sides of her car at the same time, foot hovering, always ready to brake in case someone appeared in the narrow roadway. Miles of dreading meeting something big or something that couldn't reverse back to the nearest wide spot to pass. Squeezing through the rush hour was a cinch, that was usually all forward movement, she never had been too brilliant at reversing. This smelled a lot better though, thought Jo as she crept along the lane that had confidently pointed to Bodrigga farm, and the scenery couldn't be beaten, wonderfully bright clumps of gorse, brilliant flashing views of sky and sea, rolling fields of grey-green sward or tall swaying cereals.

A small herd of goats stared inquisitively at her car as she edged in through the farm gate. She pulled up and looked about her. A tight group of stone buildings, a large barn to the right, a row of smaller ones to the left and ahead a pleasantly proportioned building that looked as if it had grown from the landscape with flowering shrubs and ivy-like plants climbing all over it.

Alex opened his door, and Jo followed suit. As they did so a door opened in the farmhouse and a large shambling man approached, his long ginger hair straggling out in the breeze, his clothes fighting him at each step as if trying to escape. He tucked his shirt in absent-mindedly, then, as he reached them, thrust out a hand.

'Pete Austin!' he said and his face transformed itself with an enormous smile.

Jo took his hand briefly, 'Jo Smart.'

'Alex,' added Alex as he took his turn to shake the enormous paw.

Pete rubbed his forehead, as if he couldn't remember what came next. 'I'll show you the chalet – then, if you like I'll show you round the farm,' he said and turned to lead the way. Abruptly he stopped and gave a short laugh. 'It'll be best if we go round the other way first, it's not so messy,' he added, as he made them retrace their steps and pass out of the farmyard gate and head towards the cliff edge.

The view was breathtaking, the whole sweep of the bay spread before them. They turned to the right and ahead Jo noticed a group of three Scots pines, and as they walked towards them the chalet appeared, a long low wooden building in a slight dip in the land.

'That's it,' he grinned, 'you can get the car along the outside to the end of the main farmyard, but I'd not recommend taking it right down here, though.'

He opened the door. The room smelled freshly cleaned, with the hint of wood smoke.

'There's a wood-burner for all hot water, it's lit, there's logs out back, just keep it filled up and it shouldn't ever go out. Any problems, just ask. Look, our usual – the people who usually come here want to live like this. It's a bit basic, not holiday-world stuff – I'll show you what else there is. You see – there's milk, veg, fruit, all organic,' he shrugged. It really had been a long time ago since anyone new came, and Julia had always been the one who ran this side of things.

'It's lovely – it really is lovely,' Jo said sensing his discomfort and remembering Rod saying that he'd lost his wife.

'Right – er – would you like to come and have a cup of tea – before we unload the car?'

'That would be lovely,' Jo said and laughed a little, partly from embarrassment and partly at herself, her needle seemed to have got stuck.

'I've been through all the trades – can't find a tool that quite fits the bill though,' James said despondently, 'Such a shape – I felt it had to be a tool, you know?'

'What'd you get?'

'Huh, marlin spike, that's for spicing rope, jeweller's ring sizer, not sharp enough by miles, and a basket-maker's bodkin – which isn't big enough – usually anyhow.' It was his favourite, but still seemed highly unlikely. He looked at the list thoughtfully again.

Glenda couldn't help feeling sympathy for him, he thrived on the active police work, sitting round looking up books wasn't his way.

'None of them sound as dramatic as an ice-pick – it couldn't be something else I suppose like a piece of machinery or something specially made.'

'Specially made to stab a tart?'

'Not – '

'Sorry, Glen – I'm just not in a good mood today.'

'Anything particular?'

'Nah, just – forget it, I'll be okay.'

'Sure?'

'Sure!' he raised a grin for her. Glenda, so understanding, so easy to talk to, it was hard to believe she was a woman. It was woman trouble that was getting him down again. Why did he always fall for someone who was heavily tied up in some way. The new little Lucy had seemed so cute, so appealing, just asking for someone to look after her. How was he to know she already had a steady boyfriend over at Crownhill nick. He'd not meant to tread on toes and she'd accepted his offer of a drink quickly enough. It was a 'friendly' word from the desk sergeant that had put him wise, he'd offered the same response that Lucy did when he complained about landing him in it, 'she was a grown woman, she could make up her own mind'. However she'd added that 'as he appeared to be less than a grown man perhaps he'd better just go f…himself,'.

'Take this, can you?' a face appeared around the door and flicked a file on to the nearest table.

'Where to? We're in the middle of a murder case.'

'Dead one – can't hang on to it forever – got to get back to work sometime, you know,' he said and disappeared.

Glenda picked up the file and read the sheet inside.

'Man's just been picked up and taken to hospital – both legs broken – says he argued with his wife and walked out, next day his brothers-in-law turned up, laid him out across the edge of the pavement and drove a car over his legs. Sick. Shall we go and pay them a visit?'

'Yeah – where's the missus?'

'Hospital – all forgiven on her part apparently.'

'Women,' muttered James under his breath as he followed Glenda out of the office.

*

'Find a pair of wellies that fit – there's just about every size there,' Pete said as he led them out to his utility room, 'and we'll go and meet the animals.'

'So are you self-sufficient here then?' Alex asked as he stuffed his jeans in the top of a pair of large black Wellington boots.

Pete laughed, 'We'd wanted to be – impossible really, but we do – I do, loads of organic veg – trying to make it grow all year round, and the animals – you'll see – but I still have to use the supermarket.'

'So do you sell organic produce as well, as the chalet – I mean, I'm not complaining, but the chalet can't bring in much and with all the other bills,' Jo's voice trailed away, conscious that she sounded very inquisitorial.

'No the place doesn't pay its way at all really – ' he took a deep breath as they stepped out into the back garden of the house,

'I work from home – computer work, very handy – no office to go to.'

'What do you do, Mr. Austin.'

'Pete, please,' he said as Alex fell in step beside him, 'Interested in computers are you? Really interested, not just playing games on them?'

'Yes, matter of fact, I am,' Alex said defiantly,

'Good – I'll show you later what I do – now come along here and meet the ducks first.'

The ducks dipped their heads coyly and trotted along behind the drake making little ducky sounds, nothing as blatant as a quack. Pete explained that they were Khaki Campbells, one of the best egg-layers in the duck world. Suddenly, in an onslaught of feathers and honking, the geese charged over to see-off the intruders. Jo found herself stepping back involuntarily as the gander advanced his neck snaking, a vicious hiss sounding from his beak. She was glad of the fence between them.

'They're always like that with strangers. They say they make good guards, always make a racket and pretty frightening in their way. You're okay really though, aren't you Nelson?'

Nelson hissed and reared his long neck making himself seem twice the size.

As they wandered back, towards the field in front of the farm, chickens darted around them, pure white with black tips to their tails and a fringe of fine black feathers at the neck. A flurry of chickens appeared from one of the low barns followed by a cockerel, magnificent with his great sweep of blue-black tail feathers glowing in the sunlight, his comb and wattle bright, blood-red and trembling as he moved.

'Light Sussex – one of the older breeds – more hardy for free-ranging,' Pete explained as Rockerfella stalked past, disdaining to acknowledge them. 'And here are the goats,' he added opening the gate into the field.

A curious kid bounced over towards them but stopped just short, legs quivering, ready for quick flight. Slowly, the older goats began to walk forward, then they all stopped to squat and water the ground, then strolled on again.

'It's always the same, it's a form of greeting- I think,' Pete grinned. He reached out a hand and rubbed the large brown, black and white goat between the ears, 'this is Jasmine – she's the matriarch of the herd, no one gets by you do they, Jas?' Nor did it look as if anyone could, a big goat anyway, Jasmine seemed almost as wide as she was high.

'Is she expecting?'

'No, Jas always looks like this, you can barely tell the difference when she *is* expecting. And this is Hyacinth – has great pretensions does our Hyacinth – part Angora, that's why she's so soft,' he rubbed her head too, Jasmine began to move off. Jo reached out a hand, Hyacinth didn't seem to mind. The hair was both coarse and soft beneath her fingers, a guard layer of hard hair with soft, fluffy fibre beneath. The goat looked up at her with its golden eyes, the strange long pupil making a dark slit in the gold.

Other goats noticing the extra attention Hyacinth was receiving decided to come forward and be introduced, Snowdrop, a pure white Saanen, Tulip, a black and white British Alpine, and Rosie, another British Toggenburg, Jasmine's daughter. Jo was delighted, they crowded round her mouthing the edges of her clothes.

'Hey, mind,' she said to Tulip as the goat gave a determined tug at Jo's tee-shirt.

'It's okay, they don't really eat anything! They'll *try* anything but there's nothing so fussy as a goat – only actually eat certain things and then only as long as no one has dropped it on the ground!'

'And you milk them?'

'Yes, by hand, twice a day. You're welcome to come along and have a go – that's what I was saying, the people who usually stay come here to do that sort of thing.' He shrugged, 'It's not compulsory though.'

'No – I'd really like to try – be different, Alex?'

'Yeah – sure.'

'Great – I'll give you a hand to get things down to the chalet and I'll leave you to settle in, milking's done at six, scruffy gear,' he added as they left the field and headed back towards the car

*

Alex swore at himself as he fought his way through the gorse. He was sure that Pete Austin had said he just had to follow the path that ran down beneath the chalet and it would take him down to Millendreath beach. He'd agreed to meet Tamsin down there as soon as she came off work at five and he didn't want to be late.

He'd only had one girlfriend, unlike many of the lads, and Hazel had been more of a companion, an intellectual equal, easy to be with. They'd held hands, touched and kissed but when it came to devoting hours to study for exams they'd drifted apart. Tamsin was something different, from the moment he saw her he wanted to touch her translucent skin, smooth that wild hair, hold her tight. He was frightened to think beyond that, and it made him nervous in her company, finding himself tongue tied and desperate to make a good impression.

The path seemed pretty steep, steeper that he thought it ought to be, but he reasoned that it had to drop quickly to get from the cliffs to sea level. Suddenly there seemed to be nothing ahead of him, except sea and air. He teetered on the edge, held back from the drop by the gorse that he'd been fighting through. He looked round. He must be half way down the cliff, in a section that had slipped or fallen years ago and was now completely overgrown. He turned to scramble back up, finding the dry, dusty earth slippery underfoot. An opening in the gorse appeared, cautiously he took the new path, it seemed safe and led along the cliff line. The path took another dip, skidding slightly, Alex followed. The gorse line stopped, he could see the beach not twenty foot below him. Over to the right he could clearly see a long structure, looking like a harbour wall, stretching out towards a rock set in the shallows of the sea. A girl sat on the end of the wall, looking the other way. Below him lay a jumble of giant rocks, broken out from the cliff, tumbled about and smoothed by the winter waves, their white veins standing out starkly. He began to climb down, finding it fairly easy for his long limbs to stretch between the rocks, which fortunately turned out to be firmly fixed, wedged together, for all their look of careless abandon.

Tamsin had been waiting, watching, hoping that Alex would come. The path from the cliffs meant that his approach would be invisible until he reached the high spot just above the first of the houses on the valley side. It was on this spot that her eyes had been fixed. She glanced at her watch, five past. As she looked up again she scanned quickly around and her eye caught a movement. There was someone coming down the cliff-face over on Bodrigga beach. She stood up, could it be Alex? Mad fool! But it *was* the cliff beneath the farm.

She launched herself from the wall, jumping far enough to miss the pools of water gathered at its base. Standing she shook herself and tugged her Tee-shirt down before sauntering, casually, towards the cliff.

Alex paused a moment to look out along the beach. He saw Tamsin, yellow Tee-shirt, jeans, mane of coppery hair flowing out behind her and his forgotten nerves reappeared. He scrambled down more, trying to keep as dignified a position as he could.

She stood at the bottom of the rocks, arms akimbo, laughing. 'What d' you think you're doing?' she called. He turned, standing, balancing on a rock just higher than her head. He jumped, a leap that should have ended with a perfect landing on the sand, except that it didn't work out quite as planned because the soft sand slipped beneath his feet and left him ignominiously flat on his back.

'Fool! You could have hurt yourself,' she said coming over to him.

Nothing to lose now, he thought. 'Damn! And I forgot the Milk Tray,' he said, delighted to find his smile reflected in her face, as he offered a hand for her to pull him up. She tugged his hand mockingly and he leapt to his feet. 'I couldn't be late, could I?' he said, looking down at her, and not letting go of her hand just yet, Tamsin smiled softly and looked down, her heart thumping. Alex, his whole body feeling as if it were filled with lava, a burning semi-solid mass, slipped his arm over her shoulder as they turned to walk along the beach. She leant into his frame, feeling the heat of his body on her bare shoulder.

'Did you really? Come straight down the cliff – so's not to be late?' she said quietly.

'What do you think,' Alex said softly, pausing a moment so that Tamsin turned to face him. She looked up into his dark eyes, God, would Michelle be jealous! Wouldn't anyone?

His throat was tight, the lava rushed through him again making his fingers feel as if they were about to burst into flames. Terrified, he kissed her.

CHAPTER SIX

'Oh, you're back,' Jo said as he came into the chalet. Alex coloured up, he wondered, not for the first time whether all mothers managed to convey so much in so few words, or whether his mother was a specialist, being a teacher too.

'Sorry I missed the milking – how'd it go.'

Jo's eyes lit up with amusement. 'Brilliant – I really didn't think I'd be any good. Pete's great hands sort of envelop the teats, it was difficult to make out exactly how to operate them. But after a few minutes I got some kind of rhythm going. He says I'm really good for a beginner, certainly something different to talk about in the staff room. I going to have another go tomorrow, you can try then too – if you're around,' she finished with a smile that disarmed any hint of criticism.

'Okay – I'd like to give it a go.'

'Oh and Pete said something about showing you his computer set up – if you fancied going over later.'

'Yeah, great – I'll do that – er – after dinner?'

'It's all right; it's almost ready!' she laughed.

*

'Close the incident room.' Superintendent Williams said curtly. 'I've never known one yield so little information.' He pushed the file back across the desk to Rick. He tried to hide his mistrust of anyone who transferred out of the Met., even though this one had come highly recommended, he was waiting to see the proof.

'Unusual case, sir, the murder of a person who appears to have no past. It was suggested that she was a prostitute, but the PM indicates she hadn't had intercourse for at least a fortnight, so there seem to be no regular punters, as such, and despite the stash of cocaine, she wasn't a user. I don't think the men that called would ever be likely to come forward to clear their names on this one.'

'As I said – waste of time and money – and Regional Crime have stolen the cocaine lead – if you'd been able to get somewhere with the murder we'd have hung on to part of that, too.' Williams seemed to be both accusing Rick and talking to himself.

'We're still working on missing persons – and the weapon,' Rick offered. Williams grunted and waved a dismissive hand. Obviously the interview was at an end. Rick stood and picked up the file, wondering whether this transfer had been a good idea, at least he'd always seen eye to eye with his last Super.

'Right, Glenda, Andy, we're closing down the incident room on the Mount Wise murder, sort it out please,' he rubbed his forehead, 'Er, when you get back I'll see you Glenda, with James, see what we can tie up.'

'Sir, D.S. Henry was looking for you while you were in with the old man.'

'Thanks.'

Almost as soon as Lewis and Hammond left the office, Detective Sergeant John Henry stuck his head round the door. Henry had a wiry frame that he never seemed to stretch to its fullest extent, making him seem shorter than many of his colleagues.

'Okay?'

'Don't ask! What've you got then?'

'A little bird tells me that the Super's not chuffed.'

'Definitely not!'

'Can't win them all,' he said perching himself on the corner of Rick's desk. 'I thought this might cheer you up though, strictly off the record until it comes through officially,' he added with one hand held up as if stopping traffic.

Rick waited, it was obvious that his sergeant had, as he had been told, his own contacts that moved information around a darn sight faster than the official communication routes.

'That little packet of coke you found, they've found some more, out to Totnes. Seems it came to light in a standard turn over, cleaning up a bit, pro's. Sound familiar?'

'Regional?'

'In on it now – just thought you'd like to know.'

'Thanks. Every bit helps.'

You all settled now?'

'Here? Almost sorted – I think.'

'And – at home, weren't you looking to buy somewhere?'

John Henry's memory for tiny details was almost as legendary as his ability to elicit information, that much Rick had already learned about him.

'I didn't think buying a place would be so much hassle.'

'Second most stressful thing in life, they do say.'

'Agreed! God, I'll be glad when it's over.'

'So, perhaps you'd like to come round for dinner one evening.'

'I'd be delighted. Thanks.'

'How about Thursday then?' John said as he straightened up a little, head on one side like an inquisitive terrier.

'Fine by me,' Rick said, standing as John left the office. He shook his head, and wondered how come Henry had stuck at D.S.

*

'Uh – I didn't expect so many,' Alex admitted as Pete showed him into his work room. Alex had thought it'd only be one or two computers at the most. 'What is it you do?' he asked.

'I de-bug, take this,' he tapped a few keys and the opening pages of an adventure game ran through their tricks. 'The graphics are really clever on this one, watch,' he started off the characters on their journey. Alex had to agree the pictures could have been from a film, and the sweep of the vision was smooth and complete.

'It's – impressive, did you make it?'

'Hell, no. Some glassy-eyed boys up in Berkshire created this one, however if we ask for this combination of events,' he tapped in some more commands, 'you see what we get?' Alex could see all right, the top half of the screen continued its journey, the lower half remained static.

'Some bug?'

'Yep – and that's where I come in – I sort out the bugs they can't manage themselves. It's as if close-to they can't see the mistakes for looking. These disks can be worth a fortune when they're sorted, but next to nothing until then.'

'That's the reason for the bank of computers then?'

'Different systems, different RAMs, what works on the beasts they design these games on sometimes slips up on the home model. I have a range of the simpler ones to guide me,' he smiled at Alex, 'Do you have a computer at home?'

'Yes, sort off, an old Amstrad, it does, for school work and stuff, you know?'

'Want to have a go on some of these?'

'Sure, what at?'

'What d'you like, graphics work? Art work?'

'Art work sounds good, mine's really not up to much – of course we've got everything at school,' he finished lamely, trying not to sound too much of a novice.

'Not quite the Mona Lisa – but pretty good,' Pete said an hour later, as he looked over Alex's shoulder.

'It's so easy to use, to get good smooth lines, like on the hair? And the quality and definition is something else – what's the art package called again?' Alex said, so full of enthusiasm that he didn't care that Pete was scrutinising the drawing he'd made.

'Artair – do I recognise her?'

Alex blushed, he'd tried to capture the essence of Tamsin in the picture, it wasn't quite right, he knew that, but he thought it had the look of her in a cartoon way, and Pete must know Tamsin.

'Artair? Who's that by?' he asked, trying to deflect the questioning.

'Well, that is by me, trouble is it's got a little bug – ' he laughed, 'Seriously, I did write that one, and it does have a minor problem – it only runs this well on the Acorn 5000 with an upgrade to eight megabyte of RAM – market's too small to set it up, besides, things have moved on with their RISC PC – I guess they won't be doing these much more – more's the pity.' He patted the monitor as if it were a favoured dog. 'Would you like to print?'

'Please,' Alex said, finding himself colouring up again and gritting his teeth.

Pete tapped a couple of keys and a printer on the other bench began to purr into action, paper slipping sibilantly into the machine.

'I always use the 5000 for my personal stuff – fast, efficient – probably my favourite machine,' he added as he closed down the system. 'There you go,' he handed Alex the picture.

'Thanks, it's um, been really interesting – see you tomorrow?' Alex said as he left the back door of the farmhouse to stumble along the track to the chalet.

The night sky was full of stars, more than he could ever remember seeing before in his life. He held the picture close to him to prevent the stiff breeze snatching it from his grasp. When the light from the chalet came into view he stood and looked about him for a moment. The sea could be heard, rushing and whooshing far below, but only the lights of a distant seaside habitation twinkled in the dark. It was dark, so very dark, and the wind, buffeting him, spread a feeling of wildness through his mind. Today, having made a monumental fool of himself, he'd let go for the first time in his life – and taking an uncalculated risk, he'd kissed Tamsin on impulse. Standing in the dark of the Cornish sea-swept night he remembered the hot rush through his whole body as she pressed her lips on his. Even now his lips tingled at the thought, the sensuous feel of her soft lips and cool moist mouth. He shivered and forced himself to head towards the light of the chalet.

The morning sun stole across Jo's pillow and looked her in the eye at five-thirty. She lay there for a moment trying to decide whether to get up or to snuggle back down. She could hear the sea and the sounds of the distant farmyard, the odd bleat of a goat, the punctuating crowing of the cockerel. It sounded so pleasantly rural that she suddenly felt she wanted to be part of it all on such a pleasant morning. With determination she threw back the covers letting a blast of cold air wake her fully. After a quick wash she dragged on the old jeans she'd worn the evening before, and the jumper adorned with various shades of goat hairs, and set off up the path to the farm. It wasn't long before she spied Pete Austin's large frame ambling across towards the ducks with a bucket of meal, she caught up with him as he stood watching them.

'Isn't it the messiest thing you ever saw?' he said warmly. The ducks shovelled and splattered, and trotted to the water trough and gulped and gargled, only to return to the sloppy meal for another session. Soon the food trough was empty and every duck was liberally speckled with meal. 'Mucky as a duck, Julia used to say, always maintained that pigs were maligned, that ducks were the really messy creatures,' He fell silent for a moment. Jo felt almost guilty at knowing who he was talking about.

'Julia was your wife?' she said carefully, hoping he'd not guess how much she already knew.

'Yep – presumed drowned. Did Sylvia tell you?'

'Only – '

'Just as well – did you sleep well?' he changed the subject swiftly.

'Yes, thank you. I feel really refreshed – thought I'd help out, if that's okay?'

'Come on then – you can have another go at the milking if you like, I'll finish feeding the poultry,' he said with a cheerful grin as he snatched up the bucket and led the way back to the buildings.

*

'Sir!' Glenda appeared at Ricks door.
'What is it?' Rick looked up sharply from the file he was reading on the 'brothers-in-law and the broken legs' case.
'I have a possible from the missing persons – height; age; colouring – all fits our Jane.'
'Good work, let's see.'
D.C. Lewis came into his office and laid a fax in front of him.
'Kate (Catherine) Morgan, age: 21. DoB 14/6/73. Height: 5ft 5in. Hair: Dark brown. Eyes: Hazel. Other distinguishing features: None. Home address: 6 Westwood crescent, Fleetwood, Lancs. Date reported missing: 27/12/94 by Mr. Morgan, father.' A photo was attached, some-what poorer for having been faxed but the general features could have fitted those of the body in cold store at the morgue.

Rick shivered, he knew what it meant, a long trip from Fleetwood for the parents, hoping against hope that the trip would be a wasted one, yet not daring to rule out the possibility. It would make his work easier if they could at least identify the body but he hated the thought of the parents' distress.
'Well done – certainly seems a possible, would you like to get on to them, see if they can get here to ID our Jane?'
Glenda pulled a bit of a face, it had been good to pick up a lead of any kind but she was as chary of the follow-up as Rick.
'Yes sir,' she said.

*

Tamsin was miles away. Uncle Mick had to speak to her twice before she heard what he said.

'Wake up girl, too many late nights I think! Go and clear the alcove.'

'All right,' Tamsin muttered, 'keep your hair on,' she added under her breath. The alcove afforded a wonderful view out to sea, and across to the wall that divided Millendreath from Bodrigga. She smiled to herself. Alex really was something else. She could barely believe it when he'd kissed her like that. Like something from a teen romance, cool, not a slobbery hit and miss affair like John Borlase at the school disco. Just the one kiss, but oh what a kiss! She shivered with delight.

They'd walked along the beach until the waves hit the cliff, then turned and walked back and across to the cafe. By then they were only holding hands, in case Uncle Mick was looking out. It was as if Alex was a different person away from the adults, chatting easily about his life in London. Even telling her about the gang that had beaten him up, though she could tell he hadn't really wanted to talk about it, but she just had to know. Mum had told her what Aunty Sally had said and she couldn't get it out of her head. Alex had said they'd come after him because he'd named them as the gang who were pushing drugs to the new kids, eleven-year olds. The school had no proof, of course, couldn't exactly do anything about them, as such, but it had made their last term uncomfortable. He still didn't know how they found out it was him that split, but he was sure it had been the right thing to do, even now.

'Niece or no bloody niece, if you don't wake up my girl I'll find someone else,' a deep voice growled in her ear. Tamsin jumped, a knife slid off and clattered noisily to the floor. She hadn't realised that she'd been standing stock still staring out the window for the last five minutes, a pile of plates in her hands. Her Uncle moved off shaking his head sorrowfully, and scowling a grin at customers who caught his eye.

*

'Hullo – you back again, glutton for punishment are you?'
Pete said cheerfully as Jo and Alex came into the farmyard just
after six, obviously dressed to help out.

'I think I'm really hooked,' Jo beamed at him. There was
something intensely satisfying in milking the goats. The way
that the milk shot into the bucket when you got the rhythm
right, churning a froth on top as it squirted into the milk with
a satisfying sound. And they were such characters, funny and
clever. She'd quite taken a shine to Tulip, whose black hairs
stood out strongly on the cream jumper Jo was wearing, gained
from leaning against the warm flank while she milked.

'And Alex – what do you want to do?'

Alex shrugged, 'I suppose I'd better have a go at milking – I
hear it's really – real,' he grinned.

'Come on, I'll show you how, then we'll go off and see to the
geese, they're real too!'

They'd spent almost the whole day on the beach. The sun
had been ridiculously hot, making it an imperative to go
swimming in the cool water at least once an hour. They'd
straggled back up the cliff path, the official cliff path, tired and
happy, eaten a meal of fresh organic salad with soft goat's
cheese and headed up to the farmyard to help out. It had been
a perfect day, Jo thought as she settled into the rhythm of the
milking, close and squeeze down, close and squeeze down.

'As long as you face them, walk towards them, the geese are
okay, but they'll bite – goose you, in fact – if you turn your
back on them!' Pete said as they walked towards the advancing
cohort of geese, all hissing and snaking their necks. Suddenly
they broke ranks and with a hooting cry backed off quickly to
re-group. 'See what I mean.' he dumped a fresh bucket of
water down and took the bucket of meal from Alex's hand.
The geese all advanced on the buckets. 'That's fine now, we
can leave unmolested,' he smiled. Alex walked warily, one eye
keeping a watch on the geese as they left the paddock.

'Seeing our Tamsin this evening?' Pete said casually

Alex felt a blush move up his neck. 'No, not this evening – I think Mum's planning on staying up here this evening.'

'Well you're welcome to come and do some more on the computers, anytime.'

'Really? That would be great – thanks.'

'Well, your mum could come up to the house too, if she likes,' Pete added, thinking how nice it would be to have the company.

*

'Sir,' Glenda's voice was subdued and reverential.

Rick looked up and immediately stood as he saw the white faced civilians standing just behind D.C. Lewis.

'Mr. and Mrs. Morgan, sir. This is Detective Inspector Whittington, as I said, he's in charge of this case,' Glenda said as she ushered the couple into the room. She mouthed the word coffee at Rick and he gave a brief shake of his head, there would be both time and need for coffee after their trip to the cold store. He shook each of them by the hand.

'Shall we go straight down, we can discuss the case afterwards, if we need to,' he said with as much of a smile as he could muster.

They were very good at the morgue, give them enough notice and they would bring out the cadaver and present it in as sympathetic a manner as possible. Somehow it is slightly less of a shock if it is not just pulled out of a cold grey drawer for inspection, but laid out properly with discreet covers spread over it.

Rick could feel the fear that emanated from this couple. A man in his late forties, hair only just touched with grey and with a face that appeared to be shaped and roughened by the weather, and his wife, dark hair enhanced by a bottle, dark eyes rimmed with grey as if she never slept.

They stood around the head end, Rick noticed how the woman clung to her husband's arm, though he made no attempt to hold her.

'Are you ready?' he asked softly and paused momentarily for their nod, before peeling back the sheet gently, with care, as if he might wake her. She seemed asleep. A cold, white, bloodless sleep. They would not have to see the circular hole that had bled so profusely onto the broidere anglaise, but Rick couldn't help himself seeing it again in his head.

The woman barely looked, stuffed her face into the material of her husbands jacket. He stared and bit his lip.

'Do you recognise ...?'

'Aye – Kate,' the granite features suddenly crumbled and he turned his back on Rick, on his daughter. Rick gently covered her face and nodded to the mortuary assistant who came across to wheel the body away. Rick guided the grieving parents out of the sterile atmosphere back into the warm living light of the summer day.

Back in his office he offered them a chair each, stuck his head out of the door and said 'coffee' to D.C. Shepherd, who happened to be the nearest.

'Will you have a cup of coffee?' Rick asked the Morgans. They nodded, as if words were too dangerous to use. Rick flashed them a sympathetic smile and nodded to Tony Shepherd, who set off to fetch them.

'We have the date you reported your daughter missing, the twenty-seventh of December, last year,' he glanced up at them for confirmation. They nodded. 'The coffee, thanks, Tony,' he said as Tony set three cups down on the desk. D.C. Shepherd quietly closed the door behind him as he left, glad to leave interviewing the bereaved to a superior.

'Can you tell us anything that might help us – did she, did Kate know anyone down here in Plymouth?'

They shook their heads slowly.

Rick tried a different tack. 'Did you receive any communication from your daughter after she left – a card maybe?'

Another shake of the head.

'Nobody cared much,' the tight lips of the mother let out.

Rick looked up at her, her large eyes full of panic and anger.

'Over twenty-one – can do what she bloody well likes – not missing you see, if you're old enough to go off – but wouldn't she – if she were going off on her own, wanting to, wouldn't she take her money?' The woman's voice became a high pleading whine as she finished.

'How do you mean Mrs. Morgan?' Rick asked softly.

'Building society account,' Mr. Morgan found his voice, 'left it behind. Only a couple of hundred quid, but what else did she have – we thought,' he stopped. 'We thought back then she'd been murdered,' he finished softly.

'No!' his wife said sharply, 'No – you thought, you always thought that – no hope,' she waved her hands in front of her as if shooing away a wasp.

Rick thought of the building society account in the name of Jane Smith and the money she'd accumulated in it.

'When did you last see her exactly?'

'Breakfast time Thursday, the twenty-second,' Mrs. Morgan said quietly, involuntarily glancing at her watch.

'How did she seem?'

She gave a small but eloquent shrug.

'Did Kate see anyone in particular – shortly before she left, boyfriend – even girlfriend perhaps?'

'How d'you mean?'

'Meet someone new – perhaps?'

There was a ruminative silence as both parents looked at the table and thought. Rick took the opportunity to try his coffee for temperature.

As if prompted by his action Mrs. Morgan snatched up her cup and cradled it in both hands, as if drawing strength from its warmth.

'There was one – not much help though. His name was Paul – I think – Pauly she'd say. He was only visiting Fleetwood, so no one knows where he went,' she said wistfully.

'Who was he visiting?'

'No one – craft fair or something – Kate was into that sort of thing – loved arty things, decorations, things to go in her room. She didn't explain herself much to us anymore – just happened to mention this Pauly. I only remembered him because she seemed happy for a change,' she looked accusingly at her husband.

'She'd just bin sacked from the printers, same place I work at – not that I had any say in it,' Mr Morgan added.

'Did anyone try to find this 'Pauly'?'

'Like who? We did – but he'd gone and the people who ran the craft fair weren't too happy with us asking questions – and the Police wouldn't,' her voice was climbing again.

'Bunch of hippies – scroungers – travellers. Call 'em what you like – they weren't helping.' Mr Morgan grumbled.

Rick could hear all of Mr. Morgan's prejudices in his tone and doubted very much that he'd endeared himself to the 'arty-craft' people running the fair.

'Perhaps we'll get somewhere even now, if you tell us all you know,' he started.

'Bit bloody late isn't it?'

Rick could hear the man's voice breaking. 'Let me at least try to find her murderer,' he said softly.

Mr. Morgan heaved a sigh. 'Okay, what do you need?'

'Anything you know.' Rick prepared to write.

Mr. Morgan gave the few details he'd gleaned, the date of the craft fair, the name the hall was hired in and the name of the safety officer who'd been to inspect the hall while the craft fair was on. It was pathetically little.

'They move round the country – advertise for any local crafts people to join them, so much a table, and they hire a hall. They do the advertising and such and the tables hired-out pays for the hall,' Mrs. Morgan said. Her husband looked at her in surprise.

'Any particular route?'

'How would I know – it was hard enough to get anyone to speak after Ron had been in there. I was lucky though, tried on the day they were packing up.'

'So how long did the craft fair go on?'

'Just the week – but they stayed camped-over until New Year though, that's when I saw them.' It was obvious from Mr. Morgan's eyes that he hadn't known of his wife's later attempt at information gathering.

'And you asked about this Pauly?'

'Of course – seems he's an occasional – no one knows who he is,' she finished with a sigh. Rick found he'd doodled yet another box on the edge of the sheet of paper he was writing notes on. Suddenly Mrs. Morgan's head came up again from the hangdog position.

'He had a limp though – she told me that – this girl from the camp. 'What, the one with a bit of a limp?' she said. I told her I didn't know, but that his name was Pauly – she laughed but said 'yes that was him'. But she didn't know anything else, where he came from or nothing,' she finished lamely, her head subsiding once more.

'That's good, interesting – helpful.' Rick tried to buoy them up on the value of this small shred of information, to leave them with a positive sense of having done some good, before they set off on their long journey back to Fleetwood.

CHAPTER SEVEN

Pete, shutting in the chickens for the night, noticed Jo as she and Alex set off for the evening. She looked very attractive, dressed in a silky black Tee-shirt and cream jeans with a fine red belt threaded through them, her bubbly blonde hair was highlighted by the sun and set off by the rosy tan she was developing. He raised his hand and smiled, they waved back as they climbed in their car.

Sitting and chatting over a glass of Julia's home-made wine yesterday evening had been delightful, he'd been as surprised by Jo's determination and occupation as she had been by his work when it was explained. There had been only one moment he wouldn't want to relive, and that had been over a simple comment that brought Julia rushing into his head and very nearly brought tears to his eyes. 'So you could work anywhere, really,' she'd said. Just as Julia had said, had insisted, when they'd first thought about Bodrigga. He could, it was as true now as then, so why did he stay? He knew, he stayed just-in-case. In-case she came back one day.

He watched as the car drove away. With a small tug of something distantly related to jealousy he wondered who she was seeing this evening and turned quickly to shake the idea from his head.

*

Rod was already at The Smugglers, Jo recognised his Landrover and wondered how he'd feel if she offered to drive them to wherever it was he'd said he was going to take her. Her only and abiding memory of the vehicle was of feeling like death as they jolted up to Sylvia's place, and even the thought made her feel off-colour.

She needn't have worried, Rod was quite amenable to having a chauffeuse for the evening, cheerily saying that it would mean he could have a drink, and that was fine by him.

They were to leave Alex with the Golds. Tamsin was trying to be cool but her agitation showed in her flittery movements. Jo smiled at Alex, sitting uncomfortably on the edge of the sofa, and only let a small shadow of concern pass through her mind, but decided to leave it to be dealt with at a later date.

'Got enough money?' she asked.

He nodded. They were going to the local pictures, down in Looe itself, and were under orders to walk straight back up afterwards. Tom had put on an impressive 'father of daughters' act when he'd made that last comment, and Alex seemed to have taken it to heart.

Rod directed Jo as she wound the car out of the narrow lanes and on to the main road. It wasn't long before they reached the Tamar bridge and were heading into the city. Jo hadn't been into Plymouth at all, though she'd told herself that she ought to 'do' the Hoe, Francis Drake and all that, while she was down this way. They drove down a double width road, round a roundabout and disappeared down a smaller road that was labelled as the way to the Barbican. Jo smiled to herself as she noticed, through a gap in the buildings, the lines of boats in the small harbour, it was as if you couldn't keep Rod away from the sea. They drove a little way further along the road before turning into a small ill-lit carpark.

Jo shivered as she climbed out of the car, the wind was brisk and cool now that the sun had gone down. She reached back into the car for the jacket she'd meant to bring, only to find she'd forgotten it.

'Bother!'

'Something up?'

'Just forgotten my jacket – it's blown up chilly now.'

Rod grinned. 'I'll just have to take you under my wing then, won't I?' he said his grin breaking into a disarming laugh as he held out his arm as an invitation to take shelter. Jo laughed back at him, but tucked herself in beside him, feeling an instant warmth as the breeze was blocked. He smelled freshly scrubbed as his arm clamped about her shoulder, his fingers gently rubbing the bare skin of her arm.

'The Lobster Pot' was a small restaurant facing the harbour, between the fish market and the Mayflower Steps. As soon as they stepped inside, Jo could understand the name. The tables were ingeniously made from oversized lobster pots with a round glass table-top fixed to them. The chairs, presumably to be in keeping, were also made of a form of wicker. The walls were decorated with suitably sea related paraphernalia, much of which Jo was at a loss to recognise.

'Friend of mine owns it, what d'you think?'

Jo, wondering how good a friend it was and quite how to answer, just looked round in amazement as they were guided to a table. The basic idea was good, but the lack of subtlety jarred.

'How do they manage, with the food regs, to have all this stuff hanging up?'

'It all sealed, or something – well?'

'Certainly different – who's you friend – the chef?'

'Nah – Pongo doesn't cook – he just owns it.'

'Pongo? With a name like that thank heavens he doesn't cook,' she laughed.

'Nickname. He was in the army, see, a 'pongo'.'

Jo looked blank. Rod grinned.

'Haven't you ever heard that? 'Where the army goes: the pong goes.' A bloke's been in the army – he's a Pongo,' his eyes sparkled at her and she wasn't sure if he was teasing or not.

'But he's still in, is he?'

'No – invalided out as it happens. Makes this sort of stuff, he does,' he waved his hand to indicate the decor, 'What do you fancy?' he said offering her the menu.

*

'In here?' Alex asked sceptically as Tamsin pointed up to a small door set at the top of a short flight of steps, tucked in beside a cheap restaurant. But sure enough the sign immediately over the door did say it was 'THE CINEMA'. Inside the door was a tiny hatchway, behind which a plump lady sat and cheerfully took their money, her eyes twinkling at Alex as she did so.

Alex had never seen such an old-fashioned place. The old red carpets, seats and walls gave it the aura of an old time music hall, as did the musty smell. About a dozen other people were already ensconced and Tamsin led him to seats far off to the left, near, but not quite, at the back.

She'd been thinking about this carefully all day. She wanted them to be as much on their own as possible, but not in the suggestive 'back row'. She wanted to be seen by her friends if they happened to go to the flea-pit that evening, but didn't want to be in line with the entrance, to be the first people seen as soon as anyone came into the place. Everything was perfect at the moment. Alex had taken her hand and held it as they'd walked down and across the bridge. When they got to the benches, just before the town proper, Tamsin had kept a keen eye out for Michelle. Michelle and some of the other local girls and boys often hung around there in the early evening, chatting, eating chips from the chippy across the way, sharing a can of coke. She'd only been one of that crowd once or twice, living on the West side she wasn't allowed down over the bridge unless she was going somewhere in particular. In fact she knew that her Dad would go wild if he found her hanging about there, she'd heard him on that subject often enough. Disappointingly there were none of her own mates among the few who were gathered there this evening, and more particularly, no Michelle. Never mind, she might just be there when they came out. She snuggled closer to Alex as the film title rolled.

*

89

Pete coughed again. His head ached a little and he was sure now that he was going down with something. Perhaps he ought to give this evening a miss, perhaps he ought to forget all about it altogether, he may well be wrong again. No, he'd spent time on that; if he was wrong then it was only a matter of a different week. He was certain of the time and place.

He snapped his long ginger hair into a elastic band to make a pony-tail to hold it out of the way, and slipped a sweat band over his forehead to prevent the stray strands from whipping across his face in the wind. He needed to be able to concentrate out there. He used all his considerable strength and weight to pull the trailer round and hitch the Shetland motor boat to the Landrover. A last look around, to make sure the farmhouse was locked up, and he set off.

He usually tried to drop the boat in the water at different places, not always using the most convenient slipway, but this time he would use the local one as he didn't feel up to struggling to drop the boat in at a strange place this evening.

As he climbed out of the car, he noticed that the strength of the wind had increased. He checked the water at the edge of the slip-way then drove the Landrover back until the trailer disappeared under the flickering waves. Clambering on board he released the boat which, buoyed momentarily, kicked and bucked to get away from the trailer. Leaping down into thigh-high water he dragged the rope to a mooring, trotted back to the Landrover and pulled the trailer clear of the sea. Locking up and secreting the keys well inside his clothing he ran back to the jetty. A deep and rasping cough racked his body for a moment and flashes of light appeared to fire across his brain, making his head ache again. Once on board he fired up the big outboard, its deep throaty roar filling the air. Aiming the small vessel out to sea he pushed the lever forward and left the security of the land behind.

*

D.S. John Henry lived in a mid-terraced house in Lipson within fifteen minutes of the Charles Cross station. It looked better cared for than most of its neighbours, the paintwork gleaming, pot plants cramming the window space. Rick had to park a little way up the street and so had passed a few other places at close quarters to compare it with. He rang the bell and stepped back a little, the bottle of wine he'd brought swinging gently in his hand.

'Rick! Come in,' John said as he flung open the door, 'I hope you don't mind, I've invited someone else along – make it a table, as it were,' he added as he took Rick's proffered bottle and led the way down the hall to the dining-room.

'Not at all,' Rick murmured, admiring the decor, clean, simple and effective. Someone had taste.

'Rick, this is Stephen, he works up in the hospital, and this is Lorna,' he paused, as Rick shook hands briefly with Stephen and then turned to face the woman.

He'd noticed her as soon as he'd entered the room and in that instant his heart started hammering – he didn't like the sensation. So he hadn't been concentrating on Stephen as he shook the soft hand, but on looking at the woman again, to be sure. It was all right. She was about the same size as Elise with the same dramatic dark colouring, but there the similarity ended. Thankfully. Her face was so different, especially when she smiled up at him, like she did now, as he took her tiny sparrow like hand in his.

'Nice to meet you,' she said, her voice tinny and high pitched. 'John tells me you're another policeman,' she laughed, 'What else?'

Rick felt a little non-plussed by her question, if it was even a question, 'That's right.'

'Rick's my new D.I., look sit down, have a drink – we'll just finish a few things then we can eat, okay?' John said as he picked up a couple of glasses.

He handed them their drinks and excused himself, Stephen, too had disappeared. It left Rick and Lorna together.

'So, do you work, Lorna?' Rick asked, noticing no signs of children in the house, no toys, no photos.

'I'm up at the hospital too, with Stephen, he's a security officer?' She made every statement sound like a question, her voice rising in inflexion at the end of each comment.

'What's that in?'

'Hospital security? I just tap names in and record things, nothing physical,' she giggled. 'You haven't known John long, have you?'

'No I er, only transferred down here three weeks ago.' Something was odd, obviously there wasn't a lot of communication between Lorna and John.

'I thought not – I haven't seen you before, and John wouldn't have let you go that long? He told me about,' her voice dropped, 'the 'dreadful accident'? It must have been – awful for you?' she said leaning over solicitously and placing one hand on his thigh.

Rick's jaw tightened as he shifted his leg, her hand withdrawing lightly. It was bad enough that Lorna looked initially like Elise, that couldn't be helped, but that she should remind him of Elise's death was too uncomfortable. And what did she think she was doing?

'Where's John?' he said softly, dangerously softly to anyone who knew him.

'Oh in the kitchen – won't be long,' she leant close towards him conspiratorially.

'Shouldn't you – help him?' he needed to get away from Lorna or to get Lorna away from him.

'Why on earth – Stephen'll be there?'

'Stephen?'

'Yes, you know – or,' she paused, pulled back a little, head tilted to one side, then an elfin smile lit her features, 'or perhaps you don't? John and Stephen?'

'What?' he asked, but he knew, like playing snap, the cards suddenly matched – two jacks.

'Those two! They're terrible match-makers mind. Can't bear to see anyone on their own? Been trying to off-load me for ages now? Makes them happy though?' she said a little wistfully.

It probably explained a lot, although he was surprised that no one had hinted at D.S. John Henry's domestic arrangements, even in derogatory terms, though he was less pleased at the idea of being paired off with 'someone suitable' than with the revelations about Henry himself. He wondered just how much Henry knew – obviously he'd heard about the accident that had taken Elise and Louise away from him – had he known what Elise looked like too? The sense of invasion was subtle but tangible enough to make Rick feel uncomfortable.

'Okay, you two – would you like to come through?' John said appearing in the doorway, casting a swift glance over the couple seated awkwardly on the couch.

The meal was exceptionally good. Rick, however, found he could not relax. Even though Lorna looked less like his Elise the more he saw of her, the momentary shock of seeing the similarities that were there unnerved him each time he glanced up during the course of the meal. Conversation flowed quite freely, each of them making sure that he was not left out, as a newcomer, but he found himself more taciturn than was usual, trying to dislodge the painful feeling between his ribs, an ache, a pressure, like a twist of the knife.

After the dessert Stephen disappeared to make some coffee and Lorna excused herself to 'pay a little visit?'. For a few moments John and Rick were together, alone.

'I've messed it up somehow, haven't I?' John said quietly.

'What exactly?' Rick wasn't in the mood to play guessing games and John's statement could be taken more than one way.

'Lorna? I mean I don't pretend I didn't know about your wife. We know Lorna well and we really like her, she just seemed the obvious choice for a fourth for a dinner party,' he shrugged, but the tension was visible in his face. It was the first time Rick had sensed anything except a total assurance from John Henry.

'And you knew what Elise looked like – so you thought Lorna would be just right?'

'What? I don't get it?'

'Lorna – same build and colouring as Elise.'

'No? Hell! God's truth – I didn't know.'

Rick nodded, he could sense the veracity in John's reaction, 'Okay, but then – I got it all wrong too.'

'Ah! Well, the other thing – I guessed you wouldn't be funny about it, but I've found it helps people just to know us both, to accept us as we are.'

'Fair enough – ' Rick suddenly grinned, 'but for an awful moment before dinner I thought *your wife* was giving me the come-on, and that type of trouble I can really do without!'

John shook his head then grinned back as he suddenly realised the situation he'd unwittingly landed Rick in. At that moment both Stephen and Lorna rejoined the table and the scent of strong coffee suffused the air.

*

'Oh my! Phew – that's turned rough!' laughed Jo as they slammed the car door on the wind and rain. They'd come out of 'The Lobster Pot' straight into the teeth of a gale, or so it seemed. Together, Rod leading her by the hand, they'd run up a cobbled back street that afforded a little respite from the blast, and on through to the street that harboured the car-park. Puffed-out, they flopped down in the car seats and laughed.

Rod stretched his arm out across the back of her seat and Jo turned to him, feeling wild and yet in control at the same time. He gathered her to him, and she leant into his arms, into his embrace, to receive his hard kiss.

Once in his arms she could feel his strength, was aware somewhere in the depths of her mind that here was a man who could break her with little effort. It hadn't been like that with the only other man she'd let into her life since Alessandros. He, Alex's Technology teacher, had been soft in comparison, and Jo had felt as if she'd used him when she finished the relationship. Though even when she was honest with herself she knew she hadn't, not at the time. Rod was different. It was only amazing that he'd left this kiss so long, his strength of passion was tangible, like a cord wrapping itself around her heart, forcing her wary body to respond. His hand came up and brushed her cheek like a butterfly wing, soft and gentle.

'You're lovely, Jo,' he said hoarsely. She shook her head slightly, the damp blonde curls emphasising the movements, then leant forward to kiss him once more. It was only the sharp headlights of a car pulling into the car park that drew them apart. Jo shivered.

'Home, I think,' she said, pulling herself round straight in the car and turning the key in the ignition.

*

The film was really good. Tamsin hadn't expected it to be, it wasn't one that she'd been dying to see, but it was good in that it had made them laugh. Alex hadn't tried to kiss her again in the dark, he'd held her hand for a while, but not all the time, and she'd caught him looking at her sometimes, rather than at the screen. They left the little cinema and made their way back towards the bridge. Tamsin could see a small knot of people over by the benches and wondered who was there. She drew Alex closer to her, until he let go of her hand and put one arm over her shoulder again, just as Tamsin noticed that a girl who was leaving the group, with a desultory wave of her hand, was Michelle.

' 'Shell!' Tamsin called. Michelle stopped and turned round. She walked slowly towards them, as if she could hardly be bothered. She wore a tight knitted skirt that hugged her bottom, boot-like shoes and an enormous jumper, the wind tugged and messed her mane of thick, curly brown hair.

'Hi, Tams. Surprised you've been let out so late,' she said, her voice slurred, eyeing Alex up and down.

'Meet Alex, he's a friend of my aunt Sally's, from London,' Tamsin said, snuggling in a little tighter.

'Hi,' Alex said.

'What you doing in this dump then?'

'Holiday.'

'Oh, well you won't be round very long then will you?' she looked at Tamsin and shrugged her shoulders unpleasantly, 'pity about that, eh Tams?' she said.

This was not going quite how Tamsin had imagined. There was definitely something wrong with Michelle this evening. She wasn't usually so abrasive. There was definitely something strange about her behaviour. She'd expected her to be all over Alex, trying to win him away from her maybe – friendly rivalry – but not this cynicism, not from Michelle.

'See you Saturday morning Shell?'

'Suppose,' Michelle said, and began to drift off again, heading up the hill towards her home with an odd dismissive wave of her hand.

'She's not usually like that – I don't know what's up with her,' Tamsin said, hoping that Alex wouldn't think less of her for having a friend who appeared as Michelle had. Alex was looking after her and wondering if she was going to be all right, whether she'd get home before she fell down, for though he'd never met her before he was sure Michelle was high on something.

*

Once well out to sea, Pete turned out the lights, becoming a dark blur against the waves, letting the boat ride the uncomfortable swell. He ducked into the tiny cabin and pulled the night-sight glasses out. Leaning against the cabin he began to look all around, his eyes straining in the dark despite the enhanced vision which the glasses gave him. The waves grew around him, the wind whipped spray across his face. Sometimes the waves seemed to ride higher than the small vessel as he sank in a trough, then bucked and splashed as the boat was tossed on a mountain of water.

Despite being a good sailor, tonight the waves were affecting him, making him feel unsteady. Only once had he ever felt this bad at sea, and that was a very long time ago, in a wicked storm that he and Julia had run into when they had taken their yacht down to Spain one Easter. In hindsight it had been the beginnings of a mild bout of food poisoning from some cheese they'd picked up in France a few days before, but at the time it felt like seasickness.

He turned the engine on, pointing the Shetland's bow into the waves, but barely making any headway. It eased the motion but created even more splash and spray. He shivered and coughed again. It left him slightly breathless, his chest felt tight and ached for minutes afterwards.

He looked round for the last time, he'd seen various vessels heading, sensibly, into harbour, but had not sighted the one he was looking for. He turned on his lights and pushed the throttle forward a little more, the big engine roared as it leapt into life, and the boat surged forward. Pete eased the lever back a fraction to steady the boat and turned her back towards the small dark slipway.

*

There was no bright sunshine to wake Jo in the early morning and she slept on. At about eight o'clock she woke and lay there in the warmth of the bed, thinking about Rod. She couldn't help it, he was having a deep effect on her physically. She smiled to herself in amusement at the thought of the previous evening. Deeply involved in a front seat kiss and cuddle outside Sylvia's they'd suddenly become aware of voices. Alex and Tamsin. She could laugh now, at the time she felt amazingly guilty as they tried to get out of the car nonchalantly as if they'd only just arrived back.

She lay back, thinking again of Rod, finding her body aching for his touch. She pulled a wedge of bedclothes together and massaged herself through them until she lay exhausted, perspiration on her forehead, semi-satisfied, half relieved but still aching. Into the silence came the distant and repeated bleating of the goats. As she listened it seemed as if there was a different quality to their cries. Insistent, repetitive. All at once she had the image of them being in some kind of trouble, caught up, in pain, or something. Something was not right. Rockerfella crowed again, still muted. Jo looked at the clock. Half past eight. With a sudden burst of energy she left the bed and dived for the bathroom. She looked in on Alex and suggested it was time to get up and dressed, then left the chalet at a trot. The air was cool and damp, the sea grey and the wind coming in from it, to roll over the land, was laden with salt.

The first thing she noticed was the absence of goats from the higher paddock, next that the chickens and ducks were still shut in. Half past eight? The goats bleated again sorrowfully from their houses. She ran now, up to the farmhouse. The back door was shut, she tried the handle but it was locked. She tapped and rattled at the door. No answer. Stepping back she looked up at the windows. All closed.

'Pete! Pete?' she called. Silence, punctuated by pathetic bleating, was the only reply.

She stood for a moment, a chill running round her, then she set off for the front door. She shivered involuntarily when she saw the front door was open. Only just open, but combined with the crazy angle that the Landrover was in the farmyard with the boat balanced precariously on the trailer behind it, it seemed ominous. She opened the door carefully, gently.

'Pete? Pete?' she called again. Silence. Should she go back for Alex? She walked on, through the kitchen, warm from the big Aga, on through to the living room. Neat, empty, the workroom, equally deserted. She returned to the kitchen and sent herself up the wooden stairs.

The door to the room stood open. She could hear his stertorous breathing before she reached it and was almost prepared to steal out again and leave him. Perhaps he'd drunk heavily the evening before, perhaps he'd not welcome her interference. Then she saw he was still wearing all his outer clothing, boots included. He'd collapsed across the bed, his face was flushed, nearly the colour of his hair. Jo stepped forward carefully. His breathing seemed ragged, she reached out a hand to his forehead. It was burning, radiating enough heat to feel before she even made contact. She sniffed lightly, there was no smell of alcohol, just the odour of oil-cloth and salt.

She stood for a moment then made up her mind. She'd wake him and see how he felt. Leaning over him she shook him gently and spoke his name. He didn't move, his eyelids remained closed, mouth open, the rattling breath coming from deep inside his chest.

'Pete – wake up. Wake up!' she said, her voice getting louder as the idea that he might be really ill began to fill her. She shook him hard, his eyes flickered, but closed again. Another try, the eyes opened.

'Julia? Julia,' he murmured.

'Pete, no, Pete, not Julia, wake up.'

'Can't – breathe,' he murmured.

Jo looked at him, his eyelids were open just a crack, the eye a flicker behind the pale lashes.

'I'll ring the doctor,' Jo said, suddenly convinced.

She flicked hurriedly through the personal phone book, found a number beside the word Doctor, and dialled. In moments she was through to the surgery and in breathless tones she gave them the details she had. She must have imparted a degree of panic in her voice because the receptionist said she'd call up the doctor who was out on home visits to come straight over. Jo was surprised, she would have been unlikely to get that sort of response back home. There, she'd most probably been to be told to take him to the nearest Casualty.

She ran back up to Pete, saying as she entered the room that a doctor was on his way. He didn't hear her, as he'd closed his eyes and returned to his harsh sleep. She pulled at his boots, finding it all but impossible to remove them, as if his feet were stuck in the right-angles, jamming them on. Eventually they came off and she covered his feet with a section of bedclothes. There was nothing she could do about the heavy waterproof coat and trousers, she could never move his weight.

The sound of the goats' bleating came to her through the window. Something had to be done about them too, poor things. She looked at the sleeping form again and turned quickly and headed out of the farmhouse and down to the chalet, calling to Alex even before she reached the door.

Alex was in the kitchen, loading a few logs into the fire. 'Alex – quick. Pete's ill, the goats need doing – the hens, you know. The doctor's coming but – Oh come on!'
'Okay – what do you want me to do?'
'Can you have a go at the birds, then come and sit with Pete – then I'll do the milking – oh and keep an eye out for the doctor's car – give me a call. I'll go and have another look at Pete first, come up as soon as they're done,' she said as they made their way back to the farm buildings.

'Mum! Doctor's here!' Alex's voice rang out.
Jo quickly released the goat she'd been milking and, leaving the bucket in the milking parlour, ran to the main house. Her forearms hurt, she'd been trying to milk quickly and the effort

had made her arms ache and her fingers grow tense and stiff. At least each of the milkers had been relieved a bit, even if they'd not been milked out properly.

The doctor, a serious-faced young man, was standing in the kitchen with Alex as she burst in through the back door. 'He's upstairs – I – we're visiting, staying in the chalet,' she said, breathlessly, as she led the way up, 'I noticed Mr. Austin wasn't about – so I came to see and – well, this is how he was,' she stood back allowing the doctor to enter the bedroom. Jo stood by the door and watched.

The doctor bent over the bulky body sprawled on the bed, peered at his eyes, felt his head briefly. He opened the jacket, lifted the layers, listened to his chest, then straightened up and turned to face Jo.

'Is he all right?' she whispered.

CHAPTER EIGHT

'He will be, with luck and antibiotics.' The doctor actually managed a smile. 'He's got pneumonia, it's a good thing you called me straight away, it could have been much worse.'

'Pneumonia? But he didn't seem ill yesterday?'

'Bit of a chill?'

'I – I wouldn't really know.'

'Needn't have been much more than that, it can come on very quickly. Are you able to care for him at home?'

Jo looked at him blankly for a moment. Care for him? She was here on holiday! Yet – he'd shared so much in the short time she'd known him, and there was no-one else – no Julia to care for him.

'He may take a week or ten days to recover properly, but he could be up and about in three or four,' the Doctor added.

'Yes – I – we can look after him, what's to be done?'

'I'll give him a dose of antibiotics straight away and leave you with a prescription for the rest to be taken orally. Keep him comfortable, watch his temperature, ring if you've got any worries. I'll be back tomorrow in any case, okay?'

'Yes, okay,' Jo said feeling her usual calm, ordered self taking over the situation. The doctor returned to Pete's side.

'Would you help me remove his jacket?' he asked as he took a small phial and syringe from his bag. Together they lifted and struggled to remove Pete's heavy waterproof coat.

Minutes later the doctor was back in the kitchen writing a prescription out for the antibiotics.

'There you are, one every four hours, regularly and continue them until the end of the course. Try to keep his temperature constant, keep up the intake of liquids, and phone if you're worried about anything,' he finished with a smile.

'Thank you. We'll do our best then,' she said. He gave her a slightly quizzical look and turned towards the door.

'How bad is he?' Alex asked as the doctor drove his Volvo out of the farmyard.

'It's pneumonia! People die from pneumonia, but it seems it was caught early enough,' she pulled a wry face at the thought that she might have slipped away to let him 'sleep it off'. 'Antibiotics and tender loving care – he'll be okay.'

'What about the farm?'

'The farm!' She'd forgotten about that aspect of taking care of him. 'Well, we'll just have to manage that too, won't we?' she gave a brittle smile – so much for a quiet holiday in Cornwall she thought.

'Great – just hope I can remember what to feed to what.'

Jo looked up at Alex, looking for the sarcasm behind the words, but his face suggested he thought the whole idea merely a challenge, not a nuisance, and Jo's heart warmed at the thought of her lovely son.

The first thing on the agenda was to find a chemist to dispense the antibiotics, she thought, then stopped as the picture of Pete still half-dressed and sprawled untidily on top of the bed filled her head.

'Come on Alex – I need your muscles!' she grinned and led the way up stairs.

It was a struggle. It took all their combined strength to undress Pete, who tried vaguely to help as he was roused from sleep. With a sigh, Jo saw him covered lightly, feeling his forehead, brushing the stray strands of hair off his sticky brow.

'You're going to be all right, Doctor says you're going to be okay. It's pneumonia but early enough, okay?' she said earnestly. The curtain of pale lashes momentarily moved, hid the eyes altogether in a blink of acknowledgement. Jo nodded at him, patted his shoulder gently, and left the room.

When she returned from Looe with the prescription she went up to see him straight away. His forehead seemed cooler and he appeared to be sleeping peacefully, his chest still rattling with each painfully-drawn shallow breath. Alex had made a cup of tea by the time Jo came back down.

'I've been thinking,' Alex began slowly,

'Steady on,' Jo said in her usual jest. Alex looked at her and allowed a twitch of a smile to reach his lips. It was one of those funny things about his Mum, she'd always treated him like an adult in some ways and it had made the transition through his teens much easier than it had seemed for some of his friends, allowing him to be child and adult together.

'At first, at least while he's not fit – we can't just leave him here and go down to the chalet – can we?'

'I'd been wondering about that too.'

'There are two spare rooms here, I looked while you were out – if we moved up – just for the time-being?'

'It's – logical,' she hesitated, wondering if such an invasion would be understood, deciding there was little choice if they were going to look after Pete properly. 'Okay, we'll nip down now and bring up what we need, not everything, not like we're really moving in?' she looked at Alex for reassurance, he nodded to show he followed her train of thought.

*

'I know it's a hell of a drive but I think we'll get more out of it if we can root around ourselves,' Rick said as he handed the transcript of his interview with the Morgans over to D.C. Fuller. 'It's a bit thin, did you get the feeling that she might have gone off with this Pauly bloke?'

'Nothing definite – the mother said that Kate had been happy for a change – it's certainly possible, the dates almost coincide, her disappearance and the end of the craft fair.'

'Hmm,' James looked quickly at the second page, 'Do we know what he made, like, to sell at a craft fair?'

'No?'

'Just wondered. When do you want me to go, sir.'

'Yesterday!'

'I better be off then,' James said with his gangster's shrug.

'And where are you off to all of a sudden?' Glenda said when James hastily gathered up the things he'd only just dropped on his desk before going in to see Rick.

'Fleetwood – chasing up the 'man with the limp',' he said with grin and a wink.

'Want company? I'm off today.'

'So what you doing in?'

'Nothing – I'm going – I just dropped in my last report on the 'legs case'. Real waste of time.'

She sounded despondent, her voice trailing off. She didn't care to acknowledge to herself why she'd actually come in with the report, it wasn't urgent, nor why she'd taken so much trouble over her appearance just to drop something off.

James looked puzzled for a moment, there was something different about Glen today, then he grinned. 'Okay, five minutes, see you down in the car park.'

*

'Let's try the hall first – see if they can give us any ideas – like if this bunch are regulars,' James suggested as they drove through Fleetwood.

'Next right then, about half way along the street.'

They passed along a serried row of semi-detached houses which somehow didn't look like the right place for a hall, then they drew level with an enormous dense green Cypress and the hall was revealed.

'There it is, 'The Victory Hall'.'

The tall, narrow red brick hall stood a little back from the road, flanked on either side by the huge sentinel trees. The name and the date, picked out in black bricks, spelled out more than just a number, it held all the defiance of the people, a celebration and commemoration of all who had suffered in the Second World War. The pale blue door was closed and a hand-written notice pinned inside the shallow porch told them the name and address of the caretaker, a Mrs. J Holmes. It turned out to be a house almost directly opposite.

'Mrs. Holmes?' Glenda began when an enormous woman in a wild floral print dress opened the door.

'Aye?'

'Detective Constable Lewis,' she smiled, and held up her identification for scrutiny, 'And D.C. Fuller,' she added as James held out his card momentarily.

'Aye?' the woman said again with an inquisitive look in her eye.

'I understand you are the caretaker for the hall across the way?'

The woman nodded, her many chins alternately compressing and trembling as she did so.

'May we come in?' Glenda was feeling uncomfortable standing on the doorstep, like a door-to-door salesman.

'Oh yes, pet, come along in,' Mrs. Holmes said as she stepped back , then led the way through to her front-room. The well-stuffed furniture was delicately covered with lacy antimacassars, the sideboard boasted hundreds of delicate glass figures, the pictures on the wall were all tiny and set in light gilt frames. The room cried out to say how light, small and delicate it was, as Mrs. Holmes sat them down and graciously took her place in the, obviously, favoured armchair by the fireplace.

'It's about the craft fair that was held in the hall between the seventeenth and the twenty-third of December of last year? Do you remember it?' Glenda opened.

'Oh yes?'

'We understand there was a stallholder called Paul or Pauly, a man with a limp, can you remember him at all?'

'What's it about love? What's he done?'

'He may not have done anything Mrs. Holmes,' James cut in with a broad smile, 'but if you can remember him it would be so helpful,' Glenda saw a new look in the woman's eye. Her lips pursed and formed as sweet a smile as they could manage, her cheeks bulging under her make-up.

'With a limp?' she said, making a show of thinking about the question. 'Do you know if he had a beard?'

Glenda and James looked at each other, then James shook his head.

'I'm afraid we don't know – why?'

'Well most of the men did have beards, only one or two didn't, I notice such things,' she said with some importance.

'We only know a name and that he had a limp. We'd like to know what craft he was selling, if possible,' James added as an afterthought.

Mrs. Holmes thought. She held herself perfectly still and recreated the scene in her head. She walked slowly round the hall as it had been on the first day of the fair. She had taken the opportunity of her position to have a good look around before the doors opened. Pottery, the odd looking couple, he much smaller than her: shell work, necklaces, filigree work polished and mounted, pretty: Glass work from a local glass-blower, she knew them: Corn dollies and the like, some with a Christmassy theme, red and green ribbons woven in, and the fair haired woman that minded the stall and plaited the straw the whole time: 'Wood'n'things' she remembered the sign, prettily pattern wood shaped into all-sorts from eggs to platters who was there? A man, with a beard, she saw him carrying a box, no, no limp: in the corner now, a basket maker, all sorts of wares, stools, tables, as well as baskets and cornucopias filled with dried flowers, no beard and, she pictured him as he placed his items out on show, yes, possibly a limp, only possibly: she carried on round the room, but returned to the basket maker as her only suspect.

'It's only possible. You mustn't take it as gospel. There was one, I think, just think, he may have had a limp. He did baskets and things, that was it, but he didn't have a beard.'

'Can you tell us anything else about him?' James was electrified.

'No – ' she said slowly, 'Only he didn't have a beard, he was dark though, and not so very tall but strong looking,' Mrs.

Holmes gazed into the middle distance seeing him again, noticing the muscles in his forearms.

'And did you have his name – for booking purposes?' Glenda asked.

'No pet, it was the organiser that booked the hall, not individuals. The er, Crafty People? No, that's not it. The – hang on,' she said and heaved herself from her chair, pressing herself up with her arms. She left the room for a moment but came back with a bulging file and a large black desk diary.

'Here we are then,' she said, flumping herself back into the chair. She turned the pages of the diary, starting at the back and quickly came to the seventeenth.

' 'People Craft' that's it. The group was called 'People Craft', they booked up in January, look, they sent me one of these,' she held out a yellow sheet of A5 with a list of dates and venues on it. It was for the previous year's craft tour, 'To prove they were serious, I think.'

Glenda nodded.

'Did they distribute any up-to-date leaflets while they were here?' James coaxed.

'Now that you ask, there were some sent to us and the Town Hall a month before they came,' she smiled sweetly at him again.

'Any left?' Glenda tried.

Mrs. Holmes gave Glenda a withering look, 'I cleared the hall out properly,' she said.

  'Yes! Yes! What a score!' James said as he almost danced back to the car.

'A score?'

'Our man with a limp? A basket maker!' he looked at her expectantly. Glenda looked back blankly but then she remembered.

'Oh, God! The murder weapon?'

'A basket-makers bodkin! Bloody namby-pamby name – bodkin. Ever seen one?'

'Not lately.'

'Vicious looking things,' James said as they climbed in the car. 'Where next?'

'Let's give the Town Hall a whirl – maybe they don't throw everything away,' James replied cheerfully.

'After lunch?'

James looked at her, how could such a fit looking girl eat so much, they'd already snacked heavily on buns and coffee at a coffee bar in the motorway service station on the way up.

'After lunch,' he agreed, 'let's see what Fleetwood can offer,' and he winked at her.

Fleetwood offered the same as every other town in the country, multinational fast food outlets, and a selection of smaller restaurants of varying sizes and prices,

'Let's try here,' James said as they arrived at a pasta house.

Glenda paused to look at the menu outside.

'Come on!' James said suddenly and grabbed her hand to draw her inside.

It wasn't in the first moment that he held her hand, that she was holding his, but in the second. As if it was the most normal thing for them to do, to walk into a restaurant hand in hand. A mixture of emotions ran through her as they were shown to a table by an archetypal plump Italian waiter. The first was of irritation. James always irritated her, that was her creed. The second was of pleasure, she wanted him to hold her hand, she wanted him to notice her as a woman. And more than that, she knew she could, would, be better for him than all the bimbos he tangled himself up with. By the time they were seated she was regretting the fact that he had now released her hand. Finding, for the first time ever, a lump in her throat when she tried to think of something to say, she just looked at him while he perused the menu. Gangster, from his sharp suits to the swatch of long dark hair that threatened to flop over his eyes, that he would, irritatingly – attractively - flick back into place with a practised sweep of the hand. And his eyes, such a deep grey, such dark lashes. She could see why others gave him the come-on, there was something about him that would make most women want to flirt a little, but not her, no, not her. She gave herself a mental shake and picked a fulsome looking dish from the menu.

He wondered if she knew that her mouth was quite so sexy. He'd never noticed it before, but then he'd never sat tête-à-tête with Glenda before and eaten a civilised meal. Watching her lips as she pursed them gently around a morsel of pasta, created butterflies in the pit of his stomach. He drew his gaze back, to survey his colleague as a woman, not just as a damn good D.C. in competition, as well as in partnership, with him. She had a strong face, not pretty and winsome, but handsome with strong cheekbones and bright eyes, her deep brown hair held an attractive gloss and was cut well, to be, he guessed, easy to manage. He thought it would look good at any time of the day, or night. And his eyes were drawn back to her lips, he was sure he'd never seen them before and he had an almost irresistible urge to lean over and kiss them. What, Glen? He must be feeling tired.

*

Rick paced about the new house. It was cold and empty. Somehow he had the sinking feeling that it would never be warm. His footsteps echoed even though the previous owners had left carpets and curtains. He wondered how long he'd have to wait for the removal van to bring all his stored pieces. He glanced at his watch. It had been difficult enough to explain that he wanted to have the afternoon off as it was, and they were late. He looked at the phone, the only item in the room, squatting on the floor. He'd give them five more minutes then he'd phone to see what was going on.

The phone rang, sitting there on the floor the sound seemed incongruous, unexpected. Rick did not answer it as quickly as he could, deciding that it was probably the furniture storer claiming some error or hold-up.

'Yes?'

'How's it going Rick? All moved in, mate?' Kelvin's cheery voice twanged, bringing a breath of London down the line.

'Kelvin! Good God, it's good to hear your voice!'

'Your card said you were moving in today – thought I'd give you a bell, on the off-chance like.'

'Ta, mate. How's it all going, back there?' Rick said quickly before Kelvin could ask him.

'New D.I.'s a bit of a bugger, Williams. Couldn't care less most of the time – likes his paper work, likes results that make numbers, know what I mean?'

'I get the picture. Williams did you say?'

'Yeah, bald like a monk,' Kelvin exaggerated.

'Sound's like my new Super, he's called Williams too. Wonder if they're related – he's fond of being in photos, apparently.'

'God! One of them! Seriously, how're things?'

The question Rick didn't want to answer. The upset of the evening at Henry's, of being reminded of Elise in just the wrong way and finding he had so little of her around to console him. The very things he'd left London to escape from were those he now felt would have brought her back to him, like re-entering a dream disturbed by a momentary awakening.

'Bit slow,' he said taking refuge in describing the job rather than his life, 'I've got a murder with some strange circumstances and not much of a lead, and a Super who thinks I could hide half a kilo of coke from Regional.'

'Huh!'

'Wants the glory – who am I to deny the man?'

'What's the team like then?'

'Good – usual mix – plodders, doers – but I've a couple of thinkers who like the action too. They could do really well, as long as they don't get screwed up in other ways,' Rick smiled to himself thinking of the trouble James seemed to be prone to, 'Oh, and a telepathic D.S.'

'Come again?'

'You'd think so, anyhow, knows everything before it hits the official channels, ears in high places – you know the type?'

'Useful – very – as long as they're on your side.'

'Quite.'

'And is he?'

Rick thought for a moment, Henry had not taken offence once the 'problem' with Lorna had been pointed out, he thought he was probably still on the same side. The homosexuality just didn't matter to Rick, provided it didn't cause trouble in the team, and as it seemed to be so taken for granted that no one had filled him in on it, then there probably wasn't likely to be any.

'Yeah – I'd say so, on the whole. How's Josie?' he said, changing the subject.

'Fine – says she's looking forward to seeing you when we come down, just over a week to go now! Is it still okay?'

Rick laughed. 'Sure – would sir like the view of the cop shop, to make you feel at home?'

'You know what you can do with that!'

'I look forward to it – you both coming down, that is. It'll be – really good,' Rick said his throat tightening slightly. Kelvin and Josie knew Elise and Louise, were part of their life together. 'Be really good, give us a ring just before you arrive and I'll put out the red carpet. See you Monday week,' he said shaking himself out of the melancholy that had swept over him again at the thought of his wife and daughter.

*

'I'm terribly sorry Rod, I can't leave him this evening,' Jo said when she rang Rod later that day.

'No, I understand. Pneumonia! Where'd he get that from? I mean ...'

'The doctor said it just does it sometimes, develops as a complication to a cold – he probably made it worse being out in his boat last night.'

'Out in his boat – in that little Shetland he's got? In that weather – the man's got a screw loose.'

'Rod!'

'Lucky he didn't drown – what the hell possessed him?' he said, his voice trailing off oddly at the end of the sentence.

'Rod? Are you all right?' Jo said softly into the crackling emptiness.

'Yeah, sure. Just the thought of him out there last night, in that weather.'

'You understand though – don't you?'

'Oh yeah, sure, sure. Look I'll give you a ring tomorrow, shall I? I mean Pete's not likely to answer it or anything is he?'

'I wouldn't have thought so.'

'Fine, I'll do that then, okay, see you,' he finished and rang off suddenly.

'Bye,' Jo said softly as she replaced the handset. Perhaps it was a bit drastic, but she didn't feel she could go off leaving Alex alone with Pete on the first evening, when he was still quite unwell.

Alex was standing by the door, he held a bucket in his hand.

'Oh no!' Jo sighed, 'This morning's milk!'

Alex just grinned.

'What do we do with it? Down the drain? Can't be fit to drink now, can it?' she said.

'Can't put it down the drain – milk's one of the big de-oxygenators.'

Jo shook her head, 'How'd you know that?'

'Pollution control study I did last year – we could pour it over the compost heap I suppose – it's not an awful lot and it'd soak into that lot.'

'Brilliant – do it – then we'll get the animals all ready for bed. Bagsy I do the goats – you can see to the geese,' she added with an involuntary shudder.

*

Rod tucked the Landrover into a field gateway just off the road and walked the rest of the way. It was dark, the quarter moon hidden by clouds scudding across the sky. He stumped up the track to the small collection of buildings on the edge of the sea, darker blocks against the dark skyline, with just one unblinking square of light shining out towards him. He knew he shouldn't be there, that it was a risk. He tapped at the thick heavy door and called a name.

'It's open,' a voice grated out. 'What the fuck you doing here?'

'If you had a ruddy phone I wouldn't be here.'

Pongo's nostrils flared slightly, stainless steel eyes glinted in the light from the Gaz lamp. 'Go on then, spit it out,' he said, his voice rattling like crushing rocks.

'It may be nothing – you know the guy we bought the yacht from?'

'Creep on the cliff?'

'Yeah- well, he's been taking little trips out – at night like,' he paused, waiting for a response. There was none, so he ploughed on, reluctantly, afraid of what he was saying, 'He was out last night, and exactly a week before?' He waited again. Still the hard eyes regarded him, the strong brown fingers moved rhythmically, the only sound the hissing of the Gaz and the crashing of the waves.

'Well?'

'Coincidence?' Rod queried, his heart lightening at the thought that Pongo would agree.

'Fuck coincidence.'

'But – '

'You screwing that new bitch of yours?'

'What the...?'

114

'Don't forget – I don't play fucking games.'

'She's okay. She's not from round here, from London. She's – ' he threw his hands sideways, 'she's nothing to do with here.'

Pongo made a guttural grunt, unintelligible. 'I've got enough of a fucking mess to sort as it is – ' his hands stopped moving for a moment.

'What kind of mess?' Rod felt a tightening of fear in his chest.

'Had to get shot of one of my outlets. Fucking bitch was cutting the stuff – doing her own trade – killing mine. It's sorted, no sweat.' The hands were moving again, as if they possessed a life of their own, brown crabs fiddling as they danced. 'Don't you cause problems, understand?'

'Sure – I'm in it too, lot to lose, eh?'

'So get the fuck out, I'll sort it.'

CHAPTER NINE

'Worth the trip, sir,' James said as he handed in his brief report. 'Our man with a limp now has a description, of sorts, and a trade.'

'So I see. What's this 'bodkin' look like?'

'I've only seen the one, sir. That's in the Craft museum out to Sticklepath. That one was small, six, seven inches, but books have pictures of them anything up to a foot long.' He reached into the inside pocket of his jacket and pulled out a tightly folded sheet of paper, he smoothed it out and handed it to Rick. An illustration of the basket maker's tools. Rick saw the hole in the girl's chest, saw the cold words of the postmortem spelling out the shape and length of the instrument of death. He shuddered, suddenly certain that James was right.

'Well done.' Rick decided to leave the case with James as it was obvious that he was fired up about it. 'Let's get your new lead followed up,' he added, surveying the green leaflet attached to the report.

'It's last year's list, the one we liberated from the Town Hall, but there's the hope that they might follow roughly the same schedule each year,' James indicated the leaflet. 'All August's down our way, easy to check bookings for the halls.'

Rick cast his glance down the list concentrating on August: Torquay, Totnes, Newquay, St Ives. Totnes? He wondered if there could be even more of a connection, but noticed that the tour did not include Plymouth at all. 'Right, go ahead, let me know if you locate them, we'll decide how to approach it then.'

'Cheers boss,' Fuller said with a grin and, taking the green leaflet, left Rick's office.

*

'Where d'you want to go?' Tamsin asked.

Jo had dropped Alex off at Sylvia's for the afternoon as it was one of Tamsin's afternoons off. She didn't really want to leave

Pete alone in the house at all, but it was difficult to see why Alex should have his holiday spoiled, especially when he was working so hard on the farm side, really doing everything except the milking, so she'd agreed to drop him off and get back quickly.

'You can show me the sights.'

'What in Looe?' Tamsin said, her eyes sparkling up at him. Alex took her hand, she seemed to make him bolder than he'd ever thought possible.

'Anywhere,' he said softly, amazed to hear his own voice sounding gravelly.

Tamsin looked oddly at him for a moment. 'We'll walk through the town, then along the beach, how's that?'

'Perfect,' Alex said and gave her a brilliant grin.

They strolled down to the bridge and into the throng of tourists who filled town. The souvenir shops spilled out on to the pavements, interspersed with crafts and antiques, but Alex didn't really see them, his eyes were on Tamsin, on her flowing auburn hair, on her delicately translucent skin. In the warm light of the day, her cheeks fired by being with him, she seemed so fresh and happy, he just couldn't wait to escape the people and reach the beach, to be alone with her. Tamsin didn't dawdle either, keeping up a rapid pace they suddenly reached the edge of the town and the beginning of the sea. They paused at the rail and looked each way for a moment before Tamsin gave his hand a tug and led him down the steps to the sand.

'All right Tams?' Michelle said from her position leaning against the wall. Tamsin spun round, relieved to see her friend's face looking warm and interested.

'Yeah – you feeling better?'

'Dunno what you mean – how's,' she bit her lower lip in a coy pretence of remembering, 'Alex – isn't it,?' she said in a smooth voice he'd not heard before. She pushed herself off from the wall with one shoulder and sauntered over close to them. Her eyes roamed over Alex, Tamsin found herself tense up. It had always seemed amusing, the way that Michelle had of eyeing up the boys, over the top, just like the most lecherous of the boys. Now it felt coarse and threatening.

'Fine – thank you,' Alex used his best, most precise put-down English, the one that had earned him teasing at school in London. He was amazed at the time, to find that he spoke any differently at all, but had learned quickly to blend in at school. Later he'd recognised that it was the strong influence of his mother, with her 'posh' accent, that had created the difference, and that it had its uses.

Michelle raised her eyebrows a little and tossed her hair. 'We'll see you round then?' she said.

'Bye Shell,' Tamsin said, tugging Alex slightly to set off along the beach.

'Yeah – an' don't do anything I wouldn't.'

They walked in silence for a moment or two, the sand and shells crunching softly beneath their feet. The breeze lifted and blew a slight chill across the beach, then eased to let the warmth of the sun reach them once more. Tamsin didn't know what to say, she didn't really want to talk about Michelle yet she was the only topic on her mind. There were fewer people here, the sand was still damp from the last tide, the cliffs ahead still met the sea.

Alex looked at the strata in the cliffs, the strong lines in the rock where they were laid down in shallow seas millions of years ago, all grey but with shades of grey and differences in their hardness creating a striated sculpture. Here the lines pointed straight at the sky, further over he could see the lines sweep and dip like a folded Sunday newspaper jammed through a letter-box. He began to slow his pace, as the cliffs and the sea blocked their path ahead. Tamsin did not slow with him, but finding him lagging gave his hand a tug. She didn't want to be noticed hesitating, she didn't want to be noticed at all. Her heart was thumping, she just wanted to be all alone with him again, for him to kiss her again. She was sure he'd been about to kiss her when they'd suddenly realised that his Mum was actually in the car parked outside home.

'Up here,' she said, and tugged him towards the furthest corner of the cliff. The sand was soft here, right against the cliff wall, and what had appeared to be a deep shadow in the cliff sculpture deepened into a slit of a mouth, a crooked smile of darkness. Wide enough for an average adult at the base it slimmed rapidly as the smile lifted into an arc. Tamsin slipped in first. Alex couldn't help it, he glanced round the beach before he followed her.

It was dark, but only until he moved away from the entrance. As soon as he stepped into the cave the light poured in and showed him a long, narrow chamber, smelling of sea and seaweed, with pebbles and shells piled at the furthest end and soft sand nearer the front. Tamsin moved close to him and his arms wrapped themselves around her. They stood locked together, his face pressed against her hair, feeling her heart beating against his chest. She tipped her face to look at him and he kissed her. Their hands were still, holding each other, but not daring to explore. They kissed again, longer and warmer. Tamsin could feel her face glowing, she knew her pulse was racing, but didn't really know why she felt so breathless as well. Alex knew exactly how he was feeling, but knew that it was not a sensible way to allow himself to feel. Rationally he knew this, but his feelings were causing confusion. Why had Tamsin led him here? Was it 'the place' for the local boys and girls to go? Had Tamsin been here with others, was he treating her like an innocent when she wasn't? Michelle certainly didn't seem innocent – and her passing remark suggested that she knew where Tamsin was going. Would Tamsin think him a wimp, inexperienced, if he stopped this now and led the way out of the cave?

He allowed his hand to move, slipped it up to touch her neck. She shivered under his touch and he kissed her again, his hand sliding down softly to the swell of her breast. Her small gasp as he touched her was indecipherable, Alex pressed, caressed, as he kissed her mouth with a mounting passion that he scarcely understood himself. Tamsin pressed herself against him, kissing him back, hoping his hand would not stray any further than it had, feeling slightly frightened by the situation she'd put herself in. She knew that Michelle would have guessed they were going 'up the cave', knew what it sometimes meant. Perhaps she'd even flaunted it at Michelle, but she had only meant to be alone to kiss him again.

Alex's jaw began to ache, his hand no longer felt the exciting shape of a small breast, but was squashed between them. He made a decision. He pulled away from her, but took hold of her hands at the same time. He could feel himself tight against his jeans. She looked lovely, the back-lighting from the opening in the rock created a halo of deep gold through her hair.

'This is, um…… I don't think,' he murmured

'Yeah,' Tamsin said to the sand between their feet.

'Is that the only way out?' he nodded at the opening they'd come in through.

'No, we can get through the other way,' her voice muted, relieved and disappointed, she nodded to the rock behind him. He turned. The cavern sloped steeply up into darkness, yet at the top a glimmer of light showed. He smiled and looked back at her.

'Can we get through there?'

'Yeah – it's a bit of a squeeze, it takes, like, two turns, it's light once you're past the bend,' her voice lifting as a sense of normality reasserted itself within her. 'I'll go first, know the way,' she said cheerfully, and scrambled past him up the steep slope of the rock.

'Must be one really soft layer,' Alex said to her back as he followed her round the convolutions of the cavern, relieved that there had been no harm done to their relationship, and allowing his mind to return to the structure of the cliff.

*

'Are you sure you're going to be all right?' Jo asked.

'Positive. What can go wrong? Pete's feeling so much better already isn't he? Besides I only have to phone Sylvia's if there's a problem, don't I?'

Jo smiled at him. Of course he'd be all right – she was worrying unnecessarily.

'Bye, then,' she said as she left the farmhouse. It was warm and the blue light of the evening seemed to welcome her. She looked back once as she drove off up the lane towards the main road.

Alex wandered upstairs to check on Pete. He was hoping he'd be awake and let him go on one of the computers for the evening. He was.

'Come in,' he said when he noticed Alex peering round the door.

'Jo's just gone out.'

'I know, she said she was going out this evening, left me to your tender care, she says,' he smiled. 'Where's she gone?'

'Oh, down to The Smugglers. She said they wouldn't go off anywhere else, that way I can contact them if I need to.'

'Who's she with then, Sylvia and Tom?'

'Perhaps, I think it's Rod, though,' Alex said half absent-mindedly. He was wondering if he could confide in Pete. He'd always found things, personal things, relatively easy to discuss with his mum before, she was always so matter-of-fact about it all. Just now, however, he felt he wanted to talk to a man. To his father. But that was impossible. Dead before he was born. Some kind of local hero, he guessed he was going learn more when they went to Greece, something his mother hadn't been able to tell him. He wasn't sure he wanted to know everything. He'd built up his own image over the years, based solely on the small photo his mother had and the bare facts she'd told him about Alessandros.

'I said, Rod who?' Pete hissed again.

Alex, who had been unaware of the whispered question, looked up sharply. Pete's face was crumpled as if in pain. 'Are you all right?'

'Who? Rod who?'

'Er, Mr. Pentewan – has a fishing boat down in Looe?'

Alex watched the large face intently. The eyes shut. Panic flooded through Alex momentarily. 'Are you okay – should I ring – ?'

'I'm okay,' he let out a deep sigh. 'Rod Pentewan,' he said heavily, 'is not the sort of man your mother should get mixed up with.'

'What? Why? Um... I think it's up to her,' Alex stumbled.

'Not if she doesn't know,' Pete said softly. 'Never mind – do you want to work on the computers?'

Alex looked at Pete Austin. The look of pain had left his face but he seemed distracted. All thought of asking him for advice had left him.

'Yes please,' he said softly, anything to get away from the worrying idea that someone so likeable as Rod could be bad in some way.

*

'How are you feeling this morning?'

'Fit – ready to take on the world,' Pete said, his eyes brighter than they had been for days.

'That sounds good,' Jo smiled as she laid the tray of breakfast things down.

'It is Sunday, isn't it?'

'Yes?'

'Alex didn't seem to think there was any rush to get back to London.'

'Oh Lord! We were supposed to leave yesterday, weren't we?'

'Yes – but that doesn't matter. You're up here now, aren't you? If the chalet can be cleared – the Thompson's usually arrive just after twelve. What I'm saying is, could you, would you stay on for a bit, please?'

'Well,' Jo thought of Rod and she thought of the expense. If they left now she could still squeeze the trip to Greece out of her budget, the chalet had cost so much less than she'd anticipated.

'I don't mean paying – you've been so good to me – I'm not sure how I'd have coped without you two here.'

'Okay, it's a deal – until you're fit. I'll check with Alex – then we'll go and clean out the chalet,' she said smiling.

Another week at the beach would be wonderful. The farm side didn't take up much time once they'd developed a routine. All the animals were fed in the morning and the evening, the goats milked at the same time. It had taken her a while to get sorted out with the basic procedures, but once Pete was able to tell her what to do, it merely became routine.

Alex thought it was a brilliant idea. He hadn't wanted to leave Cornwall and Tamsin just yet and he enjoyed feeding the livestock so that was no hardship. Though Alex thought that the animal's houses probably needed a clean he hadn't quite got round to asking Pete about it, hoping they would be okay until Pete felt fit once more, when he'd promised himself he'd help Pete with the job.

*

'Jackpot!' James said as he put down the phone, Glenda looked over at him. 'People Craft are in Newquay – as from tomorrow.'

Glenda smiled at him. She'd found herself smiling at James more and more recently, instead of the exasperated face that he usually engendered.

He stood quickly and strode to the D.I.'s office and tapped and opened the door. Glenda watched him as he leant against the door frame and spoke to Rick. He turned suddenly, and she only just had time to switch her eyes to the papers on the desk, so that he didn't catch her looking at him.

'Got anything on?' he said, coming over to her.

'Reports ...'

'I'm going down to interview the craft mob – D.I.'s given his okay, if you'll partner me...?'

This was different. There was a tentative nature to his asking. Glenda looked up and met his grey eyes, they were not as confident as usual, more like a small boy than ever, her heart melted a little more.

'All right then,' she said, feeling a little thrill of happiness.

*

'The Thompsons are a nice bunch,' Jo said as she walked with Pete the next day, his first day out of the house. 'I took them their milk this morning, and they said they'll drop in to see you later, if you feel up to it.'

'That'd be good. Yeah they, er, they all used to come, but as the years went by one or other son dropped out, then re-joined, usually with a partner. Mister says it's become a family 'tradition', the fortnight in the farm chalet,' he laughed.

'I can understand that, it's such a change, to work with the animals a bit.'

'They don't really do any of that now – the magic wears off,' he said softly, then aware of the need to keep the magic alive, he grinned, 'But you've done so well – who'd have guessed you're just down from the big city.'

The sun was shining brightly but a breath of wind made it comfortable. Pete walked slowly up to the higher paddock and leant on the gate. The goats raised curious faces as he approached, then, as a herd they performed their greeting and ambled over to have their heads scratched and to hear a few friendly words.

'I'll move them to the lower paddock when I feel a little better,' Pete said. 'They've had enough of this.'

'Alex and I can manage that – where do you want them to go?' Pete smiled, she certainly had fire and spark for someone so diminutive. There was an aura about her that made him feel protective, yet at the same time she seemed so capable. He'd been wondering how to approach the subject of Rod Pentewan. He sensed she would not welcome interference, yet if his suspicions were anything like true, she needed to be warned.

'Alex says you were out with Rod Pentewan the other evening.' Jo stiffened, she'd not thought to tell Alex about Rod's restriction on mentioning his name.

'As it happens, yes, I met him through Sylvia and Tom.'

'You don't know him well then? Only since you've been down here?'

It wasn't the line that Jo had been expecting.

'Yes, from the first evening though, the first evening when I was at Sylvia's.'

Pete heaved a sigh. Jo was perplexed, she wasn't sure what to expect or how to react.

'If I – warned you off him?'

'What? What would I do?'

'Sort of.'

'I – I understand – I think I understand your – concern, but it really doesn't have anything to do with him and me, does it?'

'No. You're right. But if there was something – concrete I could show you. Evidence?'

Jo felt uneasy. What sort of evidence could Pete be talking about?

'Well – I'd have to take it into consideration, I suppose,' she said, finding her voice becoming stiff and formal.

'Evidence,' Pete murmured. Then he looked up brightly, 'How're my renegade ducks?'

*

'Absolutely nothing!' James sighed and stretched, linking his hands behind his head and leaning back in his seat behind the steering wheel. Ahead of them the waves rolled in, blue-green under the sun, the sky a clear blue, the breeze just enough to fan the heat from the car. They were parked at a dead-end facing the cliff edge. Down below them, somewhere out of sight, was a beach crowded with holidaymakers, but up here there were just a few other cars, abandoned by their owners for the time it takes to walk a section of the coastal path. With his heart in his mouth James had driven up here when they had left the makeshift camp of the Craft People. It wasn't that they seemed suspicious of any enquiries made by the police, they did, but one or two seemed so openly honest that it was hard to believe that anyone knew the identity of 'Pauly' as they said.

'Not quite – we know he's been to more than one of their events. We *know* he's got a limp and that he is the basket maker, it was a bit iffy before,' Glenda said slowly, an idea was building in the back of her mind, it was the way that some of them had responded to the name. Something was odd, if she could just let it work over in her mind. She closed her eyes and leant back, the sun was hot through the windscreen, she let her mind wander over the way the corn-dolly girl had answered, what was it?

He couldn't resist it, as Glenda had leant back one fine strand of hair had not fallen back with the rest but laid gently across her cheek. James leaned across and brushed the hair from her face with the back of one finger, in a single sinuous movement it fell and joined the rest of the dark block and Glenda's eyes flew open.

'A hair!' James said quickly, 'I just – '

Glenda's face was no longer startled, but neither was it angry. James reached out his hand again, fearing it would get bitten off, and touched her cheek.

'Just there.'

Her eyes were filling him, for the first time in his courting life he didn't know what to do next, his arm ached yet he did not want to move his hand. Her hand joined his, her thumb sliding up his palm, she held his hand to her lips and brushed them against his skin, then, still holding his hand she lowered it to the space between them. Her heart was thumping. A relationship between two members of the same team was not a good idea, and she told herself that he irritated her, yet at this moment, at this precise moment, there was only one thing she wanted of James Fuller and there was nothing platonic about it. She couldn't say who started the kissing; it was as if it was choreographed, as if they had kissed each other every day for the last year and were in good practice. And he was right, her lips were as sexy as they'd seemed up in Fleetwood, and she tasted so good, her skin smelled fresh and sweet as he kissed beneath her ear, down her neck.

*

Pete was up early on that Thursday morning. Alex saw him come in through the back door wearing his wellingtons, yet when Alex went out, only the geese had been let out of their house. Jo had found Pete working on a computer when she had prepared the breakfast. He looked startled when she opened the door and he quickly turned off the screen, the light fading on his face as he did so.

'Be with you in a moment,' he smiled at her, and then waited while she left before he turned the screen back on and exited from the program. He wrapped the disk up and dropped it into the pocket of the Fisherman's smock that he usually wore. He wiped all memory of the information he'd been looking at from the hard disk and went to eat breakfast.

'Are you doing anything this evening?' he asked as they scrunched on their toast.

'I've planned to go out, Alex was going to meet Tamsin,' Jo said warily.

Pete regarded her for a moment. He had no wish to upset her so he didn't push the question and ask if she was going to see Rod Pentewan.

'Oh that's okay. I just wondered where everyone would be later – that's all. Er, take a key – I may be out when you get back.'

Jo looked up at him sharply, but he smiled at her, 'I'm feeling fine now, you know. I could take over the morning milking again, give you a lie in.'

'No, that's all right – I like doing it,' Jo said defensively.

'Well, perhaps I'll get some of the sheds mucked out then.'

'I'll give you a hand,' Alex offered.

'Great, um, I'll be on the computers most of today though, tomorrow okay?'

'Right, tomorrow,' Alex agreed.

*

The day had been warm but the evening brought a cool wind. Jo and Alex had seen to all the livestock early. Earlier than was usual, Pete had been surprised to see Alex with the food for the geese when he'd come out of the house. The Thompsons appeared to be staying in and around the chalet for the evening. Jo and Alex had left at seven to go to Looe.

Pete dressed ready for a cool evening and set to fixing the Shetland's trailer on the back of the Landrover. He was sweating by the time he had hitched it up and stood a moment allowing his rasping breath to steady itself. There were just these few bursts of energy required, when he was out at sea it wasn't so much trouble, he'd be all right.

He ran through the words in his head. His call sign, which had been their call sign, followed by a single sentence, a verse, 'eight bells, thunder and no light, George's well, eight marks right'.

It had been in an idle moment that he'd turned on his radio and a shock when he heard someone use his designated call sign. Julia had used it too, of course, when they were out together in the yacht, but it was allocated to him, and it came over loud and clear twice, there was no mistake. He wrote down the words, stupid words, words that could get him in trouble for messing around on the air.

The words had nagged him. Julia? No body had ever been found, just a few of her things, washed up on the shore. He worked at the words, he wrote programmes to analyse them. The more he thought about it the more they appeared to be like a code. And who was using it?

Rod Pentewan had bought the yacht from him, well had a buyer lined up, he'd said. At the time Pete had only wanted to be rid of it. The yacht was Julia, without Julia he could not bear to sail in her. Rod Pentewan, who'd seemed so friendly before Julia disappeared, who'd been so helpful afterwards, who'd seemed such a friend.

Not now. Not since he'd been sorting out the code and thinking. He started up the engine and steered the Shetland out to sea.

CHAPTER TEN

Stupid words. Nonsense rhyme. 'Eight bells', he'd thought it was a time – nautical time. It wasn't. He'd exhausted that lead. Now he was sure it was August, the 'bells' being of no consequence, part of the rhyme, part of the smoke-screen. He'd played word association games with the computer – he'd fed in his own words, he responded to the words the computer threw back. 'Thunder' – he'd settled on Thor – God of Thunder – Thor'sday. So here he was again, the third Thursday in a row, the third in August. Perhaps he was wrong. He'd wait, as he had the other two evenings, riding the dark so that St George's Island lay between him and the coast, so that he could see if the yacht, his yacht, came anywhere near. 'Eight marks right' still had him lost. Marks, on the chart? On the coast-line? To the right of St. George's Island? That had been the easiest bit, Looe Island had been known, still was known, as St George's. There again it might just have been a stupid rhyme.

The wind had picked up even more, blowing strongly off the land, carrying with it the scent of flowers and sand, a dry smell that seemed incongruous out at sea. The light was beginning to fade, the stars appearing on the horizon. He cruised up the coast, far out to sea, a speck to any casual observer from the cliffs. He'd driven quite a way to drop the boat in the water, not wanting to be seen going in locally again. The engine roared as he allowed it full rein. As darkness swamped the boat he pulled the throttle right back and trickled towards the land, keeping the island between him and Looe. He turned off the engine. He turned off his lights. Amid the pitch and toss he picked up the night-sight glasses. It really was dark tonight. Clouds, driven swiftly across the sky played hide and seek with the stars. No moon shone. No moon tonight, Pete thought casually to himself. A jet of adrenalin, a spark of electricity, and he was at once more alert, tingling with recognition. No moon: Thunder and no light. No light! He'd first pursued the idea that it might be short for 'lightning'; had wondered about it as an instruction – to show no light, or meaning just 'at night'. He'd eventually dismissed it like the 'bells' as part of the rhyme. It would be tonight – whatever- it would be tonight. August, Thursday and *no moon.*

*

'Come-on, Sylvia will look after those two when they get in. He'll wait,' Rod voice was low and persuasive.

'All right. But just coffee,' Jo said, as deadpan as possible. She wasn't at all sure it was a good idea. The words that Pete had used nagged at her, had sown seeds of disquiet in her. Nothing she could put her finger on, nothing she could easily verify and dismiss. Rod had been as charming and amusing as he'd been every other time they'd been out, but there seemed an edge to him as well, a wariness.

'Of course!' he smiled wolfishly, 'What kind of bloke do you think I am?' totally calming her concerns. His place, a ground-floor flat within walking distance of The Smugglers, cried out for a woman's touch. Furnished with other people's cast-offs it was a hotchpotch of styles and qualities. Yet it felt warm and lived in. An empty used mug sat in the fireplace next to the most comfortable looking of the chairs and opposite this was the television. The rust coloured settee faced the blank fireplace, a fluffy rug at its feet.

'Sit down, I'll just be a tick,' he said and disappeared down the hall to a back room, the kitchen. Jo prowled the living room. Had Rod brought Julia back here? Had there been something between them after all – despite Rod's assertion? There were two photos, both of the same child. One at about six months, the other at about eleven years. A round-faced dark haired girl, his hair, not his face.

'It's my Michelle,' he said as he came into the room, a mug in each hand, 'like the song, 'Michelle, my belle',' he sang, 'Remember?'

'I'll not own-up to knowing that one,' Jo said, a smile creasing her face, 'it'd show my age!'

'Nor should you, come on,' he indicated the settee, 'sit down, have some coffee,' his voice soft and welcoming.

*

Her body slid over his, smooth as silk, skin on skin. James played his fingers along her backbone, across her back, feeling the muscles flex beneath the silk. If he hadn't already seen the personal gym in the spare bedroom he would have guessed she was a fitness freak, doing a regular workout or something, she was so – toned. As it was he was just being nosy, while she fixed them some supper, and had seen it. The spell on the cliff had shaken him. He'd driven back with a feeling of being high. Of being slightly lost within his own feelings. He had to make sure it wasn't some kind of fluke – she wasn't his type – too capable by half – but he'd want to be with her again, just the two of them, just to be sure. It had been his idea to meet this evening; hers to make some supper for them both – at her place. It had all happened so quickly, he could scarcely believe it himself. Glen had taken over. He wasn't quite used to that, it didn't quite fit his role model, but he could get to like it, oh yes, especially when she did that. And that.

Glenda kissed his eyes, nipped his earlobe gently with her teeth, and flickered her caressing tongue down his body, pausing at nipples to tease, and enjoying the sensations his fingers were creating on her skin. He had a good body, no flab, smooth, unusually as good looking in the raw as he was clothed. He'd been cheeky about her appetite for food earlier, she wondered secretly if he'd be so cheeky about this. Not often allowing herself to give in, she knew he was in for a tiring night, and she was looking forward to it so much. She could scarcely believe she'd been working alongside this same man for so long, or that he could possibly ever have irritated her. She wasn't smitten. She wouldn't allow that, no, not that. If he forgot her name tomorrow she'd cope. No bother. It was the only way – being on the same team. Oh God! She hoped he wouldn't forget.

*

There it was! Gone again! A blur of a yacht, a smudge, then swallowed by the sea. His eyes strained. He was sure. It had to be. A yacht on course for the island and *without lights showing*. Lowering the glasses he looked again at the outline of the island, so small. He was drifting badly, the wind was blowing him out to sea, away from the island, away from the yacht. He started up the engine. It fired into raucous sound, whipped away by the rushing of the wind. As soon as he was under way he settled the engine down to a trickle, the boat steadied herself as she made headway through the wind and waves.

Pete leant against the cabin and trained his glasses on the dark shape of the island and began a sweep to take him towards the last place he'd seen the ghost of the yacht. There it was! And gone. There! There! His heart seemed to be thumping so hard that it made the glasses jump and throb as he struggled to keep the elusive yacht in sight.

He steadied the throttle so that he crept forward, a small unlit shape on a great unlit sea, creeping towards a ghost that was only discernible with the night-sight glasses.

He nudged the boat forward, keeping the engine low, yet knowing its sound was being carried away from him and away from the yacht.

Close enough now. He could see people, two, no three people working over her stern, pulling something from the sea. Backs bent, straightened, a movement, a cascade of water, a bent back, a straightened one. Dark marionettes. Shadow puppets.

He trickled a little closer, one hand on the throttle the other steadying the glasses. He wanted to see without being seen, not that they were looking in his direction, faces turned away from him. Bent backs, slightly straightened, bent, he had the impression of someone lifting and packing, moving from A to B, small movements now.

For a second the wind eased, a tepid quality washed over his face, the sound of his engine magnified in his ears.

Suddenly so loud? He turned his head as it hit.

The vast dark bulk of the fishing boat shuddered into his fibreglass hull, throwing him forward. His hand still on the throttle, the night-sight glasses clattering to the floor as he tried to stop himself falling. In the bright frightening flash of the moment before his head smashed against the cabin Pete knew he recognised the boat. The pain came with a brilliant light and was gone, slammed into oblivion. His frame slumped and was tossed back into the filling well of his boat by the full-power surge from his wildly raging engine.

There came a shuddering, creaking smash, a splintering in the dark amid the roar of the thrashing motor. The out-of-control Shetland crunched into the side of the yacht, twisting and writhing, a knife boring into its wounded side, driven on by the big outboard.

Shouts, unintelligible against the wind and engine's roar, and the shape of the fishing boat bearing down, slicing the motor-boat from the yacht. A scream high and thin. Panic and clamour among the waves; between the stricken craft. The open gaping wound sucking in the sea. Boiling water as the Shetland finally submerged.

Only the wind and the relentless steady throb of the diesel remained as the merciless sea swept away her spoils.

*

Jo's room in the farmhouse did not face the sun, so she slept on happily until seven. Lazily she tugged on the 'smelly' clothes she kept for the milking, looked in on Alex to wake him as she passed, and went downstairs. She went out through the back door, milking bucket in hand, and set off for the goat sheds. The wind was fresh, blowing out to sea, whipping the tops of the Scots pines over by the chalet.

'Morning Ladies,' she said as the goats stretched their necks and peered over the wall of the pen to look at her with a bleat or two of greeting. She let Jasmine out first, head of the herd, straight into the tiny milking parlour, up on the stand, head in the bucket. Same routine. Jo milked steadily as Jas munched the concentrate. And the next, the fluffy Hyacinth, ambling down to take her turn, leaving more traces of angora on Jo's jumper. Alex appeared. She noticed him moving across and back as he carried buckets of water or meal to ducks, geese and hens. Snowdrop. Tulip. Rose.

'All done?' she called, bucket of frothing milk in her hand.

'All done, five eggs today.'

They walked together back to the farmhouse. Jo strained the milk and put it to cool, Alex placed the eggs in the large rack in the dairy.

'I'm grabbing a shower,' Jo said as she trotted upstairs.

The water was nice and hot. She washed her hair then, enjoying the massaging of the water, she just stood under the jet while the bathroom filled with steam.

All dressed she came down to find Alex had put out most of the breakfast things, and was munching contentedly on a slice of toast.

'No Pete yet?'

'MmMm,' Alex shook his head, mouth full.

Jo stood still for a moment. She had just remembered. He was going out. Was going to be late, he said. She'd not thought to check if he was back, besides they were back before twelve themselves, late enough for him to have returned and gone to bed, early enough for him to still be out. So why did she feel so worried? No Landrover! It wasn't out the front, and if it had been round the back she should have been able to see it from the goat shed, shouldn't she? She could usually, between the boat and the house. No boat! She was sure. No boat! Tightness gripped her chest.

'Alex!'

He looked up quickly, it was the tone of her voice, it stirred a memory from home, from a desecrated home.

'I'll see if Pete ...' she turned and trotted up the stairs. She didn't knock. She opened the door. The room was the same as ever. Not tidy, not untidy, just lived in. But empty.

'He's not here,' she shouted to Alex turning to find him just behind her.

'The boat?' he said and turned on his heel and dashed downstairs. Jo heard him leave by the kitchen door; certain he'd not find the Landrover or the boat. What could she have done? He was his own man – true she thought he should still take it easy after the pneumonia, but she could hardly stop him could she? It wasn't as if she was responsible for him, just because she'd been helping out, looking after him.

Alex returned, slewed himself through the door, hanging on the doorpost.

'Not there!' he gasped as if he'd been running. Had her anxiety affected him, or did he feel the same sense of foreboding? 'What do we do?' he added, straightening-up and returning to the table.

'I don't know,' she said slowly. What to do? He might be happily chugging around on the water somewhere. He might have driven over to visit someone after his fishing trip, or whatever. What to do? Who to ask?

Rod. There might be bad feeling between them but Rod had seemed genuinely worried about Pete when she'd told him about the pneumonia. She moved to the telephone and automatically looked through the small book for P. He was there! She had just thought that she wouldn't find him listed in the personal phone book when she saw his name. There hadn't always been this unease between them then, or had Julia put his name in the book, would she, if there had been anything between them? She pressed the numbers in, and listened as his phone began to ring.

'Yeah?' His voice sounded thick with sleep.

'Rod? It's Jo. It's about Pete. He went out last night – said he was going out – he's not back – I.' she stopped, she knew she was sounding incoherent. 'It may be nothing – of course – but with him not being very well I'm – concerned.'

'It's all right. Look, calm down. Where did he go – did he say?' Rod's voice rolled solidly down the line, infusing his words with calm.

'He didn't say – but he took his motorboat again. Isn't there anyone I could notify?'

'I'll ring the Coastguard for you, and I'll take a look at the slip-way. If the Landrover and trailer are still there then we know he's out at sea. Hang around – I'll ring you back, Okay?' Something would be done. Jo felt a sense of relief settle over her turbulent anxiety, suppressed but not dispersed.

*

He drove fast, skating his Landrover round the bends. The slip-way was clear, no sign of Pete's Landrover or trailer. He headed back up to the harbour. Something was wrong. Before he even reached 'The Merlin' he knew she'd been moved, her prow swung a little wide and he was always careful to have her lashed tight. As he drove nearer he could see the damage. Not much, others might not even comment on it, but he saw it, scrapes of the underpaint exposed, showing up against the coloured paintwork like knife wounds. His heart felt leaden. *I'll sort it.* What the hell had he done?

He drove to the cliff edge and parked between a campervan and a saloon car, but he didn't head down the path to the beach. He walked back along the road, then when there appeared to be no traffic, he clambered over the stone hedge and landed in the field. Once hidden he ran, ran hard, something in the force of the movement was comforting. He'd find out what the bastard had done. He'd get it out of him. He wanted out. It couldn't be impossible. Out. Out. His lungs felt stretched and tight, the field rose relentlessly to the higher hedge. Over the hedge and in the distance the grey rooftops that had been Pongo's family farm, long ago, before everything else was sold to pay mounting debts. Everything bar the buildings, Pongo had seen to that, found the money somehow to hang on to them. God knows why.

Deserted. He banged on the door. Not a sound. He looked round the barns, not a sign of life. No vehicle. He felt deprived. He'd been ready to sort out what had gone on. He felt deflated. He walked the short distance from the barn to the sea and looked down. The waves crashed against the rocks, sending frail fans of water to spread their lace in the air. Bays of sand were exposed on either side, but this small headland never offered a beach even at low tide as it was now, still the water crashed against the rocks. There had been more of a headland once, Rod mused, as his eye took in the line of jagged rocks stretching away from him into the depths of the sea, it will all be beach one day, it was sheer luck that the buildings still stood.

'Don't jump,' a hand thumped him on the back, almost causing him to lose balance, to fall, the voice harsh but amused. 'Shit!' Rod steadied himself and turned. Pongo's face wore a grin of sorts, he found the situation funny in some way.

'Though, I thought I'd said?' his voice now laced with menace. 'Something's happened,' Rod's anger had wasted, replaced by fear. Pongo did that to you. There were times when you'd think he wasn't the same bloke you'd grown up with.

Pongo turned his back and walked back towards the barn, his gait uneven but strong. Rod followed.

'Did you take 'The Merlin' out?'

'What of it?'

'She's scraped – what – '

'So she's fucking scraped, what's a bit of paint?'

Rod looked at him again. 'Pete Austin went out again last night,' he said softly. Pongo's face cracked into a smile of sorts, but he didn't say anything. 'Do you – what happened to my boat?'

'Had a little accident.'

'That's it? You won't tell me – what am I going to say to Jo. She already wants to notify the Coastguard, police, the lot.'

'Stupid bitch. Do it.'

Rod gaped at him.

'Make sure you've scraped up your pretty boat on something legit then, fucking do it.'

'You've .. he's …?' Rod felt unstable. Dead. Had Pongo killed Pete. That soft man. His eyes must have betrayed him for suddenly Pongo's hand was on his face. Fingers and thumb on either side of his jaw with a grip of iron. The fingers alone felt as if they could crush the bone.

'*Your* pretty boat. You did it. Get it? Don't even think of doing anything else,' he hissed, his breath hot against Rod's face. He released his grip, flicking Rod's jaw as he let go. The blood pulsed back into Rod's face, he moved his jaw experimentally, it wasn't broken. 'Listen – you've got a little problem. The creep may have had notes, something. You weren't his favourite person – understand?'

Understand. Shit. If Pete's body landed on his doorstep where would he be? Notes. Yes, he was the type to keep notes. A wash of heat, sweat, then cold poured through him as he realised the problem and the solution. Jo would let him look, if he was looking for ideas of where Pete might have gone, Jo would help.

He was in a real sweat by the time he'd reached his Landrover again. He drove with a sense of detachment down to the harbour. He rang the Coastguard from a phone box and gave as many details as he knew, he'd be out looking he'd told them.

139

He phoned Jo and told her he'd found nothing but he was going out to sea to look. Alex, in the background, offered to come with him. Refused. Not this time. This time he had to find some convenient place to scrape up his boat, somewhere convincing. He clambered on board The Merlin and set out of the harbour too fast, disturbing the sediment as he went.

He ploughed down the coast, binoculars out each time he came to a slip-way. He was just about to give up and turn back when he saw it. A Landrover and trailer pulled up to one side. He couldn't make out the number plate so he chugged in towards the small sea-side village. There was a tiny jetty beside the slip-way, he glanced at his watch, perhaps he'd be able to get in far enough to pull alongside. It worked out well. He lifted one of the fenders from the side of his vessel. One should be enough. He turned on the echo-sounder and crept closer. He could see it now. The number on the back of the trailer hung crookedly as if it hadn't been replaced properly, but the letters and figures he could see seemed familiar.

He edged his boat closer to the jetty. Just about enough water. A couple of old men were standing on the steep village street, faces turned towards him, watching his approach. He misjudged it. Carefully. He saw their faces light up with a perverse sense of satisfaction as his prow grazed the jetty, shuddering to a stop. As if he'd just realised the problem, he pulled off a little, ran forward and threw the fender over the side, and came in again, carefully, properly. He leapt ashore and tied her up. The old gents had arrived at the jetty too late to help but in time to see his concerned inspection.

'Damn! Scraped her up good and proper,' he said over his shoulder to his audience. He stood up. 'Do you know who's that is?' he said pointing at the Landrover and trailer.

'No,' the word drawn out in consideration. 'Not local.'

'Friend of mine's gone missing you see – we're out searching,' he walked towards the trailer. He straightened the number plate, all part of the charade. 'Yep – looks like his. Is there a phone round here? I'd better ring the Coastguard,' he said.

He cruised up and down the coast after that for an hour, looking for something, the Shetland, wreckage, a survivor, a body. He didn't really know why he was doing it. He was convinced that Pongo had made sure of the job, had 'sorted it'. He watched every shade and shadow in the waves, eyes tiring to a glazed stillness. He turned the boat back to harbour, time to report back to Jo. Time to have a look around.

*

'I found his Landrover and trailer and I rang the Coastguard. Then, just in case, I've been going up and down, looking,' Rod sighed. He sank his head onto his hands, elbows propped on Pete's kitchen table. 'If only we had an idea of where he was going?'
'He didn't say,' Jo's voice sounded flat and bleak.
'He didn't leave a note – something – anything about being out at sea?'
'I haven't seen anything. He said – '
'What?'
'He said he'd take over the milking again, muck out the animals.'
'Have you looked?'
'Looked?'
'For anything he's written down – notes about the sea? Anything?'
'No – well, I've not looked at anything personal – he may have come back any minute – he may.'
'Come on then – let's have a look,' Rod said rising.

'What're you doing?' Alex asked from the doorway as he came in.
'Looking for something that might say where Pete went last night,' Jo said, not looking up.

141

'I've found his Landrover and trailer way down the coast.' Rod said flicking through the address book.

'I'd have thought he'd keep everything on disk,' Alex suggested moving towards the shelves.

'Of course! Of course he would.'

'What, in that lot?' Rod asked eyeing the shelves of disk-boxes.

'I'm sure most are work but he'd have personal ones – wouldn't he?'

Rod was looking from box front to box front. Some were headed up with letters like a filing system, some with strange words. It would take forever to sort through that lot, even if he knew exactly what he was doing. He'd seen the disks being fed into the machine and a quick tapping of keys that brought up the information, but he'd never operated one on his own before.

'This might be it,' Jo said pulling out a box labelled 'Bod'.

Alex turned on and pushed the first disk into the Acorn nearest the door, Pete's favourite machine. He was right, up came a listing for everything to do with Bodrigga Farm, from the annual accounts and the animal movement record to the names and addresses of their visitors. He opened a couple of files that had unusual titles to find out what was in 'RotAn' or 'SedLst' only to find a Rotational crop system described and a seed list for the previous year. The other disks in the box proved to be just as mundane. Household, domestic and farm doings, bills to be paid, income from his bug-busting, bank account, insurance. Nothing about the sea except notes on the sale of a yacht, 'The Miniver' and the insurance on the Shetland. Nothing. Rod was disappointed, he was sure that anyone who kept so many files would have something down in writing, he was more worried than he had been before they started looking. He prowled along the wall lined with boxes. Reading and re-reading their titles. Every now and then he'd lift the lid and flick through the disks, taking in the strange names they had on them. Diary. Dear Diary, he wanted to see. He'd have snatched something like that away regardless. But nothing.

'He may be all right,' Alex said, 'He may just have run out of petrol or something,' he sounded genuinely optimistic. That's it thought Rod, knowing what I know I'm playing this too down-beat. Funeral before there's a body – bit of a mistake. 'Of course! I – we were just a bit worried, with the pneumonia and all, weren't we?' he looked at Jo. She managed a smile, she wasn't convinced, but she had no idea why not. And in the meantime there were goats to be milked and hens to be fed. 'Thanks Rod,' she said laying her hand on his arm. He put his arm round her small shoulders and pulled her to him. 'He'll be okay, don't worry,' he said as convincingly as he could manage.

*

Jo stood in the dark on the cliff path, in the deep dark of the moonless night. She looked out to sea as if in the dark she could see his boat, invisible in the daylight. Below her the unseen waves rumbled and smashed and sucked back their spoils. She thought of Alessandros. Never ageing in her mind, always drowning. The wind breathed in her face bringing its salt to mix with her silent tears. The wind had changed.

CHAPTER ELEVEN

It was a beautiful morning. The clouds had all been blown away and the sun burned hotly in the transparent blue sky. At half past seven it was already warm.

A small crowd of early morning dog-walkers, workers and ghouls had collected against the wall of the Barbican, beside the entrance to the Sailing Club. Twenty-five foot below them was a tiny beach between the rocks, no more than a triangle with six-foot sides. Two heavy rusted chains stretched out from some hidden mooring and disappeared into the depths. Between them was lodged the body. Face down, a mass of dark ginger hair like wild seaweed anchoring the body to the sand, legs still partially water-borne.

'Has anyone been down there yet?' Rick asked, standing on the platform that ran down beside the Sailing Club building. It was a steep drop but not impossible to clamber down from this side, it looked only a little better from the other direction. 'No, least not officially,' Tony said. D.S. Hammond had taken the initial call barely ten minutes before, the informant was obviously not an official.

'Okay, let's get down there,' Rick said. He climbed with ease over the railings, letting them take his weight as he gained a good foothold on the rocks below. He smiled to himself at the thought of making a complete ass of himself with such an appreciative audience. He didn't. Climbing down the rocks he suddenly felt himself a child again. It wasn't something you did as an adult, unless you were kitted up to the eyeballs on a proper climb. This was kid's stuff. His foot reached the sand, gritty beneath his city shoes. He looked up at the wall, it seemed even further up than it did down. He turned to the body. There had been no doubt in his mind from up top but now the corpse had a solidity and fluidity that could only be human. He took a step towards the body. It had to be a man, despite the length of the hair, he was big, a good six-foot and at least fifteen stone. He had to be dead, but Rick had to check. The hair was stiff with salt and clammy. It stuck to his hand as he drew it away from the mortuary-cold flesh. He gave an involuntary shudder and pulled out his radio.

'As a doornail. Call up the other services – I think they'll be best to take him off in a dinghy – Oh and Tony.'

'Sir?'

'Clear that lot.'

'Sir.'

Rick watched as Tony moved the onlookers away then turned back to the corpse. He stood to one side and tried to tip the body up. It was heavy as if glued to the shore. It seemed irreverent to coerce the leaden flesh to move with too much force. He only managed to rock the frame on the padding of the life-jacket. He was curious. Why should a strong looking man wearing a life jacket drown?

The tide was coming in. The wavelets lapped the body's knees now, the dinghy had better get a move on. He glanced round again, a face disappeared from the Sailing club window, Tony stood guard by the wall. He turned to the body once more. Standing carefully on the other side he moved the arm closer to the body, crouched and pulled. Like a wellington boot stuck in the mud, the suction of the wet clothes gave sluggishly then was free. There was nothing to see. The face was white between the patches of grit that stuck to chin, cheeks, lips, forehead and eyes. Wide open, clear grey eyes with sand adhering to them. Rick stared, finding himself shocked. Almost nothing he had seen before, no bloody death, had seemed so dead as those sand covered eyes. He let the body tip back down as he heard the phutting noise of a powered dinghy come round from the harbour.

*

'Coastguard, can I help you?'

145

'I – A friend of mine went missing, yesterday – at sea. Um, Mr. Pentewan contacted you, I – I wondered if he's been found?' Jo felt flustered. She so wanted Pete to turn up at any moment, yet as the night had passed and she'd heard nothing she began to wonder. Please, please say Yes he's safe and well, she pleaded in her head.

'Could you let me have the details please.'

'But?' hadn't Rod told them? 'It's Mr. Pete Austin of Bodrigga farm. He was out in a motor-boat, went out on Thursday night.'

'Austin.' There was the sound of computers keys being tapped. 'Yes, I've found it, Mrs?'

'Smart, I'm staying at the farm, with Mr. Austin.'

'Nothing's come in yet – the contact number we have is – Looe 263281.'

'That's here.'

'Then we'll be able to notify you if we find anything.'

'Thank you – thank you.' Jo said hastily, as if by letting him off the phone he'd be able to get on with searching for Pete.

*

'Sorry to keep you waiting Mrs. – Minchington,' Rick said as he made himself comfortable in his chair.

'Not at all.' The bright eyes of the elderly lady danced in her small face.

'Quite briefly, you noticed the body while you were out walking your dog?'

'Bruce, yes, it was such a nice morning, I don't sleep as well as I used to, so I got up and took Bruce out for an early morning walk.'

Rick smiled, the first time he'd felt like smiling since seeing those dead eyes. Mrs. Minchington could have stepped out of an Agatha Christie, and she was enjoying it.

'At what time would this be?'

'Six-thirty, you see – '

'You saw the body at six-thirty?'

'Oh no. I went out at six-thirty. I didn't see the – body, until just after seven, and by the time I'd decided my eyes weren't deceiving me and found a telephone box, and rung the police, well, it was at least a quarter past seven.'

'Thank you. You saw no-one else, no boats nearby, nothing?'

'Absolutely nothing, just some other dog-walkers – but that was after, I don't know if any of them looked over and saw it, you have to, you know, look over, deliberately.'

'Yes, I do know, thank you very much for your assistance, I'll find someone to show you out. Thank you again.' Rick said finding himself becoming garrulous in the face of her quick patter.

*

They'd cleaned him up. Thank God. The sand had been hosed from his face, he lay large, white and cold. Rick, suspecting something untoward had decided to check up on the PM rather than waiting for the written report. Luckily the pathologist had finished and they were just clearing up.

'Anything?'

'He drowned.'

'Just like that – with a lifejacket on?'

'No, not just like that. He was probably unconscious at the time, he'd received a severe blow to the temple shortly before his death, enough to start the contusion, but not long enough for it to develop fully. He appears to have been in the sea for at least twenty-four hours, judging by the condition of the skin. He'd eaten last, properly, at least eight hours before his death.' The pathologist grinned, 'That's all for now folks, I'll put the fiddly bits in the report.'

Rick stood and looked at the corpse for a moment. 'Any guess as to what he'd been hit with?'

'I don't know that he was hit – such a broad line, he may have fallen and hit his head instead,' the pathologist chuckled, 'they can't all be murders you know.'

'Have we got any information from the Coastguard yet?' Rick asked as he arrived back in the office.

'Yes, sir – looks like a positive ID,' Tony said, offering Rick a sheet of paper.

Rick took it, perching his long frame on the edge of the desk he read. 'Name: Peter Austin; Bodrigga Farm Nr Looe. Contact number Looe 263281. Description: Male: mid forties, six-foot; well built: long ginger hair.' He could see what Tony meant – the description certainly fitted the body. He noticed that the man was said to have been out late at night in a motorboat, a Shetland, on Thursday evening and that he'd been reported missing on Friday morning. An extra note said that his Landrover and trailer had been discovered abandoned at a slipway a few miles down the coast. It all fitted, perhaps the pathologist was right; it was just an accident at sea.

'Okay, get on to the local bobbies, send someone round to the farm, see if we can bring someone in to give us the positive ID.' Rick told Tony letting the sheet of paper fall back to the desk as he pushed himself off the edge.

Glenda arrived, she flung down her bag and landed in a chair. She looked flushed and there was a sparkle about her this morning, Rick thought, she looked more attractive in some way today, though there didn't seem to be anything specifically different about her.

'Any further progress with the basket-maker lead? It'd be nice to get somewhere even if certain people have written it off.'

'You'll have to ask James, sir,' she said, her voice sounding softer than usual.

'Taking my name in vain?' James said as he came in, his eyes finding Glenda's, 'Did you want me sir?' he added turning to Rick, but not before Rick had noticed the interaction.

*

It was such a beautiful day, Jo couldn't quite remember seeing a sky such a translucent shade of blue. The wind had eased to a gentle breeze, a breath of air now and then to take the strength from the heat of the sun, a welcome relief. Alex had gone out with Rod, to look, two pairs of eyes are better than one, he'd said. She was alone. It would have been a day for the beach. Instead she sat, on the small lawn directly behind the house in an old deckchair she'd found, careful to be within hearing distance of the telephone – just in case. She was tired. She felt as if she'd lain awake the whole night listening to the wind and waiting to hear a sound, any sound that might have been Pete coming back, and all the time the sense of despair grew within her, malignant, defying good fortune with its pessimism. She closed her eyes, and saw red, blood red, as the sunlight forced its way through her eyelids. Her mind drifted, the sounds of the sea bringing her memories closer than she wanted them to be.

There was a knocking. She sat up suddenly, awake, listening. Yes, a knocking, she scrambled to her feet and dashed through the house to the front door. She pulled open the heavy oak door just as the policeman had turned away. Hearing her he turned back. His instant smile at seeing her was replaced by a small frown.

'Morning, Ma'am. Does Mr. Peter Austin usually live here?' he opened.

'Yes, yes – this is his place, have you – '

'May I come in?'

'Come in – yes,' Jo was flustered, she just wanted to ask him what it was about, why he'd come, yet she felt constrained by some kind of protocol, 'In here,' she said leading him through to the living-room. He glanced at the seats, she took the unsaid hint and sat, indicating that he should sit as well. Here we are, she thought, scene set, for what? She knew. His face had become marble. Her heart went out to him, young, fresh-faced and now colouring up as he fingered his helmet. He took out a notebook.

'I'm informed that you reported Mr. Austin missing at sea,' he said referring to his notes.

'Yes, he went out on Thursday – hasn't come back yet,' her voice caught.

He took out his pencil.

'And you are Mrs. Austin?'

'No! No – I'm, we, we're staying here with him. He wasn't well … '

He raised his eyebrows. This was no good, Jo thought, I can't go through this rigmarole to find out.

'Have you found him? … Please?'

'Would you just give me his description, then.'

'He's – ' she saw him as he'd welcomed them to the farm, as he'd taught her how to milk, as he scratched the goats heads, 'He's – oh about six-foot or more. He's a big man, heavy – not fat. And ginger hair – long, ginger hair. He's a computer programmer works from here,' she looked at his eyes. They told her he knew this already. They told her that Pete had been found.

'But you're not a relation?' His voice was gentle and local.

'No – I …'

'Is there a relation, next of kin nearby?' He glanced round the room as if Jo had hidden someone there.

'Not that I know of – his wife died – a while back. I don't know – he never mentioned anyone.'

'So how long have you known Mr. Austin?'

It seemed like years. So easy to get to know, easy-going, gentle with the animals, friendly. 'About two weeks.'

The eyebrows twitched again.

'And for part of that I nursed him while he was getting over pneumonia.' She wanted to defend herself, and him.

'Do you think you would be able to identify him?'

She knew it. This entire charade for the one question she knew would come. She felt leaden, her arms weighing more than her strength to lift them. Solid, unable to move.

'Yes, of course,' she said soberly, his picture fixed in her mind's eye.

'A body was taken out of the sea at Plymouth, they think it may be him.'

She looked at the poor man, fingers working the edge of his helmet again. But she couldn't help him, she said nothing as the certainty grew and burst within her, filling her with a kind of despair.

'If you can come now, I'll drive you into the Plymouth station, is there someone who could come with you?'

'No, they're all out – looking for him,' Jo took a deep breath and blew it out sharply, pulling herself together. She stood quickly. 'I'll leave a note, then I'll be ready,' she said. Ready as I'll ever be. Never ready.

*

'Sir.'

Rick looked up, Tony Hammond stood uneasily in the door way.

'They say they've found someone to ID the floater, bringing her in now sir, should be here in a couple of minutes. Do you er, want me to deal with this sir, or will you?'

The temptation was great. The faces of Mr. and Mrs. Morgan were still clear in Rick's mind. It caused such an ache. He glanced at Tony Hammond again, young yet, looking at the floor.

'It's all right, Tony, you can show her in to me when they arrive.'

'Ta, sir,' he said straightening up and leaving.

'Mrs. Smart, sir,' Tony said as he opened the door to his office. Rick stood, ready to shake hands and create a bond of concern. Tony stepped back and let Jo come in.

Rick stuck out his hand, began an in-drawn breath, and stopped. He couldn't help it. Something, something about this woman made his heart stop. Or feel as if it had. A sensation that had hit him only once before, in a folk club in London. His mind stopped, fused, as she took his hand in formal greeting, sparks flying in all directions. Then, on automatic pilot, the hand was released and he heard himself offer her a chair, and take his seat himself. Shorted to earth he was brought back with a jump to the situation, and a dark place appeared in the light.

'Mrs. Smart, I'm sure you understand we wouldn't want to put you through the upset of viewing the body unless we were pretty sure it was the right one, so, would you please describe Mr. Austin for me. Again, I know, please?' Mrs. Smart? And was there a Mr. Smart, and what was she to the man who was laid out in the mortuary? The man she was describing so accurately to him.

Jo repeated her information. It had to be so, it was a thankful, unthinking, repetition. Her head had been so full of Alessandros on the journey to Plymouth, that she'd been frightened to take the hand the D.I. held out. But it was only the darkness of the hair, the deep brown of the eyes, the tall and slender frame. He was, of course, much older than Alessandros had been.

'If you're ready, I'll take you to the mortuary,' he said softly, his eyes fixed on her blonde curls. She looked up at him, grey eyes magnified by imminent tears. He swallowed. Oh, God, what twists of circumstance.

The body seemed so large, an enormous mound beneath the cloth. He tried to blot out an image of the vast bulk of the deceased and this petite woman by his side. Just him, and her and the body.

'Are you all right?'

She nodded.

You were never all right for this sort of thing. She felt apart from the world around her, alone in an island of mist. Not alone, there was this Detective Inspector masquerading as Alessandros and there was the cloth. The cloth. He was lifting the cloth.

Up, like a bird taking off, a seagull, white lifting from the sea. A sea of blood, bright rust red blood that swathed round the head, the face, the large soft face, flabby in total repose, white beyond life. Pete Austin. Washed by the sea, a gaping mouth, filled by the sea. She moved her head, faces transposed, Alessandros filled by the sea, the bird flapping its wings, the sea roaring in her ears, the bird, the sea, the sea.

He caught her. He had looked away from her for a moment, looked at the man's deep rust coloured hair that someone had brushed and laid neatly on either side of the pale moon face, so when she crumpled he'd only just be able to prevent her hitting the floor. But he'd caught her. She was light. He crouched there for a moment, supporting her collapsed frame, her head tipped back over his arm, the slender pale neck stretched, a tiny throbbing vein close to her jawline. He wanted to kiss her. He was shocked, by the thought, by himself. Surely he loved Elise, only Elise.

A mortuary assistant materialised beside him and helped to revive the woman in his arms, speaking to her gently and touching her cheeks with his cold hands. He felt the shudder of returning consciousness before she opened her eyes.

Alessandros? Holding her again? No! No – the detective. What! What was he doing? She struggled as he helped her to her feet, held her.

'Let go!' her voice echoed loudly in the bare room.

'Are you all right now?' he still held out his hands as if ready to catch her if she fell again, her eyes were wide with anger and shock.

'Quite.' She suddenly realised what had happened, 'I'm sorry,' she glanced around at the mortuary attendant feeling stupid.

'It's all right Miss, quite normal down here – fainting. We gets used to it,' he said and smiled at her.

Jo looked at the body, covered again.   Anonymous. Acknowledged. Named.

'Can I go now?' she still felt waves buffeting her gently.

'I'm afraid you have to come back and make a statement.'

She nodded.

They returned to his office. Tony, writing up a report, watched them come across the outer room with an appreciative eye on Jo, until Rick asked him to fetch the coffees.

'Come in, please, Mrs. Smart, take a seat,' he said, starting things off as formal as possible. It was hot and stuffy as he walked in. He'd forgotten to close the blinds again! He threw open the window and the roar of the traffic from the roundabout nearby filled the room like a swarm of bees, but only a little fresh air came with it. Forgetting himself, he took off his jacket and threw it over the back of the chair and sat.

Jo, aware now of the tricks her tired mind had been playing, found herself watching him in a different way. He was an attractive man, in a casual way, unselfconsciously. He had a grace about him, uncommon in tall men, and his clothes wore him well. And, of course, he had that same dark colouring as Alessandros, the firm jawline, dark, inviting eyes, and dark, almost black, curling hair, though this was trimmed and tamed into a neat style.

He pulled some papers over towards him and looked up at her, those deep brown eyes meeting hers. Something within her responded, a fragile flask squeezed until it shattered, shards piercing small points of pleasure and pain, the contents released in a wash of desire. She looked down, it was obscene, improper, too much.

'It won't take long,' he said, 'we just have to affirm that you knew the deceased enough to identify him, and that you did so.'

'Well, we, that's my son Alex and myself, came down for a holiday. Huhm! To get away from things,' her eyes were filling with tears. The irony of it had just struck her. They'd come down here to escape a home that had been desecrated and the thugs who'd beat up Alex, and they'd walked into a drowning. 'So you were just on holiday – I understood you were living with the deceased, Mr. Austin?'

'Not – not like *that!* He'd been ill – had pneumonia – we only moved in to look after him!' she retreated into indignation, using anger to fight her own emotions.

'Oh, I see. I'm sorry,' he paused, it was nothing to do with the case, he just had to know, 'And Mr. Smart?'

'There is no Mr. Smart,' she said, her voice clipped, taking on a superior tone, dismissive and final, her eyes fixed on his pen as he wrote.

'So you looked after him, I guess you'd got to know him well enough then. There was no next of kin I see. Wife deceased?' Jo let a sigh escape. 'Believed drowned – so I'm told. I can't remember when they said – more than a year ago.'

'Do you think – just a possibility – could it have been deliberate?' Her bright eyes looked straight at him again; he felt a tightening in his stomach.

'You think someone killed him?'

'No I – well possibly – but I wondered about suicide?'

'I don't think so – he wouldn't.'

Rick looked at her; he didn't have to ask the question.

'If – if he was going to kill himself he would have left things right on the farm, he wouldn't have just left the animals. He'd have found them all new homes or something. I don't – ' she stopped.

'You don't?'

'I don't know what he was thinking, how he was feeling. I know there was some reason he wanted to go out on that Thursday night – but I'm sure it wasn't to kill himself, I'm sure he'd never leave the animals like that.'

He nodded, and passed her the form to sign, watching her small delicate hands on the pen, watching the script flowing from the pen.

'We've his clothes and things, next of kin would usually take them, but I'd like to hold on to them for a short time – just in case there's something…' he left it hanging in the air. She nodded.

'I'll take you home,' he said softly.

She nodded again.

He made the journey last as long as he could. It seemed right to drive slowly, steadily, part of the formality, like leaving a funeral, but it was partly because he was trying to find a way to see her again, but couldn't find the right words under these circumstances.

'Where's your son, at the moment?' he asked after a few miles of an uneasy silence.

'Out – out looking for Pete, with a friend.'

'How old is he then?'

'Sixteen. Seventeen in September.'

He took his eyes off the road to look at her, she was gazing out of the window, her face tilted slightly away from him.

'I had a daughter,' he said softly. 'Louise. She would be nearly twelve now.'

Something in his voice dragged her eyes from the passing greenery. Jo turned to look at him, his eyes firmly fixed on the road ahead.

'Would be?' her voice sounded hollow in her ears, she didn't want to know.

'Car accident. Elise and Louise, both,' as if saying their names in her presence would release him from her spell.

'I am sorry,' she said. What else could you say.

'Yeah, sorry. Shouldn't have said anything – not today anyway.'

The silence returned. It filled the space between them, filled his head with wondering at his ineptitude and filled her mind with a sense of death.

'Down here,' she said, directing him down the lane for Bodrigga Farm.

They jolted along for a while until they reached the group of buildings round the farm house. Jo noticed Rod's Landrover and felt her spirits lift. Before she even had time to climb out of Rick's car, the door of the house opened and Alex came quickly towards her.

'Have they found him?' he called.

Jo looked down, back in the car and held on to the door. Her throat was too choked to say the words. Rick opened his door and came round to be beside her, taking in the good looking youth, noticing another man coming out from the house. 'He was – washed up on the shore,' he said.

The boy stopped, his face which had been alight with hope, suddenly darkened.

'Oh, Alex. It was him,' Jo said, tears very near. Alex ran to Jo and they hugged.

'If there's anything I can do,' Rick said softly, Jo turned to look at him. 'If you need any help – please give me a call. Charles Cross station, Rick Whittington, they'll find me.' He closed the passenger door and walked round to the driver's side.

'Thank-you, you were – most kind,' she said absently. What was the right thing to say at times like this? Things like they said back then? They'd all said they were terribly sorry, but it wasn't for her. They'd all said that it was fate, and yet blamed her. Then, even though she and Alessandros had gone to Greece to announce their wedding day, she didn't belong to his family, and when her own family knew the secret she was carrying, she didn't belong to them either.

She watched Rick go, then turned and clung to Alex, fearing the feelings she'd experienced when she'd allowed herself to look into Rick's dark eyes.

Rick drove away from the farm with a sense of defeat. He just hadn't been able to ask to see her again. It seemed so wrong in the circumstances. He pulled off the road and followed a track that wound towards the sea. It came to a dead-end at a farm gate. He left the car and walked along the edge of the field until he stood almost on the cliff's edge. Hands thrust deep in his pockets he stood and stared. Pictures running before his eyes. The more he thought about Elise and Louise the more Jo's face appeared, tearing his mind away from its purpose, diverting him from conjuring his loved ones up in this wild place. The light was losing its intensity; great grey clouds were sliding in from the sea.

Suicide. He picked up a stone and flung it as far as he could out to sea. He knew what losing someone could be like – but Jo'd seemed certain it wasn't that. What had she said? 'Do you think someone killed him?' Why should they? Did she know something that he hadn't brought out because – because she'd affected him so much. That was it. He didn't like to face it, but she had affected the way he thought! Hopeless! He'd have to look through the paper-work again, he felt sure he'd missed something. He glanced at his watch, he'd go through it again, in the morning – early!

CHAPTER TWELVE

Her eyes snapped open. It was light. Early, she felt, but light. All this in an instant as she grappled for her watch to peer at it, to make out the time.

The knocking sounded again, louder, repeated, insistent.

Five o'clock! Five o'clock in the morning? Adrenaline rushed through her system, instantly clammy she leapt from bed and wrapped a towelling robe around her. She flicked back the curtain. There was a haphazard row of police vehicles, vans, cars, blocking the entrance to the farmyard, pulled off the lane on to the grass. Bang, bang, bang. The knocker on the door beneath her feet rang out again. She flung open the window. 'Hold on!' she shouted. A figure came into view, stepping backwards.

'Open up, if you please,' he shouted, nothing polite about the tone.

Could they have found out something about Pete? How he'd lied? She ran out of her room, almost colliding with Alex at the top of the stairs, and down, in her bare feet, to the door. She unlocked it and had scarcely time to move out of the way before it was pushed open. The man before her was ruddy-faced and large, in plain clothes, at his elbow stood two uniformed police officers. He waved a piece of paper at her.

'D.S. Pearce, Regional Crime Squad, this is a search warrant for the house and farm belonging to Austin.' His voice sounded loud in the house, reverberating, threatening. 'You are Mrs. Smart – and son?'

'That's right – but what are you doing here?'

'And you are 'just visiting' I'm told.'

Told, told by who? Jo wondered. 'Why are you here?' she repeated hearing her voice begin to rise.

'Searching – like the warrant says.'

'What for?'

'Well perhaps you can help me there. We can have a nice little sit-down and talk about it.'

'Can't we get dressed first?' Alex said, wearing only his jeans. 'Don't be cocky with me, lad. All in good time.' He flicked his hand at two policemen nearby, 'Upstairs!' he ordered. They pushed past Jo and ran up the stairs.

Jo took a deep breath to calm herself, thinking, there had to be some mistake, some mix up. 'Look, Inspector,' she guessed a title, having been too stunned to remember what he'd said before, she offered him her most reasonable, well modulated voice. 'Why exactly are you here?'

His face softened a little as he tried a face of incredulity, a grimace of a smile. He scratched his thick neck. 'Detective Sergeant Pearce.' he corrected her, 'Well, perhaps you can tell me, it'd save my officers getting up to their armpits in shit.'

'I'm sorry – I just don't know what you're on about.' The sound of something crashing to the floor came from upstairs. 'What the hell?' Jo started looking up, 'What are they doing up there?'

'Looking, searching if you want it that way. Look Mrs. Smart, let's go and sit down. When they've finished up there you can both go and get dressed, until then we may as well talk about it.'

Jo sighed. 'I'll put the kettle on, then. May I?'

'Yeah, why don't you?' he said and followed her into the kitchen.

The kettle boiled, she pulled it off the Aga and, holding it with a tea-towel, poured all the boiling water into an enormous teapot, heavily laced with tealeaves. She stood there a moment, watching the steam rise, wondering what exactly could be happening. She'd treat this man as if he were an irate parent, too angry to be coherent. She was rattled, she'd admit that to herself, but only because she couldn't understand quite what was happening, it was all too soon after the shock of seeing

Pete dead. So definitely dead. What could they want with him now?

'Milk, Sergeant Pearce?'

'And two sugars. How long have you been here?'

Weren't you told that too? she thought. 'Two weeks,' she said brightly, as if they'd been the most relaxing two weeks of her life.

'Where d'you live then?'

'What's that got to do with it?' Alex asked.

Pearce looked at the boy, flicked his glance up to the mother, back to the boy. 'Just answer, eh? We'll get on ever so much better that way, we will.' Alex folded his arms and looked towards the Aga. His jaw clenched, his bare foot tapping in frustration. He felt so vulnerable and so angry, how could his mum just answer so sweetly?

'London. We came down here for a little peace and quiet,' Jo said allowing the sweetness of her voice carry all her irony.

'Where? Exactly.'

Alex recited their home address before Jo could answer. Pearce wrote, but did not even look up at him.

'And you've known Mr. Peter Austin for how long?'

'I said – two weeks.'

'You're not one of the regulars here then?'

'No.'

'Unlike the Thompsons? The Farquahars, the Robins, the Stewarts, the Tailors and the Roaches? All regulars. Not you?'

'No – I don't know who else comes, the Thompsons are here now.'

'We know.'

'Well I don't – I don't know who else comes.'

'He kept records though?'

'I'd imagine so. It was a small business – I suppose he'd have to,' she didn't feel like telling him she'd been through the files with Rod and that she knew the names and addresses were all there.

*

Rick arrived early in the office, tired faces greeted him, a casual wave of the hand.

'A word?' D.S. Henry said. Rick nodded and John followed him into his office. 'A little bird tells me that Regional have come across some more of your coke.'

'Really – where?'

'It seems they've had a yacht washed up. Over on Rame Head. Regional are delighted, there was quite a quantity of coke on board. Thought you might like to know.'

'Cheers, thanks John.'

'There's more,' he said rubbing his chin as if considering the wisdom of parting with his information. Rick leant back in his chair and waited. 'A name came up. It rang a bell from Tony's report. Austin, Peter Austin?'

'Go on,' Rick said leaning forward, too interested now to play cool.

'It seems that, believe it or not, the yacht was registered. So they called up the yacht's registration at Swansea and up comes the name of your floater. Figures, I guess, must have come off the yacht when it got holed.'

'But he wasn't on a yacht – she said he'd gone out in a motor-boat,' Rick said a little too intensely.

Henry's eyebrows nearly hit his hairline. 'So she said!'

'But why should she – ' Rick began, and stopped as he heard himself, as he realised that even after a night's sleep, his thinking was still being affected by her. 'Thanks, John, I'll look into it – circumspectly, of course,' he added as he saw a flash of warning in his sergeant's eyes.

He picked up the reports from the previous day. His report. Her identification. Where were those words that had troubled him? Here they were, exactly; "You think someone killed him?" Yesterday he'd ignored them, pursuing his own idea of a suicide. Today they seemed so much more ominous. If he had a yacht loaded with high grade coke there might be plenty of reason for someone to kill him – and if she knew about it, she might have reason to suspect murder. He didn't like his thoughts, he hated his mind for working round to such a conclusion. There was no way that he wanted to believe that Jo had anything, even remotely, to do with drug smuggling. Drugs? What would he do if it were his lead. He'd be up there, at the farm. Oh God. His stomach turned over.

He left his chair and was in the main room even as he thought it. D.S. Henry was just leaving. He ran after him, catching up with him in the corridor.

'Is there a raid on?' Rick said.

'Where?'

'Don't play the fool, John. I need to know.'

'But is it a good idea, sir?' D.S. Henry said. He stopped walking. Rick pulled up beside him. 'It's none of my business – but I'd hate to see you get a black mark so early-on down here.'

'It's not like that – I know it sounded like that but I can see past – you know.'

John Henry regarded him for a moment, then appeared to make a decision. 'Regional worked their butts off to get a warrant, they should have gone in this morning at five.'

'Should have?' Rick said quickly, his hopes raised.

'That was the plan – I've heard nothing more yet – either way.'

'Oh, I see. Thanks. I mean it. Thanks,' Rick said as he turned away and headed back to his office. James Fuller had just arrived in, he greeted Rick cheerfully as Rick was wondering how to bust in to another force's raid and not get lynched.

'James, anything specific on?'

'Paperwork, sir.'

'We may just have a small lead on your 'bodkin' murder, I'll tell you about on the way, come on.'

'So you see Regional are probably up there now, giving the place the once over. I'm afraid I'm going to upset them a bit, sticking my nose in, but it's our murder even if it's their dope. What I'd like you to do is to try the local hostelries, shops, whatever. See if you can pick up anything about Mr. Peter Austin of Bodrigga Farm, anything, lifestyle, friends, you know.'

'Won't that be treading on their toes a little too hard?'

'Not at all. We've a legit interest in him too – he was the body we had out of the Sound yesterday.'

'Neat.'

Rick looked at James. He certainly had a strange turn of phrase at times.'Drop me at the farm, you go off, come back in a couple of hours,' Rick said. He wanted no means of escape for at least that long.

*

'Look, Sergeant Pearce, just tell me what you're looking for, all these questions mean nothing,' Jo said, her voice even more reasonable now she'd been able to get dressed. And yet it was while she was getting dressed that the answer came to her. There could only be two things that they would go to so much bother over; arms or drugs. Why didn't they say? Were they waiting for her to slip up and mention one or the other, to implicate herself?

'It'd be just as well for you to just answer.'

'Ohwhh,' a sigh of exasperation, 'Go on?'

'Did you notice any regular pattern to Mr. Austin's life style?'

'You are joking?' This from Alex.

'I am beginning to think that it might be better if we talked to you later,' Pearce said, looking at him from under his heavy eyebrows.

'I know what he means.' Jo intervened, 'If you keep animals – your life is a regular pattern – of looking after them! Talking of which, the goats need milking – it's past their time.'

'The – livestock will be all right. Now, a pattern, other than domestic routine. Going off the farm, visiting or visitors?'

Jo thought. There had been so little time to notice anything, but the Thursday evening trips on the motor-boat were significant. So significant that she knew she'd already told one policeman about them. That one, Rick Whittington, and now this lot. There was no point in trying to hide the knowledge, it would only seem like she was hiding something else, something greater.

'He went out in his motor-boat. The Thursday before last, and last Thursday, when he didn't come back,' she said quietly. Didn't come back. Died. Drowned.

'Who was he going to meet?'

'I don't know.'

'But he was going out to meet someone?'

'I don't know!'

'How did he seem, after he came back from the first trip?'

'Sick.'

'Pardon?' It was obvious that D.S. Pearce thought she was having a go at him, his anger showed in his face.

'He was sick. He had developed pneumonia. I called the doctor. I can give you his name. He prescribed antibiotics and we looked after him until he was better – almost better,' she didn't know why she was using her best teacher-to-very-slow-child tone, it was the wrong thing to do.

Jo heard the front door open and looked up to see scruffy looking man at the kitchen door.

'Dry barns are all clean, sir,' he said to Pearce.

'Damn,' he said and sighed. He turned his bulk back to Jo. 'Come on. I hate to shift shit to find the stuff, but we will. We'll find it. Co-operation would be – appreciated.'

'What stuff?' Jo said. The more she denied knowing anything the guiltier she sounded, even in her own ears. What did you say if you were guilty 'it's a fair cop' – no way – you'd just keep saying, 'what stuff, I don't know, I don't know what you mean'.

It was ludicrous, there seemed to be no words that she could find that would be any different to those that someone steeped up to their eyeballs in crime wouldn't use. It was all just words! D.S. Pearce stood. Towered above her. 'Perhaps a little walk round might jog your memory. You might just have seen something. Noticed, quite innocently of course, Austin, tucking something away?'

Jo and Alex both slipped on their wellingtons. In the short time they'd been at the farm it had become de-rigueur for them. Farmyard equals boots. Pearce pulled a slight smile and shook his head. His own feet were protected by stout shoes, he obviously thought them enough.

*

'You can't come in here.'

'Want to bet?' Rick said flipping his ID out. The young constable standing guard at the entrance to the Farm stiffened slightly.

'Sorry, sir. I wasn't expecting anyone else.'

'Obviously. Who's in charge of this operation?'

'D.S. Pearce, sir.'

'Where is he?'

'Just a moment sir,' he turned away from Rick and shouted to a scruffy looking man just leaving the farm house. 'Bill!'

Bill arrived, eyeing Rick up and down.

'D.I. Whittington, Charles Cross,' Rick said, 'I'd like a word with D.S. Pearce.'

'He won't like it.'

'I wouldn't expect him to, but I'm in the middle of another case. The cross-over seems to be here. With Austin.'

'He's in the house, talking to the woman, seeing if she'll save us the bother.'

'Mrs. Smart?'

'Yeah.'

'Well, she's the one I need to see,' Rick said and began to pass, as he did so he saw her. Small and light beside the hulk of the man. Her head turned once in his direction, but snapped back to looking where they were going. Rick followed slowly.

They stepped out of the door into the bright sunlight. A shiver ran right through her. Whittington was standing by the gate, talking to the scruffy plain-clothes policeman. So he was involved. Her heart squeezed as she looked at him. Judas. He'd seemed so caring. She'd felt herself attracted to him, had told him everything, and now this. This!

She heard the commotion first, the bleating, like a child crying.'What the hell do you think you're doing!' Jo shouted, breaking into a run.
Two policemen were man-handling Tulip. Hands under her front legs, back hooves dragging along the ground. The goat bleated miserably.
'Put her down!' Jo tugged at an arm.
'Shove off!'
'Let the poor thing go! Can't you see you're upsetting her!'
A hand gripped Jo around the upper arm. The fingers met. They pulled. Pearce.
'Leave off, Mrs. Smart, you don't want to be done for assaulting a police officer, as well.'
'Assaulting a police officer! They should be done – cruelty to animals, make them stop!'
'Well, we wouldn't have to search their stinking houses if you'd co-operate.'
'Don't be so stupid!' she snapped, 'I don't know anything!'
'So we have to look, then, don't we?'
'Look,' Jo said, bringing her voice back down. D.S. Pearce looked, the glint in his eye hopeful. 'Just let me, and Alex, get the animals out of their houses, quietly.'

His expression fixed itself in a sneer. 'Oh that would be convenient. What do you think I am?'

'Insensitive,' a voice said softly. Pearce wheeled round to look Rick in the eye. 'D.I. Whittington, Charles Cross,' Rick said, flicking his ID again.

'What're you doing here?'

Rick stepped aside, Pearce followed him.

'I need to talk to Mrs. Smart, about Mr. Austin.'

'What's it got to do with you?'

'We took Mr. Austin out of the water yesterday.'

'Tough, we're in the middle of an operation.'

'So I've been informed. Why don't you let the lady get the animals out. One of you could watch her every move . You know it doesn't do to antagonise the public.'

'Public be damned. Do you know what's involved in this? Five kilos of coke on that holed yacht, it's a lot, but I'm certain to God there was more.'

'Get the animals out quickly then,' Rick looked hard into the other man's eyes. He saw the shift in them.

'Bill! Jock! ' Pearce snapped. The men hurried over. 'Let Mrs. Smart and her son get the animals out, one of you with each of them and you're all eyes. Okay?'

'Sir,' they said together.

*

James Fuller was getting nowhere fast. There was little to report on Mr. Austin. He was generally thought to be a 'nice chap'. The lady in the local Post Office had said she'd been 'a little wary when he'd first come in, all that long hair, but he was just a 'nice chap' and his wife had been ever-so nice. Joined in with lots of village events, a member of the WI, everything. Everyone was so upset when she disappeared. Drowned they said. Just like him, only her body had never been found.' Word had got round quickly about Austin, and the missing wife was obviously one of the local mysteries that no one was too mystified by. No suspicious circumstances, no threats or rows to throw suspicion onto anyone. The guests who'd stayed at the farm were also given a general clean-living bill of health by the Post Office, despite some of their appearances. 'You get used to seeing all sorts with these holidaymakers,' she confided to him. The views of the pub landlord where Pete Austin had been known to drink occasionally were much he same, though couched in slightly different terms.

James looked at his watch. Three-quarters of an hour left. He decided to take a swift drive over to Looe and pick up something for brunch. He'd missed out on breakfast. It was that or be late. He'd wanted to get up early enough, but Glenda didn't want him to, just then, and who was he to deny her? It was her day off, it was all right for her, she could breakfast at any time. Somehow they'd have to get their days off synchronised.

Looe seemed busy already, the sun pulled the visitors to the sea like wasps to an open jam pot. He parked the car and walked quickly along the main street. There used to be a shop down there that sold real fresh pasties, just how he liked them, if it was still there, it had to have been at least three years since he'd walked through Looe. He found himself looking at the tourist trade shops, the antiques and the crafts. He stopped. A craft shop, goods piled on the pavement, hanging from flower-basket hooks outside. Basketware. 'Local made' the sign said. He flexed his shoulders and walked in. The shop was jammed with different types of craft, but only a few more bits of basketry, flutes with dried flowers in them. He approached the counter, a drippy looking girl stood up from her wicker chair, tucking a paperback under the cushion as she did so.

'Can I help you?' she said in a light, lazy, bored voice.

'The basket-ware. Local it says?' he paused.

'Yeah, made locally.'

'Where? I mean who makes it?'

'I'm not sure – Miss Britain would know.' The image conjured up was of some beauty queen.

'Miss Britain?'

'The owner, she buys everything in.'

'Have you ever seen the basket maker?'

'No, why?'

'Never mind. If I – if I wanted something made up specially, could it be done?'

'Oh yes!'

'Could you give me Miss Britain's number – I could call her.'

The young woman's eyes clouded. 'No, I couldn't do that. I could take your number, for her to call you.'

James smiled at her. She managed a small smile back. He wrote his number down, then added Glenda's as an option. 'As soon as possible, please,' he said. The girl smiled again.

'I'll let her have it today,' she said.

James looked at his watch again. Just time to grab that pasty then he'd better be off, back to the farm.

*

'Thank you,' Jo said icily when she returned from putting the goats in the paddock. 'You do realise I'll have to milk them soon, the poor things'll be bursting.'

'Can't spare anyone at the moment Mrs. Smart,' Pearce said as he watched his team start on the goat houses, the police dogs' tails wagging.

'I'll go,' Rick said, 'perhaps I can get my few questions answered at the same time.'

Pearce looked at him. Rick could read his mind, it wouldn't be the first time a bent cop was in on a drugs deal. 'It's been searched, hasn't it?' he added.

'All right,' Pearce said gruffly.

'Come on Mrs. Smart, can I help bring the goats down for you?' Rick said, softening his tone.

'No. Thank you,' Jo said, voice as icy as before. Judas. Traitor.

'Fine, I'll follow you then,' he said and sauntered after her as she fetched Jasmine from the paddock and led her quietly down to the tiny milking parlour.

'Oh no! Stupid, stupid people!' she spat as she lifted the lid of the feed bin. Every sack of feed had been tipped out. All mixed together, all poured into the vast box. Goat mix, wheat, mixed-corn.

'What is it?'

'A bloody mess,' she muttered scooping up a tub-full of mainly goat mix and putting it into the bucket. Only then did Jasmine happily step up onto the stand and start to munch. Jo settled down on her stool to milk and began to talk softly to the goat, her shoulder pressed against its flank.

'Good girl, there now, let's have some milk,' she murmured. Rick closed the door slightly. They were alone. The air filled with the rhythmic sound of the milk squirting into the bucket. Rick perched himself on the edge of the feed bin, looking down on her back, on her blonde curls. She looked even more diminutive crouched there.

'I came to ask you about Pete Austin,' he said.

'Of course. Bully boy first isn't it? Then mister nice guy,'

'What do you mean?'

'Pearce, and you.'

'I'm not even part of his squad. I really did come to talk to you about Pete Austin. Something you said. 'Did I think he'd been killed?' you said. I wanted to know why you asked that.'

'Hah!' it escaped more like a stifled sob. 'I don't know! That's all I've been able to say this morning. I. Don't. Know!'

'But yesterday?'

She stopped milking. Her hands were still. Yesterday, when this man made my mind flip.

'Jo?' he dared to use her name. She turned her head, a quick glance at him. He saw her tears, tracking down her face. He slid from the edge of the bin and was crouched before her in one movement. He looked into her startled face. He wanted to brush the tears away, to kiss her trembling lips.

'Jo,' he began gently.

The door crashed open! The frightened goat twisted and kicked the bucket over, sending the white frothy milk in a sweeping arc of brilliance to soak them both. There was a second of stunned silence, and then Jo laughed.

CHAPTER THIRTEEN

She laughed. She could feel it getting away from her. The sound changed in her throat, turned sour and stretched into sobs. Open cries that mocked laughter. Her hands covered her face. She felt arms around her, strong arms, that held her as she rocked.

'Sorry, sir!' James said inadequately, 'They just said you were in here.'

'It's all right,' Rick said, thinking that he had probably just been saved from himself. 'See if you can find something to clean this lot up.'

Jo shook herself. Took a deep breath, recovered her composure. 'I'll do it. I'll get something,' she breathed. Rick stood up, his trousers sticking to his legs. It suddenly seemed very cramped in the tiny milking parlour. James backed out, Rick following. Jo led Jasmine away.

'Did you get your answers, sir.'

'I don't know,' he said watching Jo. That was the answer she gave, and that was it, he didn't know.

Alex was leaning against a barn. It wasn't a comfortable, lazy leaning. It was as if he were pressed against the stone. His hands were thrust in his pockets, he stared straight ahead. Rick came and stood beside him, looking in the direction he was looking. The geese were out, in their paddock. They hissed and shouted at the springer spaniel and his handler as they crossed over to their house. The gander made a rush, a waving of wings, his neck outstretched. The dog-handler turned to face him. The gander subsided and circled away, scolding his wives for not backing him up. The handler stepped inside the house, then withdrew. He was looking at his feet. He sent the dog in with a wave of his hand and a wag of its tail. The white and brown face appeared at the door, disappeared, reappeared. The dog-handler seemed satisfied, they stomped back across the paddock. Alex suddenly seemed to notice Rick, he glanced at him, then back to the scene.

'What're the dogs looking for?' he said quietly.

'Drugs. Trained to it. Smallest amount,' Rick answered. He liked this boy, it was more than who he was, it was some indefinable recognition, like looking at a photo of yourself as a child and thinking it was someone else.

'Thought so.'

'Do you think they'll find any?'

'I don't know,' he turned to look at Rick. 'We really did come here to get away from things, nasty things back home, so I don't know. Pete seemed really cool, didn't talk down to you like some. That's it. Who knows?'

'What's your name?'

Alex looked at him. 'Alex,' he said looking away again. What on earth was he doing talking to this policeman like this. Fuzz. Pig. The derogatory terms filled his head. He'd always heard the names called, used, spat out. Now he felt them.

Rick turned the name over in his mind, and smiled.

'Bet you loved that when they called the register.'

Alex looked at him sharply. 'Oh yeah.'

'Like mine, Richard Whittington ... '

'Dick? Dick Whittington?'

'You got it, pain eh?'

Alex smiled. 'They did that,' he indicated the other policemen. 'Said, surname? Smart. First name? Alex, Alexander. It happens every time. Smart Alec. I don't know what Mum was thinking of,' he sighed.

'Well my father was named John and was called Dick all his life, so he named me Richard, he figured it would be better if it was at least a shortening of my real name – you see even the best reasons can go haywire.'

'I guess,' Alex said, thinking of the proposed trip to Greece. There was a moment of quiet between them.

'What 'nasty things'?' Rick asked casually.

Alex's head bowed, he gave it a little dismissive shake. 'Nothing – I got – mugged. Our house was broken into, really upset mum.'

'Not nothing though?'

'Nothing anyone could do.'

Jo reappeared around the end of the building. Alex pushed himself off the wall and went to meet her, Rick following closely. Jo gave him a hard look, wary and embarrassed.

'They say they're going soon,' Jo said.

It looked like a scene from the Jungle Queen. A line of assorted bearers were carrying out boxes, only these boxes were computers worth thousands of pounds and boxes of computer disks.

'You can't take all that!' Jo said hurrying forward, 'It's his work, it's just his work,' she said finding her words catching in her throat.

'Don't mum,' Alex's arm was about Jo's shoulder. 'He won't need it anyway.'

Jo felt something inside herself deflate, a balloon of indignation. 'Of course. They'll want access to the hard disks as well as the floppies. It's obvious I suppose,' she sighed and looked up at her tall son, 'We'll go home. First thing, pack and go, get away from this,'

'Okay.'

'Oh God no! We can't!'

'What?'

'The animals? I can't just leave them, we've no idea who,' she stopped and hurried over to D.S. Pearce. 'Excuse me,' she said stridently, gaining his attention. 'Perhaps, as you look through that lot you might find out who his solicitor is – we've go to hand over the place to someone.'

'Thinking of leaving?'

'Of course! Do you think I want to stay – after all this?'

His eyebrows raised. 'We'd prefer it if you didn't leave – just yet.'

'Prefer! Look we were on holiday and holidays come to an end. You've taken our address. Just let me know who to contact – I doubt there's a record of it anywhere else.'

'We'll see,' Pearce said and turned his back and walked away to where the last set of boxes were being put into the van.

Rick followed him. 'Any joy?' he asked.

'Nah. But one of the Thompson boys has got form for drugs. Ideal set up, visitors taking it away. Could be he'd run out and the yacht was the new consignment.'

'The yacht bothers me. I would have thought it'd worry you too. He went out in a motor boat, one of those that you can put on a trailer and drop in off a slipway.'

'Or someone did – to pick up from his yacht.'

'Would you register a yacht in your own name and then run drugs on it?' Rick suggested, as he turned away and strode over to where James was waiting for him with their car.

'Sorry about that, back at the farm,' James said as they took off along the bumpy track.

'One of those things.'

'Good looking lady, wouldn't think she'd be old enough to have a lad that old.'

'He's only sixteen.'

'Huh, looks older, anyway.'

'Never mind, look, did you get anywhere?'

'Not exactly. Seems Mr. Austin was a well-liked guy, you know, and his wife before she disappeared.'

'Drowned?'

'So people believe.'

'Something suspicious?'

James shrugged, 'No body, that's all.'

'What, you think we need to dig over the farm?'

'No, no one seems to even think that.'

'So there's no lead to follow up, that's what you're saying?'

James flicked a glance at Rick. He seemed to be in a bad mood, James felt disinclined to mention the very vague possibility of finding a basket maker – any basket maker.

'No, sir. I mean, yes sir. There's nothing to follow up.'

They drove the rest of the way in an uneasy silence. Rick sank into a brooding contemplation of the mess he was getting into over this woman. He couldn't let himself seek to become involved with someone who might be tangled up in drug smuggling, yet even as he sat in the car heading back to the station he could feel her body as he'd held it for those few precious moments when sorrow had overtaken her. He felt annoyed at himself and it was affecting the way he dealt with everyone else, and that annoyed him all the more. Thank God his annual leave started from today.

*

Alex waited. He was sure they had all left at the same time, but he waited. There would be time enough when he put the birds to bed later. It would be be most natural time for him to go into the goose house.

Just after six he took the soaked grain and a bucket of water and walked into the paddock surrounding the goose house. They swept over to him, chittering and complaining. He dumped the bucket of grain, took a few steps and dumped the bucket of water. The noise from the geese turned to a pleasant warbling as they tucked into their evening food. His heart was beating fast, he could feel it as a throb in his temple. He felt wound up.

The memory had come back to him as he watched the policemen search the goat houses, something about the way you could see all of them, except their heads, when they stood up inside the shed. So he'd watched and waited as they'd searched the goose house. He'd watched the small dog dive in and out and come away empty, so he guessed that whatever it was, it wasn't drugs.

As he ducked in he was greeted by the semi-acrid smell of the building, the floor thick and slippery with green droppings. He and Pete were going to do the mucking out. But Pete hadn't come back. He thought of the evening that Pete went. It was that evening that Alex had seen him. Carrying the buckets up to the paddock he'd seen Pete standing in this house, or rather had seen him from the chest down. He'd seen him reach into the pocket of his smock and take out a packet of some kind. Not large, it was almost completely masked by Pete's big hand. The hand disappeared up into the hidden roof space, then Pete ducked out of the goose house. He'd seemed surprised to see Alex there.

Alex stood, as much as the low roof would allow him to. He waited while his eyes adjusted to the reduced light. He ran the picture in his head again. Pete's body had been facing the door, the hand moved straight up. Alex looked. There it was, a thin pale line pressed in over the door frame. He worked one edge out with his fingers until he could pull it out. He knew what it was. Wrapped in plastic and sheathed in card it still had the shape and weight of a disk.

Remembering how Pete had been observed by him he held the hand with the package above his head as he looked out. He was alone, he slipped the package into his back pocket and left the geese to their feeding.

Once in the farmhouse he kicked off his boots and ran upstairs. He was right. A disk. He stared at it for a moment willing it to reveal its secrets. He suddenly remembered seeing a portable computer in Pete's room. He dashed in there hoping that the police would have missed it. They hadn't. He had to get this disk to a computer. He wouldn't worry Jo about it until after he'd found out what it said, she might just make him hand it over. It could be anything, it could be nothing. He just couldn't let it go until he knew what was on it. When he knew that, he'd know what to do with it.

'Kelvin! Josie! Great to see you, come in, come in,' Rick said, his heart feeling full at seeing such old friends again. Josie leant forward and kissed him on his cheek.

'God! What a drive!' Kelvin said as he flopped down in an easy chair.

'Tea then, or something stronger?'

'What y' got?'

'Bitter, lager, wine, scotch.'

'That'll do me – a small scotch.'

'Tea for me Rick, please,' Josie said. 'Shall I come and make it?'

'Certainly not!' Rick said with a grin, 'Won't be a tick – bathroom's upstairs, straight ahead,' he added as he left the room.

'Here you are – one scotch, one tea and another scotch for me. Cheers! Here's to a good holiday!'

'Yeah, I'll drink to that. You managed to sort that murder you was on then?'

'Not exactly – it's one of those. Barely any leads and those we have are tenuous and well nigh impossible to follow. I've left it with one of the D.C.s' I told you about. He seems keen on this case – he won't let it slip while I'm away.'

'So they've let you off on a long leash. What else have you …'

'Kelvin! Enough, you promised me it wouldn't be all shop-talk when we came down here,' Josie said warmly. Kelvin looked a bit sheepish.

'She's right, of course. So what else has been happening – apart from work?'

Rick took a sip of his scotch. How could he answer. There hadn't been much else except work. He'd given it almost all his time since he'd arrived, a couple of trips down to see his sister and family, an evening at a local, and disappointingly poor, folk venue, and the disastrous meal at John Henry's. Not exactly a lot of life outside the job.

'I've been over to see my other sister and her family a couple of times. You met Sally up in London didn't you?'

'Yeah, once or twice.'

'You are a quiet one Rick, I never knew you had another sister,' Josie said teasingly.

'Ah, well, I've got to have some secrets haven't I, or else you'd lose interest in me,' Rick teased back. It had always been this way between them, a totally innocent flirtation.

*

The phone rang four times. Alex was wishing hard. It was picked up, 'Hello?'

'Tamsin?'

'Yes, oh Alex!'

'I'm glad you answered.'

'They're out, just over in the pub.'

'You're on your own then,' Alex said softly, momentarily wishing he could be with her.

'Yeah.'

'Look, this is important. Do you know anyone with a decent computer?'

'Depends what you mean by decent?' Tamsin said, her voice sounding hurt.

'With a bit of RAM. An IBM compatible?' he said, but even as he said it he wondered whether the disk would run on a PC even if they found one.

'Sure! Michelle's got one. Rod buys her all sorts of things since he left home.'

'Right then. First thing tomorrow, I'll get Mum to drop me off at your place, you arrange for us to see Michelle and .. '

'Hang on, I'm working tomorrow!'

'Forget it, say you're sick. This is really important!'

'But I can't! It's my Uncle. He'd find out as easy as ..'

'Then just ring Michelle. Right. Make sure she's expecting me and that she'll let me use her computer. Tell her it's urgent – it'll only take me a few ticks to see what I want – tell her that.'

'What on your own?'

'Why not?'

Tamsin thought of Michelle and her computer set-up in her bedroom. She thought of Michelle and her infamous lecherous look. She thought of Alex.

'No! No – I'll wangle it somehow. You come here and I'll take you over there.'

'Cheers, Tamsin. You're wonderful. Miss you – see you tomorrow.'

'Love you,' whispered Tamsin, as she put down the phone.

*

'If I drop you at the bridge car park are you all right to walk up?' Jo asked Alex as they drove into Looe the next morning.

'Sure.'

'And you'll phone me when you want picking up?'

'Yes. That's what I said.'

'Fine! No need to get touchy.'

'Sorry.'

'No it's nice for you and Tamsin to get out for the day, where'd you say you were going?'

'The Monkey Sanctuary.'

'Oh, but isn't that nearer to Bodrigga than here?'

'We're going with some friends of Tamsin's,' Alex made up hastily. He hadn't expected to be quizzed.

'See you later then,' Jo said as she pulled up in the car park. Alex left the car and was soon walking quickly in the direction of West Looe and The Smugglers. Jo locked the car and watched him disappear before she set off on a slow walk along by the harbour to see if she just happened to find Rod down near his boat.

*

'All set?' Alex asked as soon as he saw Tamsin.

'Yeah. I'll really get stewed for this you know. I've sworn that you and your Mum have invited me out for the day, and Mum rang Uncle Mick to get me let off. If she ever finds out I'll really be for it.'

'How far to Michelle's?'

'Not far, look over there, see that row of houses half way up the other side. See that pink one, next to a white one?' She pointed to the other side of the valley.

'Yeah.'

'Well, it's the grey one, three down.'

'Lets go then,' Alex said allowing his long legs to increase the pace until Tamsin was almost running beside him. 'I'll tell you about it on the way.'

They knocked on the door and stood waiting, Alex felt nervous, he couldn't stop himself looking round, checking up and down the street. He wasn't even sure what or who he was looking for, but deep within his mind he suspected that the farm was being watched and so might he be. At last there was a sound and movement as the front door was unlocked.

'What'yer doing?' Michelle said, 'The back's open.'

'Well, I didn't think it was right – with a – visitor,' Tamsin said feeling slightly foolish for her decision to knock at the front door instead of just going round the back and calling out as she usually did.

'Hi, Alex,' Michelle said, turning her attention to Alex once she'd made Tamsin look silly. 'Come upstairs,' she paused for effect, 'my computer's in my room.'

'Great, let's go. It won't take a minute.'

'Your mum in?' Tamsin asked.

'Shopping, Dad's coming over later so she always makes sure she's out,' she opened her bedroom door. 'There it is,' she said.

Tamsin knew Michelle would have tidied up a bit, but Michelle had made her room look really cool. She'd draped a large black and starred scarf over the bedspread, had removed all but the Black Wolf and Guns'n'Roses posters and had swept away every trace of clutter. Tamsin wondered what the inside of Michelle's wardrobe looked like.

Alex didn't even pause to look round, he settled himself quickly on the chair in front of the screen. He switched on and waited while the computer set itself up, tapping his foot impatiently. As soon as it was ready he pushed the disk in and tapped the 'read floppy' icon. The small light on the disk drive flashed and a message came up.

'Damn! I should have known!'

'What is it?'

'Won't run on this machine.'

'Should do, it's really good, don't think anyone's got one better, eh Tams?'

'No.'

Alex smiled at Michelle. Tamsin felt herself tense up.

'There's nothing wrong with your machine, I wish I had one as good. No, it's this disk. I reckon Pete used his Acorn. There's a way to drop this info onto a PC but I don't know how, do you?'

'What?'

'Do you know how to read a disk from a different set up?'

'No...' Michelle said slowly.

'Oh hell,' Alex pushed the button that ejected the disk.

'What's so important?'

'See this disk. Pete Austin had it hidden. I don't know what's on it but the fuzz were all over the farm yesterday ... '

'They were looking for drugs – with dogs!' Tamsin threw in.

Alex shot her a warning glance.

'I just want to see what's on this before I hand it over – that's all.'

'Now you think it's out of a different type of computer?'

'Yeah, probably. He said he liked the Acorn. Do you know someone with one?'

'Sort of. The primary school.'

'Not a BBC. A bigger one – 5000 at least.'

'It is! They won it on something.'

'Lot of good it is to us though.'

'Depends who you know. It just so happens that Mum's the caretaker. We've got the keys!' Michelle smirked.

'That's a bit dodgy? Don't you know anyone else?'

'What's wrong with you? It's not like we're breaking in – not with the key. We could go along, just slip in, try the disk and out. You said it'd only take a tick.'

'Yeah,' Alex bit his lower lip. It didn't feel right but there seemed no alternative if he really wanted to read the disk before he handed it in. 'Okay – where is it?'

'Not far – come on,' Michelle said her face flushing with excitement.

'You sure 'Shell?'

'Course I am – chicken? I'll take Alex along on my own if you like – might be better anyway.'

'No,' Tamsin said sulkily as she followed them down the stairs. Michelle took the big bunch of keys from her mother's bureau and pocketed them, she picked up her own house keys and dropped the latch as they left the house.

*

Just as Jo had hoped, Rod was down at his boat. The boat was facing in the opposite direction to the way she'd first seen it and Rod was touching up the paint on her prow. Jo thought he looked a little careworn this morning.

'Morning,' she said as she trod softly up beside him. He glanced up sharply, his features soon melting into a smile. 'How's things?'

'Did you hear? We had a police raid yesterday, on the farm?'

'No! Oh Jo – if I'd have known. Why didn't you call me?' he hoped he'd feigned enough surprise. Pongo had known. Pongo had let him know.

'I – I couldn't. I felt that anyone I spoke to – called – would be under suspicion too.'

Don't call. Keep away. Pongo had said. Seems he was right.

'What – what were they looking for?'

'They wouldn't say. Just kept asking me what I knew, as if I should know. What could I say? "I don't know anything." What else?' she felt the panic returning, her breath seemed short.

'Come and have a coffee – sit down, tell me about it,' Rod said dropping his brush into a jam jar of murky liquid.

'It was awful – they woke me up, banging on the door at five in the morning!' Jo said as they sat over two steaming cups of hot coffee in a harbour-side cafe. It felt good to talk about it, cathartic, releasing the pent-up tensions that she had wrapped herself in. She continued her tale, Rod adding just the right mixture of commiseration and indignation as she went.

The coffee cups drained, she reached the point of the departure of the police, describing the exodus of the computers and their files.

'Oh God, and that's another thing. What do I do? I've rung round all the local solicitors to see if any of them dealt with Pete's will, whatever, but nothing. I told the police that they'd better look out for a disk with some personal information on, but I wasn't sure then. What do you think I should do?' Rod was looking a little blank. He'd gone still, his face rigid. 'What is it Rod?'

'What? Oh, nothing – I was just thinking – imagining.' Thinking about what might be on one of those disks. 'It must have been hell for you.' In the small silence that followed the church clock could be heard chiming the hour. Rod started, and glanced at his watch, it was streaked with paint.

'Oh, Jo. I, er, I've got to go. I'm supposed to be seeing Michelle,' he said. For a moment the name meant nothing to her. Another woman maybe. She felt herself colouring as she gathered up her things, even as he added, 'I promised to take her out shopping in the school holidays,' and the identity of Michelle clicked into place in her head.

Feeling slightly foolish she smiled and said, 'Mustn't keep families apart,' the words jumping out before she'd half formed the thought, and instantly regretting it. 'Sorry – I mean.'

He reached out his hand and rested it on her shoulder, massaging it slightly with his fingers.

'I'll come up and see you this evening – if it suits?'

Jo smiled up at him. 'It suits,' she said, thinking that she would welcome his reassuringly steady presence.

CHAPTER FOURTEEN

'Oh Shit, Oh shit!' spluttered Michelle when she heard the clock chime.

'What is it?'

'Dad! I told you stupid. He'll be at the house now, were going shopping in Plymouth. Hell! Look, take the keys. Here,' she grabbed Tamsin's hand and pressed a large brass key into it so hard that the square end dug into the softness of her palm. 'This is the door key and this,' she did the same with a small shiny Yale-type key, 'turns off the alarm. You must do it straight away! It's in the cupboard in the library. This,' she pressed a shiny square ended key into Tamsin's hand, 'is the library key. Got it?'

Tamsin, her face screwed with the effort of not crying out at the pain, nodded.

'Bring them back to me, not Mum, me. Got it?'

'Sure, we'll do it.'

'And don't get caught, go round the back way,' Michelle said turning. She left them walking quickly, but as she turned the corner she broke into a run.

Tamsin swallowed and rubbed her palm. She still held on to the three keys that had been indicated, the other unidentified keys dangling free on the ring.

'Come on then,' she said, sounding braver than she felt. She thought that she had a lot to make up for in Alex's eyes now that Michelle had gone.

They walked along the road facing the Primary school. Behind the building the hill revealed pasture land. Tamsin led them along a road until they came to a farm gate. They untied the faded orange baler-twine that held it shut and slipped through. By keeping very close to the hedge they found they could not see any other building except the school. They worked their way round the field edge slowly as Tamsin suggested, adding, 'Then we could be looking for early blackberries or late bullaces, perhaps, if we're asked, if someone does see us.'

The real danger time came when they had to climb the hedge and drop over into the school grounds. A second or two of exposure. A vertiginous view over the whole of Looe, then down onto the hard tarmac and a dash into the shadow of the building.

They stood close together, their hearts beating hard, their skin clammy in the heat of the day.

'Right. Where's the door?' Alex asked.

'Round the side.'

'Oh Lord,' Alex looked in the direction Tamsin had indicated. If someone looked out from the bungalow next door they would be seen easily. They watched the bungalow for a few silent moments. No signs of life.

*

Michelle came careering down the road to her house, glad that none of her friends could see her running like this. Dad's Landrover was there! Suddenly she saw Rod standing outside the house. He just appeared like magic, she slowed, came to a stumbling walk. Of course, he'd been round the back and had just come round the front because she wasn't in. That was it, but he'd seen her and stood watching her.

'Where you been?'

'Oh – um. With Tamsin and her boyfriend, you know, Alex, up at Bodrigga?' Michelle said, 'Sorry I was late Dad.'

'That's all right – I was a bit late myself. Funny – I was talking to that Alex's mum, they've had a bit of trouble up there.'

'Oh yeah! Alex told me about it! Police looking for drugs! And taking away all the computers, that's why they came to me.' Michelle said proudly.

'What d'you mean love?'

'Because of the brill computer you bought me!'

'What they want that for then?'

Michelle looked at her feet.

'Come on! What do they need a computer for?' Rod said, his voice taking on a hard edge, his insides feeling tight and knotted.

'He…. Nothing – just a game he'd got,' Michelle tried to bluff but her face coloured up a deep red.

Rod's hand squeezed his daughter's arm.

'Don't Dad, that 'urts!'

'Don't tell me lies.'

'It didn't work anyway! It was off another computer, couldn't run on mine. Mine's good enough – only it was different.'

'What wouldn't run?' His fingers eased slightly, he smiled patiently at her.

Michelle looked up at him, he looked worried.

'A disk he found. That bloke had hidden it. He found it – he only wanted to look at it – he was going to hand it over when he'd looked at it.'

'Where are they now?'

Michelle shook her head. This would get her in real shit.

Rod's fingers tightened again, he began to tug her towards the house.

'Dad!'

'Where?' his eyes were wild, his breathing quick. It frightened Michelle. 'For God's sake, love. Where?'

'At the school – they said. He said it needed an Acorn 5000, like the school won last year. I borrowed Mum's keys and I was going with them, to make sure it was all right. Then I had to come back to meet you. They won't do nothing. Tamsin won't. They – '

'They're up there now, at the school?'

'Yes.'

'How long?'

Michelle looked at her watch. All that in ten minutes! The run down, this crazy business with her Dad.

'Ten minutes – quarter of'n hour?'

He let go of her.

'From the school?'

'No, I left them at the top of Barbican road.'

He thought. He pressed both hands to his head and turned around twice. Michelle watched him warily.

'Go indoors. You don't know where they are. You've not given them your Mum's keys – I don't want you in any trouble. Understand love?'

Michelle nodded, this was more like her old Dad, looking after her.

*

'Okay – let's go,' Alex said and walked slowly and casually round to the door, Tamsin at his back. The key slipped in and turned without effort. A sound, like a trapped bee caught their attention as soon as they stepped in.

'Library!' Alex breathed closing the door quietly behind him. Tamsin led the way, things hadn't changed that much since she attended the school.

The library door opened, the buzzing filled their heads, making them quick and panicky, any moment the siren and bells would begin! They opened the cupboard and Tamsin tried to put the key in the slot. Her hand was shaking so much that she couldn't get it to go in at first. The key turned. The buzzing stopped. They stood there, frozen, waiting for the clamour. After a moment Alex sighed, letting out the breath he'd been holding. He looked round the room.

'Right room, at least,' he said.

All the school's computers, televisions and videos were in the library. All disconnected. All in odd positions around the room. It was easy to see that the classrooms had been emptied and their contents brought into this room and dumped on any available space.

'Which one is it?'

'Um – ' Alex looked from computer to computer. 'Here it is, 5000, look,' he said leaning round to look at the front of a computer that faced the wall. He cleared a small space on the central table, lifted the monitor off the computer and set it in the space. Then he turned the computer round and plugged it in. When he put the monitor back on the computer he had to connect the two together and then plug the monitor in. It took time. He could feel time trickling down his back, sweating the minutes away.

*

Rod slammed the Landrover round the small roads, his foot pushed to the floor, jabbing the brakes, lurching off. He drove unthinkingly straight up to Pongo's farm. He was a kid again, really in the shit and not knowing who else to turn to. He was scared. It had seemed like a game up to now. Now it seemed like hell. The cinders slid beneath his wheels as he stopped, throwing up a gritty cloud of dust. Pongo appeared as Rod leapt down from the Landrover.

'I told you! Never, fucking never, drive up here!' Pongo growled.
'I had to! Oh God – I didn't know what else to do, the boy from the farm's found Austin's computer disk. He's at the primary school now, trying to read it,' Rod jabbered, he felt sick, sweating, terrified.
'On his own?'
'With a friend of Michelle's.'
Pongo's face took on a hard look. 'Can't be helped,' he almost smiled, it sent a shiver through Rod. 'Get along there, I'll follow,' he said, turning his back and starting to lollop back to the farm house, shouting over his shoulder to the still stationary Rod, 'Now! Oh, and don't let them get away!'

*

'Got it!' Alex breathed as the disk offered him various files to pick from.
'Which one?'

'I don't know – we'll have to try the lot, let's start with the first,' he tapped the mouse on the file named 'Jnote'. The screen flickered and a picture appeared, a photograph.

'That's his wife!' Tamsin said in an awed whisper.

'Pete's?'

'Mm. Jnote. Julia?'

'Let's see what else there is,' he scrolled down. All her details, height, weight, colouring, distinguishing marks and the dates: Born, married – disappeared – 22 Dec. Alex felt a lump in his throat. He moved the page up. 'Unexplained entries in J diary: Nov 14: R. 21: R. 28: R. Dec 3: R/C? 10: R. 17: R/C!' he read.

'Doesn't tell us much?' Tamsin said, her voice small in his ear.

'Didn't tell Pete much either I think. Let's try a different file.' The mouse performed its dance and the options were offered again. Alex tapped on the next file in the line. 'JuAcc'.

'What's this?' Alex said to himself. 'It looks like the accounts for the farm.'

'Or for the holiday place – look at it for July and August.'

'Yeah – that's it. I'll try something else.' He tapped the file labelled 'MessY'. 'What's this? Looks like a rhyme? Oh! it's a game, look – some word game?'

'I don't know! Alex, time's getting on! We've been half an hour already!'

'Not in here – ' He opened the next file: 'YJRanl'. Alex stared at the screen. 'Jackpot,' he whispered.

*

Rod's heart appeared to be thumping in time to the revving of his engine as he turned and headed back towards the school. He drove right up to the school, then as he reached forward to turn off the ignition he thought it'd be wiser to park elsewhere. He quietly ran the Landrover on past the playground and parked outside a row of houses. He left the car and, without looking at the panorama, walked steadily back to the primary school, practising in his head the casual words he'd say if someone stopped him and asked what he was doing. 'Just checking up on the place for m' missus, favour like.' No one asked him. The whole road seemed deserted in the heat of the airless day. He opened the gate and without thinking let it fall shut. It clanged and shook the chain-link, a tremor that ran right along to the corner posts.

*

'You can't believe that?' Tamsin gasped.

'Why not?'

'We know him. He wouldn't!'

'Pete Austin suspected him – look,' he pointed. The words were clear enough. "R = Rod Pentewan? I now know J saw him on at least three of the 'R' dates in the diary. Where is she?"

'But the other stuff?'

'It fits though – with the police raiding the place. Perhaps it was her!'

'Drug smuggling? Mrs. Austin? Oh come on!'

'Look – ', he scrolled down again, ' "Call sign from our yacht!!! Are you out there Julia? Are you with R? On <u>our</u> yacht that <u>he</u> bought?" '

'But he's not 'out there'!'

'There's more files, let's look,' Alex was feeling excited, the fear replaced by the unravelling of the strange clues and thoughts contained in the files.

'Did you hear that?' Tamsin stood her head at an angle, trying to catch the sound again.

'What?'

'The school gate. I remember it! It makes a ringing sound.'

Alex looked at her, her eyes wide, poised like a gazelle suspecting lions nearby.

'Go and have a look,' he said, punching the button to eject the disk.

Tamsin opened the library door quietly, and listened. Nothing. A squeak, rubber on linoleum? She crept round to the corridor, softly down to the entrance hall. The front door was closed. She stood upright and sighed. With relief she turned to go back. He stepped into the corridor behind her! She screamed, a small involuntary scream.

'Don't!' Rod shouted and ran at her. 'Don't!' he cried again as he tried to cover her mouth with his hand. Tamsin felt choked and scared, she opened her mouth wider and found it full of hard flesh. She bit. Surprising herself with her force.

'Ahh, Bitch!'

'Rod! It's Rod! It's muhmph − .' her words cut off as he over-came his squeamishness and crashed her to the floor, clamping his hand firmly over her mouth.

As Tamsin had crept from the room, Alex stood by the computer with the disk in his hand. If there was someone out there he had to hide it, but where? His eyes fixed on the books. A needle in a haystack? First thing he thought of; first thing they'd think of. He looked around. Everywhere was obvious. His gaze returned to the computer. He tipped the monitor back and tried the disk in the small space beneath it. With any luck they'd not think of it, not even realise the space was there, and perhaps it was the last place they'd expect to find a computer disk − with the computer. It would be perfect if he could tape it up − he glanced round. A blob of grey stuff was curled up in the corner of a notice board. He grabbed it and, pulling it quickly, squeezed it onto the disk.

He heard Tamsin cry out. He heard a shout.

Tipping the monitor up again he fixed the disk in place.

Another cry! This time he was sure she shouted Rod!

He let the monitor down and centred it, hoping it looked like a permanent fixture, and he ran, tugging out a few books from the shelves as he passed, trying to lay a false trail.

At the end of the corridor Rod was sprawled over Tamsin, his hand pressing on her face as she kicked and writhed.

'Shut it!' Rod yelled.

Alex launched himself at Rod just as Rod's hand came down in a resounding slap across Tamsin's face. And Alex was on him. His arm around Rod's throat. Tugging. Squeezing. Yanking his head up and back. More anger and fury than he'd ever known in himself. He could feel the muscles in Rod's neck like ropes round canvas. Fingers dug into Alex's skin as they pulled on his arm.

His head felt as if it would split with the effort, but he could feel the man easing back, and it gave him hope and strength.

His head split. The darkness poured in. Pain and points of light, and nothing.

Pongo had arrived.

The air was filled for ten seconds with a wail. A vibrating, rising and rising scream from the girl.

Ten seconds.

Pongo made it stop. Rod sat back on his haunches against the wall and stared. Speechless. Shocked.

*

The phone rang in the empty flat. Once, twice three times. Then the click and short whirr before the recorded voice cut in. 'I am sorry I am unable to answer the phone just at the moment. You may leave a message, or if you leave your name and number I will call you back. Please speak clearly after the tone.' pee-eep!

Miss Britain detested answerphones, but the phone at the first number had just rung and rung. And business was business. She took a deep breath.

'Good afternoon. This is Miss Britain. I understand that you wish to place a special order. As you don't appear to be in – I suppose – you may contact me on Looe 264230 – Thank you.'

*

'What have you done?' Rod whispered.

'They'll be out for a bit – time enough. Get shifted.'

'What?'

'Find the fucking disk they was looking at – I'll see to them.'

'Are they all right?'

'Christ! No fucking use knowing how to do it if you never use it! Get shifted.'

Rod pushed himself up the wall until he was standing. He stepped past the body of the boy. So young-looking, flaked out, arms thrown wide, eyes closed. He could see the chest rise and fall, could hear the air in his mouth. Relieved he trotted down the corridor to the library to begin his search.

Pongo slipped out of the door, a shadow, and slid round to the school's kitchen door. Within seconds he'd broken the glass and let himself in. He pulled long strips of withy from his belt and twisted them to create handcuffs for the unconscious pair. He ripped off lengths of tape and sealed their mouths.

'Rod!' he snapped, looking in on the devastation that Rod was causing as he pulled out and shook open book after book, discarding them as he went. 'Gis' a hand.'

Together they carried the bodies along the corridor to the open door.

'We'll get them over the hedge.'

'What – leave them there?'

'Oh funny. I'll pick them up – look after them,' Pongo said, his eyes sharp but his mouth making a grin.

'You won't hurt them?'

Pongo looked at him as if considering the idea of hurting them. 'Insurance – that's it. Think of it like insurance.'

Rod swallowed. His arms felt like jelly as he helped hoist the sighing bodies over the hedge.

'Now find that fucking disk – then clear out. I've broken in; just make sure nothing links this to you. It was vandals, wasn't it?' Pongo said and belly rolled himself over the hedge. Rod stood for one dumb-struck moment, wondering what he was doing, wondering if prison would be better than the pit he was digging himself into. Then he returned to the library, desperation driving his frantic searching.

Pongo brought his Landrover right across the field as if he owned it. To be inconspicuous: be obvious. He pulled it up and quickly lifted the bodies over the tailgate. He drove further across the field, paused again, then drove back and out. The farmer doing his rounds.

He felt totally in control by the time he arrived back at his farm. Years of army training, specialised training, had locked itself into his mind, he operated as a machine. The army that had taught him so much that was useless in normal society. The army that had taken him abroad where he'd first made his contacts. The army that had chucked him out with a pittance when his leg had been smashed by a sniper's bullet in Northern Ireland.

They were stirring when he lifted them from the back of the Landrover and dropped them on the floor of his workshop. The workshop, a converted barn, was filled with withies of various kinds, with baskets, finished and half made, with the tools of the trade. Tall bundles of withies were arranged round the walls, each as thick as a maid's waist, standing in bundles of brown bark, stripped white and the golden tan of the boiled stems. Dust motes danced in the light from the two small windows, one beside the door, one towards the sea. A bundle of withies lay drowning in a long stone trough planted against the wall.

He closed the door. He pressed the button on the portable radio. Pop music burbled into the air. He shifted his tools, the beating iron, the knife, the bodkin, with a sweep of his hand. He hauled at a board, the width of a door and half its length, set up at an angle on the floor against the wall. The basket-maker's plank, his work seat.

Beneath it, smothered in the dust of willow bark, his fingers encountered a raised knot of wood. He twisted it with his flat-ended fingers, it un-screwed, leaving a hole the size of bottle top. He hooked his large fore-finger into the hole and pulled. The dust slithered off the planks as an unevenly shaped section lifted up. Suddenly the sea sounded much closer, filling the small barn. He listened. Not for the first time he shivered as his memory filled in another sound. Just the sea, he'd been down to look, just the sea, now.

He turned to the bodies. The girl was staring at him, eyes wide, full of fear, her hair a tangled mass of dark copper, her skin pale. The boy stirred. He'd have to get a move on. He pulled a rope from a beam and moved towards the girl. She pushed herself up and wriggled back away from him.

'Don't be stupid!' he spat. He didn't want to have to render her unconscious again. That might be too bad, down there. He lunged forward, grabbing her by a fistful of her hair. He threaded the thick rope through the withy manacles and forced her to the edge of the hole. She kicked and writhed and tried to keep her feet on the floor of the barn. But he was strong, so strong, an arm like a clamp lifted her, and her feet suddenly had nothing to push against.

He let her down, her arms wrenching in their sockets, her pulse thundering in her ears.

Hanging from her own arms, the rope and her manacles being the only thing to stop her falling into the darkness beneath. She looked down and saw nothing but blackness. She looked up past wrists that felt as if they were being sliced through, and saw only the rope and Pongo's face behind his fist. She prayed he was strong enough not to let her fall.

Her feet touched, she sank, the rope burned as it whizzed past her wrists and her arms fell, leaden, useless, into her lap.

She dared not move. She kept her eyes fixed on the patch of light high above her.

*

'We're leaving!' Mrs. Thompson said, her voice loaded with bitterness.

'I don't blame you,' Jo said, 'wish I could.'

'It's been — horrible. Nothing like this has ever happened before.' The accusation hung in the air. It was all her fault.

'I'm sorry — ' Jo found herself saying, 'It's not been much of holiday for us either.'

Mrs. Thompson looked at her with hard sceptical eyes then spun on her heel and stalked off. Mr. Thompson, small and affable, looked up from his feet.

'Don't take any notice of her. We've been through something like this before, that's the problem. Luke was prosecuted for possession of cannabis when he was at University. They brought it all up again. Take care, bye,' he said and turned to follow his angry wife. Doors slammed, the engine revved up, the dust spurted from the back wheels and the family disappeared up the track.

On some kind of automatic pilot Jo fetched the cleaning things and walked towards the chalet. If only she could leave so easily. It felt as if the place had been left in her hands, in trust, until things could be sorted out. The animals at least. Someone had to care for them until a will was found, or something. Under this influence she worked without thought to the task in hand. Cleaning, as if by cleaning she could wash the past week out of her system. Eventually exhausted she locked the chalet door and stood in the sunshine again. She felt drained. The sun stroked her face and made her bones warm. She dumped the bucket and went round to the small patio at the side of the chalet. The sun-loungers were still out, she bent to fold them up, but instead, sat down, too utterly weary. The sea sang her a lullaby, she lay back and sank into oblivion.

CHAPTER FIFTEEN

It was a few minutes before Alex realised that his eyes were open and that it was reality he was seeing. He was lying face down on the dusty floor, the grain of the planking large in his eyes, the dust strong in his nostrils. His head felt as if it had been crushed in the jaws of a vice. His face felt tight, he couldn't open his mouth, he felt the tape sealing it. His wrists ached in the angle they lay at beneath him. He began to move and suddenly realised it wasn't just the fact his hands were wedged under him, it was more, they were bound. All this in the moments of waking.

He rotated his head slowly to face the sound in the room. The radio, and beside it the hunched form of a man. He was braced over a hole in the floor. He was straining, holding something on the doubled end of a rope, the two free ends trailed across the floor, inching their way towards the man's thick fists.

He lifted his head again and looked round for Tamsin. She had been with him at the school. Where was she? He thought of the rope, letting something down into the hole. His heart quickened, he could feel it beating out its rhythm against the boards. The man grunted. He released one of the two strands and began pulling the other through.

Alex pushed himself steadily to his knees. The blood rushed into his arms. He didn't give himself time to debate whether an attack was the best form of action – he was barely standing before he launched himself at the man.

Army training is intensive – but it pays. Even beneath the drone of the radio he sensed the boy move. He spun round just in time.

Alex crashed into him. Mouth struggling to roar beneath the tape, arms thrust forward like a battering ram.

Pongo fended the arms away and clasped the boy round his waist, driving him away from the hole. Alex's force and

200

momentum carried him back a step. Enough. Alex saw the gaping hole and twisted himself, twisting the stranger, forcing the man to half stumble, to struggle to keep his foot on the edge of the hole.

Pongo tried to lift Alex, but Alex was taller than he was and so the boy's feet appeared to be glued to the ground. Pongo loosened his grip. Alex stumbled back, and Pongo hit him. He'd just have to go down unconscious. The girl could look after him.

He dragged the boy to the hole. He looked down. The pale disk of the girl's face looked up.

'Your boyfriend's coming down. Catch him,' he barked. Then he set to threading the rope and pushing the boy over the lip of the hole. Alex slithered past the raw edges of plank, his chin catching, head flicked back with the impact, then the rope caught and the arms stretched taut and the body swung. Pongo let the wild swinging ease before he inched the rope down.

Tamsin looked at her wrists, blood showed on one and they were just as firmly bound. How could she catch him? She looked up and saw his shape being lowered as she had been, and instantly saw the difference. Alex's head lolled and rocked with the swinging of the rope. He was not conscious. She stood. If she could support him as he landed, if she could lay him down and support his head, that would be best, the best she could manage.

His feet came level with her eyes, then his waist, she braced herself and with her fingers tugged him so that his weight would fall towards her. As he lowered she leant him against her front, until she cradled his head in her bound wrists and let him gently down. The rope began to snake through his arms, the end flicking her face as it whipped free.

With a thump the doorway of light disappeared, she gasped in a lung-full of dank salty air, and held it. Fine particles drifted down onto her up-turned face. It was dark. Only the sound of the sea filled her ears. The rock was cold and damp beneath her knees, his head felt heavy as it lay cushioned by her thighs. Tears began to form in Tamsin's eyes and her body shook, small tremors becoming great earthquakes of fear.

*

It was quite late when Jo woke. One shoulder and one side of her face felt tight from too much sun. She lay there a moment longer then snapped up, folded the loungers and stashed them away, angry with herself. Back in the farmhouse she chastised herself for being so stupid as to fall asleep in the sun and slapped a cool fresh layer of after-sun on her face and arm. She made herself a quick cheese sandwich and ate it silently, wondering if Alex had already rung and got no answer, concluding it was unlikely and deciding to get on with the animals alone.

One by one she brought the goats down and milked them. She took the bucket of frothing milk down to the house and strained it and set it to cool. Still only six o'clock, she turned on the television to watch the news and wait for the phone call.

*

Tamsin managed to still the shaking, to stop the desperate gulping back of tears. Her legs felt cramped. She wriggled her hands free from under Alex's head and tugged at the tape across her mouth. The fine down on her face tore out as she peeled it back. She took a few quick breaths to prepare herself. Her mother had always said 'a plaster hurts less if you whip it off quickly'. With the freed edge tight between her fingers she breathed, counted to three and pulled. A sound like tearing paper! A burning pain. She licked her lips. The saliva stung, her lips prickled like a nettle rash and tears sprang to her eyes again.

She looked down at Alex, and realised she could see him. The hole was not in total darkness as it had seemed when the

202

door had first been shut. She looked up. Above her rose a column of darkness, no light filtered down that way. It came from behind her, high up, a glow in the rock. And now, as she turned her head to look round for the first time she saw another lighter patch, low down. She looked back at Alex. It would be better for him if the tape was off his mouth too, he could breathe easier. It would be better if he was unaware of its removal, an operation under anaesthetic. She fingered the edge of the tape, peeling it up enough to hold it tightly. He moved a little, his head lolling. She wasn't sure if the movement had been him or her tugging. Tamsin counted and ripped. He cried out. A single sound. Then nothing. She felt like shaking him, like slapping him, to make him wake up. But she didn't, instead she stroked his cheek and spoke to him, calling his name.

He was on a rack. In a dungeon. A torturer's dungeon. It had to be. The rack had a rough bed that dug in as he was stretched, his arms were already pulled out of their sockets. He thought that if it went on much longer he wouldn't fit through the door of his room. And then the torturer put a fire brand to his mouth, fast as lightning so that he didn't see it coming, and said, 'tell me where it is', and Alex wanted to laugh because you can't speak at all if your mouth is burned shut, or laugh.

'Alex, Alex,' she said. 'Alex.'

'Tamsin?'

'Alex – oh thank God!'

Alex peered up. Tamsin's face seemed to be suspended above him, strangely upside down. He tried to move. It hurt. It all hurt.

'Help me up.'

Tamsin hooked her bound hands under him and pushed. Alex sat, then turned. His spine felt as if it had been bent the wrong way and had forgotten how it should be. He looked at Tamsin, then up to the place where the light came from.

'Where are we?'

'In a hole – under his workshop.'

'Whose?'

'Someone. He's a bit weird,' Tamsin shook at her own words, she hadn't even meant to tell Alex.

'What do you mean? Weird?'

'Well – no one sees him, much. He don't ever let anyone up here to his farm.'

'We're at a farm then?'

'It's not a farm any more. He's the last one. All the rest of the family died out. He didn't. He went away. In the Army, they say – ' she blew out a breath. She knew what she'd heard her mother say once, but wasn't sure if it was at all right.

'What?'

'Might not be right. He's supposed to have broken some man's arm just by holding it. He was trespassing see, he don't like that.'

'Hell, doesn't sound like someone's going to find us accidentally then.'

'No,' she licked her lips again, the stinging flamed across her mouth.

'Let's get these off – if we can,' Alex held up his bound wrists. 'What are they – they look like sticks?'

'Basket stuff. That's what he does, makes and sells baskets,' Tamsin said as she tried to unthread the end of the split withy round Alex's wrist. Her fingers felt stiff and aching, her own wrist sore as she manoeuvred her hands. She bent and bit and tugged at the worked up loop with her teeth. Alex leant forward and planted a gentle kiss on the crown of her head. She looked up at him, tears forming in her eyes.

'Oh Alex,' she said, and tugged at the loosened end until it sprang free.

Alex moved his wrists experimentally as he wriggled them free of the two looped twists that formed the basis of the manacles. The dark lines showed where they had cut into the soft underside skin, tingling more now the concentration of the untying was over. He worked the withies loose on Tamsin's wrists, noticing she had suffered the same cuts.

'The light's going,' Tamsin said quietly.

'I noticed. Let's see what there is here before it's too late.'

Tamsin looked at him in mild alarm.

'Before it gets too dark – see if there's a way out,' Alex added, stroking her arm to reassure her. 'We'll try up there first,' he said indicating the light source.

'I'll go up,' Tamsin said, 'It's narrow – I'm smaller. You can give me a bump up to the ledge,' she added. They began to move towards the light source in the gloom of the cave. The lower pale area that Tamsin had noticed appeared to have gone, replaced by a darker patch. They stepped near it as they moved forward. Tamsin sensed the movement and jumped a little, bumping into Alex.

'What?'

'There!' she pointed at the darkness on the floor of the cave. As they stared, their eyes becoming accustomed to the gloom instead of facing the light, they could both see the heaving, the fluid surface, rising and falling like some great slumbering beast, and with each breath came the smell of salt and seaweed.

'It's a hole!'

'It's the sea.'

They spoke together.

'Could it be a way out?' she asked, hope lacing her words.

'Possibly. Yeah, possibly at low tide,' Alex said, while dreading the thought that this may be low tide. 'Let's try the light. That cave we were in, on the beach. The other way out, that looked like this. Light round the bend,' he added hopefully.

There was a ledge about five foot from the floor then the shaft rose at an angle. It looked very narrow, but there was a hope that it might be wide enough. Alex helped Tamsin clamber to the ledge. She edged herself forward, blocking the dim light as she moved. As darkness filled the cave and Tamsin filled the narrow opening, Alex's heart sank. He could see that she couldn't get through.

Tamsin slithered back, biting her lip to prevent herself crying. 'No good, you couldn't get a cat round that. Oh Alex, I'm scared,' she said, her fingernails biting deep into her palm. He lifted her down and they stood holding each other, both silent in their fear.

As if Tamsin still blocked the hole, the light was diminished, barely enough for them to see the closest walls of the cave. 'I think we'd better find the safest place to sit, away from that hole, high as we can,' Alex said into her mass of hair. He felt her nod.

*

It was getting dark outside. Large blue-black clouds were trying to sink the sun before its time. Jo thought she had better see to the birds before the fox decided it was dark enough to be out. She fed the ducks and the hens, and saw them safely locked away in their sheds. Then she turned her attention to the geese. She stood at the gate to their paddock and shuddered as the gander swept over to see her off. She turned away again. Irrational it might be but she was scared of the sinuous neck and the ferocity of his attack. Alex will just have to do them when he gets back, she thought. She looked at her watch. She had a good mind to give Sylvia a ring and see if he was ready to come back yet. It might annoy him, but the geese had to be put away – though she couldn't imagine a fox being brave enough to stand up to the gander.

She dialled Sylvia's number and waited while the phone rang. Sylvia answered.

'Oh Sylvia. It's Jo. Look I don't want to mess up their evening, but do you know what time Alex is expecting to be collected?' There was a silence.

'Pardon?'

'I just need to know what time Alex is coming back. Oh you'll laugh, but I'm terrified of the gander. I can't put the beasts away. Alex always does …'

'But they're with you.'

'Sorry?'

'Tamsin – and Alex. Tamsin said they were going out with you today!'

'No – that's not right. Alex said he and Tamsin were going over to the Monkey Sanctuary with some of Tamsin's friends. He was going to phone me to get a lift back.'

'No, I wouldn't have got her off work for that,' Sylvia began.

'Precisely …'

'You're not saying my Tamsin's a liar?'

'Well I can assure you they did not spend the day with me,' Jo said. 'Please get Alex to phone me as soon as they come in,' she added, and let the phone drop.

*

They huddled against the side wall on a raised section, about the height of a table. The ribs of the cave showed as shaded lines in the dying light. The same rock formation that had created the cave by the beach had allowed water to hollow out this hole beneath the barn. The sea had driven its way in, chasing a channel through the softer layer, to spurt and blow out of the higher hidden opening, leaving this cave. They prayed that it didn't come often. Tamsin had described the slot that turned at right angles then, judging by the light, made another turn to face the sea. Fresh air and filtered daylight. It wasn't enough to survive on for long. Yet this man, this weird man, had not killed them. So he must want them to remain alive. They shivered and hugged each other for warmth. The damp and cold were working their way into their bones.

There was a noise; a different noise to the suck and roar of the sea. A hollow ringing noise from above, and suddenly a scraping sound and a shaft of light.

Minute fairies danced in the yellow glow and a hissing noise filtered down.

'Down there?' the rasping voice held a note of query as if he was not sure he'd left them there. Alex moved into the light. He could see the black form hunched over the hole, a Tilley lamp hissing by its elbow.

'Watch out, and don't think of grabbing the rope, else I'll let it come down. But then it'll be the last thing I do let down.'

A second while the whole glory of the light filled the space. Any hope of climbing up the shaft to the barn left him as he looked up. Then the light was blotted out as a bundle was lowered. Alex watched it and grasped it in both arms. The rope whipped through the loose knot at the top and snaked back up.

Alex barely had time to step over to their ledge before the light was snatched from them as the barn floor was replaced with a crash.

'What is it?'

'A blanket at least,' Alex said as he fumbled to untie the knot at the top. He had hopes. He hoped for a torch. For food, for drink. 'Here – hold this.' His hand had found a cylindrical shape, cold, glassy with small dimples and ridges on its surface. It handled like a bottle of drink. Tamsin's hands contacted his arm and moved down until they wrapped themselves around the bottle. Carefully she cradled it to her lap and jammed it safely between her thighs.

It occurred to Alex that this was like some pass-the-bag game, guessing the contents by their feel alone. He felt. His hand withdrew with a sudden shiver of revulsion. Whatever he'd just touched was squishy, wrapped in plastic of some kind and soft. He tried again, feeling the outline. In his mind the shape offered him a loaf of sliced bread. He squeezed again. Sandwiches perhaps, he lifted the packet to his knees. Two apples were easily identified bringing their fruity scent into the dankness of the cave momentarily. Another plastic package

Hard, but rubbery under his thumb. He lifted it carefully to his face, sniffing. Cheese. A lump of plastic wrapped cheese. And that was it; his hand could feel no more. No torch.

'At least we won't starve,' Alex said as cheerfully as he could manage. *At least he doesn't intend to let us die of starvation* he thought.

*

Jo hoisted the bucket of food for the geese over the fence. They came running in the dark, ghostly figures swooping across. Once they had settled to eating Jo stalked past them to their house and opened up the door ready. She stood in the dark, wrapped up well in wellingtons, heavy jeans, and an huge old coat. Pete's coat, the sleeves threatening to engulf her hands at every move despite being rolled back.

She cursed Alex. She was sure that he, Tamsin and the friends were still out somewhere enjoying themselves. She thought he could have phoned. She thought that he may have tried, but then she had to realise he was almost seventeen and quite able to look after himself.

The geese waddled over to their house and, grumbling and complaining, filed inside. Jo, standing securely behind the door watched them and swiftly shut the door before the gander could turn round. With a sense of relief she walked back down to the house. The phone was ringing. She kicked off her boots and ran. It was bound to be Alex.

'Hello?'

'Are they with you?' Sylvia's voice turned her own question on its head.

'No I told you. They were coming back to you, and Alex would phone for me to come and collect him.'

'Yes and *you said* they'd gone out with Tamsin's friends.'

'That's right, Alex said .. '

'Then he's a liar! I've rung …'

'What do you mean – Alex has never lied to me. I'd know. He's always been truthful ...'

'Huh – how can you tell? I've rung them all! All Tamsin's friends ..'

'And?'

'Haven't seen them. Apart from Michelle. They came to try out her new computer, but left at about eleven.'

Jo was silent. Alex, sixteen and the attractive Tamsin at fifteen. Where would they have gone? Somewhere to be alone together? Jo remembered she'd been meaning to have an extra word with Alex. 'Have you any ideas?' she said softly now.

'No – but if your Alex has done anything to Tams, then, then Tom'll half kill him.'

'That's not the way. Please – look, what's the time? Half nine? It's not late.'

'Late enough when you don't know where they are.'

'Shall I come over there?' Jo suggested.

'What's the point? Besides perhaps they'll come up there. Think they'll get a softer welcome from you.'

'This isn't helping, Sylvia.'

'She's my daughter! You don't know ...'

'I'm sure Alex will look after her – he's always been so ...'

'Oh sure! Never lied to his mother ...'

'Sylvia!' the phone clicked. The dead air of the cut line filled Jo's ear, she replaced the receiver. Sylvia seemed to be over dramatising things. Perhaps Tamsin had friends that Sylvia didn't know about, that might be it. Older friends – ones with a car – that Sylvia might not approve of. Jo stopped staring at the phone and went to make herself a cup of milky coffee.

The phone rang. Jo glanced at the time as she picked it up. Eleven o'clock. Even she was getting worried now. It wasn't like Alex. He'd be out late often enough but he had always told her before. To save her worrying.

'Jo?'

'Oh, Rod,' Jo's disappointment echoed in her voice.

'Sorry I didn't make it this evening. I had a bit of bother to sort out.'

Rod! Of course. With the Thompsons leaving , falling asleep in the sun and Alex and Tamsin's non-appearance, Rod's suggestion that he would come up to the farm that evening had totally slipped her mind.

'Oh that's all right,' she sighed.

'You all right, love?'

'I just thought you were Alex phoning. He's not come back yet – we're a bit concerned.'

'Where's he gone then?'

'That's the problem. Tamsin said one thing to Sylvia. A downright lie. Alex said they were off out with friends of Tamsin's. Sylvia says she's rung all Tamsin's friends and no-one's seen them, not since this morning anyway.'

Rod was silent. His heart was beating fast. What was best thing to say, he had a shrewd idea that they were holed up in Pongo's farm, what would be the natural thing to say?

'I suspect Tamsin has some friends that Sylvia doesn't know about – older ones maybe – with a car?' Jo tried out her theory on Rod.

'Possible, I wouldn't worry too much. They'll probably roll in about midnight. Anyway, sorry to miss out this evening – another time?' he suggested. Another time – never. Depending on Pongo. He had to go up there now under the cover of darkness to tell him he'd found nothing. Wrecked the whole library and found nothing. He didn't really want to go. It was not so much what Pongo would say as what he might do.

*

The farm was dark. A little light seeped between two curtains in the farm house. Rod walked slowly towards the door, his feet crunching heavily on the cinder path. He had barely let

his knuckles graze the wood when the door was pulled open.
Pongo stood black against the yellow hissing glow. He
snatched Rod in and closed the door.

'Well?'

Rod walked to the large farmhouse kitchen table, putting its
bulk between him and Pongo.

'Nothing,' he said quietly, looking first at the table with the
scattered remains of a meal. One plate, one set of cutlery.
Then back up to Pongo's eyes. 'I shook out every book, turned
out every cupboard. I found disks all right. I spent time. Shit,
an hour, feeding 'em into the computer there. Shit scared of
blowing the thing – but I'd seen the boy do it up at Austin's.
All school stuff!'

'This isn't a wind up? Finding nothing doesn't help them.'

'You know me! I wouldn't! … Where are they?'

'Safe.'

'You'll not – '

'What? WHAT?' his voice becoming a roar. Then as suddenly
dropped to a hoarse whisper, 'Oh, dear. Not hurt them?'

Rod nodded despite himself.

'You want to spend the rest of your life in clink? I don't. Don't
become a danger to me – no one does that. I'm nearly there.
We're nearly there. Two more runs and I disappear. Poof!'
he clicked his calloused fingers.

Rod stood transfixed, his eyes drawn to the glowing gauze of
the Tilley lamp. Burning but not burning away. Magic.

'What do I do?'

'Act natural, and if that disk turns up, you destroy it!'

Pongo opened the door. Rod walked towards it. He wasn't
sure what he'd expected. The children sitting round the table,
signs or sounds of life somewhere about the house. It all felt
so empty.

'They're only children,' he said.

'And you're in it up to your neck.'

The door closed. The night crowded in with a strong breeze and the scent of rain on the air.

CHAPTER SIXTEEN

Jo half opened her eyes, closed them, then forced them open again. The night had gone, light came in at the windows, the lamp in the room seemed to glow dimly, uselessly. She'd fallen asleep. Watching, waiting, she'd fallen asleep. She looked at the telephone accusingly. It hadn't rung, with her head less than a foot away in slumber she would have heard it. A chill ran through her body. Alex hadn't come back. What the hell was he playing at? It was so unlike him. It was that Tamsin! She sat up, all her joints seemed to ache, her back felt stiff. She sighed as she stretched and looked at the time, perhaps they'd got back so late to Sylvia's that they'd put him up? She decided to ring. A spasm of shivering hit her as she dialled the number. She had to stop and start again. What if they weren't back?

'Sylvia?'

'Oh it's you.'

'They've not come back?' Jo heard her voice tentative and small, knowing the answer already from the tone of Sylvia's voice.

'No – They've not come back.' Sylvia's voice sounded close to breaking.

'There's no one else? No other friends. Someone you don't know?'

'Someone I don't know?' Sylvia's voice rose in a mockery of Jo. 'Someone I don't know? hahaha,' and the defiance turned to sobs.

'Oh Sylvia! Don't. They'll be back – soon. Oh, I'll come over shall I?'

'Do what ever you like,' Sylvia sobbed. The click as she disconnected the call cut the crying, leaving Jo listening to a faint electrical hum while she stared into an inner space looking for Alex.

'Damn the bloody goats!' Jo muttered to herself as she stomped up to their pens. 'Damn you! Damn you all! It's your fault! We would have gone home – but for you – you creatures!' she shouted at them, the wind whipping her words away. They stared at her, their golden slit-eyes reminding her of the devil, their faces seeming sharper and less endearing. She rushed. They dawdled, like recalcitrant children who go into slow motion when speed is of the essence. She let out the ducks and hens, she threw open the goose-house door and ran. Back in the house she showered swiftly.

She wasn't going to let herself believe that anything bad had happened, it would be like wishing it on them. At worst the pair of young 'lovers' had run off together. So silly, but possible. Or they'd been invited to a party somewhere, at a chalet or something, and slept overnight. It would be something like that. She and Sylvia would get in a stew and the children would laugh at their needless worries.

But Alex wasn't like that. Alex had never lied to her before, had always been so grown-up, so understanding and careful. And so many bad things had happened lately. They kept creeping into her mind. Pictures of drowning people. Of Pete, of Alessandros, of Pete and the face in the photograph, Julia, of Alessandros, or was it Alex? She shook her head to clear the images and set off to drive the now familiar road to Looe.

*

James stretched and reached out an arm. No Glenda. But, he realised as he came fully awake, there wouldn't be. He was in his own bed, in his own poky little flat. Glenda would be back this afternoon though, he thought warmly to himself.

All day Tuesday to himself. Perhaps he'd get some grub in and cook Glenda up a surprise. He prided himself on the two dishes that he'd really mastered, and she always had such a good appetite. He flung off the covers and dived for the shower just off his room. Finished, he'd wrapped a towel round his waist and just about dried his hair and when the phone rang.

'Lo!'

'Ah! Oh! This is Miss Britain, am I speaking to Mr. Fuller?'

'Yes, good morning?'

'You wished to place a special order, I believe.'

James made the connection, this voice of an ageing debutante belonged to the 'beauty queen' name that owned the craft shop in Looe. 'Well – sort off. It would be better if I could talk to the man that makes the baskets myself.'

'I am sorry, that would be quite out of the question. Mr. Powley is a reclusive sort of man,' she laughed awkwardly, 'almost a hermit. He deals exclusively through me, he trusts me – you understand?'

The fine hair on James naked back tingled as he heard the name. 'Pow – ley' in Miss Britain's mouth could easily be a Pauly in less refined tones.

'Well, perhaps you could tell me something about him?'

'I'm sure I don't know what you mean. Perhaps, if you really do wish to place an order, you could come in to see me – I shall be in the shop from eleven. Good morning,' she said and put down the phone.

'Damn!' James muttered. The old bat was going to be funny about her contact – probably thought he wanted to cut her out. He'd go and see her later. Face to face was often best in this situation.

*

They woke shivering.

The light was pale green and cast a sickly glow about the cave. The hole where the sea slept was light again and Alex could see the water move within it from their vantage point on the shelf. He lay still, his back against the hard rock, wrapped tightly with Tamsin in the blanket. It had been so difficult to wrap themselves together and still manage to be up on the ledge. The floor of the cave was wet, shining slickly, high tide must have come during the night. It had been the fear of the high tide that had prodded him from sleep most often, that and the cold and the persistent ache in his shoulders and in his head.

'Tams?'

'Mmm,' she murmured, her breath warm against his shirt.

'Hungry?' Alex felt ravenous, they'd agreed to save some of the food from last night. They weren't sure when the hatch would open again.

'Yes,' she said tentatively. Truth was she desperately needed to go to the loo, and she felt more embarrassed in this situation than any other she could imagine. It was so easy for boys! 'Alex,' she said shrugging the blanket from her shoulders. Wriggling herself to a sitting position.

'Mmm?'

She lifted the section of blanket that she'd been wrapped in and dropped it over his head.

'Stay there a minute – please.'

'What for?'

'Just do it – you know.'

'Oh, sorry,' he mumbled from under the blanket, finding himself smiling in the dark.

'Boo!' Tamsin said as she slipped the blanket from his head with more light-heartedness than she felt. 'Did you say something about food?'

'What do you reckon, there's more than half of the loaf, a bit of cheese and half of the drink?'

'Concentrate on the bread. Leave the bit of cheese in case,' she stopped, in case, what? In case it had to last them? 'We've got to have some drink though.'

Alex slipped his hand into the plastic wrapping of the loaf. 'White Medium Cut' it said on the label. It tasted sticky in his mouth. The only hint of its true nature came from a vague yeasty scent that exuded from the bag each time they pulled a slice out. At least last night they'd flavoured it with the cheese. They washed the cloying pieces from their mouths with a couple of swigs from the bottle of Lucozade, swishing the sweet fizzing liquid round and round their mouths before swallowing, to savour it more.

They ate in silence. Withdrawn into their own thoughts. Concentrating on feeling full.

'Leave four slices for later?' Tamsin suggested. Alex nodded, and wrapped the bag tightly again and tucked the cheese and it into the corner, with the bottle blocking the crevice they'd found to wedge it all in. Even in the light it was the best place for it.

The hollow sound came again. Tamsin grabbed Alex's arm. They slipped off the ledge, stood slowly and moved towards the shaft, looking up as they heard echoing footsteps move across the barn. What to do. Shout? Call out? If it wasn't him, if it was someone else, just the chance. If it was him, what difference?

'Hello, up there!' Alex shouted, unconvincingly. The words sounded stupid called out loud.

'Hey, Let us out!'

'Let us out!' Tamsin took up the cry.

They stopped to listen. A faint tinny noise, background interference.

'Again, together? Two three – ' Alex said.

'Let Us Out!' they screamed. Top volume. The sound reverberated in the cave. They listened. A sound, a scraping sound, board on board amplified by the hollow beneath the barn. Then – music. Just loud enough to be heard, pop-music, the base line carrying best, the repetitive rhythm. Then it stopped. A burble, and more music.

'The radio,' Tamsin said. 'It's him – he put the radio on before – before he, he – ' she let the tears come, her whole body shaking. 'Ohhh God!'

'Don't Tams. Don't,' Alex said putting his arms round her, fighting the panic that rose in his throat.

*

'Is Miss Britain about?' James asked. The shop looked just the same, the assistant however was standing primly behind the counter and there was no sign of the wicker chair she'd lounged in on his last visit.

'Yeah, I'll just call her,' she said, her voice just as drippy. She opened a door that showed only the stairs to the upper floor. 'Miss Britain? Customer for you, Miss Britain,' she called. 'Won't be a moment?' she said with a tired smile, and resumed her station behind the counter.

Miss Britain swept open the door. She had probably been a handsome woman in her day. She had high cheekbones, covered now with wrinkled skin. She had once been tall, but some of her height was lost in a slight stoop. She drew her head up, unfortunately making her observation of James appear to be one of looking down her nose. It suited her voice.

'Can I be of assistance?'

'James Fuller, you were kind enough to telephone me this morning,' James said, adopting the woman's mode of speech, smiling and offering his hand. After all he wanted to woo her, for information.

She smiled graciously.

'I believe I informed you that any order would have to be placed through me?'

'I quite understand. I would, however, like to discuss the – er – viability of the design I had in mind. With the maker,'

'You could draw it? I would ask him at our next appointment.'

'When's that?'

'Monday, next Monday.'

'No – that's too long. Have you a phone number?'

'My dear boy,' she said, enjoying the young man's attention, 'I did say, he's a recluse. He doesn't have a – telephone.'

This was wasting time! 'Don't you even know where he lives?' James was sharper than he meant to be.

'Of course I do!' Miss Britain snapped, colouring up. 'All our craft merchandise is local! He's very local, he works from a farm just outside Looe itself!'

'Name?'

'I beg your pardon.'

James decided it was time to change tactics. He reached into his pocket and withdrew his warrant card. He leant forward, and said quietly, 'It's part of an investigation, I'm sure you want to help.'

Miss Britain peered at his card, reading each detail, her eyebrows raised.

'So why this nonsense about buying a special piece?'

'Well, dear lady, until I met you I could not tell if you were trustworthy. You might have run off and told him we were looking for him.'

'As if I would,' she said tugging her cardigan together around her small chest, 'What do you want him for?'

'It may not be him we are trying to trace.'

'I wouldn't have thought so – a recluse I said. I meant it.'

'Just tell me two things,' James made the request sound very reasonable, an easy release.

Miss Britain nodded, her head barely moving, her lips pulled tight.

'Does Mr. Powley have a limp, or something?'

Her answer leapt to her eyes before she even opened her mouth. 'His right leg,' she took a breath. 'You knew?'

'A guess, and where is the farm?'

'It's not signed. I've never been there. We always meet at a disgusting café at Tregolten. I don't know why – part of his – being a recluse,' she said, her voice catching.

'But you know where the farm is?'

'Well yes – any local could tell you. It was a family farm, generation after generation. Powley's. That's it.'

'Sorry – what do you mean 'that's it'?

'Powley's farm. Mr. Powley of Powley's farm. Up on the headland by Plaidy.'

'Thank you madam,' James said, rising and tucking his card away. He turned and caught sight of the girl. She turned away and gazed out of the window.

James left the shop and began to walk back to the car. Suddenly he stopped and looked around for a stationers or a book shop. After a few moments he found one and bought a map of the local area. He scanned it. All the farms were marked – and named. There it was! He couldn't believe it. 'Powleys' and further along the coast 'Bodrigga'. He was elated. The church chimed out twelve . He'd be late for Glenda getting back if he went there now – but as he was already over in Cornwall – what the hell. He dialled her number. Three rings, the recorded message and the tone.

'Hi, it's me, James. Answer if you're there, doll.' Silence, the purr of the tape. 'Guess you aren't. I had planned a big meal to welcome you home, but I may be a little late now. I've just been talking to Miss Britain, no need to get jealous, she's not a day under sixty, and got a lead on the Bodkin case. A man called, get this, Powley. A basket maker with a limp. He's local. I'm just going up there for a recce. See you later. Love you!'

*

Jo's knock on the door was answered. Sylvia pulled open the door and allowed her to walk in, face rigid. Jo saw Rick at once. She whirled round to Sylvia.

'Isn't it a bit early to bring in the police?' she hissed.

'He's not here …'

'Police!' Her mind performed a somersault, she turned back to Rick. 'What's happened, have they been found?'

'Sylvia's been telling me,' he began.

'What's happened?'

'You don't understand,' Sylvia cut in.

'What?'

'He's not here as a policeman. He's my brother.'

Rick. Sylvia's brother. Jo felt the ground shift under her feet. 'Oh,' she swallowed, 'I'm sorry, about that, earlier,' she mumbled.

'Like I said, Sylvia's been telling me about it. She called me this morning – thought I'd come over before we call in the local police.' Indeed Sylvia had been describing the boy who had taken Tamsin off. It was only when she'd said that he was staying up at Bodrigga that Rick had begun to suspect that the boy being spoken off was the lad he'd met up there. He'd seemed a capable sort of lad, even under the stress of a police raid. Yet the aspect of the police raid itself made him worry about the lad, wonder again if there was something a little shady about the boy and his attractive mother.

'What did she say?' Jo was aware her words sounded bitter, 'Sylvia,' she added.

'That Tamsin had asked her to arrange a day off from her summer job, so that she could spend a day with you and Alex.'

'And did she tell you that I had never suggested such a trip.'

'Yes.'

There had been more, Jo could sense it. 'What else did you suggest?' she looked at Sylvia.

'Tamsin wouldn't have done it on her own – your Alex probably put her up to it!' Sylvia snapped sulkily.

'It's more likely the other way round! Alex is careful! He'd never say he was going off with friends and do something else!'

'There's always a first time!'

'It is possible.. ' Rick began, trying to work a rational path between them.

'Of course, you'll see it her way! You don't know him! He wouldn't, he's not – he's not – *impulsive*. He ..' Jo could feel her anxiety getting the better of her control. She didn't want to break down in front of these people. 'You don't understand him,' she said and tore open the door, walking quickly back to her car.

She leant against the car, arms hugging her body, then chewing at a thumbnail. She looked at the house. It would make sense to work together, but she couldn't bear to see Alex cast as the villain. She could feel their thoughts, their beliefs. What to do?

A large man and his wife strolled almost up to where she stood. She suddenly became aware that the man was looking at her. Did she look so demented? Were her wild thoughts streaming out from her head like a beacon? She looked directly at the man, defying him.

'Excuse me,' he said, the woman at his side smiled sweetly from beneath her elaborate straw hat, 'I'm sure we've met. I'm excellent at faces.'

'I don't think so! I'm on holiday down here,' Jo snapped dismissively.

'Us too. Down from the smoke, Fulham.'

Jo looked at him sharply. Perhaps she did know him, faces out of context were often difficult to place.

'I know! Your boy was – mugged. D.S. March,' he indicated himself.

Of course. She could never have put a name to the face, but the same kindness was in the eyes. 'Yes, well hello,' Jo said.

'If you don't mind me saying – you looked a little upset – Josie noticed, didn't you?'

'Yes dear, anything we can do?'

'It's kind of you – but, I don't think so,' Jo began.

*

'How does she know you? That you're a policeman?' Sylvia said suspiciously, 'Has her boy been in trouble with the police before.'

'Don't jump to conclusions Sylvia, I met them both over the Pete Austin drowning.'

'Oh.'

'And fighting won't help, you know. Perhaps we ought to notify the local boys – ' he stopped her interrupting with a signal from his hand, 'just in case they're in difficulties, somewhere. I know what you think – but when I met the boy he didn't strike me as a tearaway. Now who's the girl that saw them earlier on in the day?'

'Michelle.'

'Right, Michelle. Is she a particular friend of Tamsin's?'

'I suppose so.'

'Come on Sylvie – what do you mean,' Rick said reverting to family pet names to get her to relax and talk.

'Well, yes, she's a good friend. If good's the word. Gone a bit – off – you know. She hangs around down the end of the bridge a lot, late, with the rabble. Mary doesn't seem to have a lot of control over her – and Rod, well she can twist him round her little finger.'

'Can you have a word with Mary, arrange for me to have a chat with Michelle – as Tamsin's uncle. Nothing to worry the child?'

'Okay. I'll phone her now, all right?'

'Yeah. Look I'll see if Kelvin and Josie are about, send them off on some proper sightseeing on their own.'

He opened the back door and stepped out into the fresh air. He drew a deep breath. What was wrong with him. He'd guessed the identity of the boy, and so he obviously knew that when the mother arrived it would be that woman again. Yet from the moment she appeared in the doorway he couldn't take his eyes off her, and her angry remarks stung him. He so much wanted to comfort her. To reach out and hold her when he sensed that she was near to tears. He blew out a sharp breath as if blowing away such thoughts and headed for the front of the house, hoping to see Kelvin and Josie back from their stroll.

They were there. Talking to her! He'd expected her to be gone. Had visualised her driving back up to the farm, angry and bitter. Now here she was, and speaking to the very people he'd come to find. She looked up. He knew she'd seen him because her face hardened, the jaw-line tightening, eyes narrowing. Kelvin must have noticed too as he swung round to see who or what she was looking at. His face, however, broke into a broad smile when he saw it was Rick. 'You'll never believe this, Rick,' Kelvin began. Rick saw Jo's eyes flick from him, to Kelvin and back again. She obviously didn't believe it. 'But Mrs. Smart is here on her holidays too. What are the chances of that – meeting here?'

Was this some crazy conspiracy? Was everyone she knew connected to this man. This man who made her feel wild and scared at the same time? Who looked at her with Alessandros-dark eyes, fearful and bold, as if he could read her soul but not her heart, Jo thought.

'I really don't know,' Rick's voice was flattened by her accusing stare. 'You mean – you already knew each other?' he said turning to Kelvin, as he suddenly realised that there was more being said than he'd first heard.

'Well – sort of. We've met,' Kelvin gave his foolish grin, it warmed Rick to see it. 'I was officer in charge of a GBH case, Mrs. Smart's son was beaten up,' Kelvin touched his eyebrow. He couldn't help it, he was unconsciously trying to stop Rick looking at Jo so intensely. 'Same day you left the Met,' he added. Rick didn't appear to be listening.

'I'm sorry about Sylvie,' Rick said, 'I've suggested we call in the local police – in case they're in trouble – no! Not trouble – difficulties. Alert the Coastguard too. I'm going to have a word with Michelle, see if she knows anything she's not telling.' He smiled, more to encourage Jo to smile than from any sense of happiness.

Don't smile at me. I can't bear it. My heart aches for Alex. I'm panicking inside, can't you tell. This lip-biting calm is the best I can manage. Alex is all I've got.

'Can I come up and see you afterwards. See if we can think of any other rational answers to their disappearance?' he continued. Jo nodded. She nodded again. She didn't trust herself to speak. Quickly she clambered into her car and drove off. The three stood watching as Jo botched a three-point turn then roared back past them.

'What's going on?' Kelvin asked.

*

The hollow scrape of wood on wood echoed down to the cave. Alex and Tamsin looked up, listening, straining to pick out the sounds from the background rumble and rush of the sea.

The footsteps sounded, knocking, wood on wood. A sudden lightening of the shaft told them that he'd lifted the hatch. Alex stepped into position, his neck craned back.

'Where's the girl?'

'Here,' Tamsin said, stepping over to join Alex. He put him arm around her, holding her protectively to him.

'You found a disk of Austin's. I want it,' Pongo's voice was laden with menace.

'Did we?' Alex said, his voice echoing within the cave.

'Don't fuck with me lad. You'll tell, better for you if you make it now.'

Alex felt Tamsin shake as his hard words fell on top of them. She tugged at him slightly. They stepped to one side, just enough to be out of his line of sight.

'Get fucking back!'

'He won't let us go!' Tamsin hissed, 'I've seen him – he knows, I know him.'

'But if we tell – I mean the disk only said about Rod, no-one else!'

'But they're in it together. I just know – he's weird – he'll do something …' An icy certainty had lodged itself in her core, yet she couldn't bring herself to say what she believed, that if they told, or perhaps even if they didn't, they would end up dead.

'Get fucking back – or do I have to come down there!'

Alex raised his eyebrows, considering the option. Tamsin shook her head forcefully. They moved back under the shaft.

'There was nothing on it.' Alex lied.

'Crap!'

'Nothing of interest – just a load of jumble – word games.' Alex tried to sound disappointed and naive.

'So much so you hid it – well, we'll see. You'll tell – with the wind this way you're in for an extra high tide tonight.' He laughed, a cross between a cough and cackle, and began to close the hatch.

'Hang on!'

'Well?'

'We need some more drink and …'

The hatch banged shut with a hollow ringing that momentarily blotted out the constant roar from the threatening sea. They clung to each other, their bodies shaking with the echo, scarcely daring to breathe.

CHAPTER SEVENTEEN

'I doubt it,' Kelvin said, leaning back into Sylvia's sofa and looking confident. Sylvia had contacted Mary and a time had been arranged when Michelle would be in to be questioned. Josie had brought a couple of cups of coffee into the living room, then returned to the kitchen to chat with Sylvia, while Rick filled Kelvin in on what he knew of the boy, of the mother and the raid on the farm. He'd finished with wondering whether the two were tied up with the drug smuggling.

'Somehow I don't think so – but it's no more than a feeling.'

'Is with me. See, she's the deputy head at Sir John Liddle.'

'What? Really?'

'What's more, you know I said her boy'd been done over?'

Rick nodded.

'Probably 'cos he found out about a gang of kids flogging dope in his school. Seems he told the school. Fat lot of good it did him – mind you, under D.I. Williams we weren't too much help either. But you get my drift?'

'Not very likely candidates for a drug smuggling ring you mean,' Rick said smiling. He looked at his watch, almost time to see Michelle. 'Right – I hate to just drop you like this.'

'It's all right – we said we wanted a proper look round Looe, and your Sylvia's offered us tea afterwards.'

'Probably do her good. Sylvie always did need to be busy. Thanks, Kelv, you've been a great help.'

'Thought I might 'ave been,' Kelvin said, 'Don't suppose I could help a bit more?'

'Busman's holiday? Josie'd kill me!'

'You're right at that, see you later then.'

'Cheers!' Rick waved as he left Kelvin. He felt good. The conflict that had been tormenting him was all but cleared, all he had to do now was find the youngsters.

*

They heard him leave. The footsteps echoing across the barn, a chime of wood on wood as the door was slammed shut. They stood still, counting the seconds between each suck and roar of the waves.

'We've go to get out!' Tamsin whispered.

'I know.'

They were silent again. Alex shook himself. He released Tamsin and looked about the dim cave. He stood on the edge of the hole where the sea would push its way up at high tide.

'There must be a way out here,' he said. 'The sea has to get in, and it's light.'

'But it might be too deep.'

'It's light! I don't know, but if it was deep, the entrance I mean, then I think the hole, this hole, the sea in it would always look black and dark.'

'Swim out, you mean?'

'Well.'

'It might be like the crack up there!' Tamsin said, her voice on the verge of panic, pointing to the filtered light that illuminated their cave.

Alex nodded. He'd thought about that, but then they'd never know if they didn't try. Just like the slot up there.

'There must be some other way!'

'The hole at the back, you mean?' Alex grasped the idea. The thought of getting soaked and still not getting out made him think of hypothermia, the thought of the waves crushing him against the rocks if he did get out worried him almost as much.

'It might lead on – just the light can't get round it?' Tamsin said hopefully.

'I wish we had a torch!' Alex said lightly as they made their way over to the dark gaping hole at the back of the cave. A smell of rotting seaweed emanated from the hole. Nothing like the fresh air they hoped it would lead them to.

Alex edged forward. His shadow removed the light that showed the first foot or two inside the hole. He stepped back again.

'Shall I go?' Tamsin offered.

'No, I'll do it, just,' he took a deep breath, 'keep to one side of the hole, let the light in a bit.'

'Okay.'

Alex crouched and crept into the hole, trying to let some light pass over his head, crawling forward feeling his way with his hands, dampness chilling his knees as it soaked into his jeans. The hole opened out into another smaller cave. He could reach both walls and ceiling with his hands as he knelt on the floor. He closed his eyes tight, then opened them again, hoping to gain some night-vision, and crawled forward into the darkness some more.

The floor of the cave dipped a little, the ice cold water splashed up his arm as he reached forward, he snatched his hand back as if burnt. Carefully he felt round the edge of the pool, trying to find a way round it without getting wet. There was none. Next he stretched as far as he could without losing balance, and reached the other side of the pool, where the cave floor rose again. Arching his back he tried to support himself on his hands as he braced his feet against the walls of the cave and edged across the pool. He made it. He could visualise this 'great hurdle' he'd overcome as a tiny puddle that would make anyone laugh in daylight, but the danger in getting soaked seemed so real in this fetid dark prison, he didn't feel like laughing.

'Are you okay?'

'Yeah, not a lot of room in here though,' Alex replied. Not a lot of hope either, he thought, but turned to work his way further into the cave.

The upward slope continued for a little way. Alex found it difficult to gauge how far he'd moved. Each forward movement was preceded by a sweep of the hand to make sure he hadn't reached the end, then a careful placing of the hands before he gingerly moved his knees forward. It was pitch black. He could see nothing. He closed his eyes, he opened them. There seemed to be more light with them closed.

His hand pressed on damp slimy rocks, his knees felt chilled into numbness. He moved forward again. His hand came down on something sharp. Quickly withdrawn, a gasp 'Oww!'

'Alex?'

'Its all right – it's a – ' He felt the offending item gingerly, closing his eyes. More parlour games. 'It's a shell – mussel shell, I think.'

'Oh?'

It was good to hear Tamsin's voice echoing along to him. Unless he looked back he could be anywhere in the world, totally cut off.

'There's more here,' he called, just to keep up the contact, as he tentatively moved forward. There were a lot more pieces here and he had to brush some aside just to rest his weight.

*

'PRIVATE. KEEP OUT. TRESPASSERS WILL BE' the last word of the notice was lost, the piece of board it had been painted on must have fallen off and been buried long ago judging by the state of the sign. It had to be Powley's farm. James had followed the map carefully and this was definitely the entrance to what appeared to be a long track down to the farm almost perched on the cliff edge.

He turned the car and drove through the entrance overgrown with brambles, their long arching suckers scratching at his paintwork as he passed. The track rose then dipped towards the sea that glittered in the bay, shining under the watery sun. Then the farm came into view, a house and a few farm buildings hunched on the edge of the cliff. His eyes scanned the place as he arrived. No other vehicle appeared to be about. He wondered whether it was tucked away in one of the farm buildings, or whether the eponymous Mr. Powley was absent.

He sat in his car for a moment, waiting to see if his arrival had been noticed. No one came. No irate hermit with a shotgun came rushing out of the house. James climbed out of the car and strolled up to the house casually, the pathway gritty underfoot. He knocked. The sound seemed to echo around the small hollow that the farm huddled in. No answer. James looked about.

'Mr. Powley? Mr. Pow-ley?' he called.

The sea whooshed and crashed, a seagull called, but that was all. He decided to have a quiet look around, peering first in the window beside the front door, then veering off to check out the barns.

*

'Well, come in then, Michelle's in the front room,' Mary said as she let Rick in. 'She told Sylvia everything yesterday, though.'

'I know – it's just that Sylvia might have got it muddled, she'd been in a bit of a state.'

'I should think so, these – well, lads from up-country think they're diff'rent somehow. In here, Michelle, here's Tamsin's uncle come to ask you about her and that boy.'

Michelle looked pale and worried. Rick noticed the way she hugged herself as if resisting giving anything away. He sat on the easy chair opposite her.

'I told Auntie Sylvia,' Michelle slipped back into childish terms in her anxiety.

'I know. She's – well she's worried. And you know how it is – she couldn't remember everything clearly when she told me. So I'd like to get it straight from you, okay?'

'Yeah, I guess,' Michelle perked up a little.

'You tell me first what happened.'

'Well, they came round about half past ten. We chatted a little bit. Tamsin was showing off like. Thought that Alex was special – just 'cos he's from London. – then, well Dad was coming to take me shopping in Plymouth, so they had to go at eleven. Well, they'd gone by then, ain't seen them since.'

'What did they come round for?'

'Just a chat.'

'You see, I'm trying to work out something. Tamsin went to a lot of trouble to get a day off work. Just to come for a chat?'

'It was that boy, if you ask me!' Mary chimed in.

'May have been. Any chance of a coffee, Mary, I'm gasping!'

'Oh, all right, won't be a mo, milk? Sugar?'

'Milk, no sugar,' Rick smiled warmly at her, she smiled back and left the room.

'Now Michelle, if it wasn't just for a chat, what was it for?'

'To look at a disk. I've got a really good PC and they needed a good one to look at some disk.'

'What was on it?'

'Dunno.'

'What, they use your computer and don't let you see what was on it?'

Michelle looked miserable, but Rick sensed that she knew something more and wouldn't let it go.

'Computer porn was it?'

'No! I don't know. It wouldn't work. It needed one like – ' she stopped. The colour flooded into her cheeks, she tightened her grip on her arms.

'Like what Michelle? This is important – they're missing! Like what?'

Michelle shook her head.

'Like what?'

'School's.' Michelle murmured.

'What school, yours?'

'What about the school?' Mary said as he opened the door.

'They said they needed to use a computer, like the one at the school?' Rick said.

'At the comp love?'

Michelle just looked at the floor.

'Michelle – answer me! Which school?' Mary said, her voice rising, showing a degree of anxiety that perplexed Rick. 'At the primary, wasn't it? What did you do, you stupid girl?'

'They made me!'

'Made you what?' Rick asked.

'Made me – give them mum's keys.'

Mary whirled round, took two long strides to the bureau and snatched down the flap. Her hand dived in and snatched up a bunch of jangling keys.

'They're here!' she said.

'You gave them the keys – but the keys are back. When did they bring them back?' Rick asked.

Michelle looked at her feet again.

'When?' her mother said, coming to stand over her.

'I dunno,' Michelle mumbled. Suddenly she looked up, and smiled. 'I found them, they left them in the milk box!'

'The milk box?' Rick wondered aloud.

'It's out by the back door. Just a wooden box for the milk to stand in – keeps the birds off you know,' Michelle said. Her face had changed, so had her voice, carrying undertones of mockery. She was lying, but felt comfortable in the lie.

'When?' Mary repeated.

'Oh, same afternoon.' Michelle said carelessly.

'I don't suppose you've been up to the school, to look for them?' Rick asked.

'No – they brought the keys back didn't they?'

'Or to see if they left it locked up proper – you'll get me the sack! And that'll be the last lot of pocket money you'll ever have off me!'

'I'll get it from Dad then, he's always got money!'

'I think a look at the school would be a good idea – shall we go up and see?'

'I'll bring the keys,' Mary said, picking them up again.

'What did you buy?' Rick asked Michelle as they climbed in his car.

'What?'

'What did you buy, in Plymouth?'

Michelle looked uncomfortable again, 'We didn't go,' she muttered.

*

Jo stood beside the Aga and hugged the mug of tea she'd just made. Not knowing what to do for the best was the hardest thing for her. Her whole life seemed to have been a battle, a way of proving herself. She had always had a direction. Now she didn't know which way to turn. She sipped the tea.

Well, perhaps not quite her whole life. There was a time when she was just following the path carved out for her by the expectations of her parents. Parents with all the airs and graces of their upper-middle contemporaries but without the finances to back them up. They grumbled incessantly about the cost of her school fees, but were consoled by her excellent results. Of course, they didn't mind her going to University, there would be a grant. She could read 'English Literature', nothing too technical, an additional attraction to the right sort of man. They did not envisage her wanting to make a career for herself – which she intended. Teaching meant an extra year – they did not approve of that either.

She'd won that battle. Her first post was as a junior-class teacher in a nice Surrey primary school, where she met Alessandros. Beautiful, caring, impulsive Alessandros. They'd fallen in love. Head-over-heels love. Totally abandoned love. Committed love. They'd told her parents just before Christmas.

But he wasn't the right type of man at all to be their son-in-law. Just another teacher, and foreign with it. There as no rejoicing at home. Then they flew to Greece for Christmas, to be with his father's family. They were happy to hear of the engagement when they told them on Boxing Day.

That afternoon they walked beside the sea, just the two of them, totally happy.

The waves looked grey and innocuous. The sky overcast. The beach deserted.

From somewhere came a call. They looked about. A cry. From the sea. Alessandros leapt up on some rocks. A head, bobbing in the waves. Gone. Back again. And Jo could see it too. Impulsive Alessandros tugged off his shirt and trousers and dived into the sea. She saw him strike out for the bobbing head. Now gone, now back. She saw him reach the form, a splashing, and they were both gone! Her eyes scanning the waves. Waiting for the bobbing head to reappear, for Alessandros to strike back out to the shore.

Sand dried on her toes.

The sun broke through the clouds.

The shapes appeared. Pale discs. Careless of the push and pull of the waves. A sound poured from her mouth, open, split from throat to heart, pouring out an agony of instant grief.

From a deserted sea, fishermen appeared in a traditional small boat. They brought them both out of the sea. The drunken, overweight ex-pat who'd taken a 'Boxing Day swim' and the youth who'd gone to rescue him.

And somehow it was all her fault.

At home it was 'a blessing in disguise' – until she told them about the baby. She wouldn't – 'get rid of it'. They felt – 'let down'.

And in Greece – her news was greeted with disbelief. That she should try to ruin the reputation of their dear dead son. It could be anyone's.

And that brought her back to Alex. If only they'd gone to Greece. They'd not have had to visit the family, a walk through the village would be enough. Everyone would think they had seen a ghost. They'd have to acknowledge him then. At the very least she could have explained it all to him properly.

The mug had grown cold in her hands.

*

Alex shivered. His hand had wrapped around a stick, but something told him that it was too smooth and not shaped properly for a stick. He sat back, trying to ease his knees. His head brushed the ceiling, the walls were less than four feet apart, and though he had not reached out to confirm it, he had the impression that he was at the end of the tunnel. He used both hands, with eyes shut even in the blackness, to feel the 'stick'. About half a metre long it was smooth, but bulged at both ends, one being topped by an angled hemisphere, the other a double ridged end. He dropped it suddenly. Shudder after shudder passed through him. It was a bone. It had to be a bone. In his mind's eye it was a thigh bone. He shuddered again. Human?

'Tams,' he called. 'TAMSIN!'

'What?'

'There's something.'

'A way out?'

He'd almost forgotten. There was no way out. 'No – I'm coming back.'

'No way out?'

'NO!'

He picked up the bone again. He'd have to see it in the light, it could be from an animal, would he be able to tell sheep from man? He put the bone back down, close to his foot. He felt the end of the tunnel, not even a crevice to give hope, then began to feel around the pile of debris. Stick after stick. Some small some large. Almost all too smooth, too shaped, to be wooden. Something moved, scuttled away from his hand. He snatched his hand back, closing and unclosing his fist as if warding off the possibility of touching something alive. Tentatively he felt around him, locating a deeper pile of debris. He felt a large pebble, tucked amongst weed behind him. The shape filled his hand, but rocked at his touch. He closed his fingers around the top, cupping it, to lift. It flew up in his hand. Too light for stone. It crashed from his fingers.

'Alex? ALEX?'

He swallowed. He'd take that back to the light. He may not know the difference between the thigh bone of a human and a sheep, but a skull was different.

'I'm coming back!' he croaked, shuddering as his fingers found holes in the skull to secure it in his grip.

*

James tried the largest building first. He peered through the circular hole in the door, large enough to get an arm through. The barn appeared to be empty. He slid his hand through the hole and felt for a catch. He found the large sliding bar that held the door fastened and drew it back. The door opened releasing a pungent dusty odour. James stepped in cautiously. It was as if the last animals had been driven out years ago and the barn had been left, untouched, ever since. The large barn, in which he imagined cows or calves would have stayed over the winter, was muffled by a thick crumbly layer of dried out straw and dung. Over the hayrack, still half loaded, the beam was stuck with the mud-nests of swallows, and their droppings piled high on the hay beneath.

He closed the door and turned to the next building, looking round the farmyard as he went, seeking any sign of life. The door stood open. A quick glance told him that it probably housed a car, judging by the small central patch of oil in the dirt, but that today it was empty.

James had left the small barn nearest the sea until last, so much smaller than the others it had seemed less promising. He tried the door. Firmly locked. Interesting. The windows were high, he had to stand on tip-toe to see through them. He could see the tops of bundles of sticks, but little else. He looked around and noticed a short piece from a tree trunk that was obviously used for chopping kindling on. With a heave and a grunt he turned it on its side and bowled it across to the barn. Now he could see into the barn. The sticks were bundles of basket willow. There was a table off to one side and what looked like a door leaning at an angle on the floor. A radio stood to one side and an old fashioned flat-iron lay beside it on the floor. It was obviously Powley's workshop. He stared into the gloom, trying to make out the jumble of tools, looking for the bodkin.

*

Alex reached the pool. This time he could see it gleaming darkly in the light that filtered in from the entrance to the hole. He stretched across, his free hand giving him support. He tried to brace his body, but found it impossible with one hand full. He looked ahead. If he could make sure that it didn't roll into the water he could put the skull down on the other side. He stretched again, he placed the skull down, steadying it with finger tips. It began to roll back towards him. He pushed it away with his hand quickly, just regaining his position before he fell into the water.

It rolled. Stretched across the pool he was powerless to stop it. The light caught it, too round to be a sheep's skull, it landed in the patch of light from the entrance. Tamsin, listening, watching anxiously for Alex's return, saw it. A human skull staring out at her from sightless holes. She screamed. The noise filled the cave. Vibrated and echoed all around Alex so he felt his position waver and his strength failing. Her scream escalated, out of control, rising and rising, fed by the echo and climbing into hysteria.

Alex, his muscles too tight to move with control, threw himself forward, one foot splashing in the ice-cold water. He swept the skull from sight and appeared himself in the light. Tamsin's screams modulated, rising and falling with the roar of the sea. Alex was out. He wrapped his arms around her, shouting, 'It's all right! It's all right!', until she collapsed, exhausted, subsiding into his arms.

James thought it was the cry of a seagull at first, but the essential human quality impinged itself on his subconscious. The scream seemed to come from inside the barn. He leapt back up onto the log. The empty barn. He ran round behind it. The sound still came from the barn – and from the sea. He looked over the edge of the cliff. Just waves crashing against the cliff-side, no trapped holidaymaker, no exotic birds. Then he heard another sound. A deeper voice. A different tone overlaying, mingling with the screaming. He dashed back to the barn. The sounds were quieter now, even with his ear pressed to the door he could barely hear them. He banged on the door!

'Anyone there? Open up!' he shouted, and tried the strength of the lock by shoving hard and fast with his shoulder. Forgetful of his reason for being at the farm he banged on the door again, his fist tingling with the impact. He stopped to listen, pressing his ear to the wood once more. Had it just been the radio? He began to straighten – but never made it.

CHAPTER EIGHTEEN

Mary opened the school door. She'd been reassured to find it locked when they'd arrived. She listened.

'The alarm's off!' she said sharply. 'It should buzz!' She led the way, half running, to the library. The door was open and she stopped so suddenly that Michelle almost crashed into her. 'What the hell?' she screeched.

'Oh – shit!' Michelle muttered.

'Just stay here!' Rick said quickly, as Mary made to move forward into the room. She stopped, quivering. 'Don't touch a thing – not even the door. Is there any other way into the school?'

'Why – we know how they got in!'

'Is there?'

'Kitchen door – out the back. Down this corridor, around the end there, look,' she said walking with him down the corridor. He felt the slight breeze before they turned the corner.

'But – it doesn't make sense?'

'Keep back,' Rick said as he surveyed the broken glass scattered over the mat. 'Where's the secretary's office?'

'Why? Do you think they were after records?'

'No, to phone the local police.'

'But the books – why did they pull out all the books?'

'I don't know? Michelle?'

'Don't look at me.'

'You let them have my keys!'

'You don't think Tamsin would do this! Besides – the place's been broken into. Might not be them at all!'

'Oh no? But they've disappeared now – haven't they?'

They had reached a pair of doors marked 'Headteacher' and 'Office'. Mary opened the office door, relieved to find it as neat and tidy as it had been left. Rick called the local station and explained who he was and the conditions at the school, specifically asking for scene of crime team. They all returned to the front hall to wait, Mary standing close to the glass door looking out, Michelle leaning back against the far wall.

Rick noticed the way Michelle hugged herself again, as she'd done earlier when she had tried to keep the handing over of the keys from him. Now he wondered what else she knew that she wasn't going to tell. He strolled over to her.

'What's up?' he asked gently.

'Nothing.'

'Okay – only, if you had some idea where they were it would help. That way they wouldn't get into any more trouble.'

Michelle kicked her toe against the floor. Tears were forming in her eyes and she didn't want to be seen wiping them away, nor dare she leave them until they fell. She turned abruptly and pinched them away with her forefinger and thumb.

'Michelle?'

'I can't – ' her voice was tight and childish.

'Who brought the keys back?'

Michelle sniffed loudly.

'They weren't left in the milk-box, were they?'

Michelle shook her head, and sniffed again.

'Well then?'

'It was just so mum – wouldn't – know,' she managed between gulping air as if drowning in unshed tears.

'Wouldn't know what?' Mary said suddenly

'Mrs. Pentewan – '

'What's she been hiding from me now? Deceitful little – '

'Nothing!'

'Nothing, my foot. You get that from your father!'

'Least he cares about me!'

'Oh yeah?' Mary said and stalked back to the door as she heard a car draw up.

'What didn't you want her to know?' Rick persisted quietly.

'That I gave them the keys. He went and got them back – right away. So they couldn't have done all this. It's just – someone else.'

'Who's 'he?' ' Rick asked, semi-sure of the answer already.

'Dad – when he found out what I'd done – to protect me,' she sobbed. 'But I don't know where they've gone!'

A uniformed constable arrived at the front door and introduced himself. Rick explained briefly why they had come up to the school and the condition it had been found in. Within minutes a D.C. and the scene of crime officers arrived. 'Stay here a moment,' Rick said to Michelle and Mary, and headed towards the D.C. 'A word?'

'Okay.'

Rick showed his card and the D.C. inclined his head as if ready to listen.

'I'm involved in looking for two missing children. Reported missing this morning. The girl here said they were trying to get a look at a computer disk and she lent them her mother's keys to try the school computer,' The DC's face lit up. 'No, I don't believe they caused the break-in or the damage – they had the keys. This disk – we don't know for sure – but it may be the records kept by a member of a drug ring. You knew about the raid at Bodrigga?'

'Regional,' he said and nodded.

'The disk was found up there. This stupid lad decides to look at it first – I think someone else got to know about it. An interested party. That's why I particularly asked for fingerprints – this may be more than just vandalism. The library looks as if it's been searched – whether anything was found is impossible to know, but I hope not for the kids' sakes. If we can identify the searcher we may have a lead on the children.'

'You seem sure – not just kids larking about?'

'Not these ones.'

'Okay,' he said and returned to the scene of crime officers and the constable. The group moved down to the library, Rick followed.

'There'll be hundreds of prints!'

'May I suggest the disks,' Rick indicated the drift of disks, obviously lying where they were dumped as they were removed from the computer. The scenes of crime officer looked at him indignantly. 'We know they were looking for a disk,' Rick expounded.

'Do you have any suggestions as to who it was?'

'A possibility – I know of one person who knew they were here, but I wouldn't say it was him, necessarily, Mr. Pentewan, this girl's father.'

'Oh yeah?'

'She says he came up to get the keys back so she wouldn't get into trouble, the keys came back all right.'

'Right – we'll bear it in mind!'

'If it's all right with you I want to get on – I'd appreciate the name of who did this if you turn it up – leave a message for D.I. Whittington at Charles Cross, I'll get in touch.'

*

Pongo leant over the body sprawled in the dust. Blood oozed from the gash on the back of his head turning his collar bright red as it soaked into the shirt. He turned the man over, the head lolling uncontrolled and heavy. Pongo looked at him. Not a face he knew. He dived his hands into the pockets and pulled out the collection of cards and folded paper he found there. The warrant card caught his attention immediately. Fuzz! Detective Constable James Fuller. He flicked through the other pieces, credit card, library card, a folded piece of paper. He opened it up and froze. There was instant recognition, the basket maker's tools, and danger. All he had to hope now was that this jerk was working on his own, that he'd been keeping the information to himself, that he was just fishing.

He stuffed the bits in his own pocket and quickly looked round for hidden observers. He'd always felt invulnerable on his own farm, his own territory. Suddenly it felt invaded. He unlocked the door and dragged the body inside. For a moment he contemplated throwing the body over the cliff. The waves and the rocks would soon put the cause of death beyond question, an accident falling down the cliff. Then again, the tides could be treacherous, could throw the man right back where he came from, and then there would be fuzz crawling all over the place. There was nothing for it – this one would have to join the other two. No one would accidentally find the body down there.

He glanced at the man's pallor and listened to his scant and ragged breathing. He wouldn't last long when the tide rose. He shoved the board aside and fumbled with the threaded knot. His finger thrust into the hole, he hauled up the boards. Alex and Tamsin stood directly below him, looking up, hugging each other, their faces pale discs below him. He ignored them. He dragged James to the hole, feet first.

Alex and Tamsin saw the feet appear over the hole above them. They expected the person to be lowered, as they had been, and stood waiting. All in a rush the legs dropped down and the torso appeared and began its downward rush. They were in the way. James crashed into a crumpled heap throwing Alex and Tamsin aside as they broke his fall. Aghast, they lay where they'd fallen, too scared to move, transfixed by the spreading area of blood that stretched from the man's neck to halfway down his back, sickly red in the weird light of the cave.

'Company for you!' Pongo coughed, and spat. 'Last chance – where's the disk?'

Tamsin shook her head.

'Find it yourself!' Alex shouted, his anger and frustration stirring him to move. He scrambled to his feet and moved over to the man lying so still before them. James lay sprawled on his face, one arm completely lost under his body, the other stuck out at an awkward angle, his legs folded sideways as they'd crumpled beneath his weight

'You want to end up like that? I don't fuck about – where is it?'

'Get stuffed!'

'Ha! Oh that's good. Punk. Perhaps I don't need it anyhow,' Pongo snarled mockingly and dropped the lid, his laughter echoing round the cave.

'Is he dead?'

Alex swallowed. 'I don't know,' he moved towards him. He listened. He couldn't hear any breathing, but thought he could perceive a movement. 'Give me a hand,' he said to Tamsin. Together they tried to gently turn the man, so he lay on his side, rather than on his face. Tamsin's hand came away smeared with blood.

'Who is he?' Tamsin asked.

'I thought you might know.'

Tamsin shook her head.

'Well he's not dead,' Alex said, his throat tight. 'What can we do?'

'Try to stop the bleeding?'

Alex peered at the man's head but could see nothing between the poor light and the darkness of the man's hair. He put out his hand gently and swept it carefully down the back of James' head. His fingers told him that he'd found the cut, wet and sticky he pulled them away.

'What have we got?' In Alex mind's eye the old Westerns flashed up – the voluminous petticoats that were always torn up to make the bandages. He looked at Tamsin, sensibly dressed in jeans and tee-shirt. 'A bit of blanket?'

'I'll try,' Tamsin said, moving 'hospital' quietly over to their ledge. She felt around the edge of the blanket hoping for a worn edge to give her a start. There was none. She moved to one of the small crannies where she'd noticed bits and pieces wedged between the rocks. Using her fingers she winkled out a half-mussel shell, and used its sharp edge to fray a small cut a few inches from one edge. She stood up and taking each side in her grip she pulled sharply as she'd seen her mother do when tearing up sheets to make rags. Nothing happened. She tried again, using all her strength.

'Huh!' a gasp of despair.

'What?'

'I can't even tear it – no, wait,' she started again, making a cut in an adjacent edge. This time when she pulled there was give, the material tore better one way than the other. The tearing went on, getting easier as she became practised. Then it stopped! The opposite edge was seamed.

'Hang-on,' she said, 'nearly there,' she sawed viciously with the mussel shell until the seam gave and the blanket released its strip.

Together they bound the strip of blanket around the man's head, one holding the head gently, the other winding the strip round and round. There was far too much, but no easy way of cutting the strip short. When they rested the man's head back down it looked grotesque in the dying light.

'I've been trying to find his pulse,' Alex said, 'I can't.'

'Let me try,' Tamsin said feeling under the jaw bone. 'It's there, seems slow – I can't tell. My heart's beating like hell,' she sighed. 'We can't leave him here, can we get him over on the drier bit?'

'We'll try,' Alex said looking round again, his eyes drawn to the watery hole, it could be that even their ledge would not be dry by morning. 'Tuck the blanket under him on this side,' he said, 'and we'll roll him back on to it, see if we can carry him over there,'

'Okay,' Tamsin said, glad to be doing something, anything to take her mind off the skull, off the knowledge that she had been right, the weird man was a killer.

They took a corner each and lifted, their whole weight thrown back as they moved the slumped shape from the ground.

'Ready? Step. Step,' Alex co-ordinated their movements. Their burden swung and rocked, and eventually reached the shelf. They stood on the end of the shelf to lift him up, their heads bent, their arms screaming with the effort. They let the body rest and let the blanket fall. For a moment they could do nothing else but stand there, leaning against the hard, cold rock, allowing their screaming arm muscles to pull themselves back into place.

The sweat began to chill on their frames, Tamsin shivered.

'Let's wrap him up again,' she said, and the stillness was broken as they moved stiffly to arrange the stranger's limbs and wrap him as warmly as they could manage.

'I wish we'd kept more food back,' Alex muttered.

'Well we didn't – we didn't know then,' Tamsin snapped.

Alex looked at her, slumped at the other end of the shelf, the wrapped body between them.

'A slice of bread, then?'

'Go on. It's the drink that worries me, they say you need – ' she lapsed into morbid reflection.

Alex pulled their meagre supplies out and offered a slice of bread to Tamsin. She took it, turning it in her hand as if she'd never seen such a thing in her life before, wondering if it was the last time she would. Alex stuffed the remaining wrapped slices and the piece of cheese back in the hole and looked up. Tamsin's body, head hung forward, was shaking with silent sobbing, the piece of bread crushed in her hand. He moved quietly, as if trying not to wake the 'sleeper' and slid into the small space beside Tamsin his arms wrapping around her.

'Tams, oh Tams, don't,' he took a deep breath and lied, 'we'll get out, they'll be looking for us, we'll be all right – you'll see.' The sobbing grew in volume, her face wet with tears pressed against his. They held each other tightly and rocked, the comfort rocking of childhood.

*

'How d'you get on?' Kelvin asked almost as soon as Rick arrived back at Sylvia's. Rick looked quickly at Sylvia and gave a slight shake of his head towards Kelvin.

'They borrowed the keys to the primary school.'

Sylvia looked puzzled, then angry.

'What do you mean?'

'Tamsin and Alex went up to the Primary school, with the keys, to try to look at a disk that Alex had found.' Saying nothing of the break-in, not wanting to worry Sylvia more than was necessary.

'And?'

'Well – unless Mr. Pentewan can tell us different – that's the last time they were seen.'

'What's Rod got to do with it?'

'He fetched the keys back, so Michelle wouldn't get into trouble with her mum, she says. Do you know him well?'

'Pretty well – Tom does, grew up with him.'

'So – what sort of bloke is he?' Rick asked softly, aware of Kelvin tensing as he recognised the intensity in the seemingly casual question.

'Oh all right. Friendly, funny, when he's in the right mood. Had his ups and downs since Mary and him split up, but okay, been like an uncle to Tamsin,' she added, a reproach to Rick.

'Do you know where he lives?'

'Of course! It's only just over the back,' she said flipping her thumb to point back over her shoulder, 'but he's out with Tom just now. They're running along the coast, Tom's got his binoculars – just in case they've got themselves stuck in some cove, or down a cliff or something,' Sylvia said, her voice rising as she catalogued the places they may be stuck, her face beginning to crumple. Josie made slight cooing noises, and Rick wrapped his arms around his bony sister and held her. Sylvia shook within his arms, trying to regain control.

'She's so young, so young,' Sylvia sobbed.

'We'll find them,' Rick comforted, but Sylvia just shook her head. It might be too late already for what she was worrying about.

*

'Sorry about that. Fine holiday I've brought you on,' Rick said as he drove Kelvin and Josie back to Plymouth.
'Don't worry about it,' Kelvin said cheerfully.
'You'd think it'd made his holiday to listen to him speculating all afternoon round Looe!' Josie said in mock rebuke.
'Seriously, there was something you weren't telling your sister, wasn't there?'
'You noticed, you always did! Yeah. Remember I told you about the drug raid up at a coastal farm – not my pigeon, but I had links to it?'
'Where you met the lovely Mrs. Smart?' Kelvin teased.
Was it so obvious, that Kelvin had picked up on his reaction to her so quickly?
'Yes – well I'd met her before – to ID a corpse,' he stopped, he'd forgotten what he was going to say, Jo had invaded his thoughts confusing them with her presence, with the feel of her when he held her as she cried. So different to holding his sister. 'Yes. Well her son seems to have found a disk belonging to that corpse – and it was his yacht that was loaded up with cocaine. What worries me is that someone else wants that disk too – and I didn't want to worry Sylvia by mentioning that the school had been broken into and the place ransacked. Apparently nothing missing though.'
'Hell! And this Rod, friend of the family?'
'Went up and got the keys off our pair – only he didn't say he'd seen them – makes you wonder,' Rick said as he pulled into his own drive. Jo was on his mind, he'd said he'd go up to the farm to talk over where they might have gone – but the afternoon had been taken up with the investigations at the school.

'I'm off out again, I promised I'd go and talk to Mrs. Smart – make yourselves at home. I should be back later – is that okay?' he said as they went indoors.

'Off you go Rick, don't worry about us,' Josie said smiling, 'Good luck.'

'Yes, good luck,' added Kelvin with a wink. Rick shook his head at his incorrigibly romantic friend.

*

Rick knocked at the door. No lights on in the house, no sound of someone coming to open it. He stood back and looked up at the place. Had she seen him arrive? Would she pretend she wasn't in? She couldn't be far – her car was in the yard. Rick knocked again and listened. The bleat of a goat and a cackle from the hens reminded him that she was probably dealing with the livestock, so he sauntered round to the milking parlour. As he approached he could hear her talking, her voice low, unintelligible. He wondered who else was there.

'Oh, my God!' she said startled by his sudden appearance. Jo sat on a low stool beside the goat, she looked tired and dishevelled, but apart from the goat she was alone.

'I knocked at the house – then came round to look for you.'

'It was getting late …'

'I'm sorry I couldn't get here earlier – something – no look, can I help you finish up here, we need to talk.'

'I'm nearly done – have you found something?'

'I'll tell you – back in the house, it will wait.'

'This isn't official is it?' she said standing, a frown furrowing her forehead.

Rick smiled. 'No – I'm here strictly as Sylvia's brother.'

'Well that's a relief – at least I think it is. Off you go girl,' she added to Tulip.

'I'll put the kettle on,' Jo said, 'then you'll have to excuse me for two minutes while I get out of these goaty clothes.'

'Fine – look, I'll put the kettle on,' Rick offered. She stopped and looked at him, his smile reached his eyes, warm and inviting 'Okay – won't be long,' Jo said and pointed out the large old kettle that stood on the back corner of the Aga, before she ran upstairs.

Rick took hold of the kettle and half filled it from the tap. His hand automatically felt the two shiny domes to see which one was hottest. It was something he'd subconsciously absorbed from his mother in their home kitchen. He lifted the heavy lid and set the kettle down on it to the accompaniment of a few hissing spurts as drips of water that had found their way onto the bottom of the kettle became instant jets of steam. The kettle had just boiled when Jo reappeared in time to put the water in the pot.

They sat down with their mugs of tea on opposite sides of the wooden, farmhouse table.

'Well then?'

'I spoke to Michelle this afternoon. She's a friend of Tamsin's. Have you ever met her?'

'I don't think so.'

'She'd admitted earlier that Alex and Tamsin had been over to her place.'

'Yes, Sylvia told me.'

'What she didn't say is more important. They went there to look at a disk that Alex had found.'

Jo looked puzzled. 'What disk?'

'It seems that he found a disk up here, probably belonging to Mr. Austin.'

'But you – I mean, the police, took all his disks.'

'It may be that this one was hidden.'

'Oh? What was on it – did this friend tell you that?'

'Well, now we have the next stage of what she didn't tell us. They tried to read the disk but it wouldn't run on her PC even though it's really quite a good one. It seems it would only run on one like the primary school had.' Jo looked perplexed.

'And as it happens Michelle's mother is the caretaker for the school – had all the keys.'

'They went there?'

'Yeah. Michelle was going to take them up there, but because she was due to go out shopping with her father she gave them the keys and left them to it. That was the last time she saw them.'

Jo was shaking her head.

'You don't agree?'

'It's so – I just can't imagine Alex breaking into a school.'

'Why do you say breaking in? They had keys.'

'But no permission!'

'Oh, I see. Well. It goes further. Michelle met her father and somehow he discovered that she had lent the keys to Tamsin and Alex so that they could look at this disk. Mr. Pentewan rushed …'

'What? Who did you say?'

'Pentewan, Rod Pentewan, Michelle's father – are you all right?'

Jo felt the blood drain from her face only to be replaced by a rush of heat and an unstable feeling as if she'd drunk too much. Her hand automatically covered her mouth.

'I'm all right. I just didn't realise who …'

'You know Rod Pentewan?'

Jo nodded.

'How would you assess him, as a person?'

'I don't really know,' she said in a small voice, memories and things that had been said crowded in on her, 'he seems a nice enough sort – bit – well, rough and ready – but amusing.' Why was it so hard to admit she'd been out with him. She knew. How could she look across this table at a man who turned her feelings so upside down that she didn't know if she was attracted to him or hated him and say she'd been going out with Rod. 'I – I've only known him a while – been out a few times, that's all.'

'That's what Sylvia says about him,' Rick said quickly, instantly wondering what the man was like in a totally different way. 'Well, he went after them, to fetch back the keys. The keys came back all right. The thing that worries me is that Mr. Pentewan hasn't said that he saw the children that day.'

Jo was shaking her head.

'What? Did he say anything to you?'

'No,' Jo said in a very small voice. A finger of cold was running its way around her body, making her flesh shrink at its touch. 'No – he said he'd look – ' suddenly she looked up at Rick, meeting his eyes, 'I wonder – '

'What is it – Jo?'

'Pete Austin – he – warned me off Rod. I'm trying to remember what he said – you see Rod had already told me that he would try to put me off, something to do with the time Pete's wife went missing, so I don't think I understood Pete the way he meant it.' Her eyes had taken on a fixed, far away look, as if she was seeing the past, conjuring up the dead man and his words.

Rick nodded in encouragement.

'It was, Pete said – he wanted to warn me off Rod – I virtually told him it was none of his business – then he said "what if there was some evidence – something concrete – he could show me – what then?". Well, I said I'd have to take it into consideration – I had no idea what evidence he was talking about.'

'Did he show you anything – or give any idea of what it would be?'

'No – this was the day before he went missing ...' she tailed off. 'You don't think this disk Alex found was – had some kind of evidence on it?'

'I'm afraid I think it did – or at least someone thinks it did.'

'Rod? But he wouldn't hurt them – surely?'

'I'm not saying he would – but with Pete Austin's yacht coming ashore loaded with cocaine we have to consider that they may have all been in something a lot bigger and more dangerous than we can imagine.'

'Pete Austin's yacht? But I thought you understood – he didn't go out in a yacht – he took a motorboat out.'

'Yes – but the yacht that triggered off the raid was registered to him.'

'But he didn't own it anymore!' Jo said suddenly, 'When we were looking through his records,' she suddenly blushed, 'When he was missing and we were trying to get some idea of where he might have gone – we looked through his disks, his records. In one it listed things like that. It had the sale of his yacht down there!'

'Who did he sell it to?'

'I can't remember – it wasn't relevant at the time and the police have it now anyway.'

'Can you remember anything else about the disk it was on?' he said as he stood and moved towards the door.

'It was labelled 'Bod' or something like that – part of Bodrigga – it held farm accounts and things – I think,' she said, following him as he picked up the phone and called Regional Crime at Liskeard. It took time and a little persuasion but eventually they came back to him with the answer.

He put the phone down. 'The yacht was sold to a Mr. R Pentewan,' he said.

CHAPTER NINETEEN

'Rod? But it was – a row of noughts in that figure, I don't know what it was, but I can remember that!'

'Twenty thousand odd.'

'But he was going on about how hard it is to even make a living – fishing down here.'

'Alternative resources, perhaps?'

'Oh God,' Jo murmured as the notion sank in.

Rick was dialling again.

'Sylvie? Heard anything yet?' he listened, 'Have Tom and Rod come back yet? – They haven't? Okay. I'd like to have a chat with Tom when he comes in, can you call me, I'll either be at home or up at Bodrigga. – Yes, Bodrigga. Well they are together – find one, we should find the other. Okay, Sylvie, it'll be okay, bye love.' He pressed the cancel button and began again.

'D.I. Whittington, I'm expecting a message from Liskeard. Nothing? Okay – is D.C. Fuller in? Day off – of course. Thanks.'

'Nothing?'

'They've not left a message so I'm presuming they've not made a match, I'll try them direct,' he pressed in numbers again.

'Is D.C. Edwards about? D.I. Whittington, Charles Cross. Fine – Ah, I wondered how the fingerprints came out on the school break in? ….. Perhaps I can help you there, he's out on his fishing boat with the missing girl's father, looking, due in anytime. Home harbour is Looe …. sorry I don't know the boat's name.'

'The Merlin,' Jo whispered.

'It's 'The Merlin', it seems. Some – corroborating testimony here suggests we may be on the right lines, – okay, thanks.'

'What's happening?'

'They have good sets of prints from nearly all the disks, matching, but no one they've already got on record. They wanted to ask Rod in 'for elimination' but hadn't been able to locate him,' he pressed the buttons again, calling James Fuller's number. It rang forlornly. He rested the phone down for a moment then, following a hunch, he consulted his notebook once more and pressed in the number listed for Glenda.

The phone rang three times, there was a click and a whirr – he recognised an answering machine and was about to put the phone down, when it was picked up.

'Hello, sorry – just got in!'

'Glenda – Rick Whittington.'

'Oh! Hello sir.'

'Um, you don't happen to know where James is, do you?' he asked tentatively, 'It is important.'

'Well, no. I er, I rather expected him to be here – look the answerphone's flashing – perhaps he's phoned,' she reached over, rewound the cassette and pressed play. She fast forwarded the announcement of her inability to answer the phone and landed at the beginning of a message about theatre tickets. The next space was taken up by a click and nothing more – yet another person who puts the phone down when they hear the recorded message – the next brought out a quavering voice, a Miss Britain with a message that meant absolutely nothing to Glenda.

'Don't know what that's about, sir! I'll go on,' Glenda said. She over-shot a bit, recognised James' voice and turned the cassette back again. They listened. Glenda feeling a blush creep up her cheek with his opening words and his promise of a big meal, hoping he wasn't going to say anything too outrageous. ' ... *I've just been talking to Miss Britain, no need to get jealous, she's not a day under sixty, and got a lead on the Bodkin case. A man called, get this, Powley. A basket maker with a limp. He's local. I'm just going up there for a recce. See you later. Love you! ...* '

'Miss Britain again?'

'Well, perhaps the message was for James,' Glenda said, thinking he had a bit of a cheek giving out her number.

Jo got up and paced the room a bit, then headed back out to the kitchen, something was nagging at her, but her head was so mixed up with the proximity of Rick, a man who stirred her blood yet reminded her constantly that Alex was missing, just by having the same dark colouring. The kitchen was warm and stuffy with the Aga running night and day, she opened the back door and let the cool of the summer's night pour in. And Rod? Could she believe these things about him, why hadn't she been able to tell. She'd kissed him, been held closely. Oh God! Was she such a bad judge?

'And would you have expected him back by now – even if he was 'a little late'?' Rick asked.

'Yes – I'm what you might call 'very late', I should have been back at noon.'

'Wind back again – get me that Miss Britain's number – I don't like the idea of James going up to visit this basket maker alone and not coming back on time.'

'Can I help sir?'

'Don't know yet, I'll ring, okay?'

'I'll be here,' Glenda said, 'the number's Looe 264230,'

'Thanks – I'll keep in touch,' Rick said and replaced the phone on its holder.

Jo leant against the door frame, wondering where Alex could have found the disk and why he'd wanted to look at it himself. What on earth had possessed her sensible son to want to do that rather than just hand it over to the police? Suddenly she heard a cry, a sound of panic, a chorus of distress. It felt as if a bolt of liquid lightning shot through her frame as she realised what it was that had been nagging at the back of her mind. 'Oh No!' she cried, running out into the darkness.

*

There was a groan, just audible over the sound of the waves. Alex left Tamsin and moved to the head end of the man. 'Hello? Can you hear me?' he said.

The body lay still. Alex could just make out the features in the failing light. Please wake up, he prayed. Another sound, a slight movement.

'Hello! Can you hear me? You've been hurt – but we've – I think we've stopped the bleeding.'

Hurt! Everything hurt! James gradually realised he was awake, that he was a mass of pain. If he tightened the muscles in any limb a pain shot straight into his head. And he couldn't move – he was tied up. 'Ohh!!' A voice? A voice! Hurt! Try to see. It's all dark, no, something, rock. He closed his eyes again. He was standing by the door of a barn. Listening. What for? Oh, yes, screams. Then? Nothing. 'Ohhh!'

'Please wake up!' Tamsin said, her eyes filling with tears again. 'His eyes opened and shut!' Alex said, peering at him. 'Wake up – you've got to wake up!'

Open my eyes. See rock, voices behind me, turn head! 'Ahhh!' 'Don't move your head!' Alex said, 'The bandage is a bit big – can you – if we help, can you sit up?'

'Try,' James said, his tongue thick in his throat.

Tamsin guided his legs, and Alex helped to lift James to a sitting position, swivelling around. He supported him by his shoulders as James struggled to get some kind of balance. It felt as if his head had been split open and stuffed with lead, heavy and painful, his neck unable to support the new weight. 'Kids,' he muttered.

'Are you all right? He – he just dropped you – ' Tamsin said, involuntarily glancing up at the shaft leading to the barn above them.

'Who are you?' Alex put in quickly.

James tried to shake his head, to fend off the questions, but succeeded only in losing the little control he did have of his head, and nearly pitched forward. Alex caught him and steadied him again.

'Arghh!' As pain shot up James' arm and lodged like a knife in his shoulder.

'Sorry,' Alex said, letting go but still ready to catch him again.

'Police,' James mumbled.

'Oh God!' from Tamsin.

'We've got a problem. Can you move?'

'Why?' James said, his equilibrium just about stabilised.

'This cave – it's going to flood at tonight's high tide – so he says.'

'No! NO! Not flood!' Tamsin said, her voice pained and sharp. 'We can't drown!'

'Oh God Tamsin. I hope not. I think we may be all right up there,' he indicated the high shelf that led to their air hole,' 'All of us?'

Alex shrugged. It was the only way – he'd been looking round the cave and it was obvious that the water did get up that high at times. So high that even being on that shelf would not help. He was banking on it not being that high tonight.

James shook his head, and wished he hadn't, it felt as if he'd left half of it behind performing a crazy see-sawing motion. 'Up there?' he said, feeling sick.

Alex looked towards the watery hole, just in time to see the water slick out of its confines and leave a sheen of wet on the rock floor. His face must have shown horror for Tamsin turned quickly as if expecting to see some awful monster at her elbow. She froze, watching the water rise and swell and lick the cave floor once more.

'It's getting in!' she cried, turning to move towards the ledge. It was too high for her to climb on her own, she turned back. 'How are we going to do this?'

'You first, then Mr. – '

'James – just James,' he pulled a face that tried to be a smile. All the time he could feel his strength returning, and his mind clearing. They might be kids but they had guts.

'James next, and you tug me up.'

'Will we all fit?' James asked, looking sceptically at the triangular ledge.

'I hope so,' Alex said. He had thought it would be tight for the two of them, but he was finding that all sorts of things seemed possible in certain conditions.

'Come on then – before the water makes the floor slippery, help me out of this,' James indicated the blanket still wound round his legs and torso.

'Yeah – we don't want to get wet!' Alex said with feeling.

Alex took James' weight and Tamsin helped to unwind the blanket.

'What're your names?' James slurred as he leant against the rock wall, trying to steady himself and his breathing.

'Alex.'

'Tamsin Gold.'

'What the hell you doing here?'

'I thought you'd know – aren't the police looking for us?' Tamsin said, her voice rising in anxiety.

James sighed deeply, his head spun a little. 'I – I hope so, but I wasn't, sorry.'

'What were you doing?' Alex asked.

'Don't you think we ought to try for that ledge?' James diverted the topic quickly. He really didn't want to tell these kids that he'd been following up a lead on a murderer – and that he thought he'd found him.

They moved over to the shelf, James supported between Alex and Tamsin, each finding that they could not avoid a long speculative look at the watery hole that one moment was quiet within its confines and the next was licking the floor of the cave, a hungry beast seeking its prey. James leant against the wall of the cave again while Alex helped push Tamsin up onto the ledge. Instantly the cave became darker.

'Get as far up as you can, brace your feet against the walls and reach forward to help – James,' Alex instructed. Tamsin shifted and wriggled herself until she was in a suitable position.

'Okay,' she said, silhouetted against the green back-light.

'If you kneel, then put one knee up, it'll make a step,' James suggested to Alex. 'Then drop the blanket over your knee – yeah – like that. I'll try to move quickly, like a step up.'

Alex dropped to one knee, the blanket folded across the other. James breathed deeply. He was sure that if he made a sudden movement all his brains would be left behind, but there was nothing else for it. Another deep breath and he stepped up on Alex, and thrust himself as far as he could up onto the shelf, one knee just hooked over the edge. Tamsin grabbed at him and tugged. His body felt as if it were being torn in two, he cried out and Tamsin almost let go before she realised that this was the only chance he had to get up, and she tugged harder, her nails digging into his skin. James felt a push. The boy was up, shoving at his free leg, pushing him up onto the ledge. Both knees on, a scramble-crawl forward and he was up. He leant against the rock wall, sweating with the exertion, his breathing ragged, the pain in his chest excruciating. He had no idea when, but he felt sure he must have got himself some cracked ribs or even broken ones, and the pain in his arm and shoulder made him feel sick.

The light was almost completely gone from the cave. Alex stood peering into the darkness, he shivered. He threw the blanket up to Tamsin and moved off. He stepped very close to the wall of the cave. Not being able to see the watery beast he was even more careful of where he put his feet, not wanting to slip into its jaws. He reached their little ledge and felt along it for the crevice their meagre supplies were lodged in. He pulled them out and edged his way back again. Suddenly his foot was drenched. His foot felt warm, then icy cold and heavy, a sensation of something tugging him, trying to pull him towards the watery trap. He gasped. He tried to move quickly. His feet slipped on the newly slicked rocks, he felt himself skid, threw out his arms to hold on, to fend off the beast. The bottle smashed against the rocks, flying glass and sweet stickiness showered him as his backbone scraped down the rock and he landed sharply on his back.

'Hell, Oh Hell' Alex cried out. Tears forcing themselves into his eyes. Then the water came again, silently, suddenly washing the floor so that his clothes clung to him with salt water as he struggled to his feet, hand still clutching the bread bag.

'Alex! Alex are you all right?'

'Don't ask!' he said, trying to sound braver than he felt. 'Take this, someone,' he added passing up the bag. He felt it being tugged from his hand. All he had to do now was get himself up on the shelf and into the small gap between Tamsin and the man, James, and that would be easier said than done.

*

'NO!! NO!! ' Jo screamed as she stumbled up to the paddocks. The geese screamed and called, filling the air with their panic. 'NO!! GO AWAY!!' As she ran, her eyes became accustomed to the gloom, the noise died as she reached the gate, subsided into concerned cackling, and in the darkness she could just make out the white ghost shapes of the geese. She counted out five white shapes in the small paddock as she fumbled at the gate not even thinking about the gander's fierceness. Rick arrived just behind her as she flung it open.

Three of the shapes moved. 'Goosy-Goosy,' she called as she'd heard Pete and Alex do. Her voice pinched and scared. Three shapes bunched and moved towards her in an arc, not coming in a straight line. Two remained in the far corner where the fence met the hedge.

'Fox,' Rick said as he caught the acrid scent in the air.

'Oh God!' Jo murmured. They made their way over to the still bodies. The gander and one goose, heads all but severed from their bodies. Jo thankful for the dimness of night vision still felt sick at the sight, 'Oh God!' she cried, covering her face her body shaking with the sobs.

They had been in her care and she'd let them down, let everyone down. An omen, a gander and a goose. Tears that seemed to be dragged up from somewhere very deep within her stung her eyes. Each one tearing out a new path as it came, burning a track through her body so that she could barely stand. Rick reached out a hand and touched her shoulder. She moved into his embrace, taking strength from him, feeling his arms around her like a supporting frame, while all her fears for Alex poured out of her heart.

'We'll find them,' Rick said softly, trying to soak up the pain he could feel from Jo. Her body shook with the effort of her tears. Not tears of frustration and anger this time, but tears of real desperation and sorrow. He understood that type of weeping. It left you feeling wretched and drained, yet somehow it also released a power within you. He understood, and held her tightly until the shaking ceased and she stood as if asleep in his arms, sighing each breath like waves breaking on a soft shore.

'Come on,' Rick said softly. He nodded towards the geese. 'I'll deal with them, you go down to the house.'

She walked as if in a trance, obeying his word. As she neared the house she realised that the phone was ringing and snapped into a run.

'Hello?' she gasped.

'Jo?'

It was Tom's voice.

'Yes, Tom?'

'Oh – bit off down here,' he started.

'Have you found them?'

'No! Tin't that. It's Rod. Police met us as we come in from looking, an' they takes Rod off for fingerprinting – for elimination – they says. Summat to do with the school his Mary's caretaker at. He went white as a sheet! Then Sylvie tells me Rick is wanting to talk to me urgent, like.'

'Oh, yes. I'll call him,' Jo stammered dropping the phone and dashing back to the door again.

'Rick!' she called, finding his name feeling comfortable in her mouth, 'Rick! Phone call for you.'

'Tom, do you remember a yacht that Pete Austin had a while back,' Rick asked.

'Yep, he and his wife used to take her out. Big 'un. She could do with a crew of three, but they used to manage her all right,' Tom's voice boomed down the line.

'Do you know when he sold it?'

'Well a little while after his wife went missing like. No point keeping her, he couldn't take her out on his own could he?'

'Do you know who he sold it to?' Rick asked as he sat himself down on the end of the sofa.

'No?'

'If I said it was Rod Pentewan?'

Tom laughed. 'What'd he want one of they for, asides, he don't have that sort of money.'

'I didn't think so – so what d'you reckon?'

'You mean he did buy it?'

'So the records say.'

'Well – for someone else, I'd say. Bit of dealing. Is that it? You was worried he'd gone and bought a yacht off Austin?'

'No – I'm more worried as to who he may have sold it to, any ideas?'

Tom made a small noise that sounded like spitting, 'Who'd we know with spare money like that?'

'Who else was Rod close to – I mean you've known him since you were kids, who else did he stay close to?'

There was a silence. Jo came and sat beside him, straining to hear the words from the telephone.

'Too many to say, all those of us that stayed in West Looe, 'cept Wadge. He an' Joseph Wadge always did hate each other.'

'Thanks, Tom.'

'Don't know what good it'll do you, mind.'

'No, neither do I,' Rick murmured as he put the phone down.

He looked round at Jo, perched on the edge of the sofa, the light from the table lamp creating a halo in her blonde curls. He wanted to kiss away the frown she wore, kiss her frightened eyes, still puffy from crying. His heart pounding, he took hold of her hand, she gripped his hand fiercely for a moment then gently. He drew her to him, his arm sliding easily around her shoulders.

Jo felt like a hurt child in his arms, as if a cuddle could make it all better. There were no more tears left. She just wanted to be comforted, to be told that it would all be all right, and this was the man she wanted to comfort her. She no longer hated him for reminding her, she wanted him to hold her tight, to remind her.

'I'm going to try that Miss Britain. Jo – ' he spoke into her soft hair, she tipped her head up to look at him. Their lips met. A tentative touch, as if it might be dangerous. Then, finding the world had not collapsed, they kissed again, tasting freedom and life. And again, and as he kissed her she took him into her mind filling it with the shape of him, driving away all her fears and anxieties for the pleasure of the moment. And as she kissed him the fragments of his life began to pull together into a new shape.

They looked at each other again. Two new people. Eyes smiling. A new beginning.

An insistent tone told them that the phone was off the hook, ready and waiting for them to make a call. 'The phone,' Jo said, not taking her eyes from his. Rick nodded. Leant forward and kissed her again, a gentle parting kiss, then turned to the phone.

It was as if her kiss had cleared his head. There was no more wondering and doubting. He made a short mental leap, one that had been coming together in his mind since the call to Glenda. The cocaine from the yacht, and that which was found at the murdered girl's flat was probably from the same source, marked by the same particularly high quality. If James had found the basket maker, the murderer, the drug dealer – then he may have found the person with the most to lose if the children had found some records. It was suddenly imperative that they find James, for he may have the key to both doors. He pressed in the numbers for Miss Britain. The phone rang and rang, and with each ring he was thinking of other ways to locate a Mr. Powley in the Looe area.

'Get the phone book, Jo, look up Powley, Pauley, Pawley, any variation that sounds like Powley, note any in the Looe area,' he said listening to the insistent ringing.

'None on any of those variations,' Jo said as he replaced the phone. 'Who is he?'

'He may be a drug dealer – we have to know, have to find him.'

'What's he got to do with Alex?'

'Well – if Austin really did have some secret records and they had links to that yacht – then – '

Jo suddenly realised what he was saying. 'So he may be the one that broke into the school – while Alex and Tamsin,' she added and her hand flew to her mouth, as if by saying it she might have made it be so.

'I'll go to the station, I have a hunch that Rod may be the link.' Rick said standing.

'I'm coming too!'

*

'D.I. Whittington, Charles Cross.' Rick said showing the custody sergeant his ID card. 'I believe you brought a Rod Pentewan in earlier – are you still holding him?'

'He's being interviewed,' he said, his small eyes flicking over Jo.

'I have a few of my own questions I'd like to put to Mr. Pentewan.'

'Popular bloke, Regional's suddenly taken an interest in him.'

'Not surprised. Is D.C. Edwards about?'

'In with them.'

'Any chance of a word?'

'You'll have to wait, sir. They don't like to be disturbed, I'm sure you appreciate that?' he said his fair eyebrows raised in mock query. A door opened and Rick instantly recognised D.C. Edwards and D.S. Pearce as they entered.

'Seems I'm in luck,' he said.

The custody sergeant turned quickly and walked over to them, Edwards peeled off and came over to Rick and Jo.

'Nice to see to you again,' Edwards said, sticking out a hand to shake.

'This is Mrs. Smart, the missing boy's mother,' Rick said as he let the man's hand go. Edwards nodded to Jo in acknowledgement. 'How you getting on?'

'Not good.' Edwards tipped his head to indicate D.S. Pearce. 'Not answering him, for certain. Not keen on my line either – though he says he got the keys back from the kids. Says he caught them before they got in, brought the keys straight back, but he's lying and sweating, we've taken his prints – it's only be a matter of time.'

'What's he held on?'

'Suspicion of breaking into the school,' he shrugged, 'anything to hold him a while.'

'Solicitor?'

Edwards smiled, 'Yeah. Quick at that for a local man.'

'It's the children I'm concerned about, as I said, I've just a couple of questions I like to put to him.'

'Fine by me, I'll take you down.'

'I'd like Mrs. Smart to wait just outside, in the corridor, that okay?'

Edwards, raised an eyebrow and looked at Jo . She didn't look the type to throw herself screaming into an interview room but you could never tell. 'A WPC can keep her company,' he said.

'Make sure you're in line with the door when it opens. If you can't see him, move along until you can. I'll try to keep the door open just long enough,' Rick whispered as they walked down a long corridor to the interview room where Rod was being held.

'Will it help?'

'I hope,' Rick said, he gave her fingers a squeeze and dropped back just behind her. Ahead, Edwards had paused by the door ready to open it. He glanced at Rick and went in. Jo reached the gap first, moving along until she could see Rod. He was slumped back in the chair his head hung so that he didn't see her. Rick drew level, saw the problem and spoke, his voice twice its usual volume.

'All right Mrs. Smart? Jo – you'll be all right there won't you?' he said as the WPC came to stand beside her. She nodded but looked past him at the figure sitting behind the table.

It worked. Rod heard her name and looked up. His eyes flashed a sea-green before he turned his head away again and the door closed.

CHAPTER TWENTY

D.I. Whittington, Charles Cross, interviewing Mr. Roderick Pentewan.' Rick said for the taped record as he settled himself down opposite Rod. 'Also present D.C. Edwards, Liskeard, and Mr. Pentewan's solicitor?'

'George Baines.'

'Thank you. Interview re-commencing at twenty-two hours thirty-four.'

'I rather think that my client has answered quite enough this evening – he has had an exhausting day – out on his boat looking for two missing children,' interposed Mr. Baines.

'I'm sure he'll want to talk to me then,' Rick said as he settled his gaze on Rod, 'it's the children that I care about.' As Rod glanced up he locked eyes with him. 'Tom and Sylvie tell me that you are like an uncle to Tamsin – better than I am – and your Michelle and Tamsin grew up together – didn't they?'

Rod's mouth opened slightly as the information sank in, as he recognised that here was someone with a special interest in Tamsin.

'Yes,' he muttered.

'So I understand your concern for them, but you still appear to be the last person to have seen Alex and Tamsin – when you left them at the school.'

'I wasn't up at the school! I just got the keys off them.'

'They still haven't been seen since.' Rick said leaving the quarrel over whether he'd actually been in the school for the forensic team to work out. 'They were going up to the school to look at a disk, perhaps a sensitive disk, certainly one that had been hidden by Mr. Peter Austin. You knew this, your daughter Michelle told you didn't she?'

'Yes.'

'Did you tell anyone else about the disk?'

Rod looked perplexed and worried for a fleeting moment. 'I dunno what you mean,' he said.

'Did you tell someone who might be interested in the contents of that disk themselves – someone who might have wanted to get the disk away from the children?'

Rod swallowed and stared at Rick, trying to keep his eyes from sliding away to a more restful spot near the floor, but said nothing.

Rick felt that the man before him was trying to blank off the question, avoiding the necessity for answer, and decided to approach the question from another angle.

'You've met Alex Smart, Jo's son?'

Rod nodded

'Mr. Pentewan has nodded – I have to ask you to speak for the record.'

'Yes,' Rod muttered, no longer holding Rick's gaze.

'Nice lad, Alex. I understand he's very bright – and he's everything to Jo, you know that, don't you? Then there's Tamsin of course – such an attractive girl, so friendly and helpful. Did you tell anyone that they had that disk? You may not even have known this person was interested in the disk. Did you tell anyone?' Rick paused, he was going to take a chance, just follow the hunch, 'Like – Powley – for instance?'

Rod's face snapped up – his eyes wide.

Bingo!

'Who?' Rod said, his voice thick.

'You know, local basket maker, has a limp. I mean, I really wouldn't like to think of the children coming into contact with him. Alex and Tamsin. I'm already looking for him in connection with a nasty murder in Plymouth. Single blow, one of those basket-maker's tools, straight through the heart and out the other side. Lovely young thing she'd been, twenty-one, deep chestnut hair, slender frame, delicate features. Her parents came down from Fleetwood to identify her – so sad – such a waste. So you see I really wouldn't like to think that he – ' Rick spelt out the horror of the murder, bringing it fresh into his memory, filling his mouth with a sour taste. He could see that the pictures were painting themselves in Rod's mind.

'He won't hurt them!' Rod suddenly burst out, his forehead a sickly glow of sweat.

'He?'

'He just said – insurance . He promised!' Rod shook his head as if he'd been told already that it wasn't true, that they'd been hurt. Rick felt the adrenaline surge through his body. He had hoped that the abductor of the children would turn out to be someone more mundane, less threatening, but at least they had an answer.

'Tell me what happened – quickly. If you really care about those children you'll hurry,' Rick said, his voice an urgent whisper. The solicitor sat statue-like, his bored expression gone.

'I told him. I – I knew he wanted some record that Austin had been keeping. He'd asked me to try to find it up at Bodrigga. We didn't find it – then the police took everything – so. So when Michelle said these kids had it – what I guessed would be it – I told him. I didn't know what he'd do.'

'What did he do?'

'Broke in the school – ransacked the disks and stuff – then he took them, the kids – saying that they were for insurance – he'd not found it you see.'

'Where'd he take them to?'

'I don't know – I suppose the farm.'

'What farm?'

'His – Powley's Farm.'

'That the one up by Plaidy?' added D.C. Edwards.

'That's right – he's all alone up there, no one'd know if he took them there – '

Rick sat motionless for a moment, his mind whirling with questions. 'If, if he's holding them we need to know as much as we can about him. At the farm, would he be armed?'

'He's got a shotgun.' Rod said quickly, then paused. He thought about Pongo, about his contacts, about his past. 'He was in the army. He may have – anything. He always said he'd learnt a hundred ways to kill, but none to make a living.' The bitterness in Pongo's statement transmitted itself through Rod's mouth. Rick looked at Edwards. He raised his eyebrows. Both men were thinking of the enormously different complexion this last little bit of information put upon the whole situation.

'I've a D.C. who decided to pay Powley a visit – not knowing any of this. He's not reported back, yet,' Rick murmured to Edwards.

'Shit.'

Rick looked back at Rod. He'd heard and his ashen face reflected his thoughts.

'What would your friend make of an unexpected visitor?'

'Depends.'

'Police officer?'

Rod just shook his head. Pongo had never really given a pleasant reception, even for him supposedly a childhood friend and partner. Rick stood up quickly, he glanced at his watch.

'Interview terminated at – ' he began.

'But I was looking for them!' Rod suddenly shouted. 'Get that on the record. I was looking for them – I was looking for a cave. He always said, when we was youngsters like, that his place had a real smuggler's cave. From the real old days. He was always promising to show us, but he never did. So I don't know where it is – but I was looking, from the sea – I was looking, truly – ' his voice tailed off.

Rick looked at D.C. Edwards.

'There's more to ask about the school – can it wait?'

Edwards nodded. 'Interview terminated at twenty-three hours, twelve minutes,' he said and they both left the room. Rick's heart was thumping, planning how they could go about finding the children. He didn't liked the idea of them being held as insurance – it smacked too much of hostages to him. Jo looked at him with wide eyes as he stepped out of the room.

'We've got a lead – come on,' he said, touching her lightly on the arm.

*

For the third time Alex's foot slipped. He was wedged on to the shelf, pressed against the man, James, who crouched hard beside the rock wall, his breathing sounding like waves on a shingle shore. Tamsin had one arm hooked under Alex's arm, trying to anchor him in place.

The shelf sloped as it led down to the cave, only Alex's upper body was lodged on a relatively level place and it didn't seem enough to hold him in place. He'd drawn his sodden legs up and dug his heels into the edge of the rock, trying to keep himself up. Tamsin had tried to spread the blanket about him when he began shivering, but now the shivering had turned to a shuddering that shook his whole body.

His foot slipped again – this time to splash into water. Panic filled him. He pulled his leg back as if it had been dipped in boiling oil, and the movement dislodged his other leg. He was slipping! He let out a cry – involuntary – panic filled. Tamsin dug her fingers into the soft flesh under his arm and braced herself against the rock.

He was slipping! He twisted and wriggled, struggling to regain his position, the unseen monster drawing him downwards into its jaws. He threw out his arm, his hand reaching for anything to pull himself back up by. He pulled at James, releasing a broken sigh; at bare rock, skinning his knuckles. He regained a foothold. He pressed his back to the floor of the shelf and eased his body up, up, until his other foot found something to lodge against. He was panting, his heart racing. The shuddering that had left him, returned shaking him with fear and relief.

'Alex?' Tamsin whispered.

He struggled to get enough breath to speak.

'Alex, was – where's the water?'

He took a breath, sucking the dank salty air into his lungs.

'Here – just at the edge of the shelf.'

'Oh God! Oh God!' Tamsin murmured, her voice tailing off, repeating the same words, a plea and a prayer.

*

'This is the largest scale we've got,' Edwards said as they studied a large scale map showing not only the site of the farm but the shape and location of the different farm buildings. 'Providing there's been no building in the last forty years then that's the layout,' he added.

'This being the farmhouse?' Rick pointed to an L-shaped block.

'I'd say so, yes, the other large building's probably a barn – it's the usual pattern. As you can see the farm's on the edge of the cliff, but it's also in a hollow,' his finger traced the contour lines.

'So there's no chance of creeping up on him – I suggest we go in as casual visitors, try not to alert him. The armed men can fan out, use what cover there is. If he comes to the door at least he should be illuminated and all our men hidden by the dark.'

'You want to go in now?' Edwards glanced at the blackened window.

'I'd rather not leave those children in his care any longer than I have to.'

'It'll make him suspicious.'

'It might just surprise him.'

'Okay, I'll sort out our armed men for a briefing, how about back up?'

'What can you manage in the time?'

'Helicopter on stand-by in case he makes a run for it.'

'Sounds good to me,' Rick said pushing himself up from the table he'd been leaning over, 'I'll just have a word with Mrs. Smart while you round up the team.'

'If we find them we'll be bringing them back here, so it's the best place for you to be,' Rick said as he held Jo tightly.
'I feel so useless just waiting here.'
'Sometimes there's nothing else that can be done, there's no way you could come along on this, we're taking in armed officers, it's like that.'
Jo nodded. She understood but it hurt her to be doing nothing. It was alien to her being, to her self-image. Years of positive action to change her situation and now she could do nothing, she had to rely on Rick. Yet she found it almost comfortable to rely on him. She nodded and they kissed, giving each other reassurance and courage.

*

The half moon lent a silver sheen to the surrounding countryside, the shadows standing out starkly like solid entities. They pulled up on the roadway before the farm track, gliding silently to a standstill with no lights showing, except on the car that Rick drove. He surveyed the broken sign in silence while the team from the all-terrain vehicle silently slipped away into the shadows.

Only when he felt they had moved far enough away from the road, did he turn his car and move up the bramble-hung farm track towards the farm. His headlights fanned the sky for a moment or two before the track took a steep dip towards the farm. Outside the yellow blaze of the car lights the moon shone on the slate roofs below him, showing a building configuration that he had expected.

Rick swallowed, his throat felt dry and painful, so tight with tension that it felt hard to breathe. He was frightened. Despite the bullet-proof vest he did not feel safe, a shotgun blast to the head at close range would leave him as dead as a bullet through the heart would – and this was a man who was trained to kill.

Edwards had been right, the block marked as an L-shape was the house, he pulled up fairly close, allowing himself plenty of time to pick out the features in the headlights and, rather as James had done thirteen hours before, allowing time for an irate old farmer to rush out and demand to know what he thought he was doing.

The building was in darkness but that might only mean that all occupants were asleep within. He turned out the lights and opened the door, distinctly aware that at that precise moment he was illuminated, a clear target. The door shut with a clunk that seemed to echo round the hollow.

Rick glanced around. From the farmhouse the fields rose up in three directions. Behind the farmhouse stood the dark huddle of barns and beyond them the silvered sea glinted darkly. It was so quiet, except for the sea, and so still, he could have believed he was the only person within miles. He could hear every step as he crunched across to the front door.

He flicked his tiny palm-held torch on for a second to locate the heavy lion-headed knocker then flicked it off before his fingers tightened round the rust-encrusted metal. It lifted stiffly. He had to push it to make it sound against the plate. The second time it moved a little easier, the crash resounding in the quiet.

He listened for anything. A sound of someone moving, of footsteps, of a door, anything would have been welcome as the silence stretched until his ears hurt. He crashed the knocker again and again, adding a thump to the thick timber door with his fist. The silence that followed the noise seemed heavy with disappointment – and relief.

He turned to face the darkness. Flicked his torch again and showed his hand in its light, beckoning part of the team to join him, then walked back to the car.

Edwards and two of the armed men joined him there within moments.

'He's either deaf, very cute or flown already,' Rick said.

'Well that knocking should've woken the dead – guess we'll have to watch our backs.'

'We'll take a look around, pairs, one searching, one watching,' Rick said quickly, his eyes flicking past the others towards the house as if he expected to see Powley appear from it at any moment. 'I'll take the house and that small barn – you two the large barn and the one beside it – for heaven's sake watch out.'

'Cheers,' Edwards said moving off with one of the armed policeman, both of them constantly turning and watching the dark shadows in the farmyard.

'Come on,' Rick said quietly to the other armed man, and set off for the house door again. He tried the door. It was locked, so they moved carefully from window to window, shielding their bodies behind the bulk of the wall, shining the narrow torch beam through the grimy panes into the rooms. Light glinted on the glass from oil lamps, soaked into the dirty red-damask of an old settee suite, flashed on the glassed over paintings. They moved on, the only sound those of the sea and their own feet crunching on the cinders. The next set of windows showed a large pine farmhouse kitchen table, a Tilley lamp perched on one end. Rick tried the door, expecting it to be as solidly locked as the front. It wasn't. The handle turned and the door swung silently open.

He listened, the armed man stood facing outwards, stiff and still.

'Anyone there?' Rick called. The scent of dry rot answered him, heavy with the musk of mushrooms, and a dead, hollow silence.

'Come on,' he hissed to the other man. They moved forwards, Rick's hand automatically searching for a light switch but not finding one. The meaning of the Tilley lamp sunk in. The place had no electricity laid on. They moved quickly from room to room, then upstairs, always knocking and shoving the door ajar before they dared to look in the room. Each time they were greeted by the same dishevelled, down-at-heel dinginess of a place long uncared for.

They shouted again! Heads tipped towards the rafters, in case the children were stuffed up into the loft. Silence, then a shout, a voice.

The voice came from beneath them. Rick hurried to the stairway. Edwards called up again. 'There's a car in the barn!' he shouted.

Rick and the armed man clattered down the bare wooden stairs. 'Unless he's got more than one car – he may still be around,' Edwards said as they appeared.

'What's it like?'

'G reg. saloon, bright red Capri, top powered job.'

'Shit! Let's get down there, I have to check.'

'What is it?' Edwards said as they jogged towards the barn.

'Sound's like my DS's I'll know when I see it.'

Rick stopped in the door-way; within a second he knew it was James'. Not quite as obvious as a personalised number-plate, he suspected James had been lucky in his find of a car to match his initials. 'G872 JAF'

'It's him – D.C. Fuller. He's here – and Powley's gone. Where else is there to look?'

'Only the small barn,' Edwards said moving off towards it as he did so. He reached it first putting his hand to the latch. He turned as Rick arrived.

'Locked?' Rick asked.

'Yeah – none of the others were.'

'House neither,' Rick said hopping up onto the log and shining the torch through the window. The circle of light showed the ranks of withies, the table, the half-door and a jumble of sticks and tools. Even with Rick's added height he saw little more than James had done earlier and was just as curious about the area he could not see.

'Let's get in there, there's room to hide against this wall,' Rick said as he stepped down from the log. One of the armed men trotted back to Rick's car and brought back the ram. After a shouted warning that echoed in the stillness of the night the ram was brought into action, the door and frame splintering around the locks. Another shouted warning.

'Armed Police!' and they were in. Torches shining round the small barn, locking on the stone trough momentarily, flicking across the bundles of withies, pausing over the scattering of tools and the gaz lamp.

James came to. He had no recollection of having allowed his attention to slip, yet he knew he'd been, if not sleeping, then certainly oblivious for a time. Just how long, he had no way of telling. At least he'd not lost his precarious position. His body felt as if someone had squeezed it in a vice, tight and painful, but even taking a deeper breath brought brightly coloured shooting pains, so he dared not move. The boy was shivering, shaking his body so much that James could feel the movement against him. He presumed the girl was still there, he hadn't the will power or the strength to turn his head to see.

The sea, a monster snoring wetly. A relentless background to their pain and terror. James wondered idly how long it would be before they became so used to the sound of the sea that they didn't notice it anymore, and whether it would be before they cared anymore. Then he heard it. A shout! A sound like tearing paper, another shout.

'Can you hear that?' he hissed. 'Girl! Did you hear?'

'I think so,' Tamsin said softly as if trying not to wake a child. Together they listened. Drumbeats. Feet on the floorboards. 'Someone in the barn,' Tamsin whispered. 'More than one!' she added as she noticed the difference between what she heard now and what she'd heard before.

'Scream, go on, scream, for heaven's sake!' James pleaded with as much breath as his crushed ribs would allow.

'I can't.'

'Shit, scream will you. I heard you! I heard you – scream!'

There was a movement beside him, the shuddering changed.

'Help us!' Alex shouted his voice slurred, 'Help-us!'

'It was the girl, the high voice,' James hissed.

'Screams Tams – you saw the skull – do you want to die? Help!'

Almost back to back the two men stood and surveyed the room with their torches. They were disappointed. Rick had been sure that they would find something in this locked place.

'Did you hear?' he began.

'What?'

'Listen – '

The sound made the hair on the back of their necks rise. Almost animal, the cry had an ethereal, all round, non-directional effect. Yet something in the modulation gave it a human touch. The two men looked at each other.

'We've found them – I hope,' Rick breathed. Suddenly he remembered Rod's plea for understanding and his assertion that he had been seeking the children, by looking for an opening to an old smuggler's cave. Suddenly he dropped to his knees, laid his ear to the floor boards and almost at once signalled Edwards to join him. At once the scream had direction, was clearer, the source had to be beneath the floor.

On his knees Rick noticed the basket-maker's board and lifted it aside. The torch flicked quickly over the dust and bits. Nothing. He swept the area with his hand and felt the small knot that stood slightly proud. He recognised it for a knot and would have passed on, except that it moved slightly under his hand.

'Shine your torch on here,' he said, 'look, it turns, hell – a hole.'

The scream leaked out through the tiny aperture pumping adrenaline into the rescuers. Rick placed his long index finger through, hooked it under and tugged. Part of him didn't expect anything to happen, so he was mildly surprised when the section lifted. The screamer had taken a breath – the sound of the sea swelled up from the black pit. They turned their torches to shine through the hole, both at once, the light reflected back at them from the water, glinting as if on oil.

'Tamsin? Alex? James?' Rick poured his roll-call into the gaping hole.

'We're here! We're here! Thank God, Thank God!' Tamsin cried back before her words were lost in breathing.

'Where are you?'

'On a ledge – the sea's filling the cave,' Tamsin said managing to control the sighs of relief.

'Are you all, alright?'

'Sort of, but be quick!'

'Tamsin! It's Uncle Rick! Is anyone hurt?'

'The policeman.'

'We'll get you out – just as soon as we can!'

Rick looked back at Edwards. 'I think this'll need a cave rescue team.'

'Nearest is the Mine Rescue group – I'll go call them up.'

'No – I'll do it – keep talking to them – I'll be back in a moment.'

Rick ran from the building, his torch swinging wildly. It took only moments to get through to Liskeard control room and pass on his message.

' ..... Right, Mine Rescue, Paramedics. I'll get an officer to stand by the farm entrance – it's a bit hidden. Where will they be taken? – Okay. Pass the message to Mrs. Smart that they've been found, and will go straight to Derriford Hospital for a check-up. Thanks,' he finished and headed back to the small barn.

*

'Mrs. Smart?' the young WPC beamed. Jo looked up and nodded briefly. 'I have a message from D.I. Whittington –

They have been found and will be taken straight to Derriford Hospital for a check-up.'

'Where were they?'

'I'm not sure – in a cave or perhaps a mine shaft – the Mine Rescue's been called out.'

'They've not got them out then?'

'I don't know – I'm sorry – I should have just passed on the message.'

'That's all right,' Jo said standing, 'Where is this hospital?'

'In Plymouth – it's on the road towards – '

'Never mind. I'll sort it out, thanks,' Jo said as she suddenly realised that Rick had only been able to get a message to her because she was waiting in the police station and that Sylvia probably didn't know yet. She gathered up her jacket and bag and left the station. There was the glow from a telephone box on the far corner of the road, opposite a small shop, so she headed for that first. To her amazement it was not only in good condition but it also worked! She pressed in Sylvia's number.

'Hello?'

'Sylvia – it's Jo. They've been found,' she said, her voice breaking as she passed on the news.

'Thank God! Oh! Where? Who?'

'I don't really know – just – we're to meet them at a hospital, Derriford?'

'Are they hurt? What's happened to them?'

'They said – a check up. Just a check up. I really don't know – they've got to have a Mine Rescue team to get them out from – to get them – I don't know!'

'I can't get there, Tom's got the car, he's gone out – looking again!'

'I'll come and get you – I don't know where this Derriford place is anyway!' Jo added with a laugh driven by sheer relief.

Jo drove swiftly from Liskeard to Looe, sweeping along the dark country lanes trusting that no headlights coming in her direction indicated that it was safe to go round the usually blind bends. She swept down into Looe and the lights of the town looked picturesque in the summer night. She turned sharply right over the bridge and up to 'The Smugglers'.

Her hand had barely touched the door when it was snatched open. Sylvia stood there with her coat on, ready to go, and Tom stood right behind her.

'What happened?' he snapped quickly.

'I don't know but Rick led a team, an armed team, up to Powley's farm,' Jo began. The look on Tom's face stopped her. 'What is it?'

'Go on!'

'This – Powley. He's the one they think took the children – and more – something to do with drugs.'

'My Tamsin! And they're looking for him?'

'Well – yes.'

'I know where he is.'

'What?'

'He was down on Rod's boat – I knew they had some dealings so I thought nothing of it – but – are they still holding Rod?' Jo nodded.

'The bastard.'

'Tom! Where are you going?'

'To see if he's still there – and then.'

'He's dangerous, Tom. Rick said – army trained or something,' Jo shouted as she followed him out into the night.

Tom tore open the door to his car, Jo jumped in beside him. Even if she couldn't do much, she could be there to make sure Tom didn't try anything silly that would get himself hurt. She was still closing the door as the car lurched forward. They screeched down round the bend in the road and down to the bridge. Tom threw the car sharply right and headed for the dead end near the harbour. It was impossible to make out whether Rod's boat was still there from the car and Tom leapt out leaving the lights blazing and began to run along the quay. Jo followed, trying to catch up with him. She saw him stop opposite the place she'd seen Rod's boat tied up. He stood like a statue for a moment before he came running back to her. 'He's taken it! Come on – we'll fix him,' he said as he screeched the car back in reverse right up to the bridge.

Tom nearly knocked over the waiting Sylvia as he tore through the kitchen heading for the phone in the living room. Within minutes he was back with them in the kitchen, a grim smile on his face.

'That's it! Police and Coastguard are after him, helicopter too – they said, just happened to have one on stand-by! They should get the bastard now.'

CHAPTER TWENTY-ONE

Tom sped through the dark lanes even faster than Jo had dared to. They were soon crossing the Tamar bridge and racing along the dual carriageway. The road signs warned of speed cameras but it did not seem to bother Tom as he hurled his car up the slip road towards Crownhill and Derriford. They pulled into the car park and were heading for the large well-lit entrance in minutes. It was only when they got inside that everything slowed down.

According to reception Alex and Tamsin had not arrived. There was nothing they could do but wait. They sat on the well stuffed benches, they walked round and round the reception area, they sat on the benches again. An hour passed, Jo looked at her watch for the eightieth time, two and a half hours since Rick had sent the message that they'd been found. She hoped the delay didn't mean that there'd been trouble with the rescue.

Another half hour.

'Are you sure they're coming here? There are hospitals in Cornwall you know?' Tom suddenly asked Jo.

'I can only tell you that I was told Derriford – I didn't even know where it was – let alone whether it was the nearest.'

'Still – we might be waiting here and Tamsin might be – anywhere!'

'Tom – it'll be here – ' Sylvia began.

'I'm going to ask again – they ought to know something – if they've got an ambulance out on something like that – something,' Tom said, turning away from them and heading back towards the reception desk.

Just as Tom was getting a little too impatient for the liking of the security man standing near reception, Rick appeared walking quickly towards them.

'Tom – it's Rick,' Jo said laying a hand on his arm. As soon as Tom saw Rick he strode towards him. Standing by the security desk Stephen recognised Rick from the dinner party and stood back deciding only to intervene if the D.I. couldn't sort the problem out for himself.

'Where is she? Is she hurt – if that bastard laid one finger on my Tamsin I'll – '

'She's fine – shaken, cold and hungry but fine – the best of the lot of them.'

'Alex,' put in Jo quickly as Tom turned in relief to hold Sylvia. 'He will be fine – at the moment they say he's suffering from exposure – he got wet in the cave and pretty chilled – they've not had much in the way of food or drink since they were taken.'

'Thank God! Can I see him?'

'They've only just got them in – I guess it'll be a while.'

'I just want to see that he's all in one piece.'

'I can assure you of that,' Rick smiled, taking her hand.

'What did he want with them? Why take the kids?' Tom snapped.

'Liskeard told me you saw Powley – thank God you did – you know they've caught him?'

'Good. Should've sunk the bastard!'

'Tom!' Sylvia said suddenly realising how far Tom's voice was carrying.

'Come on – we'll go and see how soon you can visit the children,' Rick said, leading them away towards the lifts.

Tamsin was still awake when they were allowed in, and was hugged and held by Tom and Sylvia as if they would never let her go again. Then Tamsin began to tell them what had happened; to give her account of their capture and holding. It was brief but almost more terrifying in its starkness.

' .... then Alex squeezed in this hole – in this little tunnel at the back of the cave – trying to get out. I was waiting, watching.' She stopped, and bit her lip. 'A skull rolled out – it made me scream. The next thing – that poor policeman, he – he just dropped him, all that way, all that way down!'

'What kind of skull? A sheep – perhaps?' Rick asked softly. Tamsin shook her head.

'No. No, human – not a sheep – Alex found it – in the little cave, he'll tell you,' she said, her voice becoming dreamy and her eyes sliding as she struggled with sleep.

They let her rest. They stayed at the hospital until Alex awoke from his deep sleep. His long dark lashes flickering before he managed to keep them open for long enough to remember that he wasn't in the cave anymore.

Under strict orders not to tire him out Jo asked how he was and squeezed his hand. He looked dreadful, his skin washed in green light, his hair lank, yet he was alive and Jo couldn't prevent the tears of relief rolling down her face.

It was nearly nine o'clock when Jo let Rick drive her back to Bodrigga. Tom and Sylvia were staying on because the hospital thought that Tamsin would be able to go home later that morning. Alex was sleeping again and, although the hospital said that there was nothing to worry about, they wanted to keep him in a bit longer for observation. Jo and Rick walked out of the artificial light into a bright summer's day, and despite her exhaustion and relief Jo suddenly remembered the farm, and the animals that were depending on her, so Rick offered to run her 'home' and give her a hand.

As soon as they arrived they were greeted by the sight of a strange car in front of the building and soon afterwards by a large ginger-haired young man who introduced himself as Miles Hoskin, the sole beneficiary of his Uncle's will. He seemed pleased to see Jo only in that he would be able to ask her to remove her belongings and person from the farm all the quicker. His rapid production of solicitors letters and a notice that any 'unauthorised' occupant of the farm should leave 'forthwith', annoyed Rick more than he cared to acknowledge.

His reaction was one which left the nephew expecting to receive a large bill for maintenance of farmhouse and livestock during the time between his uncle's death and his own arrival.

Rick helped Jo collect all her things and pile them in his car. Jo, who'd only really come back at all to milk the goats and check up on the remaining livestock, asked the obnoxious Miles if, before she left, he knew how to milk as the goats needed milking as soon as possible. His airy reply, that he 'would find someone to deal with it', left Jo feeling uneasy yet relieved of her 'duties'.

'Where to?' Rick asked as they climbed in the stacked-up car.

'I don't know. A hotel?'

'I've got a spare room you could use,' Rick began, then hastily went on, 'Kelvin and Josie are staying with me too – and I'm only a mile from the hospital. Would you like to stay?'

Jo took a deep breath. In one way it was what she wanted most – in another it scared her. It was only for a couple of nights, she thought, then as soon as they let Alex out of hospital they could go home.

'Thank you, I'd appreciate that – I don't think I could stand a hotel room alone, at the moment.'

Rick smiled warmly, pushed the car into gear and drove off leaving Bodrigga and the sea behind them.

*

Rick stood in his kitchen making two cups of coffee. Over in his small conservatory he could just see Jo as she sat quietly strumming his guitar. The vision was perfect, he felt so happy. For the first time since he'd moved in, the house felt like a home, and still his heart changed gear each time he saw Jo.

Kelvin and Josie had been sweetness and discretion, if you didn't count Kelvin's fond winks aimed at Rick now and then. They had engineered to be out most of the time, leaving Rick alone with Jo when he was off duty. The paperwork had been horrendous and had taken most of his time at work since he'd reported back after leaving Jo at his home that morning.

Tamsin had gone home, Alex was due out that evening but James wasn't so lucky, the head injury was causing some concern and he lay in his hospital bed, well wrapped in bandages, arm in a sling and looking for all the world like a hero, cosseted and worried over by Glenda.

The only real cloud on Rick's horizon was the fact that Jo had said she was going home as soon as Alex was released – and he wasn't sure how he could change her mind.

'Your coffee.'

'Thanks,' Jo smiled up at him.

'You play well, do you sing?'

'Not really, you?'

'When I've had enough to drink,' Rick smiled back at her.

He put his coffee cup down, his eyes not leaving hers. She let the guitar slip from her lap, resting its long neck against her thigh, her eyes not leaving his. They kissed. It was so right, a moment when the rest of the world vanished.

'Jo, after we collect Alex, would you like to stay on for a while .. ,' Rick began, before he was interrupted by the front door opening.

'Ah, there you are,' Kelvin said as he 'found' them in the conservatory, 'we've brought you the Evening Herald – thought you might like to 'read all about it'.' He laughed. 'This guy in town was shouting "Ee'en E'ruld!" and the sheet on the box says "Drug Baron Held", I guessed it was your one – makes a good yarn,' he added as he held up the paper so they could see the front cover. "Murderer and Drug Baron Held!", ran the headline beside the picture of a man's face. However, underneath the picture it stated that this was Superintendent Williams. Kelvin began to read the report out to them, 'Superintendent Williams, Charles Cross, held a press conference to announce the holding of a man believed to be responsible not only for the murder of a prostitute in

Devonport recently but also of Mr. Peter Austin, of Bodrigga farm, found washed-up in the Barbican last week, and his wife Julia Austin who vanished eighteen months ago. This evil man', Kelvin went on, 'was also believed to be the organiser of a drug-ring that supplied cocaine to most of the West-country. The man had abducted two children who had discovered evidence of his evil trade and were about to report him to the police. The children were found by, here it is, Detective Inspector *Dick* Whittington, ha-ha!, from Charles Cross station. I think that gives you the flavour of it,' Kelvin finished with another chuckle.

'Well – I was told that the man liked to claim the prizes.' Rick said smiling back at his old friend.

'Oh – and here's the TES you wanted, Jo,' Josie said holding out a thick folded paper to her.

'Oh thanks,' she said, a little blush coming to her cheek.

'What's that? TES?' Rick asked.

'Times Education Supplement.'

'Oh?'

'Well – I just thought I might see if there were any jobs going down this way,' Jo said, smiling.

END

Acknowledgements:
To the many friends with different life skills, occupations and experiences of whom I asked so many strange questions in order to help get things right, thank you! Any remaining errors are my own. Thanks also to Dorothy Silverstone for the final check through and grateful thanks also to Christine Haywood and Ian MacDonald – friends with extra special skills.

Note: In the creation of this novel I have added places to Looe and the surrounding area, so I'm afraid you won't be able to drink at The Smugglers in West Looe or stay at Bodrigga.

Thank you for reading **Nothing Ever Happens Here**
by **Ann Foweraker**
Please review this book, and the others written by the author, on Amazon, or by sending your review to Annmade.co.uk, where the books are also available to purchase in all e-formats

Other novels by ANN FOWERAKER

Divining the Line – Ann Foweraker
The first time it happened it felt like stumbling across another avenue to an ancient monument, but this one pulled at more than just his head, there was a tightness in his chest, the lights twinkled and flashed inside his mind, the intensity giving Perran a firework of a headache. Following the line - years later in the early nineties - leads him into Liz Hawkey's ordered life, and together they discover the source of the line.

A story of family, love and loss, Divining the Line brings the ordinary and the extraordinary together into everyday life.

Some Kind of Synchrony - Ann Foweraker

Faith Warren, married mother of two, is a secretary in a newspaper office. It wasn't what she'd hoped for, but her dreams of university and becoming an author were lost long ago. Telling stories to entertain her lifelong friend on their journey to work and back is all that is left, until she tells The Story. The real trouble began with the minor characters, just unfortunate co-incidences, but when do you stop calling them co-incidences and begin to wonder what the hell is going on – and how it can be stopped.

Some Kind of Synchrony is a light thriller, set against the background of the effect of the housing crash in the mid 1990's, combining romance, violence and extraordinary coincidences.

THE ANGEL BUG - ANN FOWERAKER

'These memoirs may be the only evidence left of what really happened, where it came from and how it spread.'

When Gabbi Johnston, a quiet, fifty-something botanist at Eden, was shown the unusual red leaves on the Moringa tree, she had no idea what was wrong. What she did know was that the legendary Dr Luke Adamson was arriving soon - and that he would insist on investigating it.

This is the unassuming start to a maelstrom of discovery and change - with Gabbi swept up in it. What starts out as an accident turns into something illicit, clandestine and unethical – but is it really, as Adamson claims, for the good of all mankind?

*

'The Angel Bug', Ann Foweraker's fourth novel, is set mainly at the Eden Project in Cornwall, UK. This is a contemporary light thriller combining science fact and fiction, told by the people at the heart of the discovery.

ABOUT THE AUTHOR

Step into an Ann Foweraker novel and you step into a very recognisable world, with people you know. When something extraordinary happens, as it always does, you are swept up in the events and carried along with your new friends, desperate to know how it will all end.

Ann Foweraker writes novels that resonate with readers of the boomer generation - being one herself - and setting her main characters at a similar age over the years.

Ann has always written, from stories for friends and poetry as a teenager, through books for her children and short stories to the novels she concentrates on now.

Always a teacher, by nature and training, Ann is available to give talks about writing and her novels to book-groups and other organisations. Contact her through her BLOG **annfoweraker.com**, where you can also find out what interests her and what she gets up to in everyday life - from belly dancing to sand-sculpting………. please LIKE her Facebook Page 'Ann Foweraker Author' and follow on Twitter @annfoweraker

CPSIA information can be obtained
at www.ICGtesting.com
Printed in the USA
BVHW032209061220
595070BV00010B/97